A Critical Companion to Lynn Nottage

A Critical Companion to Lynn Nottage places this award-winning playwright's contribution to American theatre in scholarly context. Covering Lynn Nottage's plays, productions, activism, and artistic collaborations, this volume displays the extraordinary breadth and depth of her work.

The collection contains individually authored chapters on each of her major plays, and a special three-chapter section devoted to *Ruined*, winner of the 2009 Pulitzer Prize for Drama. It also features an interview with Lynn Nottage and two of her frequent collaborators, directors Seret Scott and Kate Whoriskey.

A compelling, authoritative account of Nottage's work, *A Critical Companion to Lynn Nottage* is essential reading for anyone interested in contemporary American theatre.

Jocelyn L. Buckner is an Assistant Professor of Theatre at Chapman University in Orange, California.

A Critical Companion to Lynn Nottage

Edited by Jocelyn L. Buckner

Routledge
Taylor & Francis Group

LONDON AND NEW YORK

First published 2016
by Routledge
2 Park Square, Milton Park, Abingdon, Oxon OX14 4RN

and by Routledge
711 Third Avenue, New York, NY 10017

*Routledge is an imprint of the Taylor & Francis Group, an
informa business*

Cover photograph by Lynn Savarese

British Library Cataloguing in Publication Data
A catalogue record for this book is available
from the British Library

Library of Congress Cataloguing-in-Publication Data
Names: Buckner, Jocelyn L., editor.
Title: A critical companion to Lynn Nottage / [edited by]
    Jocelyn L. Buckner.
Description: Milton Park, Abingdon, Oxon ; New York :
    Routledge, 2016. | Includes index.
Identifiers: LCCN 2015039734 | ISBN 9781138822580
    (hardback) | ISBN 9781138822597 (pbk.) |
    ISBN 9781315742489 (ebook)
Subjects: LCSH: Nottage, Lynn—Criticism and interpretation.
Classification: LCC PS3564.O795 Z57 2016 |
    DDC 812/.54—dc23
LC record available at http://lccn.loc.gov/2015039734

ISBN: 978-1-138-82258-0 (hbk)
ISBN: 978-1-138-82259-7 (pbk)
ISBN: 978-1-315-74248-9 (ebk)

Typeset in Times New Roman
by Apex CoVantage, LLC

Contents

Figures

Contributors

Adrienne Macki Braconi is Assistant Professor in Dramatic Arts at the University of Connecticut where she is also affiliated with the Institute for Africana Studies and American Studies Program. Her book, *Harlem's Theaters: A Staging Ground for Community, Class, and Contradiction, 1923–1939*, was published in 2015 by Northwestern University Press. She has authored several articles and book chapters and served on the boards of the American Theatre and Drama Society and the American Society for Theatre Research.

Jocelyn L. Buckner is Assistant Professor of Theatre at Chapman University. She has published articles and reviews in *African American Review*, *Journal of American Drama and Theatre*, *Popular Entertainment Studies*, *Theatre History Studies*, *Theatre Journal*, and *Theatre Survey*, and is a contributor to *Food and Theatre on the World Stage* (ed. Dorothy Chansky and Ann Folino White), the forthcoming *Performing the Family Dream House: Space, Ritual, and Images of Home* (ed. Emily Klein, Jen-Scott Mobley, and Jill Stevenson), and *The Cambridge Encyclopedia of Stage Actors and Acting* (ed. Simon Williams).

Faedra Chatard Carpenter is Associate Professor of Theatre and Performance Studies at the University of Maryland, College Park. She has worked professionally as both a resident and freelance dramaturg and her scholarly contributions have been published in *The Cambridge Companion to African American Theatre*, *Review: The Journal of Dramaturgy*, *Theatre Topics*, *Women & Performance*, *Text and Performance Quarterly*, and *Callaloo*. She is the author of *Coloring Whiteness: Acts of Critique in Black Performance*.

Soyica Diggs Colbert is an Associate Professor of African American Studies and Theater and Performance Studies at Georgetown University.

She is the author of *The African American Theatrical Body: Reception, Performance and the Stage* and editor of the Black Performance special issue of *African American Review*. Colbert is currently working on a second book project entitled *Black Movements: Performance and Politics* and an edited volume entitled *The Psychic Hold of Slavery*.

Jennifer L. Hayes is Assistant Professor of African American Literature and Composition at Tennessee State University. She earned her doctorate from Middle Tennessee State University. Her research interests include twentieth- and twenty-first-century African American literature, Black feminist criticism, and contemporary drama. She is currently working on a collection of essays that analyzes the politics of voice in plays written by contemporary African American women dramatists.

Scott C. Knowles is Assistant Professor of Theatre History at Southern Utah University in the Department of Theatre Arts & Dance. He received his M.A. from Florida State University in 2010 and is completing his Ph.D. at the University of Kansas. He served three years as the Managing Editor for the *Journal of Dramatic Theory and Criticism*. Knowles's research interests include the intersections between violence, performance, race, and gender.

Jennifer-Scott Mobley is Assistant Professor in the School of Theatre and Dance at East Carolina University. She is the immediate past president of the Women and Theatre Program and a co-coordinator of the Jane Chambers Feminist Playwriting Contest. Her book *Female Bodies on the American Stage: Enter Fat Actress* was published by Palgrave MacMillan in 2014.

Jeff Paden is a doctoral candidate in Theatre Studies at Florida State University's School of Theatre, where he teaches courses in play analysis and human rights. His dissertation, "Starving for Attention," explores representations of starving and self-starved women in Irish drama since the 1890s. He has proudly served as co-convener for the ASTR Traumatic Structures working group. As an artist, he has performed and directed at Villanova University, Florida State University, the Hard Bargain Players, and the Port Tobacco Playhouse.

Sandra G. Shannon is Professor of African American literature at Howard University in Washington, DC. Widely recognized as a leading scholar on August Wilson, she has published two seminal books on this major playwright: *The Dramatic Vision of August Wilson* and

August Wilson's Fences: A Reference Guide. Her scholarship on Wilson also includes numerous chapters and articles and two edited volumes: *August Wilson's Pittsburgh Cycle* and the co-edited MLA *Approaches to Teaching the Plays of August Wilson.* Dr. Shannon was a key consultant for and contributor to the highly acclaimed PBS American Masters documentary *August Wilson: The Ground On Which I Stand* (February 2015). Her extensive interview and introductory chapter on Lynn Nottage and her growing body of plays were published in Philip C. Kolin's *Contemporary African American Women Playwrights: A Casebook.*

Esther J. Terry is a Mellon Fellow and doctoral candidate at the University of Pittsburgh. She writes on continental African and African diasporic performance. Her field research in Kenya and Tanzania was funded by the University of Richmond, the University of Pittsburgh, and a Fulbright-Hays Group Project Abroad grant. Her work has appeared in *U.S. History Scene* and *Journal of African American Studies.*

Jaye Austin Williams is Assistant Professor of Theatre Arts at California State University, Long Beach. She most recently served as a 2014–2015 Chancellor's Postdoctoral Fellow at UC Irvine. She has worked for over thirty years as a stage director, playwright, actor, and professional consultant, on and off Broadway and regionally. She holds an M.F.A. in Dramatic Writing from New York University's Tisch School of the Arts, and a Ph.D. from the Joint Doctoral Program in Drama and Theatre at the University of California, Irvine and San Diego.

Harvey Young is Chair of the Theatre Department at Northwestern University. He is the author of *Embodying Black Experience; Theatre & Race*; and *Black Theatre is Black Life: An Oral History of Chicago Theatre, 1970–2010* (with Mecca Zabriskie), and the editor of *Performance in the Borderlands* (with Ramón H. Rivera-Severa); *Reimagining A Raisin in the Sun: Four New Plays* (with Rebecca Ann Rugg); *The Cambridge Companion to African American Theatre*; and *Suzan-Lori Parks in Person* (with Philip C. Kolin).

Acknowledgements

This publication is the product of creative and intellectual collaboration between a myriad of individuals whose distinct talents, voices, expertise, and perspectives all contribute to the conversation playing out across the following pages. Thank you to the editorial team at Routledge, particularly Associate Editor Ben Piggott, who shepherded and championed this project from the very beginning. Multiple thanks are owed to the contributors in this collection, whose passion and persistence have yielded rigorous and engaging considerations of Lynn Nottage's plays. Special thanks and recognition are due to Aimee Zygmonski, whose enthusiasm and expertise informed the initial shaping of this project, and for which I am forever grateful. I am also much obliged to Cathy Hannabach, who created a thorough index to the collection. I owe additional thanks to my fellow faculty and the administration at Chapman University, for supporting this endeavor with their collegial spirit, as well as the precious gifts of time and resources. Thanks also to my students, for their patience, curiosity, and excitement about this project.

My profound gratitude and affection go to my family, friends, colleagues, and mentors, especially Henry Bial, Carolyn F. Buckner, Marcy M. Buckner, Drew Chappell, Rick Christophersen Johnnie M. Gaskins, Chandra O. Hopkins, Jack Jordan, Maiya Murphy, Matt Omasta, Lisa Jackson-Schebetta, Scott Stone, Heidi A. Temple, Jenny Woodruff, and Harvey Young, whose unwavering patience, sacrifices, advice and feedback, logistical and emotional support, and encouragement have helped make my own labor on this project possible.

Finally, and most especially, I extend my deepest appreciation and thanks to Lynn Nottage, for supporting and contributing to this collection, and for crafting stories we all need to hear.

Foreword

Freedom is a debt to repay; a legacy to uphold

Sandra G. Shannon

"I'm free, Tilly. I'm free" (94). This much-rehearsed final line from Marie, the dying "white" damsel in Lynn Nottage's play-within-a-play, *The Belle of New Orleans*, resonates on multiple levels – both within and outside the over-the-top theatrics of the waning, supposedly white starlet Gloria Mitchell and the ambitious African American supporting actress and maid Vera Stark in Nottage's multi-layered and cunningly deceptive *By the Way, Meet Vera Stark*. The illusive storyline of this work is based upon the struggles of a craftily fictionalized fallen actress, Vera Lula Stark (1910–1973?) who Nottage sets free from the constraints and prejudices of Hollywood's Golden Age by casting her significantly outside the shadow of the mammy figure and by endowing this African American woman with awareness, ambition, agency, and assertiveness.

With all of its mirrors, the richly layered metanarrative that Lynn Nottage sets up in *By the Way, Meet Vera Stark* is emblematic of multiple illusions of freedom that her African American female characters pursue throughout her growing body of dramatic works. At the center of each of her plays is a Vera Stark prototype who is well ahead of the times in her stubborn will to define her own terms, which often means that she breaks the mold society has set in place for her race and gender. She emerges in a string of unapologetically female-centered plays – *Intimate Apparel*; *Fabulation, or the Re-Education of Undine*; *Crumbs from the Table of Joy*, *Las Meninas*; *Mud, River, Stone*; *Por 'Knockers*; and *POOF!* – wherein this prototype makes moves to secure her own personal freedom: sexual, psychological, marital, political, social, or otherwise. Collectively Nottage's stubborn-willed sheroes, from Esther (*Intimate Apparel*) to Ernestine (*Crumbs from the Table of Joy*) to Undine (*Fabulation*), trample stereotypes and create more individualized portraits of African American womanhood. Nottage teases out their stories, whether they are the result of intended or inadvertent silences occasioned by historical amnesia or societal subjugation.

To be sure, the push to determine and pursue one's own definition of freedom extends beyond the fictional rivalry Nottage sets up between Mitchell and Stark. Since the 1990s when *POOF!* (1993), *Crumbs from the Table of Joy* (1995), and *Mud, River, Stone* (1998) secured her status as a serious playwright, Nottage has fought for and exercised her own freedom in stretching the dramatic form and narrative possibilities of theatre in the interest of venting women's untold stories in defamiliarized ways. "I'm concerned about telling stories about women whom I knew in a way that touches audiences," she told me in a 2006 interview (197). But Nottage is not exclusively concerned with impacting audiences. Her writing is also motivated by a desire to open more doors for fellow black female playwrights and by what she sees as an obligation to preserve the mythology of African American women by committing their stories to the stage. In her remarks accepting the McArthur Genius Grant in 2007, she savored the freedom that came along with being recognized by the prestigious foundation: "It is my hope that the McArthur will give me the freedom to explore, the freedom to experiment, the freedom to be a lot braver in the choices that I make as an artist" (McArthur Fellows). Clearly Lynn Nottage has not reneged on that freedom, for it echoes in the often unorthodox ways she relays the voices of her female characters and in her skill at highlighting challenges they face: "Women are my focal point," she explains (199).

What does freedom look like now for Lynn Nottage? Certainly, for the brilliant, well-travelled, avid researcher, women's activist, and critically acclaimed artist that she has become, freedom is not taken for granted. Influenced in part by her tenure in the press office of Amnesty International, where, as national press officer, she processed news of global suffering and mistreatment of women, coupled with her penchant for international travel and extensive research, Nottage brings to the American stage extreme passion and global awareness of women's issues that deemphasize borders and differences and invite audiences to contemplate a shared humanity. As a global citizen, she has created a platform in her work to expose inhumane treatment of peoples of color – especially women. The care that she takes in telling the stories of the marginalized is arguably a direct result of her global citizenry that is on display in her works such as *Las Meninas*, *Ruined*, and *Mud, River, Stone*. Indeed, one senses in Nottage's writing a profound awareness of a debt to be repaid and a legacy to be upheld.

The complexity of Nottage's plays is due in large part to her ability to be both informed by and able to harness the media in an effort to reflect real world concerns. Whether this entails incorporating aspects of cinematography into her scripts or jumpstarting her plots from particularly troubling news articles, her plays have benefited from the communicative power of the visual and written media to inform and change attitudes in the interest of women. For example, her incorporation of film as context and her seemingly random insertion of newspaper captions and historical nuggets gleaned from her own steadfast research invite a new look at gender and racial identity issues raised in plays such as *Crumbs from the Table of Joy*, *Intimate Apparel*, and *By the Way, Meet Vera Stark*. The richly layered and intensely ironic nature of these plays can be attributed to her ability to reverse the camera's lens in order to make double use of her characters as both role players and as commentators.

As one might expect, the stakes are high in this inaugural effort to lay the groundwork for formal study of the plays of Lynn Nottage. In *A Critical Companion to Lynn Nottage*, editor Jocelyn L. Buckner has painstakingly assembled some of the most respected authorities in the field of theatre, dramatic literature, and performance studies. They are flanked by an equally formidable group of emerging scholars well versed in current theory and poised not only to advance Nottage studies with incisive new ways of understanding her work, but also to significantly advance work in the field at large. While Nottage's impressive body of work has already earned her membership among America's elite list of playwrights, it is the work of the scholar/critic, such as the ones whose essays are featured herein, that will inspire additional critical inquiries, solidify her legacy, and secure her place among major American dramatists. August Wilson reminds us of the duty – indeed the obligation – of the scholar/critic in his highly provocative *The Ground on Which I Stand* manifesto: "As playwrights grow and develop, as theatre changes, the critic has an important responsibility to guide and encourage growth" (43). *A Critical Companion to Lynn Nottage* takes on this responsibility to assure the kind of steady and purposeful growth in scholarship that keeps pace with Nottage's creative genius. Collectively, each of the essays featured here paves the way for the "work" that must be done to draw serious attention to a playwright whom, for example, Jocelyn L. Buckner regards as a "dramaturgical historiographer," whom Faedra Chatard Carpenter sees as a "trickster folklorist," whom Adrienne Macki Braconi credits for thematic use of place and space in "sociospatial landscapes," and who Harvey Young asserts is "one of the leading social issue artists of her generation." The essays contained here, no doubt, will be cited often and at length in subsequent publications on the body of Nottage's published plays and on those certain to follow.

The essays gathered in this well-timed collection are a testament to what it means for an African American female playwright writing in the twenty-first century to be free – free to complicate existing dramatic forms and to create new ones, free to go in search of and create drama out of unabridged truths, free to politicize abuse and suffering, and, now – with an impressive repertoire of dramatic works to her credit and the respect of critics and audiences alike – free to continue charting a new course for black theatre.

Works cited

"Lynn Nottage: Playwright." *McArthur Fellows: Meet the Class of 2007.* January 28, 2007. Web. Accessed August 1, 2015.

Nottage, Lynn. *By the Way, Meet Vera Stark.* New York: Theatre Communications Group, 2013. Print.

Shannon, Sandra G. "An Interview with Lynn Nottage." *Contemporary African American Women Playwrights: A Casebook.* Ed. Philip C. Kolin. New York: Routledge, 2007. 194–201. Print.

Wilson, August. *The Ground on Which I Stand.* New York: Theatre Communications Group, 2000. Print.

Introduction

"Sustaining the complexity" of Lynn Nottage[1]

Jocelyn L. Buckner

This anthology is devoted to expanding and complicating the discourse surrounding Lynn Nottage's contributions to U.S. theatre and the contemporary dramatic canon through the critical and scholarly examination of her plays, artistic collaborations, and activism. As an internationally recognized playwright and spokesperson for social issues affecting women, artists, and communities ravaged by crises ranging from economic collapse to civil war, Nottage is worthy of a volume committed to the study of her accomplishments.

Considering the expanse and success of Lynn Nottage's oeuvre, this collection identifies and connects three main themes situated at the center of her dramaturgy: history, diaspora, and identity. The chapters engage in a chronological analysis of variations on these themes in each of Nottage's full-length plays, illuminating perhaps lesser known earlier works, while also working to shape conversations developing around her more recent and commercially successful plays. Scott Knowles's production chronology traces Nottage's career from the very beginning, noting significant productions, accomplishments, and awards. In addition to briefly introducing the themes of the plays and their methods of production, the chronology notes her overt social and political activism. The timeline serves as an overview of Nottage's career and is a helpful resource for scholars, students, and artists initially encountering the playwright's work.

Nottage's early plays initiate her commitment to discourse on and exploration of issues of social justice in both U.S. and international contexts. In the first essay, Jaye Austin Williams examines *Crumbs from the Table of Joy*, about a black family in post-World War II America. She reads Aunt Lily as the central figure on whom the play hinges, a woman who migrates north in search of political, personal, and professional safety in an effort to flee the continual persecution experienced by blacks in the U.S. South in the wake of increasing post-war nationalism and racial unrest. Williams uncovers how *Crumbs* complicates the lived experience of history, temporality, spirituality, and hope, and the unsettling violent dissonance they compose when engaged with blackness. Next, Jennifer L. Hayes identifies the unlikely international community depicted in *Mud, River, Stone* as a latter day, multivocal refashioning of the ancient Greek chorus tradition. Hayes argues that Nottage reimagines the dramaturgical function of the chorus into a collective reflecting diverse multicultural perspectives, using language to debate challenging postcolonial circumstances and preconceptions of Africa. In the following chapter, Jocelyn L. Buckner contends that Lynn Nottage's *Las Meninas* employs a dramaturgical historiography to replay, retell, and revise histories of peoples of African descent, this time in the context of the French court of King Louis XIV. By investigating the relationship between displacement and desire in a specific historical moment and location in the African diaspora in Europe, she examines how Nottage dramatizes a revisionist historiography of diasporic longing for home, identity, and belonging, pointing to the ways identity is contested and constructed across the porous borders of space and time.

Intersectionality and intertextuality frame approaches to Nottage's depictions of history, diaspora, and identity in the next three chapters. Drawing on theories of cultural materialism and phenomenology, Adrienne Macki Braconi traces how Nottage's dramaturgy reflects public and private spatial tensions in *Intimate Apparel*. Braconi investigates this play's rendering of gendered, racial, and ethnic boundaries by attending to Nottage's depiction of intimate spaces as sites of betrayal, unfulfilled desires, and self-preservation within the context of varying geographic and urban places as well as mythic spaces of the mind. Next, Faedra Chartard Carpenter examines how Brer Rabbit, an Afrocentric trickster character, influenced Nottage's thematic explorations of home and the complications of flawed humanity in *Fabulation, or the Re-education of Undine*. Through an analysis of how Nottage draws on previous trickster tropes as inspirational sources for her play, this chapter identifies the multiple ways *Fabulation* engages in an intertextual exchange with other authors and texts from the "Brer Rabbit canon." In doing so, Carpenter illustrates how Nottage recovers the contested cultural legacy of Brer Rabbit through the dramatization of the title character's story. Harvey Young's essay celebrates the women in *By the Way, Meet Vera Stark*, which further extends Nottage's consideration of identity in various historical and cultural milieus. He documents how these resourceful and autonomous characters define how others see them through a series of strategic acts. Importantly, this chapter also spotlights the play's call for recognition of the circumstances of artists who struggled in the film industry during the difficult years of the Great Depression, and the decisions that they faced regarding their careers, economic survival, and whether to resist or accept playing a stereotype.

In a special section devoted to *Ruined*, Nottage's most critically lauded play and winner of the 2009 Pulitzer Prize for Drama, three essays interrogate the importance of this work's efficacy as a piece of theatre for social change. Jennifer-Scott Mobley argues that *Ruined* echoes facets of nineteenth-century melodrama in an effort to realize a feminist political "dramaturgy of reform." Mobley illuminates how Nottage not only extends melodrama's patriarchal tradition to focus on nuanced female subjects, but also incorporates melodramatic conventions including music, suspense, and a sensation scene to draw audiences into the plot and evoke an affective response to the action of the piece, resulting in increased socio-political awareness and the potential for local and global feminist activist responses and interventions. Next, Jeff Paden troubles the dominant critical response to *Ruined*, which perceives the drama's romantic conclusion as in opposition to its political consciousness raising regarding the epidemic of rampant sexual violence against women during the civil war raging in the Democratic Republic of the Congo. By exploring the play's use of violence, Paden contends that Nottage's dramaturgical "hybridity of form" renders the play's ending more complex and uncertain than critical responses have initially recognized. Concluding this section, Esther J. Terry articulates how, by building a house comprised of ruined kinships and ruined bodies in the context of a ruined land, Nottage disrupts and reorders declarations of origin and belonging in Africa and African diasporas. She studies the difficult diasporic choices and new alliances the women in the play must make in order to heal their physical, emotional, and psychological wounds. Terry argues that by manipulating their languages, bodies, and homes, the women steer through the displacing chaos they encounter and shape their reimagined futures, together.

Nottage distinguishes herself in many ways as a playwright, from the intensive ethnographic and historiographic research she conducts that ultimately informs the stories she tells, to the socially engaged themes of gender, race, and class that thread through her plays, to her recent interest in transmedia projects that knit the live theatrical event to other means of audience engagement. The collection ends with a transcribed conversation with Lynn Nottage and two of her most frequent collaborators on premieres and major productions of her work, directors Kate Whoriskey (world premieres of *Intimate Apparel*, 2003; *Fabulation*, 2005; *Ruined*, 2008; and *Sweat*, 2015) and Seret Scott (world premieres of *POOF!*, 1993; *Mud, River, Stone*, 1996; and also director of *Crumbs from the Table of Joy* at South Coast Repertory Theatre, 1996; and *Ruined* at Denver Theatre Center, 2011). The artists discuss the craft of collaboration involved in developing new scripts and productions, the rigorous task of honoring the humor in and challenges to traditional dramatic structure inherent in Nottage's works, and the creative charge to "sustain the complexity" of the stories and histories found in Lynn Nottage's plays.

In over twenty years of professional playwriting, Nottage has continuously addressed themes and issues of concern to both individuals and communities. Nottage's newest play, *Sweat*, co-commissioned by the Oregon Shakespeare Festival and Arena Stage, and which premiered at OSF in July 2015, is no exception. Written at what could be considered the height of her critical and popular success to date, *Sweat* echoes her previous works while at the same time it serves as an indication of her ongoing commitment to empathetically telling the stories of oppressed people, both in the U.S. and internationally. Like *Ruined* and *Mud, River, Stone* before it, *Sweat* is staged in a bar, a communal watering hole where workers from local factories in the economically depressed town of Reading, Pennsylvania gather to blow off steam, commiserate about the declining state of industry in town, and to celebrate life events. As in *Ruined* and *Mud, River, Stone*, the public space facilitates interactions between people who might not otherwise meet, encouraging alliances and conflicts between individuals. The characters bemoan what Nottage terms the "de-industrialization" of their town which, in the first decade of the twenty-first century when the play takes place, is a few generations removed from the height of the Industrial Revolution and influx of European immigration that helped make Reading a boom town at the turn of the previous century. Now the community, composed of descendants of those earlier immigrants as well as new migrants from the global South, is struggling to survive. One long-time resident, Tracey, laments the town's deterioration, recalling a time in her childhood when her grandfather could proudly point to his intricate woodworking projects at various downtown business locations, which are now covered in sheetrock or closed completely. Such recognition of artisanal craft and the individual labor involved in its production resonates with the handiwork detailing The Imperial Hotel in *Mud, River, Stone*, as well as the reverence and appreciation for the craft and effort involved in making handmade fine garments depicted in

Intimate Apparel. The pride of the factory workers in *Sweat* reverberates with that of *Ruined*'s Mama Nadi, a fellow laborer and survivor, whose bar and brothel maintains a brisk business and serves as a haven in the midst of the war-ravaged forests of the DRC. While these earlier plays explore labor and class issues in postcolonial South East Africa, 1908 New York, and the contemporary Congo, respectively, *Sweat* asks, what now? And, what's next? What is the human cost of the millennial marketplace? How can witnessing stories of struggle from the past and present teach us to act with compassion and empathy toward one another? How can we better care for one another, and for our collective humanity? This new play, and those that are sure to follow it, only further underscores what Sandra G. Shannon and Soyica Diggs Colbert recognize as the need for ongoing scholarly engagement with Nottage's work as an expression of artistic and personal freedom, advocacy, and future possibility.

Untold stories. Unheard voices. Unseen peoples. Every one of Lynn Nottage's theatrical endeavors tells a tale of unsung struggle for survival and personal happiness amongst individuals living along and beyond the margins of society. The heart of Nottage's dramaturgy lies in nuanced negotiations of complex stories, where individuals are neither good nor bad, but rather valiantly seeking to better their lot in life. She has honed her voice and writing style, resonating with traditional influences and forms while simultaneously experimenting with and pushing the boundaries of theatre. Long admired by audiences and critics, it is time for scholars to engage Nottage's voice with an eye toward considering her impact on theatre politically, aesthetically, and topically. Lynn Nottage has changed – and will continue to challenge – the discourse of contemporary theatre. This collection endeavors to reflect upon her accomplishments to date, and to promote future study, production, and discussion of her work.

Note

1   This quote reflects Nottage's mantra of "sustaining the complexity of what it means to be a woman" in the process of crafting her work and telling women's stories in her plays. See "On Creativity and Collaboration" in this collection.

A chronology of Lynn Nottage's production history

Scott C. Knowles

"My plays often begin with an idea that haunts me."
Lynn Nottage, "History of Omission"

From an early age, Lynn Nottage was instilled with a sense of social activism by her parents Ruby and Wallace Nottage. This activism is reflected throughout her work and is one of its most impressive traits. Nottage is haunted by ideas that revolve around social injustice, silenced voices, and the forgotten. She works to imagine the history of those whose stories have not previously been deemed worthy of remembrance. As critic Randy Gener notes, Nottage's characters are "usually restless searchers, forgotten people and alienated folks who are trying to fit in or find a connection or are on a quest for identity" (24). Her plays span a vast array of themes, people, and locations, but the common thread of historical and social activism runs throughout. Nottage's creative and social agenda is evident when looking at the chronology of her plays. From violence against women, to lost histories of the marginalized, to the personal history laced throughout *Intimate Apparel*, to the contemporary social activism of *Ruined*, Nottage works within what Diana Taylor might term the archive and the repertoire: a rift that "does not lie between the written and the spoken word, but between the archive of supposedly enduring materials (i.e., texts, documents, buildings, bones) and the so-called ephemeral repertoire of embodied practice/knowledge (i.e., spoken language, dance, sports, ritual)" (19). She voraciously seeks out evidence to support the stories in her plays, for example, spending extensive time in the New York Public Library to research *Intimate Apparel*, or traveling to a different continent to collect the stories of women fleeing the war-torn Democratic Republic of Congo. Her plays live in the interstices of the archive/repertoire, as

evidenced by her description of the development process for *Ruined*,
"I did all these interviews – three years interviewing women throughout
East Africa. Once I finished the research, I never looked at it again.
I just thought, 'I'm done. I've heard it. I've absorbed it. It's in my body.'
So I sat down to write, and I literally never looked back at the notes"
(Murphy). Nottage's work creates a critical artistic intervention in the
space between official narratives and her subjects' own embodied expe-
riences. This chronology features highlights of Nottage's life and career
as a leading playwright in the contemporary theatre.

1964 – 2 November, Lynn Nottage is born in Brooklyn, NY.

1982 – Nottage graduates from New York's High School of Music & Art
in Harlem. While there she pens plays in her journal, including
her first play, *The Darker Side of Verona*.

1986 – Nottage receives her B.A. from Brown University where she also
meets her husband, Tony Gerber.

1989 – Nottage completes her M.F.A. in playwriting at Yale School
of Drama and takes a hiatus from playwriting to gain a more
"expansive experience." She begins working for Amnesty International as a national press officer (Shannon 194).

1992 – Nottage becomes a resident artist at Mabou Mines.

1993 – *POOF!* premieres at the Actors Theatre of Louisville's Humana
Festival of New American Plays in March, directed by Seret
Scott. It wins the Heideman Award and is published in the festival's yearly edition of *Ten-Minute Plays from Actors Theatre
of Louisville*. Nottage describes the origin of the play as her
response to survivors of domestic abuse she encountered while
at Amnesty International: "You could see all the anguish and
frustration in the women's faces [in photographs brought into
Amnesty International]. I had to respond in some way. So,
I closed my office door and wrote a short play called *POOF!*
There was a flyer sitting on my desk for a short play competition in Louisville" (Murphy). After writing *POOF!*, Nottage
leaves Amnesty International to focus on playwriting.

1994 – Nottage's next play, *Por'knockers,* receives a workshop production at Dance Theatre Workshop in New York City in September,
directed by Michael Rogers.

1995 – *Crumbs from the Table of Joy* premieres at Second Stage Theatre
in New York City in May, directed by Joe Morton. *Por'knockers*
premieres at the Vineyard Theatre in New York City in November, directed by Michael Rogers.

1996 – *Crumbs from the Table of Joy* is produced by Steppenwolf Theatre Company in Chicago, IL in March, directed by Leslie Holland, and by South Coast Repertory in Costa Mesa, CA in September, directed by Seret Scott. *Mud, River, Stone* is commissioned by the Acting Company in New York City and receives its premiere in November at Studio Arena Theatre in Buffalo, NY, directed by Seret Scott.

1997 – Nottage's mother, one of her great inspirations, Ruby Nottage, dies of Lou Gehrig's disease just two months before the birth of Nottage's first child, Ruby Aiyo. *Las Meninas* is produced at Brown University in March, directed by John Emigh. *Mud, River, Stone* premieres in New York City at Playwrights Horizons in December, directed by Roger Rees.

1999 – *Mud, River, Stone* is published. Nottage receives a grant from the National Endowment for the Arts and Theatre Communications Group to support a year-long residency at Freedom Theatre in Philadelphia, PA.

2000 – *A Walk Through Time*, a children's musical, is produced by Freedom Theatre in March.

2001 – Nottage joins the faculty of the playwriting program at Yale School of Drama.

2002 – *Las Meninas* premieres at San Jose Repertory Theatre in March, directed by Michael Donald Edward. *Becoming American*, a ten-minute play by Nottage, is produced at the Actors Theatre of Louisville.

2003 – *Intimate Apparel* is commissioned and co-produced by South Coast Repertory and Center Stage in Baltimore, MD, in April, directed by Kate Whoriskey. Nottage and her husband Tony Gerber found Market Road Films–an independent film company.

2004 – *Intimate Apparel* receives its New York City premiere in April at Roundabout Theatre Company, directed by Daniel Sullivan. *Intimate Apparel* wins several awards, including, The New York Drama Critics' Circle Award for Best Play, the Francesca Primus Prize, the American Theatre Critics/Steinberg New Play Award, the Outer Critics Circle John Gassner Playwriting Award, and the Outer Critics Circle Outstanding Off-Broadway Play Award. Nottage receives the Laura Pels International Foundation for Theater Award. *Fabulation, or the Re-Education of Undine* premieres in June at Playwrights Horizons, directed by Kate Whoriskey. After finishing work on *Fabulation,* Nottage and Whoriskey travel to Kampala, Uganda to interview women escaping the violence of the Democratic Republic of Congo. The stories of these women become the inspirational material for *Ruined*. Nottage's first collection of plays, *Crumbs from the Table of Joy and Other Plays*, is published and includes: *Crumbs from the Table of Joy, POOF!, Por 'Knockers, Mud, River, Stone*, and *Las Meninas*.

2005 – *Intimate Apparel* and *Fabulation, or the Re-Education of Undine* are published. *Fabulation* wins an Obie Award for Playwriting. Nottage receives a John Simon Guggenheim Memorial Fellowship for Creative Arts and The National Black Theatre Festival's August Wilson Playwriting Award.

2006 – Nottage receives the Lucille Lortel Playwright's Fellowship. *Fabulation, or the Re-Education of Undine* premieres in September at London's Tricycle Theatre, directed by Indhu Rubasingham.

2007– Nottage receives a John D. and Catherine T. MacArthur Foundation Fellowship, a "Genius Grant."

2008 – *Ruined* is commissioned and produced by the Goodman Theatre in Chicago in November. The play is co-produced by Manhattan Theatre Club and directed by Kate Whoriskey.

2009 – Nottage and her husband Tony Gerber adopt a son, Melkamu. In February, *Ruined* makes its New York City debut at Manhattan Theatre Club, directed by Kate Whoriskey. The play attains critical acclaim and wins numerous awards including the Pulitzer Prize for Drama, the Drama Desk Award for Outstanding Play, The New York Drama Critics' Circle Award for Best Play, and the Lucille Lortel Award for Outstanding Play. In November *Ruined* receives a reading at the Kennedy Center in Washington, D.C., produced by The Enough Project at the Center for American Progress. Before the reading Nottage discusses the importance of producing *Ruined* at the "seat of power" where "the audience will be in a position to bring about some kind of change in the Congo" (Olopade). *Ruined* is published.

2010 – *Ruined* opens in April at the Almeida Theatre in London, directed by Indhu Rubasingham. Additionally, Nottage receives the Steinberg Distinguished Playwright Award, the Dramatists Guild's Hull-Warriner Award, the inaugural Horton Foote Prize for Outstanding New American Play (*Ruined*), and the League of Professional Theatre Women's Lee Reynolds Award.

2011 – *By the Way, Meet Vera Stark* premieres at Second Stage Theatre in New York City in April, directed by Jo Bonney. *Ruined* is produced at Arena Stage in Washington, D.C., directed by Charles Randolph-Wright.

2012 – *By the Way, Meet Vera Stark* has its West Coast premiere at the Geffen Playhouse in Los Angeles, CA in September. *Ruined* wins the Helen Hayes Outstanding Resident Play Award for its production at the Arena Stage.

2013 – *By the Way, Meet Vera Stark* opens at the Goodman Theatre in April and is published. The Metropolitan Opera and Lincoln Center Theatre announces that they have commissioned Lynn Nottage along with composer Ricky Ian Gordon to adapt *Intimate Apparel* as an opera.

2014 – Nottage joins the faculty of the M.F.A. playwriting program at Columbia University's School of the Arts. *Intimate Apparel* makes its British premiere in May at the Theatre Royal Bath's Ustinov Studio, directed by Laurence Boswell.

2015 – *Sweat,* Nottage's newest work, premieres at the Oregon Shakespeare Festival (OSF) in July, directed by Kate Whoriskey. *Sweat* was commissioned by OSF as part of its American Revolutions initiative, in conjunction with Arena Stage and Labyrinth Theatre Company.

2016 – Nottage receives the PEN Literary Award's Master American Dramatist Award. She is awarded the Susan Smith Blackburn Prize and an American Theatre Critics Association Award nomination for *Sweat* (as of the time of publication).

Works cited

"Awards & Prizes." *American Theatre* 21.5 (2004): 11. Print.

"Awards & Prizes." *American Theatre* 22.8 (2005): 12. Print.

"Awards & Prizes." *American Theatre* 24.1 (2007): 22. Print.

"Awards & Prizes." *American Theatre* 27.10 (2010): 16. Print.

Barnwell, Michael. "Fire and Water." *American Theatre* 12.9 (1995): 10. Print.

Billington, Michael. "Review: Theatre: The War Zone in Which Women's Bodies Are the Battleground: *Ruined* Almeida, London 4/5." *The Guardian.* April 23, 2010: 44. Print.

Bradley, Jada. "Kennedy Center Stages Reading of 2009 Pulitzer-Prize Winning Drama *Ruined.*" *The Examiner.* 11 November 2009. Web. Accessed February 10, 2015.

Brown, Jeffery. "Congo's Civil War Is Rich Seam for Prize-Winning Playwright." *PBS News Hour.* July 15, 2009. Web. Accessed July 12, 2014.

Clapp, Susannah. "The New Review: Critics: Theatre: You Reap What You Sew: A Seamstress Illuminates Lynn Nottage's Beautifully Understated *Intimate Apparel*, while Polly Stenham Takes Direct Action: *Intimate Apparel* Ustinov Studio, Theatre Royal, Bath." *The Guardian.* June 8, 2014: 33. Print.

Engelman, Liz and Michele Volansky, eds. *POOF! Ten-Minute Plays from Actors Theatre of Louisville: The Best of 1993.* Louisville: Actors Theatre of Louisville, 1993. Print.

Gener, Randy. "Conjurer of Worlds." *American Theatre* 22.8 (2005): 22–145. Print.

Giuliano, Mike. "*Intimate Apparel*." *Variety* 390.4 (2003): 41. Print.

Harvey, Dennis. "*LAS MENINAS* (Drama)." *Variety* 386.7 (2002): 42. Print.

Healy, Patrick. "Lynn Nottage Awarded Steinberg Prize." *New York Times*. September 21, 2010. Web. Accessed July 20, 2014.

Iqbal, Nosheen. "Lynn Nottage: A Bar, a Brothel and Brecht." *The Guardian*. April 21, 2010: 22. Print.

Kepler, Adam W., compiler. "A New Lynn Nottage Play." *New York Times*. March 17, 2014: C3(L). Web. Accessed July 10, 2014.

Lane, Eric and Nina Shengold, eds. *Plays for Actresses*. New York: Vintage Books, 1997. Print.

"Lynn Nottage." *Contemporary Authors Online*. Detroit: Gale, 2010. *Literature Resource Center*. Web. Accessed July 12, 2014.

"Lynn Nottage & Will Eno Named First Recipients of the Horton Foote Prizes." *The Horton Foote Prize*. August 26, 2010. Web. Accessed September 29, 2014.

Marks, Peter. "'Ruined': Luminous in the Red light." *The Washington Post*. May 3, 2011: C10. Print.

"The Metropolitan Opera Announces the 2013–14 Season" *The Metropolitan Opera*. February 26, 2013. Web. Accessed July 20, 2014.

Murphy, Dwyer. "History of Omission: Dwyer Murphy interviews Lynn Nottage." *Guernica: A Magazine of Art and Politics*. May 1, 2013. Web. Accessed June 20, 2014.

"Nilo Cruz & Lynn Nottage." *Dramatist* 12.4 (March 2010): 27. Print.

Nottage, Lynn. *By the Way, Meet Vera Stark*. New York: Theatre Communications Group, 2013. Print.

———. *Crumbs from the Table of Joy*. *Crumbs from the Table of Joy and Other Plays*. New York: Theatre Communications Group, 2004. 1–88. Print.

———. *Fabulation, or the Re-Education of Undine*. New York: Dramatists Play Service, Inc., 2005. Print.

———. *Intimate Apparel*. New York: Dramatists Play Service, Inc., 2005. Print.

———. *Intimate Apparel and Fabulation, or the Re-Education of Undine*. New York: Theatre Communications Group, 2006. Print.

———. *Las Meninas*. *Crumbs from the Table of Joy and Other Plays*. New York: Theatre Communications Group, 2004. 245–324. Print.

———. *Mud, River, Stone*. New York: Dramatists Play Service, Inc., 1999. Print.

———. *Mud, River, Stone*. *Crumbs from the Table of Joy and Other Plays*. New York: Theatre Communications Group, 2004. 163–243. Print.

———. *POOF! Crumbs from the Table of Joy and Other Plays*. New York: Theatre Communications Group, 2004. 89–103. Print.

———. *Por'knockers*. *Crumbs from the Table of Joy and Other Plays*. New York: Theatre Communications Group, 2004. 105–162. Print.

———. *Ruined*. New York: Theatre Communications Group, 2009. Print.

Olopade, Dayo. "The Root Interview: Lynn Nottage on 'Ruined' Beauty." Interview with Lynn Nottage. *The Root*. March 1, 2010. Web. Accessed October 5, 2011.

Roux, Alyson. "Lynn Nottage at Steppenwolf." *Steppenwolf.* 2003. Web. Accessed June 12, 2014.

Sanders, Vicki. "Rescue Worker." *Brown Alumni Magazine.* September/October 2003. Web. Accessed June 12, 2014.

Schuessler, Jennifer. "Two Playwrights Join Columbia." *New York Times.* June 17, 2014: C3(L). Web. Accessed July 10, 2014.

Shannon, Sandra G. "An Interview with Lynn Nottage." *Contemporary African American Women Playwrights: A Casebook.* Ed. Philip C. Kolin. London and New York: Routledge, 2007. 194–201. Print.

Sheward, David. "Theatre Reviews: *Mud, River, Stone.*" *Back Stage* 38.51 (1997): 33. Print.

Soloski, Alexis. "Lynn Nottage: *Intimate Apparel* and what Lies Beneath my Plays." *The Guardian.* May 28, 2014. Web. Accessed July 20, 2014.

Taylor, Diana. *The Archive and the Repertoire: Performing Cultural Memory in the Americas.* Durham: Duke University Press, 2003. Print.

Taylor, Paul. "*Fabulation*; Theatre; Tricycle London." *Independent Extra.* September 22, 2006: 14. Print.

Weibgen, Lara. "Nottage, Lynn." *Current Biography Yearbook, 2004.* Ed. Clifford Thompson. New York: H.W. Wilson, 2004. 417–421. Print.

Chapter I

On the table

Crumbs of freedom and fugitivity – A twenty-first century (re)reading of *Crumbs from the Table of Joy*

Jaye Austin Williams

The bourgeoisie is fearful of the militancy of the Negro woman . . . [t]he capitalists know, far better than many progressives seem to know, that once Negro women undertake action, the militancy of the whole Negro people . . . is greatly enhanced.

Claudia Jones, "An End to the Neglect of the Problems of the Negro Woman!"

I never stand for the National Anthem, don't even know the words. But ya know the tune that git me to my feet every time, that Charlie Parker playing "Salt peanuts, salt peanuts." Chile, I practically conceded to God when he took his sax on up that scale.

Lily, Act I, Sc. 3, *Crumbs from the Table of Joy*, Lynn Nottage

Daniel Patrick Moynihan's celebrated "Report" [published in 1965, depicts] the "Negro Family" [as having] no Father to speak of . . . [this] is, surprisingly, the fault of the Daughter, or the female line. This stunning reversal of the castration thematic . . . becomes an aspect of the African-American female's misnaming.

Hortense J. Spillers, "Mama's Baby, Papa's Maybe: An American Grammar Book"

There is a kind of "mathematical" elegance in how these three epigraphs concertize. The first asserts the coalescent power of Black women. The third casts a "black light" to reveal that which rhetorically, legislatively, and historically, which is to say, soci(et)ally, undoes that power.[1] The second moves "fugitively" between the other two, interstitially, articulating an elegant triumvirate: Jones's wish toward effective militancy, Lily's love of (and existence betwixt) the jazz notes that sonically exceed

the (aesthetic) values that would enslave them, and Spillers's interrogation of the will to maintain dominion over them all, not least, by laying
blame upon the very "matriarchy" that is structurally denied them.[2] The
sum of their concerted effort, and more broadly, that of Black women
across generations who have labored and died while fighting for "the
(civil rights) cause," equals a violent paradox: a life constituted by a
perpetual wish for freedom that continually eludes the wisher.

I offer here a meditation on the ways playwright Lynn Nottage both
dramaturgically and theoretically intervenes in that paradox. In so doing,
I am mindful of Plato's precursory imagery of captivity in his *Allegory
of the Cave,* in which he depicts prisoners gazing upon shadows cast on
a cave wall. He constructs a cautionary exchange between the prisoners and shadows, deeming it untenable and, more implicitly, dangerous, because of the prisoners' circumscribed purviews and the shadows'
figurative departure from that upon which a sound, societal apparatus
can be constructed and sustained.[3] I posit that the remainder of Plato's
rhetorical invalidation of this confluence between captives and shadows
(cited above) manifests in modernity as beings rendered captive within
a structure girded by both literal incarceration and abject circumstance;
and that it is notable and in no way arbitrary that those so marked and
partitioned today are predominantly Black.

A dramatic exemplar of such meditation is Lynn Nottage's rendering
of the "Black family" in post-World War II America, at the intersection
of the bebop and McCarthy eras, and the "Great Migrations" north and
west by "freed" Blacks. *Crumbs from the Table of Joy* centers around a
young aspiring writer named Ernestine Crump, who recalls the painful
aftermath of her mother's death in Florida in 1950. Ernestine's bereft
father, Godfrey Crump, ventures up north to Brooklyn, New York, with
Ernestine and her sister, Ermina in tow, in pursuit of a life unencumbered
by grief and Jim Crow.

The play's title is inspired by poet and dramatist, Langston Hughes's
short poem, *Luck*:

> Sometimes a crumb falls from the table of joy,
> Sometimes a bone is flung,
> To some people love is given,
> To others only heaven.

(*Selected* 99)

Nottage situates the poem as epigraph to the play, which premiered
Off-Broadway at Second Stage Theatre in New York City in 1995.[4]

Figure 1.1 Godfrey Crump with daughters Ernestine and Ermina. Daryl Edwards (center) as Godfrey, Kisha Howard (right) as Ernestine, and Nicole Leach (left) as Ermina in the world premiere production at Second Stage. Photo by Susan Cook, ©1995.

Her deployment of Hughes as tone-setter is keen, as the poem posits a quadrangle of loci: a crumb, a bone, love, and heaven. Hughes's quantifier "only" in front of "heaven" paradoxically pinpoints heaven as the locus of death – the place for "others." It is distinct from the "love" (a presumably greater value here) that "people" get. The "crumbs" that fall suggest a scavenging of the "bone" that is cast to beasts and those presumed to be beasts. The resultant questions and implications surrounding the "table of joy" are vast and anything but joyous, suggesting Nottage's affinity with Hughes to be savvier than meets the (Platonic) eye, prompting me to read Plato's rhetorical move as a scandalizing of the captive-shadow relation in order to set soci(et)al practices and political constructs in contradistinction to what he presumes a vacuous exchange. Moreover, this move redacts the "intramural" details of that exchange from historical and epistemological legitimacy across time.[5]

One of the most stunning aspects of Nottage's oeuvre – in addition to her remarkable facility for distilling historical segments into dramatic storytelling – is her apprehension of temporality as a perpetually collapsing, paradoxical vortex for her Black characters. It follows then, that she would look to Hughes's sensibility. His scathing, prescient 1935 satirical one-act play, *Soul Gone Home*, for example, anticipates the Moynihan Report that Spillers observes to "misnam[e]" the Black matriarch and her daughters, encumbering them with sole culpability in the failure of the Black "family."[6] In the following excerpt, Hughes's grand satire crackles, as the Son lies dead, coins placed over his eyes, in ancient Greek tradition, and the Mother wails with grief. The Son rises from (within) the dead and upbraids her:

SON: Mama, you know you ain't done me right.
MOTHER: What you mean, I ain't done you right? [*She is rooted in horror.*] [. . .]
SON: [leaning forward] [. . .] You been a bad mother to me.
MOTHER: Shame! Shame! Shame, talkin' to your mama that away. [. . .]
SON: You never did feed me good, that's what I mean!

(*Soul* 536)

Hughes is acutely aware that the mother's inability to care for her son adequately is a matter of her *incapacitation* rather than her *incapability* to do so, and his broad, farcical gesture signifies accordingly. Nottage clearly apprehends Hughes's critique of romanticized tracts about equality and progress and the attendant presumption of racial slavery's obsolescence, such that the fact of its afterlife slices through the veneer of such violent obfuscation, denial, and displacement of culpability onto the slave-descended. The direct correlation between the Mother's structural incapacity in Hughes's play, and father Godfrey's paralysis in *Crumbs*, epitomizes the function of the Black feminist and Black radical dramatic. Together, they confront the paradigmatic (structural) condition that so intricately and violently impacts Black existence *at every level*. In other words, as Hughes sets the suffering wrought of incapacity into deathly satiric relief, so does Nottage situate her characters, with the very first utterance, at the place of death, such that the blur between its literal and figurative contours comes sharply into focus.

The protagonist, Ernestine Crump, remembers: "Death nearly crippled my father, slipping beneath the soles of his feet and taking away his ability to walk at will. Death made him wail like a god-awful banshee. *(Godfrey wails like a god-awful banshee.)*" (Nottage 7). Godfrey Crump is grieving his wife's recent death. However, banshees are said to *foretell* death with their wailing.[7] In establishing Godfrey as at once already grieving *and* wailing in anticipation, Nottage, taking her cue from Hughes, uncovers a locus-continuum for death and time, at the fulcrum of which are the illegible pain and paralysis that constitute Black suffering. This is to say, she collapses time through Ernestine's quip about a banshee, in the "present," which Godfrey then repeats with the action in the "past." The dramatic effect resonates almost soni-cally, resembling a scratch in an old record's groove that repeatedly trips the needle back to the same spot. Particularly profound here is that Ernestine does not immediately attribute her father's crippling condi-tion to her mother's recent death; inferring instead that it is *already* his condition at the play's opening. It is not until several lines later that she references her mother's passing when she recalls, "Death made strang-ers take hold of our hands and recount endless stories of Mommy" (Nottage 7). With this "subluxated" textual ordering, Godfrey and his daughters become "strangers" to those gathered in mourning; presum-ably, members of a community to which they and the mother have belonged.[8] This is to say, Ernestine's remembrance of her first cog-nition of death might well be read as an adolescent's experience of adults, particularly in a context as disorienting as a parent's funeral. Nottage's labor is far more sophisticated, however. Ernestine's label-ing of the mourners as "strangers" opens a compelling fissure through which the loss of the mother pierces, resonating beyond literal mater-nal loss, toward the severance from Mother Africa to which Saidiya Hartman refers; a repetition of the cutting through the Atlantic waters by endless slave ship bows, and the subsequent retelling of slave narra-tives by the slave-descended in the Americas. Its dramatic performance echoes as one slave remembers and the other wails in remembrance . . . the needle skips and skips, forward, back, back, forward . . . within the same no-place.[9]

Ernestine's opening incantation continues: "Death made us nau-seous with regret. It clipped Daddy's tongue and put his temper to rest. Made folks shuffle and bow their heads. But it wouldn't leave us be, tugging at our stomachs and our throats" (Nottage 8). With this opening litany, Nottage enunciates death as a perpetual, unrelent-ing state of being, and Ernestine, her father, and sister, as its coordi-nates. This move pinpoints literal death as one of several terms within an overall (relational) condition of what Orlando Patterson terms "social death;" namely, civil society's refusal of Black *being* as both a variable within the expression of social life writ large, and a direct outgrowth of Transatlantic (racial) Slavery, to which Patterson applies his analysis.[10] The Crump family indeed experiences death and loss affectively, but Nottage opens a rhetorical space – akin to Suzan-Lori Parks's formulation of "the great (w)hole in history" – wherein a correlation between the exponential gravity of Black folks performing their response (grief/suffering) to literal (already) death, and an overarching rhetorical expression of symbolic (always) death, can be examined.[11]

Ernestine's soliloquy at the play's conclusion prompts a theorization of the play by way of her Aunt Lily. Ernestine tells us that she has just arrived in Harlem from Brooklyn, where she had settled some years before with her father and sister. She is searching for her mother's sister, Lily, who ventured to Harlem immediately after Ernestine's mother's death, in fervent quest of a movement that might prove Black people's salvation. She found Communism, the only apparent political framework that espoused any semblance of "equality for all" in 1950. I posit Lily as the fulcrum of the play precisely because she exemplifies the Black woman of so many "confounded identities," as Spillers observes, and one whom Ernestine will become ("Mama's" 65). Ernestine tells us, in both homage and lament:

> Years from now I'll read the *Communist Manifesto, The Souls of Black Folk* and *Black Skin, White Masks* and find my dear Lily amongst the pages. . . . [Y]ears from now I'll ride the Freedom Bus back down home, enraged and vigilant, years from now I'll marry a civil servant and argue about the Vietnam war, integration and the Black Panther movement. Years from now I'll send off one son to college in New England and I'll lose the other to drugs and sing loudly in the church choir.
>
> (Nottage 88)

Here, Ernestine enters the aporia of years passing yet somehow standing still; marking the "precarious life of the ex-slave" that Hartman memorializes (*Venus* 4). She exists in perpetual migration, in search of the unfindable, and labors within the railing of political movements that later fall into the impasse of her past. Nottage thus forges a rethinking of "Great" migrations as but fugitive parries in response to the structured violence from and toward which the slave-descended are always running. In so doing, she hurls into urgent question the notion of the Black as a migratory "agent" given, as Spillers and Hartman remind, the literal and symbolic severance from origin and heritage that slavery exacted upon the (née) African[12] ("Mama's" 67, "Venus" 3). This ruptured relation to life is compounded by the unremittingly rehearsed abjuration of Blacks' attempts to enter the "civil" space – the very attempt being regarded as scandalous and even criminal.[13]

Lily would appear to be the Communist activist Claudia Jones's fictional doppelganger. Jones's 1949 manifesto (from which the opening epigraph is drawn) attests to the indignities of, among other things, the invisibility, exclusion, and inferior pay scale for Black women, noting, "the low scale of earnings of the Negro woman is directly related to her almost complete exclusion from virtually all fields of work except the most menial and underpaid, namely, domestic service" (Jones 110). Jones's empirical rigor exposes the unrelenting bureaucratic violence to which Black people are subjected in post-World War II America (what Patterson might describe as a residue of the "general dishonor" that he defines as constituent to slave-making). She calls attention to the extent to which Black women's "militant participation in all aspects of the struggle for peace, civil rights, and economic security" helped to galvanize the broader efforts aimed against the growing influence of fascism and imperialism upon "the bourgeoisie" (Jones 108). Jones's findings that Black women earn half of white women's under-earnings point incontrovertibly to anti-Black racism being the grammar that punctuates that disparity (Jones 110). Correspondingly, Lily puts the point on Jones's findings, by not only declaring to Godfrey her affiliation with the Communist party, but also articulating what comprises the bedrock and vitality of racism's stronghold: "This may be New York, but this still the basement. Don't none of those crackers want to share any bit of power with us. That's what it's about. Red Scare, should be called Black Scare" (Nottage 28). Lily later imparts to Ernestine and Ermina the consequences of her convictions, declaring, "babies, a Negro woman with my gumption don't keep work so easily. It's one of the hazards of being an independent thinker. If I've ever had me a job for more than a few weeks then I knew it was beneath me. You see what I'm saying?" (Nottage 31). That Claudia Jones was routinely arrested and imprisoned for her activism, threatened with deportation (she was born in Trinidad), and marked as "alien," speaks volumes to what both Jones and Lily seem to suggest: that labor inequity is but a symptom of something that in fact animates and structures this persistent hatred of both of them.[14]

Although Jones appears to isolate "Big Business" as the culprit, she determines its capitalistic machinations to be not only rooted in, but dependent upon the degradation of Black people, particularly Black women (Jones 109). Throughout the play, Ernestine recalls her Aunt Lily likewise "reading" the world, her perceptions slipping into conversation playfully, but with gravity. In this way, she calls Ernestine's attention to the rage and watchfulness she has accrued in direct disproportion to the evidence of "progress" that she cannot identify as her own. Ernestine thus sets about dutifully fighting everybody's fights, only to land squarely in a horrible and incommensurable "black zone": the topical (affective) gain of one son, and the paradigmatic (structurally anticipated) loss of the other. Both are immeasurable and illegible to the world, making Ernestine's labor to construct a legacy through both the lived and posthumous "kinship" with Lily a daunting but critical one.

To bring the devastation of Ernestine's and Lily's shared plight into even greater focus, I am prompted by cinematic theorist Kara Keeling's assertion of the need for "an investigation of the nexus at which the epistemological and ontological mechanisms of racism and the socio-economic interests that racism serves collide with the mechanisms and interests that animate cinema" (Keeling 1). I am suggesting that such an analysis is also needed within numerous other theatres; political, intellectual/academic, popular/cultural, and so on, wherein these mechanisms explode into the animus of racial violence and libidinal consumption. The boldness of Nottage's dramatic intervention is just such an analysis. This is because she casts Ernestine as one who navigates the meld of language and political activism in order to protest, to grieve her losses, and to search for Lily, whose own rhetorical moves have served as critical "intramural" engagements with Ernestine and Ermina, yet have ultimately failed Lily. This is due to the extramural, rhetorical musculature of Marxism and Communism hitting their limit in encountering the slave and by extension, the mid-twentieth century Black woman struggling to amass an ethical grammar with which to navigate racial slavery's afterlife. I say "boldness" because Ernestine's very presence as a writer and thinker in relation to the epistemic realm – which casts blackness (read: the captive-shadow exchange within the cave) as a scandal to literary and rhetorical acumen (acquired above and without the cave) – rages against what she reads through Lily's death, as a violent reduction to absence from the metonyms of episteme. These include the classroom, and by extension, the world's soci(et)al formations and intercourses.[15]

It is through this corresponding kinship-through-death formation that Nottage creates a palpable tension between Ernestine's search for

Lily and her father Godfrey's search for "life" as envisioned under the spell cast by Father Divine, the unseen but omnipresent character that Nottage has modeled on the real-life, charismatic leader of the same name. Father Divine's Harlem-based Peace Mission mesmerized thousands of Blacks from the late 1930s until his death in Pennsylvania in 1965. His overarching mission was to promote interracial relationships, and he did not ascribe to being "Black," *per se*. He shunned not only being regarded as Black, but also marriage between Blacks, suggesting, among other things, that engaging with a Black woman would proscribe his entry into the civil/social paradigm. Jared Sexton defines this strategy of multiracialism in part as one that is "about love, romance, family, and trust where these ideals are associated with the heights of racial harmony – [resulting in] *the elevation of the interracial relationship up and away from the low areas of the body*, the putative site of racism's pernicious effects" (*Amalgamation* 261, emphasis mine). Citing Fanon, Sexton further notes that "within the parameters of racist culture, to move away from the low areas of the body and the carnality of desire is also to move away from racialized blackness" (*Amalgamation* 284). Father Divine's cultivation of a predominantly Black "multiracial" spiritual caucus in which he cast himself as God on Earth, girded a rhetorical platform upon which he could enjoy – if only fleetingly – the appearance of having attained not merely human subjectivity, but supra-human ascension. The euphoria that Father Divine's followers experienced in his presence suggests a likewise fleeting respite from Fanon's formulation of the Black as a phobogenic object that attracts anxiety and dread (Fanon 132).[16] Father Divine's spell does not ultimately hold, since he is later cast down in history as not merely a shyster and cult leader, but a prototypical one. His project is a dogged attempt to alchemize the divine, the damned, and the performance of what I'll call "interraciality," into a balm for the Black disaffected.[17]

Godfrey desperately attempts to emulate the heights to which Father Divine appears to have ascended through living in the presumed peace that interracial harmony purports to bestow. In so doing, Godfrey devastatingly foils Lily's aim to enter the family formation to which her sister once belonged prior to the Crumps' migration. That aim is strong enough to compel Lily to travel from Harlem, all the way to Brooklyn, hoping for shelter from the world's onslaught, and an even better seat at the proverbial family table: "Didn't you hear me ringing the bell, nearly froze my ass out there.

(*She displays her legs*) These stockings, thank God for 'em, just ain't no competition for this weather. Remind me, take a note, need for weather-resistant stockings. Period. Stop!" (Nottage 21). Nottage's metaphoric framing of Lily's demand for refuge from the climate of anti-black racism exposes a palpable urgency to escape inside the "family home."[18] She has come running from the quarantine of non-belonging that haunts even the "haven" of Communism that situates labor as the fulcrum uniting all oppressed human beings. But as Fanon remarks about "[Marx's] . . . reaction [to the Black]: 'We educated you and now you are turning against your benefactors. Ungrateful wretches!'" (*Fanon* 18).

Godfrey, under the charismatic influence of Father Divine, repels Lily, pushing back against the memory of their illicit passion because it might unite them in (em)brace against the world he so desperately seeks to enter.[19] After this chilly reception, Lily surveys the white flight and black ghettoization that strangely conjoin Harlem and Brooklyn: "It do seem colder in Brooklyn, but don't it though? . . . Didn't see a Negro face between here and 116th. HELLO white peoples! (*Waves. A moment*) Living in their midst do have a way of wearing down your stamina" (Nottage 26).

Aiming to escape the vastness across which blacks are displaced as isolates, Godfrey and Lily *both* strain toward an inhabitation of "life" and "identity" in the face of this all-encompassing quarantining. Lily's attempt at a solution to the alienation she suffers in her quest to belong to a movement that does not ultimately claim her is evident in Ernestine's recollection of an exchange between her, Ermina, and Lily while Lily is hot-pressing Ermina's hair:

ERMINA: Sister, why ain't you been married?
(*Lily laughs long and hard.*)
LILY: You're just filled with questions. 'Cause I ain't. *(Tugs Ermina's head straight, wielding the hot comb like a weapon)*
ERMINA: Nobody ask you?
LILY: Nobody ask me . . . Besides, I never plan to marry. How you like that? I'm exerting my own will, and since the only thing ever willed for me was marriage, I choose not to do it. And why take just one man, when you can have a lifetime full of so many. Listen up, that may be the best advice I give you babies. And you needn't share that little pearl of wisdom with your daddy. Now, Ermina, sit still.

ERNESTINE: (*To audience*): We were Lily's family now, kinda like buying
    flowers from a store without having to plant the seeds.
(Ermina squirms in the chair.)
LILY: Sit still, don't fight me on this. Choose your battles carefully, chile,
    a nappy head in this world might as well fly the white flag and
    surrender.
ERNESTINE: (*To audience*): She'd talk constantly about "a revolution" from
    the kitchen. I's always wondered when this revolution was going to
    begin and would I have to leave school to fight along her side.

(Nottage 32–33)

Nottage's signifying on Plato is ingenious here: Lily as both Socrates
and Shadow; and Ermina-as-Glaucon, refusing to hold her head still
under the "press," literal and symbolic, of one of the many concessions to
blackness's erasure. Spillers's keen apprehension of "confounded[ness]"
is useful in reading the folds and collapses here between Lily's sense
of herself as a kitchen revolutionary, and her simultaneously pressing
out the (black) kinks in the "kitchen" (rear bottom) of Ernestine's head.
In other words, Lily's notion that the whitening (masking) of one's
blackness somehow ensures its survival speaks to the "locus of confounded identities" that Spillers describes as "a meeting ground of invest-
ments and privations in the national treasury of rhetorical wealth"
("Mama's" 64).

This is to say, Lily strives to fashion a self through fleeing the formidable terrain of Jim Crow, toward a (seemingly) more progressive landscape wherein she can at least fashion an amalgamation of
self-whitening and rebellion, and in turn pass on to her only "prog-
eny" the spare revenue of (sentient) survival that politically girds them
both. By the time Lily has arrived at the Crumps' in Brooklyn, however, Communism's rhetoric of equality for all is fervently eclipsed by
Godfrey's aspiration toward the peace, belonging, and abundance that
Father Divine's refuge promises. Godfrey therefore provides no such
refuge for Lily. Ultimately, Ernestine's search for her is over before it
begins. She'll neither find Lily, nor anyone who can help in her search.
Lily's suffering and consequent death will relegate her to the litany
of no-names in the lost archive that constitutes what Hartman calls "a
death sentence, a tomb, a display of the violated body, an inventory of
property" (*Venus* 2).

Meanwhile, in a desperate attempt to escape this fate himself,
guided (or more aptly, *mis*guided) by Father Divine's compass,

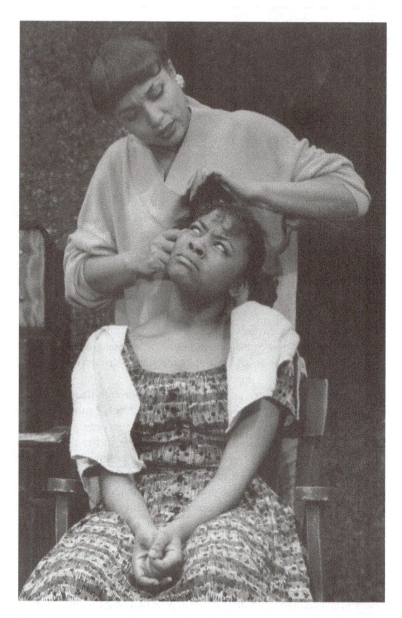

Figure 1.2 Lily combing Ernestine's hair. Ella Joyce (standing) as Lily and Kisha Howard (seated) as Ernestine in the world premiere production at Second Stage. Photo by Susan Cook, ©1995.

Godfrey meets and immediately marries Gerte, a non-Jewish defector from Nazi Germany. Godfrey's thinking around this move becomes only more fragmented with time. In a desperate prayer, his disorientation is evident:

> Can you give me some words. Sweet Father ... the boss keeps calling me 'the country nigger,' in front of the other men. They laugh and I want so badly to say something ... Sweet Father, this city confuse me, but all I know is to keep the door shut. Sweet Father, my wife's sister, she living with us and I don't know how long I'll be able to look away. Sweet Father, sometimes I think about sending my gals back home. Sweet Father, I've wed a white woman like you done, I loves her, but I don't know whether my children ever will? Do I gotta make a choice? Will you help me calm my rage?
>
> (Nottage 79)

Godfrey's need for language is posed in the form of a statement rather than a question, such that the subsequent questions are borne of the one thing about which he is sure: there is no language sufficient to reconcile this swirl of dilemmas. They comprise a recitation of social banishment and degradation, the response to which he is forced to quash; the odd tripartite folds between a dead woman he stills calls "wife;" the surviving sister-in-law whom he carnally desires but a union to whom amounts to the same death to which his past is fused; and the white woman around whom he has structured a feeling of "wed[dedness]" to (social) life. Ernestine and her sister are, as a result, encumbered with the strangeness resulting from his decision, and subjected to the terms of their new stepmother, Gerte's, making.

The deep complexities of Godfrey's marriage to Gerte, and the (relative) peace he presumes it will bring him, endure in Ernestine's memory. But so does the clarity with which she capsulizes the larger terms by which she knows she must abide in the play's epilogue: "The principal says the world is to be approached like a newborn, 'handled with care.' What he didn't say was what happens when the world doesn't care for you" (Nottage 84). It is the violence of this uncaring world, the "bad faith" to which Lewis R. Gordon refers, that circumscribes Godfrey to what he believes is a contentedness with working as a baker in Brooklyn – subject to (not so) random acts of violence, like the racist attack he and Gerte experience on their way home one night (Nottage 72). Lily's commentary on Godfrey's assault and Gerte's efforts to cast it as anomalous speaks volumes:

> You see, Ernestine, that's your America. Negro sitting on his couch with blood dripping down his face. White woman unscathed and the enemy not more than five years back. You can't bring order to this world. You can't put up curtains and pot plants and have things change. You really thought you could marry a white woman and enter the kingdom of heaven, didn't ya?
>
> (Nottage 75)

In other words, "heaven" as Hughes's poem has factored it, is as much a part of Godfrey's landscape as it is Lily's, and they both have the lumps and bruises (inside and out) to prove it. It is this "heaven" that will be Lily's undoing for daring to name and interrogate it. Godfrey colludes in that undoing, casting Lily as the locus of badness and undesirability, partly because, as Frantz Fanon argues, "the black man on his home territory is oblivious of the moment when his inferiority is determined by the Other" (Fanon 90), and partly because of his fear that Ernestine's quest will take her to dangerous places. He warns her, "Forget about Lily, you follow her you know what you'll be taking on" (Nottage 85). Ernestine ignores his warning and continues her quest to find not only Lily but also herself, despite her father's wishes that she get a job at the bakery where he works. Ernestine observes the job to have "no greater expectation than for the bread to rise," (Nottage 85) and instead dares an altogether different reading of blackness and of progress than does her father: "(*To audience*): In the movies the darkness precedes everything. In the darkness, the theatre whispers with anticipation . . ." (Nottage 86). The anticipation of what is to come is immediately followed by Ernestine becoming lost in and to the imperceptible (unthought) "darkness" of the Harlem ghetto, to where she has followed freedom's trail of crumbs, and from within which she learns of Lily's suffering and demise. Through Ernestine's sojourn/migration into the darkness that holds the "theatre" that Plato devalues, Nottage pinpoints the ways in which slavery's after-life both anticipates (already) and obliterates (always) the "kinship" relation to which Ernestine aspires, and which is anathema to that of the Peace Mission to which her father has turned.

It is here in the darkness of the proverbial cave that Nottage herself engages the dramatic, "mathematical" elegance by which I frame this essay's opening epigraphs; the "intramural calculus" that takes place outside/in excess of Plato's contemplation. For example, Ernestine declares, upon arriving to Harlem, in search of Lily: "Finally, Harlem . . . Lost . . ." (Nottage 87). In three words, Nottage not only suggests that Ernestine's trip to her destination has been laborious (for a host of reasons), but also includes Ernestine, Lily, AND Harlem within an incalculable equation that might be expressed as follows:

Ernestine + Lily + Harlem = Lost

Or, syllogistically:

If Ernestine + Lily = Lost
   And
Harlem = Lost
   Then
Ernestine + Lily + Harlem = Lost

Further still, If Lost = Points/Dimensions/Universes/Coordinates unthought and unknown, then perhaps Ernestine, Lily, and Harlem might be pulled by the gravity of a black hole or cave into a realm wherein they locate Hughes's dream deferred, behold the shadows signifyin' on a Black canonical formulation of the world above ground, and locate the dimension where slavery's archive – all those whose lives have been imperceptibly missing (willfully unseen) – can at long last be reconciled. Within the earth's gravitational pull, however, Lily, in being lost to Ernestine, is relegated to a status that exponentially exceeds what anthropologist Claude Meillassoux terms "absolute alien" by, first, her sister's death; second, Godfrey's rejection of her in favor of a white German immigrant; and finally, her own collapse under the weight of this multiple assault. Meillassoux observes of aliens (those outside of kinship structures during the formation of slavery in Africa), "a [requisite] characteristic which appears in all forms of slavery and is its very essence: *the social incapacity of the slave to reproduce socially – that is, the slave's juridical inability to become 'kin'*" (Meillassoux 35, emphasis mine).[20] The death of Lily's sister has expunged Lily from the only kin she had left, and thus propels her on a quest that proves fatally and irrevocably unfulfilling.

While Ernestine lives to tell her story in retrospect, by its end, it is a story fraught with paradox. Her hopefulness resonates with the knowledge of her own captive-fugitivity, forbidden as she is to merely wax nostalgic. Rather, Ernestine must remember a catalog of loss for which there is no index, and acknowledge that whatever happiness her creativity garners will be forever laden with the echoes of her father's complicated quest to live, and with communism's bankruptcy in the face of the unpayable debt owed to the slave-descended. Her father joins the ranks of all those who aspire to the narrative of striving. But in the end, it is dear Aunt Lily's trajectory that rises above the din of the commonplace, banging against the cave's walls and ceiling, guiding the wayward shadows, haunting Ernestine – haunting us all – from within the interstitial realm of longing to *be*. . . .

Notes

1 I move between the uses of "Black," "black," and "blackness" throughout the essay as follows: The upper case 'B' connotes cultural and racial identification; the lower case 'b' indicates the descriptive noun; and the suffix "-ness" (used in conjunction with a lower case 'b') infers a condition that is interpreted, projected (upon) or resisted in a myriad of ways. Both Lewis R. Gordon's distinction between "black" and "African American" in the introduction to his reading of antiblackness as a global condition of "bad faith" in *Bad Faith and Antiblack Racism*; and Jared Sexton's clarification of "blackness" in his Introduction to *Amalgamation Schemes: Antiblackness and the Critique of Multiracialism*, fn. 1, 259, are useful here.

2 See another of Spillers's groundbreaking essays, "Interstices: A Small Drama of Words," in which she raises harrowing questions around the ability to locate Black women's being, sexual and otherwise; so intricately are its aspects "embedded in bizarre axiological ground" (*Black, White & In Color: Essays on American Literature and Culture*, 203). The essay's title stirs the implications of Plato's allegorical imagery: shadows "performing," in effect, outside human purview, for those existing outside that purview by dint of their captivity. (See works cited for this and all subsequent source references.)

3 An accessible translation of Plato's *Republic* is edited by Scott Buchanan. Alain Badiou has also written an incisive and uniquely comprehensive contemporary translation. Lastly, to read further on my analysis of the Cave Allegory as progenitor of structural violence in the civic and epistemic spheres, see Chapter One of *Solving for 'x': The Allegorhythms of Black Feminist Playwriting*.

4 I had the supreme pleasure of serving as assistant director on the play's world premiere in the spring of 1995 at Second Stage Theatre in New York, directed by Joe Morton, which afforded me the opportunity to meet and work with Lynn Nottage. In his collaboration with the production's design team, Morton aimed to emphasize the cognitive dissonance between the stagnant conditions to which Blacks were subjected, their migratory dreams of a better life notwithstanding; and the sonic, explosive bebop style of jazz (forged by, among other notables, Charlie "Yardbird" Parker, Thelonious Monk, Sonny Rollins, and Dexter Gordon. This "untamable" style was a response to the predominance of white, big band swing during and post-World War II).

I recall Morton's conceptual aim as one of underscoring bebop's resistance to the groundswell of national pride around the defeat of the presumed fascist alliance between Germany and Japan. The drab, stagnancy of the Crumps' Brooklyn cold water flat (designed by Myung Hee Cho) in concert with this ensemble of artful resistance (sound design by Mark Bennett), called attention to the abject, violent conditions to which Blacks, no small number of whom had fought in the War, continued to be subjected.

5 The "exchange" between Blacks in the present is, in some respects, more rife than ever, given the chasm between notions of striving and respectability, and those of radical militant response to State and other manifestations of antiblack violence that do not "discriminate" between the Black off-duty executive and the Black on-duty drug-runner, any more than they recognize the particular suffering these two figures share in their immutable marking (as B/black). Once again, Spillers is helpful here in her call for the "intramural" reading (thinking) of literature (which, I suggest, must extend into our present-day readings of the media-sphere and other (often spectacular(ized) entertainments). See her essay, "Black, White and In Color: or Learning how to Paint: Toward an Intramural Protocol of Reading," the title essay in the collection *Black, White and In Color: Essays on American Literature and Culture,* 2003.

6 See Spillers's landmark essay, "Mama's Baby, Papa's Maybe: An American Grammar Book," in which she unflinchingly examines Daniel Patrick Moynihan's empiricism.

7 See "Banshee," *The Element Encyclopedia of the Psychic World,* 2006.

8 In orthopedic medicine, a "subluxation" is a misalignment of bones. While they are not literally severed, their relation to one another has become, in effect, "estranged," such that their functionality ranges from chronically to acutely compromised, posing the threat of permanent damage if not realigned. I use the term to suggest that Nottage's narrative estrangement between "death" and "mother" effectively trains our focus onto both the predicament of the slave-descended in relation to notions of ancestry and heritage; and onto the subtler, metonymic resonances of "bones." Hence, while the Black's biological roots might indeed be genealogically traceable to Africa (as Henry Louis Gates, Oprah Winfrey, Whoopi Goldberg, and other popular notables are committed to illustrating), the structure of feeling that coalesces this mission both circumvents and is insufficient to explain the immutable distinction between the *desire* to recuperate a heritage, through either a literal return to Africa, or the acquisition of genealogical evidence that one is "African-American;" and, for example, the Italian-, Chinese-, or German-American's foregone *ability* to stake heritage claims in Italy, China, or Germany *without such pronounced labor*. The implications of this distinction are vast and terrifying, and are the focus of a growing number of rife, intra- and extramural discourses.

9 At the end of her memoir *Lose Your Mother,* Hartman declares, "If after a year in Ghana I could still call myself an African American, it was because my Africa had its source in the commons created by fugitives and rebels, in the courage of suicidal girls aboard slave ships, and in the efforts, thwarted and realized, of revolutionaries intent upon stopping the clock and instituting a new order, even if it cost them their lives" (234).

10 See Orlando Patterson's *Slavery and Social Death: A Comparative Study,* in which he distinguishes the three key elements of slavery that are *constitutive* to its construct (total powerlessness, natal alienation, and generalized dishonor) from those elements that are attendant to, yet not required in the complete making of a slave. In other words, it can be argued that a slave and a migrant worker are both victims of exploited labor. However, where the migrant worker is underpaid, (s)he is also free to leave the plantation and return to whatever construct of family and/or home exists, no matter how meager. By contrast, the slave is captive, and alienated from any and all kinship constructs, as well as subject to the dishonor of, among other things, gratuitous physical and psychic violence at any moment in time. The migrant worker might draw the ire of the overseer if (s)he does not comply with the particular rules of conduct and labor output, but such punishment is contingent upon transgression of those rules, rather than gratuitous, as Frank Wilderson points out in his reading of Patterson in *Red, White and Black: Cinema and the Structure of U.S. Antagonisms.* No such contingencies exist for the slave, a distinction Wilderson clarifies throughout the book.

11 See Suzan-Lori Parks's *The America Play* for numerous references to and "riffs" on this notion. Jacques Derrida is also useful here in his assiduous conceptualization of "always already" in *Of Grammatology,* and other of his works. This in turn harkens back to Spillers's notion of "American grammar" and its structural (not to be confused with affective or performative) undoing of natal and filial kinship relations for Blacks.

12 Also in *Lose,* Hartman notes that, "The most universal definition of the slave is a stranger. Torn from kin and community, exiled from one's country, dishonored and violated, the slave defines the position of the outsider" (5). Correspondingly, in "Mama's Baby, Papa's Maybe," Spillers observes a constellation of components to that severance when she notes the ways in which the intimacy of family and belonging are annulled by and through the process of slave-making and its "externally imposed meanings and uses: 1) the captive body becomes the source of an irresistible, destructive sensuality; 2) at the same time – in stunning contradiction – the captive body reduces to a thing, becoming being for the captor; 3) in this absence from a subject position, the captured sexualities provide a physical and biological expression of 'otherness'; 4) as a category of 'otherness,' the captive body translates into a potential for pornotroping and embodies sheer physical powerlessness that slides into a more general 'powerlessness,' resonating through various centers of human and social meaning" (67).

13 See W.E.B. DuBois's exhaustive indexing of the countless labors toward civil entry and viable, normative citizenship in *Black Reconstruction in America: 1860–1880.* With regard to the Black as scandal to sociality, see Frank B. Wilderson, III's analysis of the transposition of the slave into prison inmate in "The Prison Slave as Hegemony's (Silent) Scandal." *Social Justice,* 30.2 (2003): 1. Also see numerous readings of the prison industrial complex as "new slave estate," including Michelle Alexander, Angela Y. Davis, and Ruth Gilmore.

14 For a more in-depth look at the life and work of Claudia Jones, see Carol Boyce-Davies's two books, *Claudia Jones: Beyond Containment,* and *Left of Karl Marx: The Political Life of Black Communist Claudia Jones.*

15 See "Counter-Allegory: An Imagining." in Chapter One, Part II of *Solving for 'x': The Allegorhythms of Black Feminist Playwriting* (referenced in en 3),

in which I read the violence of a teacher's symbolic absenting of a Black female child from a classroom through the repositioning of the child's chair, and the affixing to the chair of a signifier of intellectual inferiority (a sign reading "DUNCE SEAT"). The child is thereby symbolically soldered to the chair-object and thus erased from the classroom, despite the physical presence of her body, which is, in turn, also degraded (or, in Patterson's reading, dishonored). I note again, Wilderson's "Prison Slave", in en 13.

16 Fanon's research hinges on psychoanalyst Angélo Hesnard's broad definition of phobia as a neurosis manifesting from fear of an object, to fear of anything that the individual differentiates from the self.

17 For an in-depth biographical study, see Jill Watts's *God, Harlem USA: The Father Divine Story.*

18 I place this phrase in quotations to emphasize that by representing the Crumps as a "family," Nottage exposes the notions of "family" and "home," and certainly their amalgamation, as always-already ruptured by the racial hatred that prompts the Crumps' (and Lily's) migration and alienation (as Patterson elaborates it) and in turn, forecloses the possibility of their together constituting a filial unit.

19 In Act I, scene four, Lily infers that she and Godfrey had a dalliance or two during his marriage to her sister (Nottage 41, 42).

20 See again, Patterson's formulation of the three constituent elements of slavery in *Slavery and Social Death.*

Works cited

Badiou, Alain. *Plato's Republic: A Dialogue in 16 Chapters.* Transl. Susan Spitzer. Cambridge: Polity Press, 2012. Originally published as *La République de Platon.* Paris: Arthème Fayard, 2012. Print.

Boyce-Davies, Carol. *Claudia Jones: Beyond Containment.* Boulder: Lynne Rienner Publishers, 2011. Print.

———. *Left of Karl Marx: The Political Life of Black Communist Claudia Jones.* Durham: Duke University Press, 2008. Print.

Cheung, Theresa. *The Encyclopedia of the Psychic World: The Ultimate A-Z of Spirits, Mysteries and the Paranormal.* New York: Harper Collins Publishers, 2010.

Davis, Angela. *Abolition Democracy: Beyond Empire, Prisons, and Torture.* New York: Seven Stories Press, 2005. Print.

Derrida, Jacques. *Of Grammatology.* Transl. Gayatri Spivak. Baltimore: The Johns Hopkins University Press, 1997. Print.

DuBois, W.E.B. *Black Reconstruction in America: 1860–1880.* New York: Charles Scribner's & Sons, 1999. Print.

Fanon, Frantz. *Black Skin, White Masks.* Transl. Richard Philcox. New York: Grove Press, 1952; 2008. Print.

Gordon, Lewis R. *Bad Faith and Antiblack Racism.* New York: Humanity Books, 1999. Print.

Hartman, Saidiya. *Lose Your Mother.* New York: Farrar, Straus and Giroux, 2007. Print.

———. "Venus in Two Acts." *Small Axe* 26. June, 2008. Print.

Hughes, Langston. "Luck." *Selected Poems of Langston Hughes*. New York: Vintage, 1990. Print.

———. "Soul Gone Home." *The Norton Anthology of Drama, Vol. II: The Nineteenth Century to the Present*. Eds. J. Ellen Gainor, Stanton B. Garner Jr., and Martin Puchner. New York: W.W. Norton & Company, 2009. 535–538. Print.

Jones, Claudia. "An End to the Neglect of the Problems of the Negro Woman!" *Words of Fire: An Anthology of African-American Feminist Thought*. Ed. Beverly Guy-Sheftall. New York: The New Press, 1995. 108–123. Print.

Keeling, Kara. *The Witch's Flight: The Cinematic, The Black Femme, and the Image of Common Sense*. Durham: Duke University Press, 2007. Print.

Marriott, David. *On Black Men*. New York: Columbia University Press, 2000. Print.

Meillassoux, Claude. *The Anthropology of Slavery: The Womb of Iron and Gold*. Transl. Alide Dasnois. Chicago: University of Chicago Press, 1991. Print.

Nottage, Lynn. *Crumbs from the Table of Joy and Other Plays*. New York: Theatre Communications Group, 2004. Print.

Parks, Suzan-Lori. *The America Play and Other Works*. New York: Theatre Communications Group, 1994. Print.

Patterson, Orlando. *Slavery and Social Death: A Comparative Study*. Cambridge: Harvard University Press, 1982. Print.

Plato. "Book Seven, *The Republic*." *The Portable Plato*. Ed. Scott Buchanan. New York: Viking Press, 1977. 546–584. Print.

Sexton, Jared. *Amalgamation Schemes: Antiblackness and the Critique of Multiracialism*. Minneapolis: University of Minnesota Press, 2008. Print.

Sexton, Jared and Copeland, Huey. "Raw Life: An Introduction." *Qui Parle* 13.2 (Spring/Summer 2003): 53–62.

Spillers, Hortense J. *Black, White and in Color: Essays on American Culture and Literature*. Chicago: University of Chicago Press, 2003. Print.

———. "Mama's Baby, Papa's Maybe: An American Grammar Book." *Diacritics* 17.2 (1987): 64–81. Print.

Watts, Jill. *God, Harlem USA: The Father Divine Story*. Berkeley: University of California Press, 1992. Print.

Wilderson, Frank B. "The Prison Slave as Hegemony's (Silent) Scandal." *Social Justice* 30.2 (2003): 18. Print.

———. *Red, White & Black: Cinema and the Structure of U.S. Antagonisms*. Durham: Duke University Press, 2008. Print.

Williams, [née] Joyce Ann [Now: Jaye Austin]. *Solving for 'x': The Allegorhythms of Black Feminist Playwriting*. ProQuest, UMI Dissertations Publishing, 2013. Web.

Chapter 2

Guess who's coming to dinner

Choral performance in *Mud, River, Stone*

Jennifer L. Hayes

Mud, River, Stone (1998) is Lynn Nottage's first full-length play set outside of the continental United States. The play depicts the misadventures that an African American couple, David and Sarah Bradley, experience while traveling to Africa to reconnect with their ancestral roots. Recounting their journey to friends at a dinner party held after their return home to New York, the Bradleys produce a souvenir of their trip, a stone. The ordinary nature of the stone juxtaposes their romantic vision of Africa, which is altered when their vacation turns perilous. While on their journey, their car runs out of gas. Alone in the wilderness, Sarah recalls that David "picked up this stone to defend us, so brave and misguided, not sure from which direction danger might come" (Nottage 172). While David anticipates an invisible danger, one real danger he and Sarah encounter is their idealized vision of Africa. The Bradleys initially ignore the reality that many parts of the continent are struggling through the ongoing transition from colonial dependence to postcolonial independence. For the audience, this initial point of reference contextualizes the Bradleys' transformative journey.

Nottage positions these African American characters within a microcosm of contemporary African postcolonial conflict by staging the recollection of their trip within the confines of a former colonial resort, The Imperial Hotel. The Bradleys' preconceptions of Africa shift as they encounter varying characters and perspectives, and the hotel transforms from "an oasis" where weary travelers recover from a strenuous journey into a chessboard where competing voices reveal the complex political dynamics of the region's tentative peace (Nottage 173). They first encounter Joaquim, a hotel bellboy and former child soldier who was involved in a decades-long civil war that altered the political and social landscape of the "South East Africa[n]" country in which the action takes place (Nottage 168). As rumors of possible conflict in the region spread, Joaquim becomes increasingly paranoid and aggressive. His behavior impacts every other character in the play when he eventually loses his composure and takes the guests hostage, immediately establishing a bond between the diverse characters. While David and Sarah seem unaware of past political and racial tensions in the area, the hostage situation is an event that forces the African American characters, African characters, and characters of European descent to collectively consider how historical tensions and misconceptions about race and power manifest in present conflicts. Yet Joaquim represents only one view of the connection between the past and present. Mr. Blake's presence in the play signals the lingering influence of European imperialism on African politics and economics. Mr. Blake, described as "*a bombastic white African of English descent,*" consistently challenges Joaquim (Nottage 173). Blake's status as a business man compared with Joaquim's role as a hotel bellboy initially signals a clear class distinction between the two men, but their conflict eventually reveals a more complex view of the lasting relationships and fraught tensions resonating in the economic and political climates of various African nations.

Nottage adds two seemingly different characters to the complex matrix of global voices: Ama and Neibert. On the surface, Ama and Neibert represent diverse perspectives, yet they have more in common than a casual observer might initially assume. Ama Cyllah is a twenty-something "West African aid worker" seeking relief from the region's seasonal rains as she also seeks assistance for the mission where she works (Nottage 168). While the specific location of the play remains mysterious, Ama's background is known: she is Nigerian. Her experience as an aid worker contrasts with Joaquim's life as a child soldier. Nottage implicitly explores the diversity within the continent by representing different African perspectives amongst the characters. Additionally, Ama challenges the myth of the great White Savior since she, as well as other Africans, are involved in administering aid and fostering growth in villages devastated by economic exploitation and war. Her mission work is juxtaposed with her companion Neibert's philosophical mission. Neibert is a twenty-something-year-old "Belgian tourist and adventurer" who is wandering the East African jungle searching for a mythical creature known as the agogwe (Nottage 168). Mr. Blake describes the agogwe as a "little red hairy man that lives in the forest and steals vegetables from farmers" (Nottage 191). However, Neibert views the agogwe as an authentic natural force in the forest lying somewhere between "myth and reality" (192). For Neibert, the agogwe represents a quintessential African spirit, but his ambition signals the fetishization of the continent and the lingering racial stereotypes associated with cultural images of blackness. He searches for the agogwe as David and Sarah search for their roots. Joaquim searches for stability, while Mr. Blake searches for economic superiority, and Ama searches for a deeper purpose. This band of global voices emphasizes present tensions in a complex landscape. *New York Times* critic Peter Marks suggests that these diverse characters function as various political "arguments" and "talking points of view" concerning "vital global topics." Heard together, these individual voices articulate competing narratives concerning the aftermath of colonization.

Nottage conveys the global community's responsibility for recognizing and telling the region's story of political revolution by connecting the Bradleys' trip with other characters' transformative journeys. In doing so, I argue that Nottage borrows from previous theatrical traditions to produce a contemporary chorus that performs a remembered event: the hostage situation at The Imperial Hotel. Through this event, the audience is encouraged to recognize the historical roots of present political conflicts by witnessing the characters' complex interactions. In the preface to the play, Nottage recounts how an untitled October 1994 *New York Times* article concerning Mozambique inspired *Mud, River, Stone*. The article describes how "demobilized guerillas sent home after a sixteen-year civil war, demanded food and blankets from the United Nations" (Nottage 165). Nottage interprets the conflict as "the narrative of any number of African nations in the process of shedding the vestiges of armed conflict" (Nottage 164). While the article focuses on the results of decades of instability without considering the roots or the psychic impact of the conflict on the guerrillas, Nottage connects historical tensions with present conflict in *Mud, River, Stone*. The effect goes beyond merely questioning the cycle of violence and political turmoil evident in many African countries.

Kevin J. Wetmore Jr. argues that African American playwrights adapt and incorporate elements of Greek drama into their texts because the form "is distant enough to say things that audiences would not be as comfortable hearing and seeing directly" (3–4). This approach allows for the exploration of present problems through familiar theatrical traditions such as the chorus. By situating the past within present tensions, and by dramatizing them through the creation of a polyvocal chorus comprised of multicultural characters, Nottage connects diverse understandings of history to global conflict in the present moment. Graham Ley contextualizes the chorus as "a group of people expected to sing and dance," explaining that their "songs or dances accompanied decisive events in the lives of Greek communities" (30). The chorus traditionally performed as a kind of living history book, preserving the traditional myths and stories that helped form national identity. Their performances were a central component of drama. Helen Bacon argues that the ancient Greek audience traditionally interpreted the chorus as "one of the actors. It should be part of the whole and participate in the action" (7). However, some contemporary scholars reduce the choral component of ancient Greek theatre to "a source of interludes and peripheral lyrical commentary on the action performed by the actors" (7). This reduction of the chorus's importance diminishes the impact choral presence has on the scope of the performance since "what happens in such a play cannot be fully understood without taking into account the nature and function of this group of individuals . . . occasionally speaking and always there" (9). Judith Fletcher maintains that "students of choral voice tend to focus on the distinction between the authorial and characterological voices of the chorus," making distinctions between choral leaders and other less prominent members of the group (30). While Fletcher suggests audiences typically focus on the interaction between choral leaders and chorus members, Nottage encourages audiences to consider the various political and social issues her chorus introduces. Each choral member individually offers a competing perspective concerning the hostage event, which creates an opportunity for the audience to consider the historical context that has precipitated this destructive moment. Although many Greek choruses were "more or less homogeneous in age and sex and social status," the important bond that linked the members of the chorus was actually "a common interest in the event . . . [so] they represent not the community at large but some segment of the community specially concerned in the event, what we might call a constituency" (Bacon 9). Nottage's chorus challenges the homogeneity of choral groups by combining a diverse group of characters in The Imperial Hotel to expose the impact that the challenges of postcolonial Africa have on the global community.

Rootedness: Nottage's connection to and progression of Black feminist tradition

Nottage's chorus reflects the Greek performance tradition and its adoption by African American dramatists. Other contemporary women playwrights have employed the chorus or group protagonists with differing impacts. In *Wedding Band: A Love/Hate Story in Black and White* (1966), Alice Childress explores how racial communities define values. Church members, soldiers, mothers, children, and landlords all articulate specific values concerning racial and gendered expectations. When

Julia, an isolated Black seamstress, moves into a new Black neighborhood her desire to maintain a strong connection with her racial community coincides with her desire to maintain her bond with her significant other, Herman, a middle-aged White baker. Herman must manage his own familial obligations and racial pressures to discontinue his romantic involvement with Julia. Ultimately, both racial communities collide in an epic argument where Julia and Herman are encouraged to separate. The voices within the play blend together and articulate national perspectives regarding race relations. As Julia and Herman try to maintain a meaningful relationship, tensions arise as both fail to meet the expectations of their respective racial groups.

Ntozake Shange's choreopoem *for colored girls who have considered suicide/when the rainbow is enuf* (1975) represents yet another interpretation of choral performance in contemporary African American drama. Shange's achievement gives voice to seven African American female characters whose lives establish a broader context for understanding Black femininity. In *for colored girls*, the experiences of diverse Black women provide a complex definition of self that challenges reductive representations of Black femininity. The choreopoem allows women of color to articulate their experiences by examining the intersectionality of race, class, and gender. Their personal triumphs and failures are strengthened by the form of the play, and the characters are supported by the presence and verbal encouragement of the other chorus members.

Other African American women playwrights, such as Anna Deavere Smith, have explored community and racial tension via solo performance. In all of her works, Smith channels various characters in order to represent multicultural perspectives on specific political issues. For example, in *Fires in the Mirror* (1992) Smith performs a series of monologues based on interviews she conducted with members of the Black and Jewish communities in Crown Heights Brooklyn. These voices present diverse reactions to the tragic car accident that killed a young Black Caribbean youth and the subsequent riots and murder of a visiting Jewish Australian student. The monologues emphasize the clear racial divide and cultural tensions within the neighborhood as Smith shifts seamlessly between perspectives.

Suzan-Lori Parks employs the chorus to demonstrate how political and social institutions (such as welfare, religion, and medicine) have systematically dehumanized Black women. Parks presents the repetitive labeling and misuse of Hester La Negrita's body throughout *In the Blood* (1998) to highlight the ways in which welfare mothers are blamed and made complicit in their own degraded position within society. As

Hester La Negrita attempts to provide for her children, she experiences difficulty because of the bias associated with her status as a welfare mother. Parks uses a Greek style chorus, comprised of embodied social forces and referred to as "All," to announce assumptions about Hester La Negrita to the audience. These judgements belittle and undermine Hester's identity and place in society by focusing on her sexuality, perceived idleness, and hopelessness. The language and negative opinions of the chorus precede any physical representation of Hester, which implies the sequence involved in classifying Hester's identity.

The community Nottage establishes among choral members in The Imperial Hotel contrasts with the ways other African American women playwrights have constructed choral bodies. Nottage's progressive chorus brings diverse perspectives together while allowing each member to grapple with self-definition. In order to fully understand the progressive nature of Nottage's contribution to the African American women's literary tradition, one must comprehend the simultaneous development of the Black feminist theoretical tradition within the contemporary renaissance of African American women writers. Black feminist literary theory developed from the civil rights and feminist movements in the 1960s and 1970s. Farah Jasmine Griffin has documented the simultaneous development of the African American women's literary tradition with the growth of Black feminist socio-political and literary theorists. According to Griffin, "the development of African American women's literature and the criticism it spawned were a direct response to the masculinist bias of the civil rights and especially the black power and black arts movements" (485). Griffin further claims that the development of Black feminism "was also a response to the feminist movement's tendency to normalize the experiences of middle-class white women as equivalent for all women" (485). In both instances, African American women found themselves "lost in the cracks" (485). Consequently, Black feminism initially questioned the circumstances that situated African American and other women of color as subordinate members even within politically progressive groups.

In "Toward a Black Feminist Criticism" (1977), Barbara Smith suggests the connection between "the politics of feminism" and "the state of Black Women's literature" (158). The connection Smith identifies works as a tool "for the exploration of Black women's lives and the creation of consciously Black woman identified art" (158). Smith advocates critical methods that consider the specific subject positions of the characters within African American women's texts, and she further suggests that critical approaches to African American women's texts have not acknowledged "the state of Black women's culture and the intensity of all Black women's oppression," which results in a predominately racist and sexist approach to their literature (158).

Black feminist critics have answered Smith's call for "a Black feminist approach to literature that embodies the realization that the politics of sex as well as the politics of race and class are crucially interlocking factors in the works of Black women," by expanding the body of criticism surrounding texts written by African American women writers (159). Several Black feminist scholars have attempted to define the key characteristics of these texts. Mary Helen Washington suggests:

> If there is a single distinguishing feature of the literature of black women – and this accounts for their lack of recognition – it is this: their literature is about black women; it takes the trouble to record the thoughts, words, feelings, and deeds of black women, experiences that make the realities of being black in America look very different from what men have written. (35)

As Washington suggests, this distinct perspective emerges in the transmission and transformation of lived experience into creative language, in sharing the details of silenced lives in the language of literature. Dramatic literature written by African American women further advances this transformative impulse through the intentional embodiment of historical reclamations on the stage. These performances enact a recovery that encourages audiences to reconsider historical depictions of African American women by unpacking the context that promoted the creation of narrow identities reflected in dominant cultural narratives. Their plays complicate the incomplete images audiences repetitively see associated with Black femininity by emphasizing and interrogating the legacy of this reductive imagery.

Nottage applies this mode beyond stories that focus solely on African American women, exploring multiple characters' subject positions and exposing various ways people are marginalized globally. Her exploration of subjugated global voices advances the Black feminist agenda in several ways. First, it places Black women within important national and global political conversations, which acknowledges their connection to issues beyond their racial community. Second, this approach represents a redefinition of community since the issues at stake in *Mud, River, Stone* impact all people. Ultimately, Nottage illuminates the bonds that connect seemingly disparate people. Nottage applies Black feminist strategies in *Mud, River, Stone* as a consciousness raising exercise that politicizes issues of race, gender, imperialism, and power. Individuals on the margins of global society are moved toward the center of discussion to engage with business men and women as well as journalists and travelers. Nottage pushes the audience to move beyond merely hearing reports of global conflict by demonstrating meaningful conversations that encourage thoughtful introspection on global conflicts.

Muddy water: Competing voices and historical perspectives

Nottage links global issues to the Bradleys' vacation, which eases the audience into the complex dynamics of the play. The Bradleys' vacation is the audience's gateway to Africa. Visiting an exotic locale seems like a typical objective for travelling abroad, but the Bradleys' journey is more meaningful because they are trying to establish a connection with their ancestral roots.

DAVID: I'd always imagined our trip accompanied by a sound track. A perfect blend of rhythms by Africa and orchestration by Europe. It sounded romantic –

SARAH: If romance is the sound of stripped gears. Two weeks in Aruba, piña coladas on the beach, my thought. We can do Africa later.

(Nottage 170)

From the outset of their vacation story, the Bradleys manifest real tension. They offer competing agendas concerning the trip. Additionally, David's fantasies highlight a more complex problem members of the African diaspora encounter beyond the sense of loss of their ancestral home and identity: the sentimentalization of Africa. The continent begins to take on mythic proportions when David romanticizes the culture and landscape. The consequence of such a narrow view is a reduction of the complexity of current political, social, and national conflicts that resonate within the continent's varying countries and geographically distinct locales. David envisions the vacation as a perfectly orchestrated song signaling his homecoming. However, the landscape sounds more like a "modern jazz ensemble's second encore" with improvisations and constant shifts presenting challenges to the Africa he imagines (Nottage 172).

The Bradleys' objective is to claim their heritage by visiting Africa, but their affluent Western lifestyle and naiveté render them ill-equipped to anticipate the current difficulties some Africans face. As the Bradleys make their way through the forest, the arduous drive dissolves David's fantasies. "Our road became a river. Our passage back . . . was subsumed by nature" (Nottage 172). Their journey exposes them to other individuals with vested interests in Africa, which Nottage connects by place and circumstance. The Imperial Hotel hosts this coming together of various perspectives, and the conflict that occurs there shatters David's allusions of a mythic homecoming. A constant downpour initially compels the Bradleys toward the hotel for shelter and quickly becomes an impediment to their escape.

Initially, The Imperial Hotel represents "an oasis" for the Bradleys, but once inside the hotel transforms into a vestige of colonial power (Nottage 173). Mr. Blake and Joaquim offer competing origin stories that reflect historical interpretations of the hotel. Mr. Blake views the hotel as a family relic, describing it as "my totem" (Nottage 185). For Blake, the historical significance is connected to his familial identity:

> My uncle built it in the thirties. He had a vision of a railway from the coast cutting across the continent. He built this hotel not even by a river, hoping that he could bribe the officials to have the railway pass through here. . . . This hotel is the final vestige of an age. . . . It really was a splendid dream. Can you imagine the insanity that brokered this magnificence? The chandelier was brought up from South Africa. The wood, the finest mahogany imported from West Africa. The glass, from Cairo. This hotel represents the totality of the Continent. He thought he could bring it all together under one roof. Here now, the embodiment of an idea gone sour.
>
> (Nottage 184–185)

Mr. Blake's version of events focuses on colonial progress and imperial splendor, while deemphasizing the human cost of this vision. The hotel functions as a symbol of the promise of colonial power, but the current reality of the totem underscores the destructive political consequences of manipulating the land and people for economic gain. Mr. Blake acknowledges that his uncle's vision ultimately did not flourish, but he stops short of recognizing the connection between the current state of affairs in the community and his uncle's agenda with the hotel.

In contrast, Joaquim offers a completely different interpretation of the hotel's history by focusing on his community's involvement in building this image of colonial power: "He says his uncle built this hotel, but it is not the truth. Our village did. Look closely at the details throughout the rooms. You will see our history carved into the woodwork. Our stories are all here" (186). Joaquim shares this personal history with Sarah in the lobby as: "*the lights continue to flicker. Joaquim lights a candle. Darkness falls on all but Sarah and Joaquim*" (Nottage 186). His story voices a marginalized perspective and challenges Blake's version. For Joaquim, the hotel's symbolic meaning is connected to the stories of his people. Their communal history is engrained within the totem. However, Mr. Blake does not acknowledge that the history of the village is woven into his own famil-ial story. The failure to acknowledge both historical perspectives prevents Mr. Blake and Joaquim from understanding one another's connection to the space and the survival of their mutual histories. Nottage presents both stories and encourages the audience to understand the connections and resulting conflicts present within the competing narratives.

The chorus's circumscription in the hotel creates a tense atmosphere where they begin to contemplate rumors of another war. Neibert relays his percep-tion of events, claiming "drunk soldiers gathered people in the village center" (Nottage 199). The threat of another regional conflict builds as members of the chorus offer their perspectives on the causes for previous tensions:

DAVID: Hey what was the war about?
MR. BLAKE: Power. Control. Money.
JOAQUIM: Land. Food. Culture.

(Nottage 201)

The inconsistency regarding the sources of previous conflicts further increases tensions in the present moment. If community members are unsure of the reasons for past conflict, how can they hope to avoid simi-lar discord in the future? Mr. Blake and Joaquim reflect the residual ten-sion from previous clashes. David's naïve question promotes a spiral effect where other choral members offer conflicting hearsay about the possible militarization of young village boys.

As the hotel guests grapple with the possible threat of impending war, Joaquim becomes increasingly more anxious. His own past as a child soldier literally haunts him as he tries unsuccessfully to dismiss any new conflicts. "Nothing has happened, everything is okay. No Soldiers!" (201). His attempt to block out the voices of the other choral members is unsuccessful, and they do not sense his rising unease. The confused chatter concerning the impending war escalates into a stand-off between Mr. Blake and Joaquim. The men "*play a game of chicken . . . Mr. Blake reaches for the gun in his holster. Joaquim grabs Mr. Blake's arm and takes the gun from his holster*" (Nottage 202–203). This confrontation represents the turning point of the play. Generational, racial, and imperial tensions explode as competing histories collide within the lobby. Mr. Blake's and Joaquim's historical and political roles of oppressor and oppressed are reversed through the transferal of the gun. The gun grants Joaquim a new level of control over the narrative through his ability to use force to direct the language and actions of the guests in The Imperial Hotel. The meteorologically sequestered chorus suddenly transforms into a group hostage situation.

As their entrapment begins to take a toll on the chorus, tensions manifest. Specifically, the group debates the distinctions between ethnicity and race that feed and perpetuate divisions between individuals in the chorus, and entities in the region.

NEIBERT: My brother, if you relaxed, let down some of that soul brother pride, we might find a common ground, even manage a conversation, my brother.

DAVID: I am not your brother. I can't explain, but it's like you've forced your way into a private club. . . . Don't take offense, but you are a white man. (*Sings*) "You're not black, you're not an African." WHITE! When you say "my brother" you're assuming a bond that does not exist.

NEIBERT: Really? And you are an African by virtue of your color?

DAVID: And Ancestry. Yes. . . .

MR. BLAKE: Ah, but there is one thing wrong with your supposition. . . . There is my passport. It's the one thing Joaquim and I have in common. . . . That makes me an African. David Bradley, would you give up your eagle for this passport? Would you become an African? Ah, you have to think, don't you?

JOAQUIM: ANSWER!!

DAVID: I'm proud of being an African-American.

SARAH: Wasn't it you, the non-tax-paying, this country can kiss my black ass, David Bradley, who refused to vote in the last primary because you were angry? . . .

AMA: You can't just become an African, a black man, because you want to be. There is much more that binds us together than the eye can see.

(Nottage 214–216)

Neibert offers David advice regarding strategies for coping during the hostage situation, but David is unable to accept Neibert's good-intentioned suggestions because of their differing ethnic and racial backgrounds. David's ideological understanding of race and ethnicity are challenged directly by everyone within the group. His conflation of race and ethnicity provides Mr. Blake and Joaquim a platform to simultaneously challenge David's understanding of community. The racial bonds that connect the Bradleys with Joaquim and Ama are complicated by the privilege the Bradleys enjoy as American citizens. The Bradleys' national identity, symbolized through the eagle, provides them with privilege that other Black members of the chorus do not possess. Sarah's comment further complicates the discussion of identity, revealing that David has previously challenged his American identity by refusing to pay taxes or vote. Ama's declaration proposes that the substance of ethnic or racial bonds goes beyond cultural performance such as the adoption of linguistic patterns (i.e., Neibert's speech); yet, she does not clarify the source of the bonds within ethnic or racial communities. The hostage situation provides the chorus with an opportunity for discussion of these complex ideas. Nottage uses the polyvocality of the chorus to challenge deeply held views of race, class, and power during this scene. And while the tensions within the chorus are not resolved, the articulation of competing perspectives provides the audience with an opportunity to consider not only the various ideological positions performed via the chorus, but also their own.

Joaquim's new and tentative power falters when he attempts to establish order within the group. Joaquim's actions neither positively alter the dynamics in his village, nor provide a meaningful solution for any impending political conflict. Instead, he violently undermines his goals and demands that the hotel guests view him as a physical threat. In order to end the standoff between the chorus and Joaquim, David subdues Joaquim with a stone, and the gun is transferred between choral members, signaling their difficulty with Joaquim's conduct and the clear political and historical tensions that motivate his actions. Even as *"they all stare, hard and contemptuously"* at Joaquim, they do not know what to do with the gun (242).

AMA: Get the gun.
(*Sarah retrieves the gun, Joaquim, dazed, manages a smile. Joaquim laughs. . . . Sarah begins to pass Mr. Blake the gun.*)
SARAH: David, what should I do?
JOAQUIM: Throw away the gun . . . You keep it!
(*David looks at Sarah, uncertain.*)

SARAH: Even now, you're barking orders at me?
(*She slowly passes Mr. Blake the gun; he examines it.*)
MR. BLAKE: Joaquim, I don't recognize you.
(*He fires one shot at Joaquim, who slumps to the ground. Mr. Blake returns his gun to the holster at his side*).

(Nottage 242–243)

Mr. Blake fatally resolves the hostage situation, thereby releasing the chorus from The Imperial Hotel. Nottage purposefully incorporates violence at the end of *Mud, River, Stone* to underscore the lived consequences of imperialism and to highlight the necessity for discourse about the macro and micro implications of such conflicts for the global community. The Bradleys' testimony, and the weight of the stone they bring home as a reminder of their experience, provide an opportunity for thoughtful reflection. The memories that they share reflect Nottage's agenda to represent the legacy of imperialism, while encouraging others to move beyond "the moral indignation of an armchair activist" (Nottage 164).

Significance of choral performance

Although David ultimately uses the stone to subdue Joaquim, when recounting the event to his friends, he redeploys it as a teaching instrument to convey the seriousness of the experience. The stone signifies the Bradleys' dangerous adventure, but it also suggests the fragmentary nature of the chorus's collective experience. The Bradleys' knowledge represents only one layer of the stone. The stone's intricate layers emphasize that complex issues remain unresolved. Before they return home, Mr. Blake entreats the Bradleys to "tell the truth" about their experience in Africa (Nottage 243). Part of telling the truth involves addressing the competing perspectives they encountered on their trip. While the Bradleys are unable to influence the political situation in Africa, they can help frame a more empathetic understanding of the complexity of the lives of individuals such as Joaquim, Mr. Blake, Neibert, and Ama, thereby humanizing the choral members by emphasizing their concerns, problems, and desires. By telling the story, the Bradleys transform the choral members from nameless figures in a remote, international incident, into complex individuals grappling with serious issues.

   In *Mud, River, Stone* Nottage deploys polyvocality as a meaningful strategy for addressing the residue of colonial conflict in contemporary times. Nottage's multicultural chorus advances what Lynnette Goddard calls a "Black feminist performance aesthetic" (39). Goddard claims that "from the outset, black aestheticians conceived [of art as] an oppositional practice that would foreground black experiences and the struggles for racial equality," resulting in the creation of texts "distinctly different from white American theatre in form and content" (44). Goddard presents W.E.B. Du Bois and Alain Locke as Harlem Renaissance aestheticians who "wanted to use theatre to reveal the Negro to the white world as 'a human feeling thing'" (44). This particular commitment was extended during the Black Power Era of the 1960s and 1970s as "Amiri Baraka (Le Roi Jones) and Ed Bullins argued for a black aesthetic that rejected white American norms of form and content" (44). However, the contemporary flourishing of drama written by African American women has challenged audiences to recognize the privilege associated with racial and gendered presentations of African American experience. A part of this challenge involves analyzing historical representations of race and how our understanding of history impacts our perceptions of the present.

Nottage uses the chorus to challenge the audience to see the connections between the past and present. Her chorus represents a revision of the traditional use of the chorus, transforming the group from a heterogeneous body that summarizes the action into a multicultural community of voices that uses language to consider difficult problems. As the choral voices clash, the audience is positioned to contemplate political issues represented in their dissonance. The multicultural community in The Imperial Hotel is at the center of the action in *Mud, River, Stone.* Nottage's use of the chorus represents an extension of the Black feminist agenda, politicizing current global issues by revising community without forgoing considerations of identity. In doing so, Nottage positions characters as historical barometers that reflect the ongoing influence of colonial transgressions on contemporary crises.

Works cited

Bacon, Helen H. "The Chorus in Greek Life and Drama." *Arion* 3.1 (1995): 6–24. Web. Accessed April 18, 2013.

Childress, Alice. *Wedding Band: A Love/Hate Story in Black and White.* New York: Samuel French, 1973. Print.

Fletcher, Judith. "Choral Voice and Narrative in the First Stasimon of Aeschylus *Agamemmon.*" *Phoenix* 53.5 (1999): 29–49. Web. Accessed April 30, 2013.

Goddard, Lynnette. "Black Feminist Performance Aesthetics." *Staging Black Feminisms: Identity, Politics, Performance.* London: Palgrave, 2007. 39–56. Print.

Griffin, Farah Jasmine. "That the Mothers May Soar and the Daughters May Know Their Names: A Retrospective of Black Feminist Literary Criticism." *Signs* 32.2 (2007): 483–507. Web. Accessed December 18, 2012.

Ley, Graham. *A Short Introduction to the Ancient Greek Theater*. Rev. ed. Chicago: University of Chicago Press, 2006. Print.

Marks, Peter. "Hostages With a Lot to Say." Rev. of *Mud, River, Stone* by Lynn Nottage/Roger Rees. *New York Times*. 16 December 1997. Print.

Nottage, Lynn. *Mud, River, Stone. Crumbs from the Table of Joy and Other Plays*. New York: Theatre Communications Group, 2004. 163–243. Print.

Parks, Suzan-Lori. *In the Blood. The Red Letter Plays*. New York: Theatre Communications Group, 2001. 1–110. Print.

Shange, Ntozake. *for colored girls who have considered suicide/when the rainbow is enuf.* 1975. Rpt. ed. New York: Scribners, 2010. Print.

Smith, Anna Deavere. *Fires in the Mirror: Crown Heights, Brooklyn, and Other Identities*. New York: Drama Play Services, 1998. Print.

Smith, Barbara. "Toward a Black Feminist Criticism" (1977). *But Some of Us Are Brave*. Eds. Gloria T. Hull, Patricia Bell Scott, and Barbara Smith. New York: Feminist, 1982. 157–175. Print.

Washington, Mary Helen. "'The Darkened Eye Restored': Notes Toward a Literary History of Black Women." *Reading Black Reading Feminist*. Ed. Henry Louis Gates Jr. New York: Penguin, 1990. 20–43. Print.

Wetmore Jr., Kevin J. *Black Dionysus Greek Tragedy and African American Theatre*. Jefferson, NC: McFarland, 2003. Print.

Chapter 3

Diasporic desires in
Las Meninas

Jocelyn L. Buckner

One of the contributions Lynn Nottage makes to critical debates surrounding narrative and dramatic theory is a rigorous dramaturgical historiography through which she investigates the relationship between displacement and desire throughout history and regions in the African diaspora. This replaying, retelling, and revising of histories of peoples of African descent is a project taken up by artists across disciplines, such as photographer Carrie Mae Weems, whose *Slave Coast, Africa*, and *Sea Islands* series all feature locations that were points of departure and arrival for Africans in the transatlantic slave trade and explore the affective meanings of these places. bell hooks's description of Weems's images as "diasporic landscapes of longing, a cartography of desire wherein boundaries are marked only to be transgressed, where the exile returns home only to leave again" also speaks to the revisionist projects enacted by Lynn Nottage (*Art on My Mind* 73). In many of Nottage's works, including *Intimate Apparel, Crumbs from the Table of Joy, Fabulation*, and *Ruined*, characters' lives are hemmed by circumstance, preventing or challenging them from easily achieving belonging, safety, and love. As a result, characters transgress boundaries in search of home – the place, the idea, and the feeling – often ultimately ending up back where they started, only to strike out once more, in continuous search of their desires. Such physical, psychological, and emotional nomadism uniquely marks the African diaspora, and is a recurring theme in Nottage's plays.

Echoing hooks's evocative description of diasporic longing, this chapter examines how Lynn Nottage adopts a visual aesthetic metaphor in *Las Meninas* (2002), creating a dramatic portrait of the movement of diasporic peoples across geography and temporality, and by extension desires for home, identity, and belonging. I explore how Nottage deploys language and bodies to evoke displacement as a critical component of

characters' identities. I next analyze how the play converses with previous art works, especially Diego Velazquez's *Las Meninas* (1656) and
the unsigned portrait *The Black Nun of Moret* (c.1680), and how these
images manifest visual representations of perception and diasporic
desire. Finally, I identify how Nottage engages with official and contested primary source evidence to radically re-envision and reposition
diasporic identity in the historical record. In the very act of writing *Las
Meninas*, Nottage troubles the questions: How can theatre revise histories from which particular individuals, relationships, and acts have
been erased? Why do we search for our roots across boundaries of time
and place? How does knowing about our past help imprint and map our
contemporary lives? By exploring such questions, Nottage contributes
to ongoing dramaturgical dialogues surrounding pan-African displacement, identity, and self-definition that resist Eurocentric and Afrocentric
notions of place and identity. Through an interrogation of language and
bodies, imagery, and evidence, Nottage enacts her own revisionist historiography in which identities are constructed in a liminal space and
time, suspended by displacement and connected by desire.

The mystery and erasure of a secret child, the offspring of a rumored
affair between Queen Marie-Therese and a court fool, an African
dwarf named Nabo Sensugali, is the historical core of *Las Meninas*, Nottage's imaginative retelling of this European court scandal.
Their union produced a daughter, Louise Marie-Therese, who is the
thirty-one-year-old narrator of the play. She has been sequestered and
raised in a convent for her entire life, and seeks to tell the story of her
birth before she is forced to take a religious vow of silence, thereby
further erasing her voice and existence from official historical records.
Nottage frames this portrait of displacement with two important ideas.
In an epigraph to the script, Nottage cites the familiar Yoruban prov-
erb: "The white man who made the pencil also made the eraser" (Nottage 246). In the last line of the play Louise Marie-Therese laments,
"And now I too will be lost to history" (Nottage 324). Between these
bookends, Nottage beckons the audience to critically consider her representation of the past, which Louise Marie-Therese describes as "the
true story of the seduction of the Queen of France" (Nottage 252).
Her emphasis on her tale as truth positions *Las Meninas* as a revisionist history, new consideration of lives erased from record. In the act
of writing *Las Meninas*, Nottage performs the historiographic exercise
of re-envisioning her characters' lives from a previously unconsidered
perspective by granting Louise Marie-Therese a public embodiment, a
voice, and a stage on which to share her story.

Language and bodies

Louise Marie-Therese's story of displacement and disappearance begins with her parents' respective departures from their home countries. Her mother, the Spanish-born Queen, was married to the French King Louis XIV in 1660 to help establish and sustain peace between Spain and France. Living far from home was difficult for the Queen, and was made more so by her husband's open and prolific extramarital affairs. Nottage captures the dissonance in their marriage during the opening scene of the play, in which the King and Queen are sitting for a royal painter. During the creation of one of the most symbolic representations of their union – an official portrait, an icon of peace between countries and love between individuals – the rulers are anything but united. In fact, they quite literally do not speak the same language, as the King points out:

KING: I'm sorry, did you say something Marie? Speak French, for God's sake I don't know what you are saying.

QUEEN: I'M TALKING OF DE BOX DAT ARRIVED FOR ME DIS MORNING!

KING: Not louder Marie, in French. Please, my ears are dying! . . .

QUEEN: [*upon opening the box*] Ay Dios mio. Es un African. A little one at that. Look Louis, es fantastic.

(Nottage 253)

The "box" that has arrived is the inciting incident in the play. The monarchs are stymied in their strained marriage and being painted for posterity, when a distraction arrives. Inside the box is Nabo Sensugali, a displaced man, sent to serve at the pleasure of a displaced Queen. She heralds his arrival with a greeting that echoes Franz Fanon's famous recounting of his own racial hailing – "Look, a Negro!" – immediately marking Nabo's difference and displacement in the context of the court (Fanon 112). In the moment he is hailed, emerging from his shipping container and gasping for breath, Nabo evokes ideas and memories of black bodies contained and transported in other contexts and epochs, from the belly of slave ships heavy with human cargo, to Henry "Box" Brown's spectacular 1849 escape from captivity by shipping himself in a box from Richmond, VA to Philadelphia, PA. In this way, Nabo is not treated as an individual but instead signifies long-held ideas of blackness beginning before, and extending beyond, his own experience as a diasporic individual. As Harvey Young explains, "When popular connotations of blackness are mapped across or internalized within black people, the result is the creation of *the black body*. This second body, an abstracted and imagined figure, shadows or doubles the real one" (*Embodying* 7). From this initial moment when his body is set in contrast to the foreign environment of the court, Nabo must endure and negotiate assumptions about his behavior – from cannibalism to carnal instincts – based on preconceptions and stereotypes, rather than clear understandings of blackness or his own individuality.

Furthermore, Nabo's foreign and racial identities intersect with his identity as a little person. His physical stature, in addition to his racial and outsider status, marks him as triply othered in the royal household. Paradoxically, his difference was the very reason for his delivery to the court. As cultural historian Betty M. Adelson notes in *The Lives of Dwarfs: Their Journey from Public Curiosity toward Social Liberation*,

> the history of dwarfs is embedded in the history of civilization in general. . . . for many centuries, those dwarfs whose history was recorded were employed as court dwarfs – owned, indulged, exploited, traded, and sent as gifts. Far from representing a single, monolithic experience, each of the courts offered a milieu that sprang from the characters of its monarchs and citizens. (3–4)

African dwarfs in particular were rare in the royal courts of Europe and as such were symbols of imperial power, whiteness, and colonial expansion. Dwarfs were regarded as integral members of court and often well clothed, fed, housed, and sometimes educated. Yet dwarfs, particularly those identified as foreign, were regarded as playthings, knick-knacks, and living curiosities; not necessarily human. Adelson explains that Diego Velázquez's painting *Las Meninas* (1656) famously features dwarfs integrated into life in the Spanish court, making them among the most well-known (13). As Sandra L. Richards notes, and I will expand upon later, Nottage's depiction of Nabo's experience "recuperates and redirects – 'repeats with a critical difference' in black cultural terms" the questions of perspective, representation, and relationships presented in Velázquez's painting (100). The portrait of court dwarfs is echoed in the play's title, and serves as primary evidence for the experience of court dwarfs reflected in the Queen's attempted explanation of Nabo's position of doubled difference and disenfranchisement. "[M]y cousin gave you to me. He knows how much I love little . . . back in Spain we had a number of . . . but none of dem were . . . De court was always filled with laughter and little people" (Nottage 262). The Queen's false starts reveal rather than mask the intersecting components of Nabo's physical novelty, and underscore how ill-equipped the court is to understand and respect his identity. Indeed, language fails the Queen in this moment, as she searches for words to describe the stranger in the box.

Nabo, like most literary and historical fools, is a truth-teller. But his truth, rather than pointing out the humor in life in order to entertain and disarm the court, instead offers a disruptive depiction of his own experience, one of unwilling migration from West Africa to France. He is a resistant fool, interested in the truth as a means of self-preservation rather than entertainment or placation of the ruling class.

QUEEN: Oh goodness, I wonder what he does. . . . Sing for me!
(Nabo, the African dwarf, does not respond. He stares incredulously at the Queen.)
Well? . . . Sing, little man!
(Nabo still does not respond.)
SING! COMPRENDE?
NABO: *(Timidly)*: I can't!
QUEEN: Oh?
(A moment.)
Give us a dance then!
NABO: I don't.
QUEEN: . . . Then what is it dat you perform?
NABO: What can one perform after being in a box for three days? I was promised six goats and some beads, and I closed my eyes and I had crossed the ocean. And now I'm scented, powdered and stuffed in a box. . . . Each place I go, they expect me to perform. What? I don't know. And they pack me back in a box and send me on. I've traveled halfway across the world in this box. And I'm tired, tired, tired . . . of it! . . .
QUEEN: He's tired, Louis! Delightful!

(Nottage 254–255)

By refusing to sing and dance and instead explaining his discomfort, Nabo unwittingly enacts a dystopic diasporic performance of blackness and difference. Kennell Jackson, in describing performance as a critical component in black cultural traffic, explains that "the performance moment is key because it is the instance in which some representation of blacks, black cultural material, or blackness is offered" (4). From his initial entrance, *"dressed as a French footman,"* Nabo's very resistance is interpreted as a cultural performance, including his vocal protests that he is displaced and longing to go home (Nottage 257). In so doing, Nabo and Nottage give voice to a history of subaltern experiences long silenced.

As his captivity in the court extends indefinitely, Nabo labors to survive in the foreign culture. In order to do so, he adopts the outer trappings of the court in dress and diet, while simultaneously maintaining and manifesting his own identity and sanity through the stories and dances he chooses to perform publicly for the court and privately for his own self-preservation. Such performances of cultural expression, hooks notes, are enacted and "emerge as a response to circumstances of oppression and exploitation. . . . One may engage in strategic performances in the interests of survival employing the same skills one uses to perform in the interest of ritual play, yet the performative standpoint alters both the nature and impact of the performances" ("Performance Practice" 210–211). Nabo seeks solace in the familiarity of remembered cultural practices as the lonely Queen pursues him day and night, finding comfort and reassurance in his presence. At moments when the Queen's demands and advances overwhelm him, Nabo prays before a *"small makeshift altar with cowrie shells, a small clay pot and several burning candles,"* and *"does a warrior dance as if evoking a distant spirit for strength"* (Nottage 272, 275). Nabo's private performances of ritual ground him and connect him to his point of origin, in Dahomey. Finding himself at a crossroads about how to navigate this strange context, he prays to Legba, the West African trickster god associated with destiny and decision-making, asking, "Please mighty Legba, why am I here? If I do as she says will she let me go? If I'm very funny will they give me more food? If I kiss her will she free me?" Reflecting on her father's pleas for guidance, Louise Marie-Therese describes Nabo's forlorn sense of utter displacement, "in his small room facing the darkness, he stood wondering how he had gotten so far from home" (Nottage 275).

In contrast, during his public performances at court Nabo fashions himself as a storyteller, which the rulers initially resist ("A story? No, no, no!"), but eventually enjoy ("Nabo told me de absolutely most funniest story this morning. I nearly spoiled myself with delight.") (Nottage 261, 276). All of Nabo's stories in some way reflect his experience of diaspora and the search for home, family, and a sense of belonging. He enthralls the Queen with the tragedy of his abduction, to which she reacts, "it's too sad . . . imagine if something like that were true," and wins the King's favor with a hilarious fictional story about his early days in Europe, when he misunderstood the upper class custom of wearing makeup and wigs, and as a result mistook his unadorned master for an intruder and chased him out of his own house (Nottage 266, 277). As part of the court's notorious fetes and festivals, Nabo at one point even dresses as "*Bacchus/Legba . . . wear[ing] an African mask and a huge phallus strapped to his front*" to entertain the court with the West African myth of Ananse spider. Accompanied by "*a simple drum beat*," Nabo enacts the story of how Ananse, seeking to spread his seed and keep his trickster traditions alive, seduces the moon's wife and impregnates her, a telling metaphor for Nabo's own affair with, and resulting pregnancy of, the Sun King's wife (Nottage 292). As Richards observes, the performances of these stories, along with Nabo's confession to the court painter that he actually first heard the humorous tale of mistaken identity while on his travels between Dahomey and Paris, offers "an interesting critique on class, cultural circulation, and the sophistication of the early African diaspora to Europe that has largely been forgotten" (101). Nabo deploys the oral traditions of West Africa as a survival tactic. By listening, retelling, and revising stories, he participates in the diasporic circulation of language and culture from continent to continent and court to court, making visible his transcultural and transtemporal movement through performance.

The need to perform conscious acts of self-definition is further underscored in interactions between Nabo and the Queen. Echoing the earlier exchange between the Queen and King, Nottage deploys ideas of home and language to evoke the sense of Otherness and isolation felt by both the Queen and Nabo. Thrown together by circumstance and recognizing their need to rely on one another in order to survive the expectations of the court, the Queen and Nabo attempt to establish a common language of exchange:

NABO: You call me fool, but it isn't my name.
QUEEN: Well? I will give you a name then.
NABO: I have one.
QUEEN: You do?
NABO: Nabo Sensugali. (He bows again)
QUEEN: I don't like it! I can't say it! Jorgito or Pedro, you like Pedro?
NABO: No!
QUEEN: You're indignant for a man that came in a box. I could put you
    back in dere and ship you home.

NABO: Indeed? I welcome such punishment, for this liberal tongue
deserves no mercy. Send me home!

(Nottage 257)

Neither is understood by those around them. Later the Queen asks, "Who
are you?" to which Nabo responds, "Someone not unlike yourself" (265).
Nottage underscores their disparate identities: the Queen, who "arrived in
Paris drawn by a hundred grey horses," is confined to the palace by marriage and political diplomacy, while Nabo was trafficked there trapped in
a box, but she also works to align these social misfits as fellow travelers
in a world in which they do not truly belong (Nottage 262). When Nabo
enters the Queen's sphere, his embodied difference as African and dimin-
utive in size, as well as her dominance over him, gives Queen Marie-
Therese the confidence and desire to cross the barriers of nations and
marriage bonds in order to traverse new corporeal borders. Eventually,
"with a kiss he tasted empires past and future. With one tender kiss she
drew him in and they faced the possibility of freedom" (Nottage 286).
Nabo, as court attendant, is obliged to join the Queen in these transgressions, which begin innocently and lead to the exchange of carnal knowledge, the creation of a new life, and the erasure of his.

Exiled from their homes due to circumstances beyond their control,
the Queen, Nabo, and later their child Louise Marie-Therese, experience and understand the profound sense of displacement Edward Said
describes in *Reflections on Exile*:

We take home and language for granted; they become nature and
their underlying assumptions recede into dogma and orthodoxy.
The exile knows that in a secular and contingent world, homes are
always provisional. Borders and barriers, which enclose us within
the safety of familiar territory, can also become prisons, and are
often defended beyond reason or necessity. Exiles cross borders,
break barriers of thought and experience. (185)

In their exiled states, the Queen and Nabo each recognize the value of
language, and fight for their right to use it to define themselves and their
circumstances. Queen Marie-Therese insists on speaking her mother
tongue, to the frustration and displeasure of both Nabo and the King. By
insisting on being called by his African name and by weaving stories of
his abduction from home as well as African myths into his courtly repertoire, Nabo Sensugali maintains a connection to Dahomey and attempts
to preserve his subjectivity. Their efforts at self-preservation are further

reflected in their daughter Louise Marie-Therese's tactics as she deploys language and the storytelling tradition to narrate the tale of her parents' love affair, give voice to her own existence, and illuminate the strategies of displacement and diasporic desire that manifest a provisional sense of home.

Imagery and evidence: Portraitures of truth

The task of the painter and the cultural function of portraits are significant, and serve as a productive metaphor for Nottage's own imaginative repainting and reframing of history. As noted, the title of the play, meaning "maids of honour," echoes Diego Velázquez's 1656 painting of Queen Marie Therese's half-sister, the Infanta Margaret Theresa, long hailed by art historians as "an icon of Baroque Naturalism" (Stratton-Pruitt 5). In this canvas, the young royal is attended by two ladies-in-waiting and two dwarfs capturing, as Adelson notes, "how intertwined were the lives of the royalty and the dwarfs depicted" (13). The Infanta is nearly perfectly centered in the middle of the composition, posed standing next to the painter himself and in front of her parents, King Philip IV and Queen Mariana, who are only seen in the reflection of a mirror hanging on the wall behind their daughter. Their image, as well as the image of Don José Nieto Velázquez, a court attendant looking into the room through a doorway at the back of the painting, draws the viewer further into the piece, encouraging our consideration of the variety of perspectives portrayed in the image. Indeed, as Estrella De Diego observes, "Velázquez needed the complicity of the spectator for the painting to function the way it did. The spectator was the essential part of the work and in his *mise-en-scène*" (167). In response to the painting such questions emerge: With whom are we to align our viewpoint, and which is the "right" perspective? The unseen King and Queen looking into the painting? Their child looking out of the painting? The painter looking at his undisclosed canvas-within-the-canvas? The attending members of the court? The dwarfs poking the resting dog who also inhabits the painting? The *dog*? Is this a multi-layered and multi-positioned painting of the Infanta, or a painting of the portraiture of the monarchs, or a painting of the creation of *Las Meninas* itself?

In addition to formal studies of the painting's composition, questions of perspective and representation have dominated artistic adaptations and discourse surrounding the painting for the last two centuries. Gertje R. Utley notes that in contemporary responses to and reinterpretations of the painting, "the quoted art work [is] used as a template for the modern

Figure 3.1 *Las Meninas* or *The Family of Philip IV*, c.1656 (oil on canvas), Diego Rodríguez de Silva y Velázquez (1599–1660) / Prado, Madrid, Spain / Bridgeman Images.

artist's inquiry into areas of . . . artistic, philosophic, social, or political concerns, and even as a tool for the artist's critique of contemporary sociopolitical or artistic conventions" (171). Nottage's *Las Meninas* is in chorus with these aesthetic queries (and others) on perspective and subjectivity, which she stages in the French court portrait session that opens the play and in her own depiction of the court's inhabitants. By staging her *Las Meninas* in another European court, Nottage aligns herself with Velázquez certainly, but also with a multitude of visual artists, Pablo Picasso perhaps most notably, who have created new meditations and interpretations on the famous painting and the questions of absence and presence it evokes.[1] Each reinterpretation explores both what is seen *and unseen* in the painting, recognizing and acknowledging that which is not made manifest either in Velázquez's work or written historical records.

Michel Foucault's essay about the canvas in *The Order of Things* specifically troubles that which is *in*visible in the painting, and the meaning that this unseen presence evokes but does not reveal. He writes, "the invisibility that [this painting] overcomes is not the invisibility of what is hidden: it does not make its way around any obstacle, it is not distorting any perspective, it is addressing itself to what is invisible both because of the picture's structure and because of its existence as painting" (8). In *Las Meninas*, Nottage also questions the surface meanings of paintings and records of Western history, recognizing that "the essence of critical memory's work is the cumulative, collective maintenance of a record that draws into relationship significant instants of time past and the always uprooted homelessness of now" (Baker 7). By interrogating these canonical artifacts in radical ways that engage and insert heretofore invisible diasporic and subaltern lives into the frame of the public sphere, she seeks to locate and create a new portrait of diaspora, identity, and history.

In the play, when the King exits the opening scene's portrait painting session to attend to "affairs of state" with his mistress, the Queen commands Nabo to sit with her in order to avoid the humiliation of having her "portrait painted alone" (Nottage 256). As Louise Marie-Therese recounts, "there it began in the King's chair . . . with the image of Nabo lightly drawn in, uncommitted . . . a mercurial impression barely perceivable" (Nottage 258). The provocative stage picture of Nabo sitting on the King's throne foreshadows his romantic replacement of the King. It also illustrates how Nabo's thumbprint in history has been painted over – made invisible – with a dominant portrait of court life. By sketching Nabo into the early layers of the painting, Nottage encourages audiences to wonder not only at *this* man's story, but also the countless others literally brushed over, and out of, portraits of history. She invites audiences, as cultural historians with infrared eyes, to examine the image *she* is painting, to recognize layer upon layer of the image being restored before our eyes on the page and stage.

The idea of the painterly perspective and the evidence of portraiture drive Nottage's revisionist dramaturgy. As Harvey Young notes, the performance of the painter and paintings themselves are significant sites of possibility for "the study of nontextual remains as the basis for writing performance history" ("Writing with Paint" 138). Over the course of *Las Meninas*, Nabo is eventually recorded in a portrait painted by the same court artist who captured the likeness of the King and Queen. Like Nottage herself, the court painter sees the man beneath the courtly costume he wears. He entreats Nabo, "Let me paint you. Without the adornments. Your face" (Nottage 281). Years later, the artist visits with Nabo and the Queen's daughter Louise Marie-Therese and shares, "you know who it is you remind me of, an African, yes, a dwarf of very fine character from Dahomey. . . . You resemble him" (Nottage 280). As omnipotent narrator, Louise relays that there was "a sketch, colors selected, hues blended. Frustration. And finally found in a damp cellar, a portrait of a nameless African man" (Nottage 281). By recording Nabo's portraiture and its subsequent dispatch to a basement, Nottage simultaneously identifies Nabo, preserves his corporeality on canvas, then subsequently scripts his further displacement and debasement into the bowels of history.

The intersections between representation and reality are further complicated in the dramatized exchange between the painter and Louise Marie-Therese when considered alongside the existence of an actual extant unsigned portrait, this one of a subject known as "Louise Marie-Therese, the Black Nun of Moret (1664–1732)," believed to have been painted by a court artist who also painted Louis XIV.[2] The portrait is preserved in the library of St. Genevieve in Paris, making Louise Marie-Therese's existence, according to African American ex-pat writer Anita Thompson who penned a short story about the nun's scandalous birth in 1929, "as true as historical record . . . can make it" (Sharpley-Whiting 110). In addition to this connection to the palace, the subject of the historic painting was born in the same year Nottage begins her play, and takes the veil in 1695, the year from which the character Louise Marie-Therese narrates. These courtly connections and chronology, as well as the mention of the Queen's black baby in journals and other writings of the King's mistress Madame de Montespan (whose so-called memoirs were written by Philippe Musoni years after Montespan's death), Duchess de Montepensier, the Duke of Saint-Simon, and the French writer Voltaire, while debatable in accuracy, all stand as evidence to her very real, yet displaced, life.[3] The character Nottage scripts is literally out of place, removed from the court to the convent because of her race and gender, reflecting Radhika Mohanram's question: "If woman is the scaffolding upon which rests the identity of the nation and its male citizens, what do you do with her materiality," particularly when her identity is demarcated by the single

Figure 3.2 Portrait of Louise-Marie-Therese (1664–1732) *the Black Nun of Moret* (oil on canvas), French School / Bibliothèque Sainte-Geneviève, Paris, France / Archives Charmet / Bridgeman Images.

fact that she is viewed as out of place, since "the category of the 'black body' can come into being only when the body is perceived as being out of place, either from its natural environment or its national boundaries" (xvii, xii)? The character of Louise-Marie Therese embodies and illuminates the subject of "The Black Nun of Moret's" erasure, validating her contentious yet persistent archival record by reimagining the events that bring her into existence. Nottage firmly places her in a historical moment and context, thereby dramatizing her exile from court and her disconnect from the diaspora from which she descends.

Revisiting and revising the record

Numerous official records exist which document the public and private activities of Louis XIV's court. Yet secret lives and silenced scandals seldom endure the censure of sanctioned court historians. To recover these stories is to enact a radical historiography of reckoning with unofficial records and anecdotal evidence to revise the catalog of past events. One such exemplary source that Nottage leans on in cultivating her historiography is the Marquise de Montespan's memoirs. Her journals detail life in the court of Louis XIV, recall her experiences as the King's mistress, and record early court gossip. Nottage cites her in the preface to the published script:

> My readers remember the little negress who was born to the Queen in the early days – she whom no one wanted, who was dismissed, relegated, disinherited, unacknowledged, deprived of her rank and name the very day of her birth . . . it was wished that this young Princess should be ignorant of her birth, and in this I agree that, in the midst of crying injustice, the King kept his natural humanity. This poor child not being meant, and not being able, to appear at Court, it was better, indeed, to keep her from all knowledge of her rights, in order to deprive her, at one stroke, of the distress of her conformation, the hardship of her repudiation, and the despair of captivity. The King destined her for a convent when he saw her born.
>
> (Nottage 247)

Nottage paints such evidence onto the canvas of her play, simultaneously relying upon and challenging evidence to underscore themes of diasporic longing embedded psychically, physically, and spiritually into Louise-Marie Therese's life.

For example, upon learning about her parentage from one of the King's jealous mistresses sent to the convent to report on the condition of the secret ward, Louise Marie-Therese reveals the psychic loss she has attempted to fill with religious iconography – portraits – and stories about paternity and belonging. She laments her lost connection to her father, and to her sense of home, crying:

> Papa! I'd never seen an African other than the stained glass windows of Balthazar bending over Christ with a gift, wearing his

azure turban more magnificent than the others. As the light shone through the window at noon I imagined he was my father, casting purple hues across my forehead. I'd pray to him, a King from a far off land who ruled countries more beautiful than France. A King who'd been in the very presence of Christ. In Madame de Montespan's version my father was not a King. In mine, sometimes he is.

(Nottage 307)

By reimagining the circumstances of Louise Marie-Therese's birth and lived "condition of perpetual captivity," Nottage publicly interrogates the accuracy and reliability of the historical record in performance (Williams 73). She demonstrates the power and potentiality of performance as a site of "reclaimed subjugated knowledge and historical memory . . . a space of transgression where new identities and radicalized black subjectivities emerge, illuminating . . . history in ways that challenge and interrogate, that highlight the shifting nature of black experience. . . . [P]erformance [is] a site for the imagination of future possibilities." (hooks "Performance Practice" 220). In doing so, she manifests the physical, emotional, and psychic burdens of diasporic desires for freedom and home.

Nabo's separation from his family in Dahomey and from his newborn child in the foreign court echoes countless stories of generations of Africans removed from their homelands and families and carried to foreign ones in service to colonial masters. The gossip and mythology surrounding these historic figures – human commodities in circulation, products and purveyors of black cultural traffic between Africa and points North and West – reflects the simultaneous curiosity and anxiety inherent in the consumption and sacrifice of black lives and stories for pleasure and entertainment. Upon learning of the royal infant's "discoloration," the King christens the baby Louise Marie-Therese, thereby marking her with his and the Queen's names, and erasing Nabo's paternal claim to her. He then banishes the child to the convent and a life of displaced captivity. Next, he summons Nabo to his chambers to deliver the news that Nabo will be executed for his "very penetrating look," the euphemistic explanation for the biracial baby (Nottage 315). In an attempt to defend himself and save his life, Nabo recounts his capture and transportation to Europe, bitterly describing his travails in defense of his relationship with the Queen:

NABO: I gave a woman a few moments of love. I should be thanked for that. I was shipped to and from empires bizarre and unwelcoming in a box no full size man could survive. Bought, sold, bartered and brokered until I do not know who I am. Laughed at, kicked and disgraced, I've learned more than most men about this human race. And if my tongue were acid you'd now be dead. I've made kings weep with joy and queens whine with delight. Months of pleasure I've given your court, and I am to pay for the one moment I stole for my own.

KING: Yes, unfortunately, that seems to be the case.

(Nottage 323)

Nottage's dramatic portrait of diasporic displacement and desire embodied in Nabo and Louise Marie-Therese exemplifies Saidiya Hartman's description of "rescuing and recovering the black subject," through the enactment of a "resolutely counterhegemonic labor that has as its aim the establishment of other standards of aesthetic value and visual possibility. The intention of the work is corrective representation" (quoted in *Art on My Mind* 67). Many historians and scholars discount the stories of Nabo and the black baby born to the Queen. But by challenging the systemic dismissal of these individuals, Nottage performs the nuanced work of reinscribing value and possibility for their lives. To remember is radical, and Nottage's dramaturgy recognizes that "there is revolutionary power within black memory. It can spotlight the past assaults on the black body within both public and private settings and can name the culprits responsible for those abuses" (Young, *Embodying* 18). *Las Meninas* serves as a microhistory of one such injustice, and in doing so underscores the violence of colonialism and Western cultural imperialism. Ultimately, Lynn Nottage aligns with fellow playwrights, artists, scholars, and historians of diaspora, cultural memory, and identity. She labors to recreate and paint into the present moment diasporic identities through the historiographic portraiture of *Las Meninas,* interrogating history and provoking new inquiry into what – and who – is remembered.

Notes

1 Pablo Picasso first saw *Las Meninas* in 1895 at the age of fourteen, and painted a series of forty-five variations (and thirteen related works) on Velázquez's masterpiece during the fall of 1957. See Gertje R. Utley, "*Las Meninas* in Twentieth-Century Art" for more on Picasso and other artists' works inspired by Velázquez.

2 See Honoré Champion, ed. *Mémoires de la Société de l'histoire de Paris et de l'Île-de-France.*

3 See Françoise-Athénaïs de Rochechouart de Mortemart, marquise de Montespan, *Memoirs of Madame la Marquise de Montespan, Written by Herself Being the Historic Memoirs of the Court of Louis XIV* (Boston: Grolier Society, 1900); citation of Voltaire's claims about Louise Marie-Therese's parentage in the biography by Joëlle Chevé, *Marie-Thérèse d'Autriche: Épouse de Louis XIV* (Paris: Pygmalion, 2008); Duc de Saint-Simon, *Memoirs of Louis XIV and His Court and of the Regency*, vol. 2, digitized version; and Duchess Anne-Marie-Louise d'Orléans, *Memoirs of la Grande Mademoiselle: Duchess de Montepensier*, vol. 2, June 1664–66, digitized version.

Works cited

Adelson, Betty M. *The Lives of Dwarfs: Their Journey from Public Curiosity Towards Social Liberation*. New Brunswick: Rutgers University Press, 2005. Print.

Baker, Houston. "Critical Memory and the Black Public Sphere." *The Black Public Sphere: A Public Culture Book*. Ed. The Black Public Sphere Collective. Chicago: University of Chicago Press, 1995. 5–38. Print.

Champion, Honoré, ed. *Mémoires de la Société de l'histoire de Paris et de l'Île-de-France*. Paris: Société de l'histoire de Paris et de l'Ile-de-France, 1924. Print.

De Diego, Estrella. "Representing Representation: Reading *Las Meninas*, Again." *Velázquez's Las Meninas*. Ed. Suzanne Stratton-Pruitt. Cambridge: Cambridge University Press, 2003. 150–169. Print.

Fanon, Franz. *Black Skin, White Masks*. New York: Grove Press, 1952. Print.

Foucault, Michel. "Las Meninas." *The Order of Things*. London: Routledge, 2002. 3–17. Print.

Hartman, Saidiya. "Roots and Romance." *Camerawork* 20.2 (Fall/Winter 20013): 34–36. Print.

hooks, bell. "Diasporic Landscapes of Longing." *Art on My Mind: Visual Politics*. New York: The New Press, 1995. Print.

———. "Performance Practice as a Site of Opposition." *Let's Get It On: The Politics of Black Performance*. Ed. Catherine Ugwu. Seattle: Bay Press, 1995. 210–221. Print.

Jackson, Kennell. "Introduction." *Black Cultural Traffic: Crossroads in Global Performance and Popular Culture*. Eds. Harry J. Elam, Jr., and Kennell Jackson. Ann Arbor: University of Michigan Press, 2005. 1–39. Print.

Mohanram, Radhika. *The Black Body: Women, Colonialism, and Space*. Minneapolis: University of Minnesota Press, 1999. Print.

Nottage, Lynn. *Las Meninas. Crumbs from the Table of Joy and Other Plays*. New York: Theatre Communications Group, 2004. 245–324. Print.

Richards, Sandra. "Spreading Sweetness: Storytelling in Contemporary Black Theatre." *Worlds in Words: Storytelling in Contemporary Theatre and Playwriting*. Eds. Mateusz Borowski and Małgorzata Sugiera. Newcastle Upon Tyne: Cambridge Scholars Publishing, 2010. 90–106. Print.

Said, Edward W. *Reflections on Exile*. Boston: Harvard University Press, 2000. Print.

Stratton-Pruitt, Suzanne. "Introduction." *Velázquez's Las Meninas*. Ed. Suzanne Stratton-Pruitt. Cambridge: Cambridge University Press, 2003. 1–7. Print.

Williams, [née] Joyce Ann [Now: Jaye Austin]. *Solving for 'x': The Allegorhythms of Black Feminist Playwriting*. ProQuest, UMI Dissertations Publishing, 2013. Web.

Young, Harvey. *Embodying Black Experience: Stillness, Critical Memory, and the Black Body*. Ann Arbor: University of Michigan Press, 2010. Print.

———. "Writing with Paint." *Theater Historiography: Critical Interventions*. Eds. Henry Bial and Scott Magelssen. Ann Arbor: University of Michigan Press, 2010. 137–147. Print.

Chapter 4

Intimate spaces/public places

Locating sites of migration, connection, and identity in *Intimate Apparel*

Adrienne Macki Braconi

This chapter employs the lenses of cultural materialism and phenomenology to interrogate Nottage's treatment of space and place as elements that both define and fracture the identity of her characters in *Intimate Apparel* (2003).[1] It argues that tracking the "sociospatial" sites that shape Nottage's narrative yields fresh insights about the interwoven private, public, and mythic spaces that create and contest a sense of belonging and identity for each of her characters in this play (Westgate 4). A close examination of the thematic and dramaturgic manifestations of space and place in *Intimate Apparel* is productive for several reasons. First, it provides ways to understand the trans-historical significance of Nottage's storytelling. Second, it highlights how her plays resist stylistic categorization, despite some critics' desires to brand her work in specific ways.[2] Third, this approach illuminates the intersection of form and function in her playwriting. In an interview with Sandra Shannon, Nottage enlisted spatial metaphors to describe her intentions with this play, explaining that she "wanted to bridge the gap between women at the turn of the nineteenth century and at the turn of the twentieth century. They were very focused, very hard-working women, and because of the choices they made, they were being punished, which I think is what's happening to a lot of African American women today who have taken a career path" (197). She also observed that there were "fewer cross-cultural conversations [during this era]. People could exist in the same space but not have certain kinds of conversations" (199). In what follows, I trace how *Intimate Apparel* pivots on the politics of space to delineate how the play's representation of space shapes not only discourse but also identity and community formation. *Intimate Apparel* renders space as geographically and culturally specific locations (including Esther's boarding house room, her friend and client Mayme's brothel bedroom, her customer Mrs. Van Buren's boudoir, her fabric supplier Mr. Mark's tenement, her correspondent and future husband George's tent, and finally the letters themselves exchanged by Esther and George) to demonstrate that each place in the play, at different moments, serves three spatial capacities. I limn how the slippery borders of these private, public, and mythic spaces manifest in each site to inject and/or dislodge a sense of belonging and identity for Nottage's characters. Against the iconic backdrops of New York and Panama that showcase the "expression of power relations," the urban and the rural contexts operate as more than a setting (Kilian 116). Dramaturgically, the city plays an explicit role in "social transitions or transformations," shaping the characters' motivations and providing a source of conflict (Westgate 2). The urban landscape is the fodder for obstacles and opportunities, dreams and escapes, as in Esther's plan for an upscale beauty salon east of Amsterdam Avenue where "a colored woman could go to put up her feet and get treated good for a change" (Nottage 54). Correspondingly, for George, the city emerges as an incontrovertible foil that cannot be reconciled or overcome. For Mayme, an interlocking system of oppression in New York's red-light district traps her in a vicious cycle of prostitution; she resorts to turning tricks all the while hoping to break into a big musical revue show. For Mr. Marks, the Jewish ghettoes of the Lowest East Side replicate the expectations of the old country as he yields to rabbinical law and family traditions. For Mrs. Van Buren, the social and gendered stratifications of the Upper East Side accentuate her loneliness, infertility, and the failures of her marriage. As I will show, the tension between the rural and urban landscapes informs the "psychological and social lines of [each] character" in distinct ways to demonstrate how the city becomes a site of unfulfilled expectations that links all of these characters in their individual and collective border-crossings, ultimately determining how identity is constructed and dislocated in and through place and space (Fuchs 31).

I draw on Henri Lefebvre and others to examine how *space* is expressed in *Intimate Apparel* as "physical locales" (concrete, material space), "mental space" (abstract, conceptual space), and "social space" (locations for human interaction) in order to parse how these spatialities emerge as "dialectically interconnected processes of production" (Lefebvre 11; Schmid 42). This triad constitutes the representation of space as " 'absolute space' [which] refers to a conception of space as a field, container, a co-ordinate system of discrete and mutually exclusive locations" and "meta-space" (where the private and public realms are fused and "civil life" takes place) (Smith and Katz 75; Tétreault 81–97). Neil

Smith and Cindi Katz, referencing Lefebvre, posit that modern notions of absolute space became bound up with capitalism and "increasingly hegemonic" (75). This dynamic is integral to the sociospatial relationships and concomitant exchanges of power evident in *Intimate Apparel*.

In concert with these theorizations of space, I also use the term *place* to indicate a concrete, material location and probe *Intimate Apparel's* conception of place in terms of concretizing consciousness of identity, connection, and community. I agree with Michael Keith and Steve Pile that our perception of place is evolving and evocative of a "very real sense about location and locatedness" (5). For Keith and Pile, "our 'place' (in all its meanings) is considered fundamentally important to our perspective, our location in the world, and our right and ability to challenge dominant discourses of power" (6). For Nottage's characters, establishing a sense of place alternately denies or ensures their personal fulfillment; it disenfranchises or enables them to root themselves in order to safeguard their interests; leaves them immobilized; or pushes them to transplant themselves for self-preservation and survival.

To better articulate the representation of place and space in Nottage's plays I turn to a 2012 production of *Intimate Apparel* at Connecticut Repertory Theatre (CRT) that offers a particularly illustrative example of the tensions between rural and urban spaces and intimate and public places within a period rife with racial, gender, and economic segregation. With direction and scenic design by Michael Bradford and Maureen Freedman, respectively, the production aptly reflected Nottage's delineation and disruption of the color line in terms of physical locales, mental spaces, and social spaces. CRT's design incorporated the director's production concept of "constructs, constraints, and slippage" (Freedman). Set designer Maureen Freedman explained that she attempted to reflect the period's "*social constructs* (the social structure created and endorsed by society and the perception of an individual or a group through social practice); *social constraints* (the repression or control imposed on actions, feelings, and impulses because of social constructs); and *slippage* (crossing of otherwise strict social boundaries)" (Freedman, emphasis added). With sharp, box-like configurations of the play's physical locales, the production's visual demarcations of space clearly instanced the material reality of Samir Kawash's premise that "racial politics are spatial politics" (Romeyn xxi) (see Figure 4.1). This approach reflected the ways in which space was configured in the period's urban dwellings, according to Freedman, who was influenced by visits to the Tenement Museum in New York City and canvassing the Lower East side of New York. Likewise, her nuanced use of levels,

Figure 4.1 Connecticut Repertory Theatre's set for *Intimate Apparel* as designed by Maureen Freedman. Photographed by Greg Purnell.

planes, color, and texture manifested the hierarchical chasms segregating Nottage's characters in terms of class, gender, ethnicity, and religion. Thus, the show's mise-en-scène illuminated a crucial aspect of Nottage's dramaturgy by crystallizing the relationships between space, place, and race (Lefebvre 33). In this way, the rich scenography called attention to how these dynamics contribute to and complicate the intersectionality of racial identity, gender, and economic status. Furthermore, with a group of raised platforms spotlighting the play's hierarchical stratification in terms of class and ethnicity, it expressed specific "architectural definitions of [the] mise-en-scène" (Garner 56). CRT's production of *Intimate Apparel* delineated how "space . . . becomes a depository of meaning" in which the performance of everyday life and an accumulation of everyday domestic objects "inscribe dominant social and cultural values and thus create the city as a space of community" (Romeyn xv).

Placing *Intimate Apparel*

Una Chaudhuri's theorization of "platiality," which may be understood as "a recognition of the signifying power and political potential of *specific places*," prompts generative ways to read Nottage's intimate yet highly stratified settings as meta-spaces in which the private and public realms (consisting of physical locales, mental space, and social space) coalesce within the absolute space of New York and Panama (5). The Connecticut Repertory Theatre production's representation of locations shed light on Nottage's articulation of identity in relationship to place and space – particularly in terms of racial, ethnic, and class lines – and the sociospatial construction of the city that confined and restricted black Americans during this historical moment.

Set in the early 1900s primarily in New York, *Intimate Apparel*'s story of migration, love, and betrayal follows the life of Esther, a lonely thirty-five-year-old seamstress who, in a rented room where she has resided for the past eighteen years, makes fine intimate garments for ladies. With the help of friends and clients, an illiterate Esther exchanges a series of letters with a West-Indian man, George Armstrong, stationed as a laborer on the Panama Canal. Despite never having met, their short correspondence consummates in an abrupt marriage proposal. Still strangers, they begin a new life together that quickly unravels. Possibly pregnant, alone, and in search of a safe space for connection and community, Esther retreats back to the all-female boarding house.

Throughout the play she is surrounded by an array of border-crossers who come to New York in search of a better life, such as her landlady, Mrs. Dickson, the widow of an opium addict, who used marriage to advance her position, and Mr. Marks, a Romanian Orthodox Jew and fabric importer. The seamstress's customers are also transplants: Mrs. Evangeline Van Buren, a white, high-class Southerner, and call girl Mayme, a "colored girl from Memphis" (Nottage 23). Each character essentially mirrors Chaudhuri's argument that one's geography profoundly informs identity, be it regionally, nationally, or transnationally (3).

Nottage situates her characters in the most intimate of spaces – their bedrooms – as a way to draw attention to the characters' more private dimensions. Likewise, owing to the fact that their bedrooms serve multiple purposes, from personal sleeping quarters to sites of social companionship and commerce, these places complicate the resulting sociospatial relationships by providing an alternative social space to investigate "the silence between the lines – what's unspoken" (Shannon 199). The fact that several characters conduct business in these locations further confounds the customary discourse that might occur in such public exchanges. As a result, Nottage's choices also unsettle the power dynamics that might transpire in more utilitarian public spaces. As a result, unforeseen relationships and new patterns of negotiating differences are realized as the ensemble attains unanticipated levels of intimacy when class, gender, religious, and racial barriers are temporarily dropped.

In the stage directions, Nottage calls for the set to be "spare to allow for fluid movement between the various bedrooms" (5). CRT's production included a fixed floor plan with detailed, realistically rendered scenography that included iconic props and set pieces for each unique place that kept the play "grounded" in a concrete place while suggesting how these meta-spaces produce and reproduce social hierarchies (Freedman). The CRT production featured square tiered platforms for each character's representative place (see Figure 4.2). These staggered scaffolds were arranged vertically (in part to fit within the confines of CRT's studio theatre) and fortuitously echoed the social stratification endemic to the play and to the period. Mrs. Van Buren's status as a high society lady from the "top echelon of society" situated her at the center with the largest and highest platform (Freedman). Mr. Mark's tenement room was placed below her platform, stage right, as his identity as an Eastern European Jew relegated him to "the lower echelons of society

Figure 4.2 An image of the set's model box platforms and central staircase for CRT's *Intimate Apparel*. Photographed by Maureen Freedman.

yet still higher than Esther" (Freedman). Esther's bedroom (oriented toward stage left) was across from, but still slightly below Mr. Marks's. Correspondingly, because Mayme's status as a sex worker was lower, her abode was situated beneath Esther's (on stage right). As George was perceived as having an even lower status as a black immigrant, his quarters were on the ground level (and his belongings were tucked directly underneath Mayme's platform).

Freedman remarked that the platforms overlapped to some degree to suggest how "each class depended on the existence of the lower class to define itself" (Freedman). Accordingly, the platforms' "sharp geometrical shapes and varied platform heights conveyed society's irrational need to define the quality of a person's humanity in terms of ethnicity, gender, finances, and abode" (Freedman). This design approach also aptly illustrated how the characters often overstep their bounds, behaving more candidly in such deeply personal confines. The resultant social slippage was brilliantly enabled by a central staircase with landings that served as the vertical axis of the set and visibly bridged these segregated spaces. Together, the distinctly graded staircase and platforms reinforced the play's explicit racial, class, and social hierarchies. For example, the steps, primarily used by Esther, not only provided a cohesive link tying these spaces together, but also conveyed how she bypassed sociospatial borders through her journey to the various places in the play.

The fact that each body mainly appeared within his/her specific realm spotlighted the relatively fixed nature of these sociospatial relationships. The tiered set, from the ground level (where George dictates his letters), to the uppermost platform (where Mrs. Van Buren sits at her vanity table), imparted the palatial dimensions of Jim Crow segregation as well as the divisions across class, ethnic, and religious lines. At the same time, the mise-en-scène evoked a sense that the specific platforms constituted individual adjoining rooms in one large unit building; this deliberate choice visualized a spatial metaphor for race relations in the United States circa the early twentieth century. The set gestured to how the public space of the urban city became more contained and domesticated, thereby conveying a kind of meta-space conjoining public and private locations while still preserving the color line.

The play's representation of spaces and particular places reveals much about each character's place in this world. Spatially, the physical locale of Esther's bedroom is a private residence; it is also a social space for conversations with her landlady, a professional space where she works, and a mental space where she imagines a more emotionally fulfilling future with a husband and a family. Disappointed with her personal life,

Esther quips that she fears she has become "just another piece of fur-
niture" because she has resided in the rooming house for "so long"
(Nottage 9). This exchange signals the ways in which place has informed
her identity, and that she views herself as worn, overlooked, and static.
Yet, CRT's production showcased Esther as the most mobile figure in
the play. Because of her wage work, she passes freely between these
stratified places and spaces, from taking the trolley to Orchard Street
with its enclaves of immigrant tenements, to visiting the luxurious home
of her wealthy client in the capitalist center of Fifth Avenue. It is important to point out that female mobility became more common given the
rise of working women in New York at the turn of the century (Clement 50).
Like many working women who "used the streets, trolleys, and subways," Esther's public identity as an independent working woman legiti-
mized her presence in the public spaces of New York (Clement 50).

Nevertheless, as Nottage indicates, women's participation in wage
work (and the public sphere in general) was fraught. The fact that Esther
designs corsets which "symbolically and literally restrict women's
mobility in both private and public spheres" speaks to one of the innate
tensions surrounding women's mobility during this economic and social
transition (Fields 47). Paradoxically, Esther's economic freedom and
relative social mobility pivots on making and selling these restrictive
garments. Moreover, her participation in wage work foretells the contradictions Lefebvre hints at when theorizing how "money and commodities" hinge on the use of space (367, 265). This overlap of personal and
work space, restriction and mobility is intrinsic to Esther's character and
is a source of power, contradiction, and conflict.

Significantly, as realized by the CRT production, the most prominent items in Esther's sparsely furnished bedroom included her Singer
sewing machine atop its wooden cabinet, a stool, and spindle post bed
adorned with a handmade patchwork quilt that stores all of her earnings
(which she saves toward her dream of opening a beauty shop catering to
black women). These props are equally important in establishing place
and identity. As Stanton B. Garner, Jr. argues, "props constitute privileged nodal points in the scenic field, asserting a powerful materiality
and a density both semiotic and phenomenal" (89). For example, on
one level Esther's "colorful crazy quilt" essentially mirrors in microcosm the square shapes of the tenement rooms and society's attempt to
map and confine what Jacob Riiss had described as the "extraordinary
crazy-quilt" of New York City (Nottage 7; Riis 22) (see Figure 4.3).
In addition, the way this coverlet, a seemingly simple domestic art, is
used to contain her savings complicates how viewers might understand

Figure 4.3 *Intimate Apparel's* "dream scene," which was the only non-realistic scene in CRT's production. Light penetrated the floor boards. Notice the detailed squares of the quilt which replicate the cubed confines of the tenement spaces. Photographed by Maureen Freedman.

the ways in which her work has afforded her social mobility within society's narrow parameters. That she rips open the quilt's tightly sewn seams to turn her money over to her husband shows that she would gladly sacrifice her savings for the feeling of being loved. These objects – her quilt and the sewing machine – are especially symbolic as they impart the private/public aspects of the mise-en-scène and anchor the production in a specific place. These domestic items are the tools of her trade, enabling economic independence.

Equally important, when pressed to share something about herself in her first letter to George, Esther describes herself in terms of place (in other words, her physical locale) and her profession. She says "I live in a rooming house with seven unattached women and sew intimate apparel for ladies . . . Sure I can tell him anything there is to know about fabric, but that hardly seems a life worthy of words" (Nottage 16). If Esther's self-definition is tied to her work, domestic abode, and solitary status, then the meta-space of her bedroom appears initially as a site of stagnation, disenchantment, and loneliness. However, this room becomes a space of acceptance, resilience, self-love, and community reflecting the

journey that Esther undergoes over the course of the play. Her transformation is reinforced by the laying on of hands in the final scene,
from when Esther takes Mrs. Dickson's hand and gratefully accepts an
invitation for tea, to when she "lightly touches her belly," to Mrs. Dickson's parallel action when she "lovingly takes Esther's hand, giving it
a supportive squeeze;" these moments point to how this physical locale
engenders a sense of community, connection, and what bell hooks terms
a "homeplace," a site of resistance, within the city's bounds (Nottage 74, 73;
"Homeplace" 41). In this final quiet moment as Esther touches her
abdomen and begins to sew a second quilt, I posit that she envisions a
new future for herself (and unborn child), entreating a mythic space of
potential and possibility.

In comparison, spatially, Mayme's boudoir in the red light district
serves as her private sleeping quarters, a site of commercial, interracial
exchange with clients, a social space for entertainment and intimate conversation, and a mental space where she daydreams about a doting suitor
and about becoming a concert pianist. The CRT production featured a
compact but inviting boudoir, a neatly furnished interior with a faded red
floral upholstered love seat strewn with pillows, an accent table, area rugs,
and an upright piano which signified her mediated agency and material
success in the "stratified economy of sex" (Clement 78). Honing in on
Mayme's precise location in New York is important to parsing her position in society. If we are to believe that Mayme's quarters are located in a
brothel rather than a rented room in a tenement building in the Tenderloin
district, her domain reveals a great deal about the spatial and racial politics of the time and how her presence potentially challenged the status
quo. Given that Elizabeth Alice Clement's study of prostitution reveals
that "some forms of prostitution, like brothel prostitution, discriminate[d]
against racial or ethnic minorities," then it is significant if Mayme occupied a space often denied to black women (78). Mayme's place in this
social space and physical locale ultimately signifies what Kevin Mumford refers to as "interzones," a way to describe these "black/white
sex districts termed vice districts by urban authorities" (20). For Mumford, these sites' "spatial and ideological definition" at the dawn of Pro-
gressivism's era of social reform hint at how these spaces were "marginal
and central . . . [and] understood foremost as areas of cultural, sexual,
and social interchange" (20).

Esther compromises "the politics of respectability" when she visits her
friend in the red light district (Higginbotham 185–230). Mayme warns
Esther that once she marries "it won't be appropriate to visit a place like
this" (30). However, in this meta-space, Esther ignores the social and

class rules to share secrets and dreams with her friend; ultimately they test the boundaries of female friendship, especially when Esther realizes that Mayme is her husband's lover.

Initially ignoring Esther's knocking at the top of the scene four, Mayme beats out a "frenzied upbeat rag" on the piano in an attempt to transform this public space of commercial exchange. Her absorption in the music (and dismissal of the knocking) speaks to her desire to invoke her own mythic space in order to escape the day-to-day drudgery of work (Nottage 20). But, Esther enters and demands acknowledgment. By way of explanation, Mayme declares her exhaustion and frustration, clearly bristling at the way her clients treat her. She quips, "For a dollar they think they own you" (Nottage 21). Her comments suggest that Mayme resents her own commodification in this space, but feels trapped by the dearth of alternative choices available to a black woman in the city. Thus, Mayme's escapism through her music, a portal to the mythic space of her imagination, is especially important for self-preservation and maintaining a sense of hope about her future. She recounts, "so many wonderful ideas [have] been conjured in this room. They just get left right in that bed there, or on this piano bench. They are scattered all over this room" (Nottage 25). Like Esther, her dreams and sense of self are rooted within the confines of her meta-space and unable to develop due to an exploitative system of racial and gender inequity. Speaking literally and metaphorically about her chances to change her fortune, she admits "I see the dice rolling, and I think Lord, God, wouldn't a place like that [Esther's vision for a beauty shop for black women] be wonderful. But every time the dice roll, that place is a little further away" (Nottage 70). She admits that she had envisioned a different path for herself, but her status as a prostitute has doubly confined her to the bedroom and marred her reputation, making it difficult for her to pursue an alternative course.

On the other side of the tracks, Mrs. Van Buren's boudoir signifies the upper echelon of society. Located on Fifth Avenue in Manhattan, symbolically representing "America's wealth generated by 'free' capitalistic entrepreneurship," her place appears spatially as an ultra-sensual bedroom designed to entice an emotionally distant husband, a site of transaction between the elite matron and Esther when Esther brings intimate goods for her to try on, and a mental space where she sits at the vanity table with a glass of brandy contemplating her reflection and imagining a new life with a child, a loving partner for herself, and for Esther when she helps the seamstress write to George (16). Her room bears the signs of material wealth: an elegant chandelier (hers is the only space with electricity), a lushly carpeted floor, and upscale furnishings including a

carved wood dressing table with an oval mirror and bright scarlet jacquard upholstered stool, a Victorian-style gossip bench (sans the phone)
with matching luxurious, vivid scarlet and gold floral jacquard uphol-
stery, and a coordinated four-panel mahogany and silk dressing screen.
An array of perfume bottles, cosmetics, and a brush, comb and mirror
set line the table.

Several scenes with Esther and Mrs. Van Buren revise the expected
distance between vendor and customer given that their professional
exchange occurs in the privacy of a bedroom. Obviously, the nature of
Esther's work leads to intensely intimate encounters as evidenced by
the stage directions which indicate that Esther gently touches Mrs. Van
Buren, from running her fingers down the front of the woman's corset to
adjusting the woman's breast in the bodice. Meanwhile, Mrs. Van Buren
grabs Esther's hand with "an unexpected tenderness" (Nottage 32–33).
It is in this meta-space that Mrs. Van Buren helps Esther read and
respond to George's letters and alludes to her own husband's emotional
and physical abandonment. These exchanges complicate the power
dynamics of how Mrs. Van Buren views Esther – is she an employee,
a friend, or a potential lover? One of the most provocative exchanges
occurs in Act Two, scene three when Mrs. Van Buren draws Esther near
and kisses her on the mouth. In response to Esther's shock, Mrs. Van
Buren explains how she hoped to show "what it's like to be treated
lovingly" and asks for them to be friends (59). Mrs. Van Buren pleads
with Esther to stay and reveals that "it's only in here with you, that I
feel . . . happy" (59). She declares her love for Esther, which Esther dismisses by reminding her of the color line that separates them. According
to the stage directions, Mrs. Van Buren angrily throws a wad of cash
on her bed for the unpaid work which underscores the failure of this
intimate encounter (60). Though the CRT production did not include
a bed, the setting's material objects concretized the elegant personal
confines while the performers' movements enunciated how this codi-
fied space remained mired in the power dynamics of a "capitalist mode
of production" and ultimately manifested the ways in which space is a
"social construct" (Harvey 3, 5). This exchange would not have trans-
pired in quite the same way had not the intimacy of the bedroom lay
bare such profoundly personal revelations and potential for interracial
queer landscapes.

Situated spatially and socially below Mrs. Van Buren's posh boudoir
is Mr. Marks's Orchard Street tenement apartment. His locale is indica-
tive of the "Lower East Side's Jewish community [which] occupied a
new type of urban space" (Hadassa 81). Annie Polland and Daniel Soyer

claim that "two and a half million eastern European Jews" emigrated to the United States between 1880 and 1924, and nearly "85 percent of them came to New York City, and approximately 75 percent of those settled initially on the Lower East Side" (111). As Kosak Hadassa puts it, in this "tightly defined area, where life was identifiably Jewish and separate from the rest of New York, private and public spaces merged" (82). Accordingly, the fabric merchant's physical locale appears spatially as a simple sleeping space that also serves as a site of commerce, a social space where he weaves fantastic background stories about the cloth he sells, and a mental space where he reflects on the unknown wife to whom he is betrothed, and entertains fantasies about his unspoken attraction to Esther.[3]

Freedman's representation of Mr. Marks's domicile is best described as "austere and fairly monochrome" (Freedman). It featured bare wooden floors, a ladder chair, a "coat hanger" chair, and a large wooden armoire with a drop down counter that doubled for eating and displaying his wares (see Figure 4.4). The most dominant piece, the armoire, was designed to "show a living/business space on a tiny platform . . . without limiting . . . movement in that space" (Freedman). Like the figure of Mr. Marks who repressed his inner feelings, the armoire "represent[ed] his clear control of emissions" (Freedman). These symbolic set pieces conveyed information about his identity which is bound up in his connection with his faith, homeland, and traditions. Tucked within its compact shelves were bolts of "vivid fabric colors and fluid materials," which the actors manipulated as a way to "express these suppressed emotions" (Freedman). And, as the performers engaged with the gorgeous flowing fabric, the space seemingly transformed into a more playful, imaginative site of social exchange.

In this private bedroom space, the exchanges between Esther and Mr. Marks are rife with resonant silences, gestures, and glances. Their sexual tension is palpable, particularly in the penultimate scene of the play when Esther presents him with a Japanese silk smoking jacket, once a wedding present to her now estranged husband, George. This scene culminates in a stirring, visceral moment in which she dresses Mr. Marks. As her fingers align along the drape of the shoulders and straighten the lapels, their eyes remain locked upon each other; he neither moves nor stops her touch during the silent encounter. The stage directions indicate that "*Esther reluctantly walks away, exiting the boudoir without a word. Marks is left alone onstage to contemplate the moment*" (Nottage 72). While dramatized love scenes in bedrooms typically involve disrobing as a way to achieve intimacy, this scene reverses expectations on the

Figure 4.4 An image of the model box section of Mr. Mark's armoire, ladder chair, and "coat hanger" chair. (He and Mrs. Van Buren would be the only individuals with a hanger; the others could not afford the luxury.) Photographed by Maureen Freedman.

grounds that intimate attire is put *on* rather than taken off. Moreover, it resists "normative" physical displays of affection (or even sexually explicit or romantic dialogue) to suggest how ingrained racial boundaries remain impenetrable for the characters, despite their deep desires for more intimate connections. This scene is especially powerful in contrast to their first scene together, when Mr. Marks's explains his religious beliefs and why he cannot touch a woman to whom he is not married. While Esther's gestures ostensibly "crossed the sexual color line," Mr. Marks's tacit nonverbal response articulates a contradiction in abstract space "between liberation and repression" (Mumford 19; Lefebvre 353). For, as Lefebvre posits, "spatial contradictions 'express' conflicts between socio-political interests and [religious] forces; it is only *in* space that such conflicts come effectively into play, and in so doing they become contradictions *of* space" (365). Therefore, these unexpected gestures construct this contradictory intimate social space that reified their sociospatial distance. In this way, the representation of Mr. Marks's place works to define and confine his identity.

The next space, the physical locale of George's territory, presents itself as a semi-private temporary shelter from the harsh environment of the public Panama Canal labor site, and a social space in the corner of the camp from which he dictates the letters containing intoxicating myths of Panama, and a mental space where he fantasizes about the "promised land" of New York. His trajectory is typical of those Barbadians who left harvesting sugar cane in search of opportunity (Greene; O'Reggio; Frederick).[4] In both Panama and New York, George's identity and self-worth are deeply impacted by "space relations [which have been] revolutionized through technological and organizational shifts" via the production of "turnpikes, canals, railways," subways, and skyscrapers (Harvey 6). Whereas his labor was central to the project of building the Canal, the opposite is true in New York, where he may only "watch buildings going up left and right, steel girders as thick as tamarind trees, ten, twelve stories high" (Nottage 51). Here, George's nostalgia for rural Panama serves to amplify his alienation in New York. The construction occurring around him mirrors the American dream of upward mobility and provides a constant reminder of his inability to scale these heights.

The play tracks his "crisis of homelessness," which bespeaks the loss of connection to his homeland, and the ways in which he is marginalized, differentiated, and "othered" due to his race, further distancing him from establishing a sense of place (Harvey 11). Ostensibly, this constellation of issues leads to his inability to root himself in the North and drives him to violate the sanctity of his marriage vows. Consequently, this situation results in a crisis of identity for Esther who has been clutching at a phantom marriage. She realizes "at least I knew who I was back then," before she married a myth of a man, a stranger, "a duppy," or "a spirit" (Nottage 54). In short, George's dislocation in urban space adversely affects his marriage and Esther's conception of herself in this union. Certainly audiences can find fault in George, but by exploring the complexity of his emasculation within the platiality of the city, Nottage complicates George's character and challenges stereotypical views of black masculinity.

The CRT production effectively visualized George's status at the base level of the social strata. His bunk was nestled below the other platforms. As George moved along this subterranean surface, it conveyed the aura of dirt and gravel. Freedman explained that "the inspiration came from both the neglected streets on the Lower East Side and the natural environment surrounding the build of the Panama Canal" (Freedman). This stark contrast of the spaces and places in the play helped define George as a character grounded in the soil, poverty, and otherness; these design choices registered how capitalism foments a "strongly differentiated landscape" (Harvey 6). In short, the scenography crystallized how urban space "has a symbiotic relationship with that rural space over which . . . it holds sway. Peasants [like George] are prone to restlessness . . . the towns have always found it hard to contain them" (Lefebvre 234–235). When George bounds into their bedroom, frustrated with his experience in the streets of New York, he declares "I want to build t'ings, not polish silver or port luggage. I ain' come 'ere for that!" (Nottage 52). Viewers became keenly aware of his passage to the United States, which was staged as a vertical ascent from the lowest platform to Esther's and Mayme's scaffolds. The exchange of letters between George and Esther anticipates and accentuates George's journey.

Finally, I turn to how the letters operate as liminal spaces connecting people and places, as shared documents forging personal/transactional alliances between the senders in the form of a marriage proposal and arrangements, and as seductive sites of storytelling about individuals and foreign places. George's letters bridge the geography of North and South America and foster a particular composite of his identity. In addition, his letters contain much of the play's most vivid, evocative platial imagery that gestures to Lefebvre's conception of absolute space in terms of its description of "levels: surface, heights, depths . . . the earth, as worked and ruled by humanity; the peaks . . . and abysses or gaping holes" (236). Take for example Nottage's haunting depiction of Panama at the turn of the century, which George details as "this great fissure across the land that reach right into the earth's belly. Indeed, chaos is a jackhammer away" (17). Such glimpses of a site where "one man drops for every twenty feet of canal dug, like so many flies" lead Esther to imagine George as a daring, "good noble man from Panama," braving the wild landscape (Nottage 11, 67). In another letter he proclaims, "Today we severed the roots of a giant flamboyant, and watched it tumble to the ground. I stood thigh deep in crimson blossoms, swathed in the sweet aroma of death and wondered how a place so beautiful could become a morgue . . . If you take a moment to listen to the forest around us there is so much life just out of sight" (Nottage 17). In these moments, George's letters craft a heroic, romantic mythology that captivates Esther by engendering a mythic space they share in their imagination and express in their written communication. The play's otherwise more confined locales stand in stark relief against the unbounded territory depicted in George's letters.

If the representation of this absolute space in George's correspondence emerges as a mythic place, then these letters foretell his conflicted "pastoral nostalgia" for the unchartered dangerous territory of the Panama Canal which leads to his restlessness in the urban space (Fuchs 31). Just as the language of George's letters points to multiple levels of abstract space, CRT's scenography in turn represented Lefebvre's description of such dimensional differences by highlighting the distinctions between "horizontal space [which] symbolizes submission, vertical space [as it signifies] power, and subterranean space [which signals] death" (236). For instance, standing aloft in a tight sphere of lush light and shadows cast by the tropical plants surrounding him, George verbalized his missives to Esther from his base-level camp site. The crunch of stone was ever apparent as he stepped along the outskirts of his domain.

In equal measure, Esther's letters to George invoke a similarly seductive mythology about urban life in the U.S. North. He claims he was beguiled by the promise of the city's bounty in Esther's letters: "She tell 'e about the pretty avenues, she tell 'e plentiful. She fill up 'e head so it 'ave no taste for goat milk. She offer 'e the city stroke by stroke. She tantalize 'e with Yankee words" (Nottage 64). His reply suggests how Esther's letters (actually written by Mayme and Mrs. Van Buren) convey an auspicious view of the city which engages his interest.

That the authorship of their letters is an illusion amounts to another aspect of this mythologizing: both Esther and George rely on ghost writers (and readers) to express their respective mythologies. This deception comes to a head in a climatic confrontation between George and Esther that illustrates a "space of truth" and transformation (Lefebvre 236). Following Lefebvre, the outburst of truth in this exchange "destroy[s] appearances . . . and other spaces," namely the mythic sites imagined in their letters (236). Esther admits that though she cannot read, she clung to his letters because it is in this liminal space that their relationship took hold. Up to this point, the liminal space broached by their correspondence neutralized their isolation and alienation. Instead these notes tendered a semblance of belonging for Esther and George via constructing a mental space which had distinctly diverged from the hegemonic reality of the private and public spaces surrounding them. Correspondingly, these letters participated in a discursive, idealized identity formation which reimagined their day-to-day personas. Consequently, the mythic spaces fabricated in these letters engendered an unknown past and uncertain future that concealed or fragmented their actual identities.

Intimate Apparel's sweep from Panama to New York at the turn of the century offers a fitting microhistory through which to plumb the intimate stories of the urban American landscape with its ever present social barriers. Its bedroom settings gesture to and complicate "notions of environmental determinism which meant that race, class, assimilation, and social mobility were, of necessity, configured in relation to and enacted through and upon, the body and space" (Romeyn xix). From the personal bedrooms in New York to the wide terrain of Panama, Nottage expresses how place informs identity and affects a sense of community. Excavating the representation of these private/public realms illuminates how the characters mediate multiple boundaries and invoke a mythology of space and place as a way to reconfigure their identities. Staging the risks, successes, and failures of their departures, Nottage points to how her characters have much to gain (and lose) as they cross the borders of their particular geographies. Parsing the deeply imbricated relationships between identity, space, and place acknowledges the ways *Intimate Apparel* pivots on the effects of migration, the importance of finding one's place, and the consequences of placelessness.

Notes

1 This thinking draws on the work of many, including Chaudhuri, Westgate, Fuchs, Harvie, and Carlson. I also want to thank Jocelyn L. Buckner for her patience and constructive input and Lindsay Cummings and Thomas Meacham for their helpful comments as I developed this essay.
2 Nottage herself articulates that though she does not "totally reject 'kitchen sink dramas,'" she views her work veering more toward expressionism rather than naturalism (Shannon 196).
3 That Mr. Marks provides his services within a cramped flat rather than a retail showroom or factory was in keeping with the majority of Jewish immigrants who first worked in the garment industry and set up shop in their homes (Polland 119). During this period, the garment industry (especially the quickly growing industry of women's garments) was spread out among "tenement contract shops throughout the neighborhood" and subdivided between workers focused on different aspects of the process from designing, cutting, sewing, pressing, to assembling (Hadassa 64; Polland 119).
4 Historian Julie Greene notes that a 1912 census reported that nearly half of the Zone's 62,000 residents hailed from the Caribbean islands (126). At a major recruiting site in Barbados, the U.S. contracted 20,000 Barbadian workers to assist the American government with building the Panama Canal (Greene 30).

Works cited

Blocker, Jack S. "Writing African American Migrations." *The Journal of the Gilded Age and Progressive Era* 10.1 (January 2011): 3–22. Print.

Carlson, Marvin. *Places of Performance: The Semiotics of Theatre Architecture.* Ithaca: Cornell University Press, 1993. Print.

Chaudhuri, Una. *Staging Place: The Geography of Modern Drama.* Ann Arbor: University of Michigan Press, 1995. Print.

Clement, Elizabeth Alice. *Love for Sale: Courting, Treating, and Prostitution in New York City, 1900–1945.* Chapel Hill: University of North Carolina Press, 2006. Print.

Fields, Jill. *An Intimate Affair: Women, Lingerie, and Sexuality.* Berkeley: University of California Press, 2007. Print.

Frederick, Rhonda D. *"Colón Man a Come": Mythographies of Panama Canal Migration.* Lanham: Lexington Books, 2005. Print.

Fuchs, Elinor. "Reading for Landscape: The Case of American Drama." *Land/Scape/Theatre.* Eds. Elinor Fuchs and Una Chaudhuri. Ann Arbor: University of Michigan Press, 2002. 30–52. Print.

Garner, Stanton B. Jr. *Bodied Spaces: Phenomenology and Performance in Contemporary Drama.* Ithaca: Cornell University Press, 1994. Print.

Greene, Julie. *The Canal Builders: Making America's Empire at the Panama Canal.* New York: Penguin Press, 2009. Print.

Hadassa, Kosak. *Cultures of Opposition: Jewish Immigrant Workers, New York City, 1881–1905.* Albany: State University of New York Press, 2000. Web. Accessed July 22, 2015.

Harvey, David. "From Space to Place and Back Again." *Mapping the Futures: Local Cultures, Global Change.* Eds. Jon Bird, Barry Curtis, Tim Putnam, George Robertson, and Lisa Tucker. New York: Routledge, 1993. 3–29. Print.

Harvie, Jen. *Theatre and the City.* New York: Palgrave Macmillan, 2009. Print.

Higginbotham, Evelyn Brooks. *Righteous Discontent: The Women's Movement in the Black Baptist Church, 1880–1920.* Cambridge: Harvard University Press, 1994. Print.

hooks, bell. "Homeplace: A Site of Resistance." *Yearning: Race, Gender, and Cultural Politics.* Boston: South End Press, 1990. 41–49. Print.

Jones, Jacqueline. *American Work: Four Centuries of Black and White Labor.* New York: W. W. Norton & Company, 1998. Print.

Keith, Michael and Steve Pile. "Introduction Part 2: The Place of Politics." *Place and the Politics of Identity.* Eds. Michael Keith and Steve Pile. New York: Routledge, 1993. 22–40. Print.

Kilian, Ted. "Public and Private, Power and Space." *Philosophy and Geography II: The Production of Public Space.* Eds. Andrew Light and Jonathan M. Smith. Lanham, MD: Rowman and Littlefield Publishers, 1998. 115–134. Print.

Lefebvre, Henri. *The Production of Space.* Trans. Donald Nicholson-Smith. Malden: Blackwell Publishers, Inc., 1991. Print.

Nottage, Lynn. *Intimate Apparel.* New York: Theatre Communications Group, 2003. Print.

O'Reggio, Trevor. *Between Alienation and Citizenship: The Evolution of Black West Indian Society in Panama, 1914–1964.* Lanham: University Press of America, 2006. Print.

Page, Max. *The Creative Destruction of Manhattan, 1900–1940*. Chicago: University of Chicago Press, 1999. Print.

Polland, Annie and Daniel Soyer. *Emerging Metropolis: New York Jews in the Age of Immigration, 1840–1920, vol. 2 of City of Promises: A History of the Jews of New York*. Ed. Deborah Dash Moore. New York: New York University Press, 2012. Web. Accessed July 21, 2015.

Riis, Jacob A. *How the Other Half Lives: Studies Among the Tenements of New York*. New York: Dover, 1971. Print.

Romeyn, Esther. *Street Scenes: Staging the Self in Immigrant New York, 1880–1924*. Minneapolis: University of Minnesota Press, 2008. Print.

Rutkoff, Peter M. and William B. Scott. *Fly Away: The Great African American Cultural Migrations*. Baltimore: John Hopkins University Press, 2010. Print.

Schmid, Christian. "Henri Lefebvre's Theory of the Production of Space: Towards a Three-dimensional Dialectic." *Space, Difference, Everyday Life: Reading Henri Lefebvre*. Eds. Kanishka Goonewardena, Stefan Kipfer, Richard Milgrom, and Christian Schmid. New York: Routledge, 2008. 27–45. Print.

Shannon, Sandra G. "An Interview with Lynn Nottage." *Contemporary African American Women Playwrights: A Casebook*. Ed. Philip C. Kolin. New York: Routledge, 2007. 194–201. Print.

Tétreault, Mary Ann. "Formal Politics, Meta-Space, and the Construction of Civil Life." *Philosophy and Geography II: The Production of Public Space*. Eds. Andrew Light and Jonathan M. Smith. Lanham: Rowman and Littlefield Publishers, 1998. 81–97. Print.

Westgate, J. Chris. *Urban Drama: The Metropolis in Contemporary North American Plays*. New York: Palgrave Macmillan, 2011. Print.

Chapter 5

"It's all about a rabbit, or it ain't"

The folkloric significations of Lynn Nottage

Faedra Chatard Carpenter

> I'm exploring the role of the trickster in American Mythology. I am using Brer Rabbit, classic trickster . . . We love, but we despise him. We admire, yet rebuke. We embrace, yet we push away. This glorious duality enlivens and imprisons him. Because ain't he only hunting for "a way out of no way," as it's been said. And so you know, the poem is not about Brer Rabbit, he is merely a means to convey a truth . . . It is open-ended. A work in progress. A continuous journey.
>
> Flow, *Fabulation, or the Re-education of Undine*

Lynn Nottage's *Fabulation, or the Re-education of Undine* (2004) takes the ever-popular "rags-to-riches" story and inverts it, thereby offering its audience a comical yet thoughtful tale about a young woman who goes from rags-to-riches – and then riches-to-rags. The woman in question is named Undine Barnes – or, at least, that is the name she is known by when she is first introduced to the audience. When the play opens, Undine, described as a *"smartly dressed, thirty-seven-year-old African American woman,"* is at the height of her career as an exceedingly successful public relations executive (Nottage 79). However, soon after the audience is introduced to this seemingly self-possessed figure, we discover that Undine's husband, Hervé, has left her. The unrest Undine exhibits after this disclosure is quickly exacerbated when Undine's accountant delivers even more devastating news: Hervé has not only run out on her, but he has taken all of Undine's hard-earned money with him. To make matters even worse, Undine – abandoned and now bankrupt – takes a pregnancy test and learns that she is carrying Hervé's child. Thus, in a traumatic twist of circumstances, Undine no longer envisions herself as an incredibly accomplished entrepreneur. On the contrary, Undine realizes that she has suddenly transformed into the very thing that she was trying desperately *not* to become: poor, single, and pregnant – the stereotypical welfare mother; a walking statistic.

These are the unsettling (yet surprisingly hilarious) events that Lynn Nottage crafts in order to cast *Fabulation*'s protagonist on a self-reflexive and soul-searching journey. Central to this life-altering quest is Undine's eventual discovery of the liberatory possibilities of "home." For Undine, home had long been a contested space – a struggle evidenced by the fact that she spent over a decade running away from her familial ties and personal history. It takes fourteen years and a state of destitute desperation for Undine to return to the origins that she had relentlessly denied. The journey of *Fabulation,* then, chronicles Undine's ability to heal both her familial relationships and her own torn and troubled psyche.

Notably, this theatrical trek toward healing and cohesion takes great inspiration from the illusory and layered literary figure of "Brer Rabbit," a character that, while made famous in the late 1800s by a white American journalist, also boasts folkloric roots traced throughout the African diaspora.[1] These folkloric manifestations of Brer Rabbit are simultaneously evoked and reimagined through the various dramaturgical components of Nottage's *Fabulation.* By signifyin(g) on well-known portrayals of Brer Rabbit within American literary and film history (as encapsulated by the work of Joel Chandler Harris and the Disney Corporation),[2] Nottage's play establishes itself within the continuum of Brer Rabbit adaptations. Subsequently, the playwright's use of Brer Rabbit lore not only nuances *Fabulation*'s broader ruminations on perverse realities and duplicitous identities, but it also imbues the play with critical commentary by restoring obscured aspects of Brer Rabbit's Afrocentric roots. By illustrating how the trickster trope serves as inspiration for the whole of Nottage's theatrical tale, this chapter explores the intertextual structure of *Fabulation* and reveals how Lynn Nottage deftly recuperates the contested cultural legacy of Brer Rabbit while dramatizing her central protagonist's personal journey.

From past to present and back again: The many musings on Brer Rabbit

When referring to Brer Rabbit's cultural legacy as contested, I allude to the way that Brer Rabbit, as a folkloric figure, is characterized by contesting qualities and expressions; as a classic trickster he is typified by paradoxes and seeming contradictions. No less significant is the fact that, for many audiences, the audible utterance of "Brer Rabbit" will most certainly conjure contentious images related to a *very specific* rendering of Brer Rabbit tales: those popularized in the 1880s by the white Georgia native and *Atlanta Constitution* journalist Joel Chandler Harris, a writer whose literary oeuvre was permeated with dueling qualities of righteousness and racism. Thus, by explicitly calling forth the name of Brer Rabbit in her play, I contend that Lynn Nottage purposefully reveals a dramaturgical lens that encourages her audience to recall the dueling tensions bound by Brer Rabbit narratives. Affirming the complexity of Brer Rabbit, Nottage invites her audience to recognize the complexity of her own fictional characters and, concurrently, offers a critical response to those who shun Brer Rabbit folklore due to problematic elements within Joel Chandler Harris's appropriations.

The stories transcribed and disseminated by Joel Chandler Harris often depict how Brer Rabbit, through sheer wit and will, escapes or conquers his primary rival, Brer Fox, in a seemingly neverending game of "cat and mouse." A host of critters are featured in Harris's tales, and their antics and adventures are crafted to both entertain and educate. There are a handful of these stories that stand out as being particularly memorable, serving as oft-repeated representatives of the collected canon. Such is the case of "The Wonderful Tar-Baby Story." Detailing one of Brer Rabbit's most famous victories against Brer Fox, "The Wonderful Tar-Baby Story" goes something like this:

Brer Fox, always scheming to catch Brer Rabbit, came up with an ingenious idea: he decided to use black, sticky tar – shaped like a small child – to lure and trap the ever-elusive rabbit. After placing his "Tar-Baby" on the side of the road, Brer Fox hid in some nearby bushes and waited for Brer Rabbit to pass. Sure enough, just as Brer Fox predicted, Brer Rabbit came by and stopped to greet the Tar-Baby – but the Tar-Baby didn't answer. Slightly annoyed, Brer Rabbit once again extended warm greetings. The Tar-Baby still didn't answer. Assuming that the Tar-Baby was hard of hearing, Brer Rabbit spoke up, but the Tar-Baby *still* didn't answer. Offended by the apparent aloofness, Brer Rabbit started shouting verbal threats in an effort to intimidate the Tar-Baby into responding, but to no avail. Increasingly frustrated by this blatant disregard, Brer Rabbit worked himself up to such a frenzy that he began punching the Tar-Baby. After getting his fists stuck, one by one, Brer Rabbit entangled himself even further by kicking the Tar-Baby. Absolutely incensed (and none the wiser) Brer Rabbit finally resorted to head-butting the inanimate figure – only to find his whole body thoroughly and completely stuck in the now-disfigured, sticky pile of tar.

At this point, Brer Fox sauntered out of his hiding place, taunting Brer Rabbit with his plans for "rabbit barbeque." Brer Rabbit began pleading with his smug captor, insisting that he could face almost any means of torture and suffering with one exception: "Please, Brer Fox," the rabbit asked, "you can hang me, drown me, skin me, snatch out my eyeballs, tear off my ears, cut off my legs – but whatever you do, just *please* don't fling me into that briar patch!" Hearing the rabbit's fear and trepidation, the fox didn't hesitate to take action: he threw that rabbit right into the briar patch!

And then there was silence. But not for long.

While Brer Fox was basking in his triumph, he heard someone call his name. He looked up across the horizon and, to his surprise, he could see Brer Rabbit, laughing, on the *other side* of the briar patch! "Don't you know," said Brer Rabbit with fulsome glee, "I was born in a briar patch, Brer Fox – bred and born!" And with that, Brer Rabbit hopped out of sight.[3]

At once harrowing and humorous, tales such as "The Wonderful Tar-Baby Story" brought Brer Rabbit to widespread national attention. While a hungry public devoured Harris's tales through newspaper columns and published anthologies, the Atlanta journalist always – and readily – admitted that his beloved trickster tales were not of his own divining. Rather, Harris always acknowledged that his stories drew heavily from the African American folklore he had heard as a young man.[4] What *was* wholly original in Harris's work, however, was "Uncle Remus," the now famous character that Harris created as his story-telling mouthpiece.

When initially hired by *The Atlanta Constitution,* Harris's journalistic duties extended to writing comedic content and it was from this appointment that Uncle Remus was born. Harris created Uncle Remus in 1876, using his personae to humorously observe or comment upon the politics and social happenings of the day. By 1879, however, Uncle Remus had blossomed into a teller of Brer Rabbit tales. Harris's Uncle Remus stories became so popular that they were reproduced widely and earned a regular place in the *Constitution*'s Sunday paper. Predictably, the demand for these tales eventually led to a publishing offer, resulting in the 1880 release of *Uncle Remus: His Songs and Sayings.* The popular collection – which sold 7,500 copies in its first month – featured folktales, proverbs, songs, and character sketches. Following the success of this initial publication, Harris went on to publish a number of additional Uncle Remus volumes, even managing to distribute a monthly Uncle Remus magazine for two years immediately prior to his death in 1908 (Hemenway 7–15).

Despite the ways in which Harris's Uncle Remus tales have been historically embraced, they have long had their share of disparagers and dissenters. As these detractors are well aware, the vivid storytelling for which Joel Chandler Harris was lauded also bears an undeniably unflattering aspect: the character of Uncle Remus (as opposed to the actual stories about his non-human cohorts) reflect, as gently phrased by Robert Hemenway, "an author with a sentimental attachment to a plantation memory" (8). Crafted according to the racial stereotypes of the late 1800s, Harris's Uncle Remus was devised as a simple-minded, ever-content former slave whose docile cadence denoted a ready acceptance of the Old South and old Southern ways. Uncle Remus's easy devotion to the social hierarchies of the era is epitomized by the way he dotes on the child of his former white master. Although the obsequious nature of Uncle Remus's character was undoubtedly welcomed by most whites (especially in the wake of America's tumultuous post-Reconstruction era), the racist elements imbued in the character eventually became the subject of modern-day contention and debate among both blacks and whites alike. Of course, it is also important to note that critics on both sides of the racial divide have also championed positive aspects of the Uncle Remus character, highlighting, for instance, the relationship Remus has with the white child under his watch. To this end, some argue that Uncle Remus is crafted as a positive paternal figure, one that represents – albeit problematically – the potential and possibility for racial and national harmony.[5]

The precarious history surrounding Brer Rabbit vis-à-vis Harris's Uncle Remus tales is, in part, suggested by Lynn Nottage when Flow (Undine's brother in *Fabulation*) philosophizes on Brer Rabbit's duality: "I'm exploring the role of the trickster in American Mythology. I am using Brer Rabbit, classic trickster . . . We love, but we despise him. We admire, yet rebuke. We embrace, yet we push away" (Nottage 97). Observing how the things we cherish and admonish are often one and the same, Flow animates these worldly reflections by channeling the narratives of Brer Rabbit, thereby prompting us to recognize that Harris's prejudicial lens (as embodied by the character of Uncle Remus) can be distinguished from the cultural significance of the Brer Rabbit folktales themselves. This distinction, that is, the role of *Brer Rabbit* in world folklore versus *Uncle Remus* in American folklore, is an incredibly important one. Brer Rabbit is historically linked to both African American *and* African oral traditions while the Uncle Remus character is a modern literary figure, born out of the imagination of a single white American author.[6] Accordingly, the full history of Brer Rabbit is both deep and wide; its cultural cachet is distinct from the way its imagery has been usurped and applied in more modern times.

It is this latter fact that Lynn Nottage deftly highlights in her own recuperation of Brer Rabbit folklore. While Nottage's play recognizes the "sticky" history of Brer Rabbit, *Fabulation* capitalizes on the knowledge that Brer Rabbit is a long-surviving trickster figure in the storytelling traditions of black people. Stressing the depth of Brer Rabbit's history, Nottage slyly reminds us that as a trickster figure, Brer Rabbit's ancestral roots can be traced throughout the African Diaspora, including to the West African deity, Elegba.[7] She does this by conjuring and connecting *both* of these figures within the bounds of her theatrical treatment, explicitly naming Brer Rabbit as a "classic trickster," while also depicting a dubious Yoruban Priest who speaks on (and claims to speak for) Elegba (Nottage 94–95).

The linking of these two iconic tricksters not only encourages audiences to recognize Brer Rabbit's rich lineage, but they also serve as emblematic characterizations of "doubleness," thereby rooting one of *Fabulation*'s central motifs. Similar to Brer Rabbit, Elegba is ever-shifting and mischievous. Elegba's multifarious character is implied, in part, by his many names (Esu, Exu, Legba, Esu Elegbara, and Echu Elegua, to note a few), as well as his many ancestral homes: his presence can be traced throughout West Africa, the Caribbean, and South America (Gates 4). Strategically indecisive, Elegba stands on the cusp of the divine and the abominable; he is neither "sacred" nor "profane," neither "good" nor "bad," but rather *all* of these things. An instrument to express satire, ambiguity, chance, betrayal, loyalty, closure, and disclosure, he is appropriately known to be "double-voiced" in act and deed (Gates 6–7).

These qualities, shared by Elegba and Brer Rabbit (as well as many other trickster figures), may be understood as simply contradictory *or* they can be understood as reflecting a decidedly Afrocentric cosmology that resists absolutisms. When considering the latter in reference to Brer Rabbit, the sociologist Annie Ruth Leslie posits that:

> Theoretical conceptualizations of Brer Rabbit are limited in that scholars have not theorized about Brer Rabbit in terms of an African-centered moral perspective. Instead, they have criticized or justified the Rabbit's antics in terms of Christian patriarchal assumptions about tricks and about "good and evil" behavior. (62)

Resisting a rigid assessment of being either "good" or "bad" when framing trickster figures, Leslie further explains that many African cosmologies understand "bad" as nothing more than an *aberration* versus the Western understanding of "bad" which is more aligned with notions of intentional ill-will or intrinsic evil. Moreover, there is the belief that a "purposeful good" can result from the *balanced merging* of so-called negative and positive energies (64). Subsequently, Leslie suggests that trickster figures within the African diaspora should never be interpreted as amoral, morally deficient, or self-serving. Rather, their antics and behaviors are designed to emphasize values (such as wisdom over physical prowess) that are traditionally championed in African societies (64 and 78). As figures that challenge expectations while also satisfying communal values, tricksters are often the perfect fodder for both dramatic and comedic narratives – as suggested by their inclusion in Nottage's *Fabulation*.

Fabulation's conscious and deliberate invocations of Elegba and Brer Rabbit encourage audiences to recognize the tie that exists between past and present, African and American. Moreover, Nottage's conscientious reclamation of Brer Rabbit folktales is endowed with even greater value when one heeds the folktales' significance within *African American* expressive culture. Stories such as "The Wonderful Tar-Baby Story" continue to captivate audiences, yet a fuller consideration of the Brer Rabbit tales (and their more sobering, sometimes violent narratives) suggest that these tales also provide insight into slave life and culture. Within the Brer Rabbit stories, the rabbit trickster often represents the enslaved African American while the treacherous fox can be seen as representing white enslavers. Reflecting upon the multi-layered subtext in these stories, historian Lawrence Levine notes that:

> The white master could believe that the rabbit stories his slaves told were mere figments of a childish imagination . . . [but] Blacks knew better. The trickster's exploits, which overturned the neat hierarchy of the world in which he was forced to live, became their exploits; the justice he achieved, their justice; the strategies he employed, their strategies. From his adventures they obtained relief; from his triumphs they learned hope. (114)

That is to say, the tales *themselves* – just like Brer Rabbit (and his ancestor, Elegba) – are "double-voiced," presenting different life lessons for those willing and able to interpret their folkloric mediations.

Through their coded fictions these stories revealed strategies for physical and emotional survival. Many of the Brer Rabbit tales evolved from African cosmologies, but in their transition into American folklore they were crafted to serve a populace that routinely experienced life's sweetest joys and most bitter horrors. Cultivated by and for a subjugated population, Brer Rabbit tales reflected the harsh realities of slave culture through their colorful fictions. The stark truths they dramatized reflected the precarious environment and circumstances that enslaved people faced on a day-to-day basis. True to these perils, some tales depict Brer Rabbit as a proverbial underdog confronting and conquering domineering forces. Others frame him as a denigrated subject whose very survival relies on questionable ethics and dubious actions. Sometimes Brer Rabbit is a friend to his community, sometimes he is a foe. Consequently, audiences must consider a character who, like Elegba, is exceedingly ambiguous: neither wholly good, nor wholly bad. It is this inherent ambiguity of the historic trickster character, exemplified through the conjuring of Brer Rabbit and Elegba, which is aptly applied and appropriated in Lynn Nottage's *Fabulation.*

Importantly, Nottage's conjuring of Brer Rabbit's cultural history does not simply end with the way *Fabulation* pays homage to West African mythology. Rather, there is yet *another* inter-textual layer that establishes *Fabulation, or the Re-Education of Undine* as a contemporaneous corrective within the canon of Brer Rabbit folklore. Demanding that we move our attention away from the power of the written word to also address the power of visual images, Nottage's structural crafting of *Fabulation* also implores audiences to (re)consider the way in which her play responds to the problematic call of Disney's 1946 film, *Song of the South.*

Unsurprisingly, when it came to modifying Harris's Brer Rabbit tales for *Song of the South*, Walt Disney made no effort to shed light on their folkloric heritage, nor did he make any attempts to unpack the significance of Brer Rabbit in the context of African American artistic expressions. What Disney did do, however, was emphasize the levity to be found within Joel Chandler Harris's stories – a lightness that expunged the less-than-flattering aspects of the original Brer Rabbit narratives, yet created unique controversies of its own by glorifying America's race-based social hierarchies.[8]

Although there is much to protest about the racial politics of *Song of the South*, I contend that Disney's film still stands as a text worthy of attention, not only because the movie (and the responses to it) continue to provide evidence of America's ever-changing social and political landscape, but also because the film's thematic ruminations on home inspire students of *Fabulation* to recognize the centrality of this motif in Nottage's play. Similarly imbued by their treatments of home, Nottage's *Fabulation* resonates with compelling correlations to *Song of the South*, a text that – for good and bad – holds a prominent place in cinematic history and public consciousness, thereby inscribing its unequivocal place in the canon of Brer Rabbit lore. However, to best understand the particular intertextual parallels found between *Fabulation* and *Song of the South*, one must first revisit the overarching story of Disney's now (in)famous film.

Song of the South revolves around a young boy, Johnny, who travels with his parents from their home in Atlanta, Georgia to his grandmother's provincial plantation. Soon after arriving to the plantation, Johnny's father retreats back to Atlanta (no clear explanation is given as to why), leaving Johnny to simultaneously wrestle with his father's absence and the feelings of dissonance related to his relocation. Simply stated, Johnny doesn't feel "at home" on the family plantation; he wants nothing more than to run away from this less-polished suburban territory and return to the comforts of the city.[9]

Johnny's travails on the plantation, a place that seemed so foreign and unwelcoming at first, are eventually eased through the forging of new relationships. First and foremost is the bond that develops between Johnny and Uncle Remus. When Johnny attempts to run away from the plantation the first night of his arrival, it is Uncle Remus who finds him, protects him from being punished, and assuages his anxiety by telling him a story about Brer Rabbit. By intermittently sharing his folktales and guarding Johnny against bullying (from kids and adults alike), Uncle Remus gains Johnny's trust and affection – a paternal savior amidst life's uncertainty.

Another unlikely comrade and comfort to Johnny is a young white girl named Ginny. Ginny comes from a family of little means. Her ornery brothers delight in harassing her and despite constant chastisement from their mother, the brothers continuously think of ways to make Ginny's life miserable. Through Johnny's interactions with Uncle Remus and Ginny, the audience witnesses a privileged child create unexpected allegiances with those who, according to the hierarchical ranking of the Old South, fall far below his social status.

Although Johnny forges new friendships and allies, he still finds the tensions within his home and community distressing. In the end, however, it is a traumatic physical injury that helps heal Johnny's emotional wounds. After a raging bull charges at Johnny and causes serious injury, a forceful display of familial solidarity and support among Johnny's blood relatives and the plantation workers implore the film's characters (and the viewing audience) to understand that an ideal home has nothing to do with luxuries and accouterments; that home is not a site, but rather a sense of community and connection.

Despite *Song of the South*'s "happy" ending (an ending that is forged, in great part, due to the unconventional friendships highlighted in the film) one must take care to underscore that the social schema presented in the movie is far from a utopia. On the contrary, Johnny's relationships with Uncle Remus and Ginny clearly reveal that post-war plantation life is fertile ground for interpersonal conflicts marked by race, as well as class and gender. For example, by introducing the viewing audience to the communities in which both Uncle Remus and Ginny belong, *Song of the South* inevitably discloses the devastating divides that separate the "haves and the have-nots." And while whiteness is clearly privileged over blackness within the world of *Song of the South*, the film does cast notable attention toward the class differences among its white characters, thereby also suggesting that issues of economic insecurity and belonging extend beyond racial parameters. Also of interest is the way in which the film's white characters – from Johnny's well-to-do mother, to Ginny's disadvantaged brothers – run the gamut from being unreasonably impetuous to down-right cruel (Bernstein 234). Thus, in revealing both the fiscal disparities and ethical fractures within white communities, *Song of the South* does offer a subtle challenge to any undue correlations between race, economic status, cultural capital, and moral authority.

Similar to Disney's *Song of the South*, Nottage's *Fabulation* also challenges any undue correlations between moral authority and one's social and cultural capital. In *Fabulation,* surface assumptions regarding characters' inherent value within both personal and professional ecosystems are taken to task, thereby disrupting all-too-familiar stereotypes and trite notions based on race, class, and gender. Strikingly, one way that *Fabulation* unhinges surface assumptions bears witness to the intertextual dialogue between Nottage and the works of both Harris and Disney. Taking a cue from its predecessors, *Fabulation* – a recent addition to Brer Rabbit lore – pays homage to the complexity of earlier trickster-indebted tales by animating paradoxical qualities within Nottage's own characters.

Framing her characters according to an Afrocentric cosmology that resists absolutisms and aspires toward holistic balance (and, therefore, a more purposeful good), Nottage creates a dizzying collection of double-voiced characters that work to underscore the paradigmatic duality of *Fabulation's* central protagonist, Undine. Among this supporting cast, of course, is Undine's husband, Hervé, the smooth-talking Latin lover who tricked Undine with his own double-life. He swept Undine off her feet – and then swept her bank account clean, leaving her both pregnant and penniless. Looking for comfort and counsel after this emotional blow, Undine seeks ethical guidance from a Yoruban Priest – but the priest's morality proves suspect when he insists that Undine satiate an angered Elegba by offering him a thousand dollars *and* a bottle of Mount Gay Premium Rum. Undine's grandmother also belies initial appearances: she is not only a housecoat-clad, wheelchair bound, doily-crocheting senior citizen, but she is also an easily incensed heroin addict. Doubleness continues to abound as the play unfolds: we meet Undine's best friend, Allison, who – like Undine – has been living under a pseudonym; we are made privy to the drug-addled behaviors of a seemingly-respected college professor; and we encounter a social worker who betrays any expectations of helpfulness. Adding to the reversal of expectations is the unforgettable story of Velvet Whitehead, a porch-step philosopher who, despite appearances and his humble position in life, demonstrated his genius when he figured out a $50,000 math problem on a napkin. If these characterizations weren't enough, Nottage introduces us to Prison Inmate #2, who may appear to be a prostitute, but in reality works at the Metrotech *and* is a proud, high-heel-wielding feminist. Similarly, Devora, who grew up in the Walt Whitman projects and still favors "ghetto fabulous" attire, challenges assumptions when she discloses that she is a senior financial planner for JPMorgan. And then there is Guy, a former drug addict, who is revealed to be the most promising life-partner for *Fabulation*'s equally complex protagonist, Undine. As evidenced by this lengthy (yet not exhaustive) character sketch, the deliberate abundance of *Fabulation*'s surprising portrayals enables the playwright to complicate her characterizations and detract audiences from making surface assumptions. In doing so, *Fabulation* avoids absolutisms and invariably highlights the strategic equilibrium and truthful representation that comes from the merging of both negative and positive qualities within her characters.

While the merging of both positive and negative attributes makes the characters in *Fabulation* more nuanced (and, correspondingly, echoes the trickster trope in *Song of the South* vis-à-vis Brer Rabbit), Nottage's dramaturgical strategies also speak to the way that both *Fabulation* and *Song of the South* frame ideas of home. Like *Song of the South*, *Fabulation* champions a nuanced meaning of home, one that recognizes that virtue can be housed within imperfection. Even more specifically, both texts reveal how sanctuaries of security can be created through healthy relationships rather than by acquiring social status or material goods. In so doing, both *Song of the South* and *Fabulation* ultimately assert that the fortunes of home are found in the comfort and experience of familial support and acceptance rather than within the physical confines of an idyllic locale.

Notably, in privileging a more abstract yet emotionally substantive notion of home, both *Song of the South* and *Fabulation* feature characters that run *to* and *from* their homes. In both texts, the cosmopolitan city is perceived by the protagonists (Johnny and Undine) as a favored setting; a respite from the grittiness represented by, respectively, the plantation and the projects. With time, however, both Johnny and Undine come to appreciate what these seemingly abject spaces have to offer. Neither the plantation nor the projects boast material goods that either protagonist favors, but both reveal themselves to be rich repositories in terms of the ultimate sense of security and comfort they offer to Johnny and Undine.

This revelation, that one can find sanctuary by embracing one's roots, not only links the plotline of *Fabulation* with *Song of the South,* but it is also tellingly traceable to the central message within Joel Chandler Harris's popular and widely recognized tale, "The Wonderful Tar-Baby Story." All three texts (the Tar-Baby story, the Disney film, and Nottage's play) champion the tranquility and freedom experienced by embracing one's past. Moreover, the resounding influence of Harris's "The Wonderful Tar-Baby Story" is clearly delineated throughout *Song of the South*: aside from the film's thematic ruminations on home, the Disney movie also offers a much-touted, animated treatment of the tar-baby story. Even more striking about this intertextual trio is that a closer consideration of the tar-baby story reveals how Nottage uses the folktale to create a template for Undine's own narrative and behavior. Ultimately, Undine's personal saga, as well as her actions and reactions, echo those within the tar-baby story, further disclosing her as the definitive "Brer Rabbit figure" within *Fabulation.*

Framing Undine as a Brer Rabbit figure recalls the fact that Undine is not *really* Undine Barnes, in name or professed biography. On the contrary, Undine's real name (which was never legally changed) is Sharona Watkins, and rather than being born with a proverbial "silver spoon" in her mouth, Sharona was born and raised in the Walt Whitman projects of Brooklyn, New York. Sharona left that world behind when she earned the opportunity to attend "an elite boarding school in New England" through a "better chance" program, followed by collegiate studies at Dartmouth College (Nottage 86). Despite recognizing the socio-economic disparities between her family life and her college life, Sharona maintained a tie to both – until the day of her college graduation. On that day, Sharona reinvented herself by rechristening herself as Undine Barnes and claiming that she had tragically lost her entire family to a house fire.

Like Brer Rabbit, Undine chooses to use manipulation, word play, and performance as a means of negotiating her way through potentially delimiting obstacles. While this alone may align *Fabulation*'s protagonist with Brer Rabbit (and his ancestor, Elegba), Undine's personal narrative also reveals very specific parallels to the tar-baby story. Just as Brer Fox (once a representation of the slave master, an instrument of a racist economic system) entices and traps Brer Rabbit with the tar-baby, Undine is enticed and seduced by the fixtures that are produced and promulgated by a material-minded, capitalistic society. Although not physically enslaved like her forebears, Undine is psychologically enslaved, ideologically subjugated to a perverse value system. Thus, just as the rabbit is drawn to the tar baby, Undine finds herself lured by tempting – and enfeebling – entrapments.

After all, it was Undine's covetous desire to be a card-carrying member of the black bourgeoisie that led her to prioritize status over substance. While a student at Dartmouth, Undine "subsequently acquired a taste for things [her] provincial Brooklyn upbringing could no longer provide" (86). Accordingly, she became increasingly strategic and far less sincere when it came to her life and relationships. She "mingled with people in a constructive way" and "built a list of friends that would prove valuable" to her future professional interests (Nottage 86). She purposefully disavowed her family in favor of more prestigious circles and made a particularly ill-formed decision when she married her Argentine lover, Hervé. Reflecting upon that ill-fated path, Undine admits: "He permitted me to travel in circles I'd only read about in *Vanity Fair*. . . . He gave me flair and caché" (Nottage 87). Of course, the flair and caché of that union fades and falters, fully revealing how Undine got caught within the sticky snare of a skewed value system.

In light of her status-climbing strategies, Undine's professional success is neither heroic nor villainous, just as she is neither wholly good nor wholly bad. Instead, Undine proves to be both a victim and victimizer; she used her cunning ways to concurrently hurt and help. Undine climbed the ladder of success, but left her family – and her own psyche – wounded in the process. And while the fruits of Undine's cut-throat labors were temporarily sweet, her thoughtless words and actions eventually worked against her as she got herself stuck deeper into the trap of appearances. In the end, Undine is bound in a snare of lies and deceit, forced to wrestle with the sham of her divining, the façade of fake friendships, and the layered consequences of Hervé's betrayal. Yet, like Brer

Rabbit, Undine recognizes that there is hope to be found in home. She returns to the Brooklyn projects and discovers that – despite its thorns or perceived unsightliness – it is a sanctuary. She was "bred and born" in Walt Whitman and regardless of what she achieves or attains, she learns to acknowledge the beauty and strength that comes from self-acceptance.

In short, the same summarizing conclusions that humanities scholar M. Thomas Inge offers in relation to *Song of the South*'s depiction of the tar-baby story (a rendition that includes the musical number, "Everybody Has a Laughing Place"), can be just as easily applied to Undine's experience in *Fabulation*. Inge asserts that the Disney film offers audiences two important lessons: 1) "you cannot run away from troubles, that you must rely on your own native wit to overcome physical force," and 2) "everyone needs a place of refuge, 'a laughing place,' which comes from self-confidence and people who love you" (228). Taking their cues from Harris's "The Wonderful Tar-Baby Story," both *Song of the South* and *Fabulation* pay due tribute to these simple, yet profound, beliefs.

Lyrical abstractions: Flow's poetic précis

Bursting with allusions to duality through a plethora of characters, *Fabulation* may focus on Undine's healing, home-bound journey, but in doing so it also offers a particularly notable and layered treatment of yet another prominent character: Undine's brother, Flow. On the outset, Flow may seem to be a simple-minded, would-be poet/rapper, but we learn that he is a young man with unfulfilled promise. Once a student at West Point and a member of the Green Berets, Flow found himself cast into the turmoil of Desert Storm, an experience that relegated him to a security guard position at the local drug store, side-tracking him from loftier dreams. While such a turn bears no shame, it does represent a "dream deferred" – deferred, most poignantly, by the irreversible horrors he witnessed in battle. Thus, Flow, like so many of *Fabulation*'s characters, proves to be much more complex than surface impressions may initially suggest, effectively symbolizing *Fabulation*'s attention to paradoxical personalities. Even more significantly, however, Flow's presence in the play is particularly important because it is *his* articulated musings on Brer Rabbit that offer audiences *explicit* insight into the nuanced narrative created by *Fabulation*'s overall structure and characterizations.

Elicited in a pinnacle moment of prose and posturing, Flow spouts forth a lyrical abstract, a poetic précis that succinctly speaks to the complexities of African American experiences. Flow's revealing ruminations, a layer of *Fabulation*'s signifiyin(g) storytelling, comes in the form of a metaphorically rich rap – a poem that has been brewing in his mind for over "fourteen years and nine months" (Nottage 132). In a climactic moment within the play, after familial frustrations rise to an all-time high, Flow suddenly recounts his hip hop soliloquy with unbridled fervor:

> This ain't the beginnin' you wuz expectin'
> It ain't a poem, but a reckonin'
> Be it sacred and profane,
> Or a divine word game.
> It all about a rabbit,
> Or it ain't.
>
> (Nottage 130)

Immediately alerting the listening audience to the seriousness of his treatise, Flow dismisses the paltry notion that he is simply delivering a mere poem, claiming his verbal deluge as a "reckonin'." Subtly conjuring the figurations of both Elegba and Brer Rabbit, he rejects models of ethical absolutism when he posits that the poem could be "sacred *and* profane" but then relishes in rhetorical devices when he seems to turn back on this stance by stating "It all about a rabbit, *or* it ain't" (emphasis mine). With the consciously placed "or," Flow affirms that his poem (as a revelatory treatise about life itself) is about making life choices, yet his careful contextualization still resists a mandatory adherence to absolutes. Flow's oscillating commentary forces his listeners to confront their own conceptual crossroads, encouraging them to take their own path. His audience must come to their own determination: *is* this critical computation all about a rabbit – or is it not? The wisened audience will recognize that it is *either and both*: the mythologies around Brer Rabbit stand alone as significant, but they are also a means to explore a much greater end.

Assuring us that "It ain't a myth so old/That it been whole-saled and re-sold," Flow asserts that his poem – and, for that matter, the entirety of *Fabulation* – is not simply rehashing old narratives, but rather has currency and present day relevance. It is this latter point that Flow addresses when he exhorts:

> It that ghetto paradox,
> When we rabbit and we fox
> And we basking in the blight
> Though we really wanna fight.
>
> (Nottage 131)

Reminding us of the paradoxes found in Brer Rabbit tales (for example, the way in which behaviors elicit both celebration and condemnation), Flow makes a link to a "ghetto paradox," thereby translating the tales' personifications into real-life, present-day terms. Flow concisely articulates the dilemma in which many young, urban African Americans find themselves. Media moguls and every-day malefactors perpetuate self-serving myths (in movies, television, and popular music) that encourage young people to "bask in the blight" of their disadvantages and poverty. Rather than recognizing that a dearth of resources are obstacles that must be conquered, signatures of struggle are often packaged and commodified as markers of authenticity and "realness." Furthermore, a compromised sense of hope can overwhelm young people, rendering feelings of powerlessness and immobility despite their desire to fight against dire circumstances. Thus, as pronounced by Flow, "basking in the blight" may also be interpreted as the experience of self-induced paralysis.

Yet and still, history reveals (and Flow reiterates) that despite the obstacles faced, even the most impoverished among us can retain a spirit that resists psychological subjugation and oppression. Flow embodies this refutation; he renounces the cultural stereotypes that hinder progress while also championing the cultural capital gained from a discrete sense of communal identity.[10] He champions self-acceptance and admonishes self-denial, recognizing that the choice between the two is the difference between being your own best friend or your own worst enemy:

It 'bout who we be today,
And in our fabulating way
'Bout saying that we be
Without a-pology
It's a circle that been run
That ain't no one ever won
It that silly rabbit grin
'Bout running from your skin.

(Nottage 131)

Acknowledging the manifold maneuverings that are made when one faces life's challenges, Flow offers a deceptively simple resolution, "'Bout saying that we be/Without a-pology," thereby echoing the sentiments penned by another bard: "to thine own self be true."[11]

Flow's rabbit poem is a meditation on choices. It is about the ways in which life and its conundrums confront us at the crossroads, and the consequences of our decision-making (or lack-thereof) at these significant junctures. It reminds us that life's journey is full of deviations and aberrations; good and bad will not always be clearly defined; and regardless of our origins or obstacles, our greatest sense of comfort can come from embracing ourselves. By dramaturgical design, the whole of *Fabulation,* a journey to home and self, underscores what is transmitted in Flow's brief recitation. Flow's poem serves as a lyrical abstract for the entirety of Nottage's play and, in fact, even the arrangement of Flow's microcosmic monologue craftily mirrors the open-ended conclusion we are left with at the end of *Fabulation.*

In the very last scene of *Fabulation* Undine finally gives birth to her child, and it is this long-awaited delivery that punctuates the close of the play: *"A baby cries. Blackout"* (Nottage 140). Thus, at the play's end, audiences of *Fabulation* are left with questions about what will commence beyond the close of the curtain: what will become of Undine and her "rebirth" in the light of her child's arrival?

Correspondingly, Flow's rap, as a poetic précis, echoes the open-endedness suggested by this close to Nottage's play. Although Flow initially offers his poem with fierce urgency, his propulsive ponderings soon transform into a whimpering whisper and he *"stops mid-sentence as abruptly as he began, struggling to find the next word in the poem"* (132). Flow gets stuck – and despite his family's encouragement, he cannot find the words to finish. Instead, he explains in frustration: "It ain't finished. It ain't done 'til it's done. A fabulation takes time. It doesn't just happen" (Nottage 132). And he is right. According to literary expert Robert Scholes, a fabulation not only takes time, but it also fails to adhere to the tenets of typical "storybook endings." Rather, the conclusion of a fabulation may suggest a sense of closure, but it is purposefully constructed to linger in the mind of its receiver, prompting audiences to reflect upon the story's end with speculative wonder.[12]

Aptly analogous, Flow's recitation seems to cease prematurely, leaving us to wonder about what is "supposed" to happen next; how the poem is "supposed" to end, thereby ingeniously echoing the open-ended conclusion of Nottage's play, and thereby serving as yet another signifyin(g) moment. *Fabulation* closes with the sound of a newborn's first cry, simultaneously dramatizing an ending *and* a beginning, leaving its audience with as many questions as answers. Significantly, Flow foreshadows this dramaturgical strategy when he *first* mentions, earlier in the play, that he was working on a poem and that Brer Rabbit is his muse. "[T]he poem is not about Brer Rabbit, he is merely a means to convey a truth" [. . .] "It is open-ended. A work in progress. A continuous journey"

(Nottage 97). The same, of course, could be said of Nottage's play. *Fabulation, or the Re-education of Undine* is not a play about Brer Rabbit per se, but Nottage methodically uses the tropes and narratives of Brer Rabbit – both good and bad – to convey truths. And, as an artful adaptation within an ever-expanding oeuvre of Brer Rabbit lore, *Fabulation* is part of a proliferating "work in progress," thereby demonstrating the continuous journey of Elegba, Brer Rabbit, and other diasporic influences.

Notes

1 An oft-cited study by Florence E. Baer reveals that approximately two-thirds of Harris's Uncle Remus stories "have close analogues in African traditional oral literature." See Florence E. Baer, "Joel Chandler Harris: An 'Accidental' Folklorist." Critical Essays on Joel Chandler Harris. Ed. R. Bruce Bickely, Jr. (Boston, MA: G.K. Hall & Co., 1981): 192.

2 I use the term Signifyin(g) as employed by Henry Louis Gates, Jr., *The Signifying Monkey: A Theory of African-American Literary Criticism* (Oxford: Oxford University Press, 1998).

3 My retelling of the Brer Rabbit story is based on the Harris tale as told by Julius Lester, *The Tales of Uncle Remus: The Adventures of Brer Rabbit* (New York: Dial Book, 1987).

4 For a critical interrogation regarding the oft-cited claim that Harris gleaned his stories from his encounters with black people and their storytelling, see Opal Moore and Donnarae MacCann, "The Uncle Remus Travesty." *Children's Literature Association Quarterly,* 11.2 (Summer 1986): 96–97.

5 For a discussion of these opinions, see Annie Ruth Leslie, "Brer Rabbit, a Play of the Human Spirit: Recreating Black Culture through Brer Rabbit Stories." *The International Journal of Sociology and Social Policy* 17.6 (1997), and Robert Hemenway, "Introduction: Author, Teller, and Hero." *Uncle Remus: His Songs and His Sayings* (New York: Penguin Books, 1982): 19–21.

6 A distinction made by many, including Hemenway, "Introduction," 8.

7 Innumerable scholars and cultural curators have made the connection between Brer Rabbit and Elegba, both explicitly and implicitly. See, for example, William Jelani Cobb, *To the Break of Dawn: A Freestyle on the Hip Hop Aesthetic* (New York: New York University Press, 2007): 22.

8 For a more detailed discussion of the controversies and early critical reactions, including formal reviews and black communal protestation regarding *Song of the South,* see M. Thomas Inge, "Walt Disney's *Song of the South* and the Politics of Animation." *The Journal of American Culture,* 35.3 (2013); Matthew Bernstein, "Nostalgia, ambivalence, irony: *Song of the South* and race relations in 1946 Atlanta." *Film History* 8 (1996); and Jason Sperb, *Disney's Most Notorious Film: Race, Convergence, and the Hidden Histories of Song of the South* (Austin: University of Texas Press, 2012).

9 In her essay, "Rural as Racialized Plantation vs. Rural as Modern Reconnection: Blackness and Agency in Disney's *Song of the South* and *The Princess and the Frog,*" Esther J. Terry speaks to how *Song of the South* reveals the stratification between urban and pastoral spaces." *Journal of African American Studies* 14.4 (2010) 469–481.

10 Notably, Flow references this tension earlier in the play when he first discusses working on his Brer Rabbit poem. He explains that he is using Brer
Rabbit "as a means to express the dilemma faced by cultural stereotyping
and the role it plays in the oppression on one hand and the liberation of the
neo-Afric (to coin a phrase) individual, on the other." Lynn Nottage, *Intimate
Apparel* and *Fabulation, or The Re-education of Undine* (New York: Theatre
Communications Group, 2006): 92.
11 William Shakespeare, Act 1, Scene 3 of William Shakespeare's *The Tragedy
of Hamlet, Prince of Denmark.*
12 It is worth noting that Lynn Nottage's *Fabulation* adheres to a number of
the descriptors Robert Scholes offers when defining a fabulation as a literary
genre. According to Scholes, a fabulation is similar to a fable (they both reveal
some moral truth), but while fables usually employ animals or inanimate
objects as their central characters, fabulations generally feature the exploits of
people in fantastical situations. Also of interest is that a fabulation chronicles
a journey that abounds with the unexpected (which is also true of fairytales),
but in the course of a fabulation an author often *offers a tale within a tale,*
thereby revealing "an extraordinary delight" in the design of her storytelling
(8–10). And finally, another defining aspect of a fabulation that resonates with
Lynn Nottage's play is that a fabulist's work relishes in satire and comedy as
well as pain and discomfort; she balances humor with tragedy because she
knows that "an excess of the horrible is faced and defeated by the only friend
reason can rely on in such cases: laughter" (43). Robert Scholes, *The Fabulators* (New York: Oxford University Press, 1967).

Works cited

Baer, Florence E. "Joel Chandler Harris: An 'Accidental' Folklorist." *Critical
Essays on Joel Chandler Harris.* Ed. R. Bruce Bickely, Jr. Boston: Mass, G.K.
Hall & Co., 1981. 185–195. Print.

Bernstein, Matthew. "Nostalgia, Ambivalence, Irony: *Song of the South* and
Race Relations in 1946 Atlanta." *Film History* 8.2 (1996): 219–236. Print.

Cobb, William Jelani. *To the Break of Dawn: A Freestyle on the Hip Hop Aesthetic.* New York: New York University Press, 2007. Print.

Gates, Jr., Henry Louis. *The Signifying Monkey: A Theory of African-American
Literary Criticism.* Oxford: Oxford University Press, 1998. Print.

Harris, Joel Chandler. *Uncle Remus: His Songs and His Sayings.* New York:
Penguin Books, 1982. Print.

Hemenway, Robert. "Introduction: Author, Teller, and Hero." *Uncle Remus: His
Songs and His Sayings.* New York: Penguin Books, 1982. Print.

Inge, M. Thomas. "Walt Disney's *Song of the South* and the Politics of Animation." *The Journal of American Culture* 35.3 (2012): 219–230. Print.

Leslie, Annie Ruth. "Brer Rabbit, A Play of the Human Spirit: Recreating Black
Culture through Brer Rabbit Stories." *The International Journal of Sociology
and Social Policy* 17.6 (1997): 59–83. Print.

Lester, Julius. *The Tales of Uncle Remus: The Adventures of Brer Rabbit.* New
York: Dial Book, 1987. Print.

Levine, Lawrence. *Black Culture and Black Consciousness: Afro-American Folk Thought from Slavery to Freedom.* Oxford: Oxford University Press, 2007. Print.

MacCann, Donnarae and Opal Moore. "The Uncle Remus Travesty." *Children's Literature Association Quarterly* 11.2 (Summer 1986): 96–99. Print.

Nottage, Lynn. *Intimate Apparel and Fabulation, or the Re-education of Undine.* New York: Theatre Communications Group, 2006. Print.

Scholes, Robert. *The Fabulators.* New York: Oxford University Press, 1967. Print.

Shakespeare, William. *The Tragedy of Hamlet, Prince of Denmark.* Ed. Barbara A. Mowat and Paul Werstine. New York: Simon & Schuster, 2012. 3–287. Print.

Song of the South. Dir. Harve Foster and Wilfred Jackson. 1946. VideoDisc. Walt Disney Home Video, 1986.

Sperb, Jason. *Disney's Most Notorious Film: Race, Convergence, and the Hidden Histories of Song of the South.* Austin: University of Texas Press, 2012. Print.

Terry, Esther J. "Rural as Racialized Plantation vs. Rural as Modern Reconnection: Blackness and Agency in Disney's *Song of the South* and *The Princess and the Frog.*" *Journal of African American Studies* 14.4 (2010): 469–481. Print.

Chapter 6

Vera Stark at the crossroads of history

Harvey Young

At the close of *By the Way, Meet Vera Stark*, playwright Lynn Nottage shares a secret with her audience. Every female character within the world of her dark comedy – from the "white" starlet who was once widely regarded as "America's Little Sweetie" to her maid Vera Stark – is African American. In prominently featuring black women within her play, Nottage invites audiences to consider the role of performance in the fabrication and maintenance of social identity. This chapter spotlights the women in *Meet Vera Stark* and chronicles how their manipulation of speech, dress, and gesture enables them to reveal the artifice and thin construction of racial and class categories. These agentive and authoritative characters determine and structure how others see them through a set of calculated acts. Additionally, this chapter explores how the play offers an opportunity to consider the real experiences of performers who labored in the film industry during the bleak years of the Great Depression and the difficult choices that they had to make concerning whether or not to play a stereotype.

Meet Vera Stark premiered in May 2011 at Second Stage Theatre in New York City. The first Nottage play since her widely acclaimed *Ruined*, the 2009 winner of the Pulitzer Prize for Drama, *Meet Vera Stark* faced high expectations. Would this new play similarly address the abuses and atrocities endured by women of color in a truthful and unflinching manner? Would it provide further evidence of Nottage's ascendance as one of the leading social issue artists of her generation? Certainly, some critics and audiences wondered whether *Meet Vera Stark* might be another Pulitzer contender. Whether or not Nottage sought to dampen expectations, she very clearly asserted that her newest work possessed key differences from *Ruined*. Although both plays explore the lived experiences of women of color, the characters in *Meet Vera Stark* are fictional. The playwright, in interviews surrounding the premiere, often mentioned her passion for film comedies and pointed to that genre as a significant influence on the aesthetic structure of *Meet Vera Stark*. Nottage also revealed that she began writing her comedy as she was revising *Ruined* and realized that she needed an escape, an outlet, from the bleak environment of that play: "*Meet Vera Stark* . . . was also a matter of needing to go somewhere while I was writing *Ruined*" (Murphy).

The marketing and promotion of *Meet Vera Stark* further distinguished the play from the one that preceded it. For the Pulitzer Prize winner *Ruined*, the Manhattan Theatre Club produced a publicity image consisting of a photographic close-up (head to shoulders) of actress Condola Rashad. With hands crossed protectively over a seemingly bare chest and eyes directed downward away from the camera, Rashad hints at the objectification and mistreatment of the women who dwell within Nottage's play. Her pose suggests abuse and victimization. In contrast, the *Playbill* cover of *Meet Vera Stark* at Second Stage centers actress Sanaa Lathan (figure 1). In that image, she is dressed in an elegantly designed, immaculately tailored black-and-white maid's outfit, reclining on a fainting couch and holding a film script. She looks directly at the camera with a hint of a smile. Unlike the *Ruined* image, this one projects a sense of play. The only potentially (and perhaps intentionally) confusing element within the picture – one that neatly sums up the experience of the fictional character – is whether the woman pictured is a maid who aspires to be an actress or whether she is an actress performing the role of a maid.

Meet Vera Stark tells the story of the title character, an African American domestic worker and struggling actress during the opening years of the Golden Age of Hollywood. The first act centers on Vera's relationship with her employer Gloria Mitchell, her friends Lottie and Anna Mae, and her efforts to break into the filmmaking business by being cast in the film *The Belle of New Orleans* as the character Tilly, a rare and widely coveted role – a "slave with lines" – enabling a black performer to be seen and heard (Nottage 22). The second act fast forwards to 2003, where a group of public intellectuals attending a symposium debate Vera's career and attempt to discern what could have prompted her to abandon show business after appearing on a television talk show in the 1970s. The talk show scenes are presented live on stage, and clips of Vera's film debut in *The Belle of New Orleans* are screened and discussed by the symposium panelists. Less nuanced than *Citizen Kane*, the most highly regarded text of the fictional investigative documentary genre, the second act similarly borrows the convention of inviting spectators

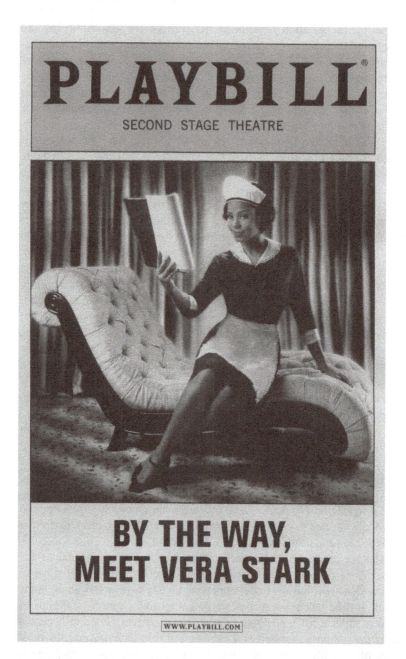

Figure 6.1 Sanaa Lathan in *By the Way, Meet Vera Stark*. Photo by Mark Glenn. Courtesy of Second Stage Theatre.

on a journey that introduces the protagonist from a past perspective and simultaneously privileges "experts" who, ultimately, are not as well informed as the audience. In addition, the play revisits themes present in Nottage's earlier works: self-invention (*Fabulation or the Re-education of Undine*), revisionist history (*Intimate Apparel*), and a fascination with 1930s cinema (*Crumbs from the Table of Joy*).[1] This blend showcases Nottage's dexterity as a playwright and the wide ranging inspiration for her work but, unfortunately, frequently left major theatre critics not quite satisfied.

Reviews of *Meet Vera Stark* routinely heralded one of the two acts as an example of commanding narrative form, and dismissed the other as being sufficiently problematic to weaken the integrity of the entire enterprise. Often, reviewers disagreed on which of the two acts was the better one. *New York Times* theatre critic Ben Brantley, after praising the scripting of the older Vera (as she appears in the talk show) confides, "you can't help thinking what a play this might have been if everything were on the same level." Chris Jones, the senior critic of the *Chicago Tribune* tasked with reviewing a subsequent production at the Goodman Theatre, asserted, unlike Brantley, that the first act was the stronger of the two and declared that "Nottage's impulse to lampoon the way academics have dissected the lives and careers of real people . . . defeated this production." What critics may have missed is how the play's split structure, specifically Nottage's temporal fast forward, grants the audience a privileged insight into the racial role play of its characters. *Meet Vera Stark* offers an opportunity to interrogate racial passing and identity performance both in the entertainment industry and society-at-large.

Dramatic contingencies

Social identity categories, such as age, race, wealth, and physical ability, affect performances in everyday life as well as individuals' perception of themselves. These factors and divisions, as I outline in *Embodying Black Experience*, shape our experience in the world and the choices that we make. At the start of *Meet Vera Stark*, Gloria Mitchell and Vera Stark are attractive, healthy, twenty-eight year-old women who live in the same city but they differ in terms of race, socioeconomic status, and occupation. Mitchell is "white," wealthy, and an actress. Stark is black, working-class, and a maid. These identities inform their experiences of the body. Vera Stark is expected to work, serve, and remain (mostly) silent in the performance of her duties. There are limits and restrictions placed upon her professional, social, and physical mobility because of her social identity. Even her desire to work in the film industry is checked by the reality of her recognizable race and, as a result, she can only compete for the roles of servants and slaves. In contrast, Gloria's phenotypic "whiteness" bestows privilege, and enables her to attain her socioeconomic status through the various professional and social opportunities available to her as a young "white" starlet.

Although it can be difficult to single out a particular embodied sense of being from all others, within certain situations distinct aspects of our social identities may trigger a particularly strong affective experience of difference or otherness. As a result, it is common for our self-perception to be anchored in those identity markers that most render us potential targets of harassment, abuse, or discrimination. A woman who endures catcalls with exhausting frequency on the street continually will be reminded not only of her status as female but also the determining influence of gender on her lived experience. African Americans who consistently find themselves in the glare of extreme surveillance by the police or even shopkeepers quickly learn that their recognizable racial identity profoundly impacts their day-to-day lives. Over time, our social identities get expressed in shorthand, one that spotlights a single category that informs our perspective of the world and our sense of how we are seen by others. This has been evidenced not only within theories of double consciousness (*pace* W. E. B. Du Bois) but also by the effectiveness of civil rights and social movement campaigns that privilege only a few words and employ stative verbs: "I am a Man" or "Black is Beautiful." Individuals with an awareness of the over-determining influence of a single identity category may structure daily acts in an effort to mitigate the threat of being perceived or treated as a stereotype. Citing her habitus as a woman and aiming to avoid street harassment, a person might dress differently or elect to take an alternate walking route. Both are performance choices prompted by social identity. In *Meet Vera Stark*, Nottage presents characters who consciously invoke performance to challenge the negative contingencies of identity. Her female characters fabricate new social identities to gain socioeconomic advantages. Employing a parallel structure, Nottage presents four African American women, two of whom (Gloria and Anna Mae) "play" non-black, while the other two (Vera and Lottie) enact an extreme caricature of blackness.[2] Together, their acts not only stretch the possibilities of blackness, but also highlight the fragility of racial assumptions. Their performances threaten to shatter confidence in the stability of racial lines of discourse.

Nottage provides a compelling example of the effectiveness of racial role play in an early scene set in Gloria's living room in which Maximillian von Oster, the German director of *The Belle of New Orleans*, talks about his vision of the type of actors who will play the slave characters in the film. As he speaks, Vera and her friend Lottie, who previously spoke in standard English and stood with proper posture, slowly transform themselves into the mythic, stereotypical black body of the director's imagination. Sitting in Gloria's living room with the two maids attending to him, Maximillian declares:

> It is time to capture the truth. For instance, I vant the Negroes to be real, to be real Negroes of the earth, I vant to feel their struggle, the rhythm of their language, I vant actors that . . . no, I don't vant actors, I vant people. Negroes who have felt the burden of hard unmerciful labor. I vant to see two hundred years of oppression in the hunch of their shoulders.
>
> (Nottage 46)

He subsequently adds, "I vant to hear the music of the fields. The songs of strife and struggle." In response, Vera and Lottie, seeking to attract the attention of the director and transform the scenario into an impromptu audition, "*morph into slave women.*" Prompted by Maxmillian, they "*hunch their shoulders*" (46). Vera invents a stereotypically tragic origins story – Nottage reveals its fabrication by noting that Vera is "*lying*" in a stage direction – and delivers it in an exaggerated "black" dialect that aligns with Maximillian's sense of authentic blackness: "My mama died in child birth cuz there wasn't no doctor there to birth me proper, and you see my pappy wuz a blues man, and he guitar was the onliest thing he luv." Lottie aids Vera's performance. She "*softly hum[s] a spiritual*" as her friend speaks (Nottage 47). The scene is filled with humor, as the contrived nature of the excessive stereotypical performances are readily apparent to audience members, and as the characters compete with one another to play the most extreme version of the director's imagined slave. The performance proves successful, as evidenced by the appearance of both Vera and Lottie in an excerpt from the film *The Belle of New Orleans* that opens the second act. They won the roles, triumphing in the impromptu audition. In the moment of the living room performance, the convincing nature of their racial role play is made apparent through Maxmillian's response: "Just as Anna Maria conjures the flavors of Carnival in Brazil. This broken Negro woman [Vera], her sad mournful face, the coarse rhythm of her language tells the story of the South" (Nottage 48).

Nottage sneaks in a joke here. "Anna Maria" is also a role being played. She is really Anna Mae, "a very, very fair-skinned African American woman" (Nottage 17). Possessing a similar desire to be cast in Hollywood films, Anna Mae crafts a new identity with the aim of avoiding the contingencies that limit opportunities for black women. She adopts an inconsistently exercised Brazilian accent and the result is a faltering performance, like Vera and Lottie's, but one that somehow works. Even though the artifice is apparent, as evidenced by Maximillian's black chauffeur Leroy telling Anna Mae, "I knew there was some pork fat in that hello," the illusion holds (Nottage 53). In the first act, considerable attention is given to Anna Mae's labored efforts to not be seen as African American. Anna Mae justifies her role play as merely a part of the larger Hollywood scene: "everyone in this town has an angle" (Nottage 51). She comments on how other competing interests might motivate people not to enforce racial lines of division. Referring to her relationship with Maximillian, she declares, "Oh, he's buying what I'm selling, even if it ain't the real thing. Trust me, in the bedroom a horny joe ain't so particular about the accent" (Nottage 51). Anna Mae is refreshingly unapologetic for her actions. She views her act as existing on a continuum of social identity performance. She notes, "Some broads dye their hair blond. And some of us are a little more 'creative'" (Nottage 53). A brunette pretending to be blonde to win a role, in her estimation, is not significantly different than an African American woman playing Brazilian or white. Both are performances that demonstrate the fragility of identity categories. It is Anna Mae who ultimately delivers the line that best summarizes the play, "I ain't the only colored girl masquerading for a living" (Nottage 53). The success of her racial performance is revealed in the second act. None of Nottage's public intellectuals question "Anna Maria's" South American roots.

In comparison with Vera, Lottie, and Anna Mae, the masquerade undertaken by Gloria is more covert. Throughout the play, Nottage drops hint after hint that Gloria harbors a secret. In addition to the stage directions that identify her (within quotation marks) as "white," there are multiple instances in which her identity is called into question. When we first meet the film star, she enters and speaks with a southern accent. Seconds later, she "drops" it (Nottage 9). Later, Gloria speaks cryptically about her parentage: "No one has ever been a hundred percent sure he was my daddy" (Nottage 14). During the scene with Maximillian, she briefly has an intense exchange with Anna Mae. Nottage writes, "Gloria glares at Anna. The women have a silent showdown" (Nottage 53). The two are rivals seeking roles in *The Belle of New Orleans*, and this particular encounter occurs only a few seconds after Anna Mae's comment about "masquerading." Although the remarks are intended for Vera, who is being called out for playing Maximilian's fantasy of the black slave, Gloria herself is also a "colored girl masquerading." If Leroy can sense Anna Mae's blackness, it is conceivable that the "showdown," in part, could be a recognition of each other's cross racial performance. In the 1970s talk show scenes in the second act, Vera and Gloria reunite after having been apart for twenty years. Joyful at their being together again, Gloria reveals that she and Vera "were youngsters on the vaudeville circuit" (Nottage 80). When the interviewer replies, "I didn't realize that the circuit was integrated back when you two were performing as children," a brief silence ensues. It is broken when Vera, referring to the Theatre Owners Booking Association (T.O.B.A.) that managed a black vaudeville circuit, recalls that "we used to joke it meant Tough on Black Asses" (Nottage 81). Nottage's clues about Gloria's passing are not always subtle.

Meet Vera Stark is populated with women who pass, who strategically employ performance to create a new social identity that is legible to others. They play characters of high and low socioeconomic status: slaves and free born, black and white, and American and foreign. The mastery of their performances comes with the acknowledgment that these four women share similar attributes – all are twenty-something African American women – and possess within themselves the ability to inhabit a wide array of identities. Although fictional, they stand-in for real life actresses, the "Black Divas of Early Hollywood," as Nottage calls them in the play's dedication, whose performances were constrained by Hollywood's Production Code.

Playing the maid

Nottage sets *Meet Vera Stark* on the eve of Classical Hollywood's adoption of a set of "codes" that would define, among other things, the types of roles that African American actors could play. Some of these regulations explicitly sought to curtail the allure of black bodies in films marketed toward a white audience. Leonard Leff, writing about the negative impact of the 1934 Production Code on film narratives, observes:

> The movie industry's superego, the Production Code Administration (PCA), had been created in 1934 to regulate the moral and social

content of motion pictures. In only one section did the Code speak to treatment of the Negro: 'Miscegenation (sex relationship between the white and black races) is forbidden.' Yet the PCA's 'black book,' a compilation of Code rulings on individual films, spoke to dozens of restrictions, some suggested by the Code and others not. (147)

The play opens in 1933 in a pre-Code Hollywood. It exists as a passing narrative and, in a way, falls into a long tradition of literary, theatre, and film works that center on the challenges facing men and women who are racially indeterminate. Literary scholar Valerie Smith observes that "[s]tories of racial passing have long captivated the attention of American viewers and readers" (43). In stage adaptations of *Uncle Tom's Cabin*, the scene that most captivated audiences was Eliza's escape, featuring a mulatto woman, typically played by a white actress not in blackface, who dashes across a frozen river. Certainly, *Imitation of Life*, which featured Louise Beavers and Fredi Washington as her daughter, might exist as the most recognizable twentieth-century text on racial passing, with the emotional register assuming melodramatic overtones in Douglas Sirk's later remake. In these performances on stage and screen, mixed characters prove dramatically interesting because they covet more opportunities, greater acceptance, and recognition in the societies in which they live. *Meet Vera Stark* joins this canon. It is a play about passing, not only the desire to play a particular role onscreen but also the personal efforts and sacrifices required to fabricate a new social identity. Gloria becomes "white;" Anna Mae, Brazilian. Although both performances prove successful, as neither the white characters nor the future-residing black characters in the play question the authenticity of their racial role play, it is evident that the maintenance of their identities requires a consistent and carefully executed performance. It requires never (or rarely) returning "home" or acknowledging one's own blackness.

In interviews, Lynn Nottage notes that she found inspiration to write about the experiences of black female actresses in the Hollywood studio era after watching the film *Babyface* which stars Barbara Stanwyck and prominently features Theresa Harris as her maid. Film critic Manohla Dargis, writing for the *New York Times*, asserts:

Curious to know more, [Nottage] set off on an intellectual investigation that became an aesthetic revelation, as she searched for Harris's traces in the Hollywood histories of African-Americans, in biographies, online, on YouTube and DVD. She didn't find much, save for movies like *The Flame of New Orleans*, a period confection directed by René Clair in which Harris somewhat reprises her role in "Baby Face," but with more lines and real glamour shots.

("Just a Maid")

Dargis continues, "[w]ith little to go on but the movies, Ms. Nottage began filling in the blanks with her imagination. The result is *By the Way, Meet Vera Stark*." The playwright places a spotlight on actors like Harris or, more memorably Hattie McDaniel and Butterfly McQueen, who appeared frequently in the role of domestic worker (slave, nanny, or maid) in the classical Hollywood era. Using their careers as inspiration, Nottage scripts fictional backstories for her characters that resemble that of historical performers whose personal narratives were lost and, except for a few cases, have not been reconstructed by film, theatre, and African American studies scholars.

In *Meet Vera Stark*, Nottage incorporates snippets of film history into the fabric of her characters' lives. It was not uncommon for black actors who appeared onscreen in the 1930s to have also performed in the various vaudeville circuits, including (but not limited to) T.O.B.A. On the circuit, future film stars such as Ethel Waters, Bill Robinson, Hattie McDaniel, and Lincoln Perry (Stepin Fetchit) performed an array of non-stereotypical roles that exceeded the limited opportunities available to them on Hollywood sound stages. Although some actors, such as Perry, used the network to cultivate and refine the caricatured portraits that would bring about their celebrity on celluloid, they presented these roles alongside a considerably more diverse line-up of characters. The vaudeville circuit, unlike Hollywood, did not limit African American actors to being a maid, butler, or slave onstage. In her play, Nottage uses this history as Vera's and Gloria's backstory. She scripts a scene in which the women not only revel in their past as "youngsters on the vaudeville circuit" but also sing "an old African-American vaudeville song like 'I'm Just Wild About Harry,'" a comic tune about the desirability of a black man (Nottage 80–81). In so doing, the playwright gestures to the more inclusive and better representative narratives available on the theatrical stage.

Although professional theatre and performance circuits created opportunities for actors to embody a range of types, Hollywood studios attracted performers thanks to the promise of comparatively high pay. Leonard J. Leff, in "David Selznick's *Gone with the Wind*: The Negro Problem," notes that the compensation was too appealing to be ignored or declined. He writes, "studio paychecks and the prevailing conservative climate within the film industry encouraged blacks to lend moviemakers their personas, not their opinions on racial images" (157). Hattie McDaniel, in an oft-cited quote, defended her decision to play "mammy" and maid roles with the following retort: "I'd rather play a maid and make $700 a week, than be a maid for $7" (Saltz; Zeisler 32). Certainly the effects of the Great Depression in the early 1930s and the difficulty of life during the Depression years prompted many actors to check their politics at the studio lot. Others (such as McDaniel) accepted the menial film roles offered, and sought to refine them from within. In a manner not dissimilar from earlier generations of black blackface performers, as theatre historian David Krasner has observed, these artists helped to revise and render slightly more positive the caricatures of black folk (36). Referencing the historical experiences of black actors, contemporary theatre critic Chris Jones notes:

> Actors have to find work in their oversubscribed profession. And if all they're offered are slaves with lines, then, well, the only real options have been either to take the role and sell your dignity, or take the role and try to quietly subvert the stereotypical mindset of the studio.
>
> ("*By the Way*")

Real-life actors like McDaniel, Harris, and arguably Lincoln Perry created performances that, decades later, allow informed audiences to feel as if the actors are winking from beneath the stereotype mask. Lynn Nottage, speaking about Theresa Harris, asserts, "she played very marginal roles, but she would shine above them and make herself known" (Levitt). James McBride, in a 1971 *Film History* feature interview with Lincoln Perry, notes that actors like him "played the game – it was the only game in town – but they were, somehow above it: Step with his other worldly eccentricities and Hattie McDaniel with her air of bossy *hauteur*" (21). The weight of the mask as well as Nottage's desire to render the character visible beneath it can be felt in *Meet Vera Stark*.

Nottage places Vera Stark within this history. Vera exists not only as an underappreciated talent who worked during the golden age of Hollywood, but also as a figure whose decision to play servile roles receives belated critical and scholarly attention in the second act of the play. As an audience, we are not asked to evaluate Vera Stark's desire to play a maid. Nottage inserts a series of value judgments that, unfortunately, foreclose this possibility. Not long after she pretends to be the down-and-out maid of Maximilian's imagination, Vera announces, "I actually did something

I vowed I'd never do, and I did it so easily it frightened me. And I got to thinking about what I'd be willing to do to have a taste of what Gloria's got. You know, be a star!" (Nottage 56). Later, Nottage reveals the toll of Vera's having "crossed a bridge," having left behind her personal ethics to become a star, when she re-introduces the actress, now older, as "sexy, ebullient, and *hardened* by booze" (Nottage 66, emphasis mine). Alcohol for Vera, similar to the other women within the play, acts as a salve to ease the pain of racial role play.[3]

Nottage frames the scholarly characters' revisionist analysis of Vera Stark within a symposium tasked with recuperating the actress's artistic contributions. The most outspoken character in defense of Vera is Afua Assata Ejobo, "a very hip and slightly masculine woman" and a "journalist, poet, and performer" (Nottage 63). Ejobo hears the ghost notes of Vera's militancy. Commenting on the actress's television interview in which Vera Stark appears as an engaging guest who seems content to be back in the public spotlight, Ejobo finds her to be "fearless. Fearless!" (Nottage 73). She continues, "[Vera Stark] is a volcano on the verge of erupting, ready to release the years of battling patriarchal hegemony . . . She is saying, whitey, WHITEY! Pay attention to this 'nigger' woman" (73). The staging (of the talk show) does not support Ejobo's interpretation. This extreme reading lends the scene its humor. The critic overextends her argument and projects her politics onto Vera Stark, whose comments on race relations – from her involvement in the Civil Rights Movement to interracial relationships – are delivered in a measured tone. Although Ejobo is framed as a parody of a humanistic scholar or public intellectual, her analysis echoes the assertions of some black actors who worked in the period. Lincoln Perry, who became a millionaire by shuffling and mumbling, took a similar tack. In his interview with McBride, he declares, "I was the first Negro militant" (22). Nottage's second scholar, Carmen Levy Green, provides balance. She exists as an alternative to Ejobo. In addition to relaying valuable biographical information that helps to bridge the time span between acts, Green offers the most astute reading of the challenges facing African American actresses. Referring to her own prior experiences, she recalls, "At the academy I played Juliet, Nora, Medea, classical roles, but in the professional world I'm offered the same crumbs that in many respects defined Vera's career" (Nottage 73). She sympathizes with Stark and senses "the internal tug-of-war, between what she was and could have been, and what she has come to represent" (Nottage 74).

It is noteworthy that Nottage avoids presenting Vera Stark as a "mammy," a popularly presented caregiver in the classical Hollywood era. Perhaps in an effort to avoid reinscribing a stereotype, she is less interested in the full figured, nurturing caricature that appeared in the major Hollywood films of the period, from *Imitation of Life* (1934) to *Gone with the Wind* (1939). Film scholar Sybil DelGaudio notes that "the Mammy image reflected the opposite of social mobility for blacks" as it gestured toward a past, perhaps a mythic past, of content blacks working on plantations and rearing white children at the expense of their own. The popularity of mammy roles had a devastating effect on actresses (23). DelGaudio notes that Louise Beavers, who starred in *Imitation of Life*, "went on force-feed diets to increase her size and her marketability as an actress, and affected a Southern accent to mask her Los Angeles upbringing." She adds, "Beavers literally studied and ate her way into the stereotype. . . . Her size becomes a metaphor for her own social immobility, in contrast to the svelte, lithe and upwardly mobile Bea," the white woman for whom she works and to whom she gives proceeds from the selling of her massively successful pancake recipe (24). While simultaneously resisting and acknowledging the mammy stereotype, Nottage uses her play to challenge the false assumption that every black woman who appeared onscreen played a mammy and fashioned a look, like Beavers. There were actresses, like Theresa Harris and Butterfly McQueen among others, whose bodies and performances defied the asexual mammy figure. Possessing a body type that was not dissimilar from the white starlets with whom they appeared, they could have been leading actresses if not for the studios' exclusionary casting practices against artists with darker complexions. As a consequence of their recognizable racial identity, they were relegated to the sidelines in near-silent roles. Even as they appear in the background, these women, through what Clayton R. Koppes and Gregory D. Black identify as "sheer force of personality," sometimes managed to create an outsize presence in a film despite their limited time onscreen (392). They "transcended their roles. Yet remained trapped" playing characters who were marginal to the dramatic narrative (Koppes and Black 392). Their performances attract the attention of the spectator and, for brief moments, make the actors the stars of the scenes in which they appear. In *Meet Vera Stark*, Nottage highlights the subversive strategy of acting beyond the scripted part in order to gain notice. Leroy, Vera's eventual husband, recalls:

> Vera had the costume mistress take in the dress two inches around the waist and hips, so it looked real sexy. And I could tell the director dug it, cuz when you see the film there are these wonderful

close-ups of Vera bending over to pick up laundry. She knew how to work all angles, get a little more than they was willing to give.

(Nottage 76)

These acts transformed the maid from a desexualized, unnoticeable, background figure into a person to be desired, noticed, and actively watched. Although limited by the conventions of the era, Vera maintains a degree of agency over her appearance and can affect how others perceive her. In a similar manner, the *Playbill* image of Sanaa Lathan presents Vera Stark not merely as a domestic worker who inhabits a space but as a star whose luminosity demands acknowledgment. She shines. Her maid outfit is expertly tailored to reveal the contours of her body, including a dress hemline several inches shorter than a typical maid uniform that draws attention to her legs. She fashions herself to be seen.

In addition to showcasing the concerted efforts of her characters to challenge racial limits, Nottage, within her stage directions, repeatedly calls attention to the allure of blackness, especially the appeal of black women. This decision seems designed to shatter the mammy/jezebel binary. Nottage implies that there is an inherent attractive quality possessed by all black women. Black is beautiful. The playwright describes Vera as a "beauty," Lottie as "pretty," and Gloria as "glamorous" (Nottage 7, 15, 34). She notes that Anna Mae is "dressed to kill" and, later in the first act, that Vera is "dressed to impress" when she first meets Leroy (Nottage 17, 27). Even the academics look good. Carmen, a professor of media and gender studies, is "stylish" and Ejobo is "hip" (Nottage 63). The playwright wants black folk to be seen and appreciated. She spotlights the significance of their contributions to both the film industry and everyday life. Nottage, in interviews, acknowledges the important societal roles played by black women. "You take out black American women from American culture and a lot of babies don't get raised. We were at the forefront of the suffragette movement, the civil rights movement, but somehow black women get removed from the conversation" (Murphy).

Lynn Nottage has expressed concern at the fact that critics of her work tend to discuss her treatment of race and gender issues rather than attending to the formal elements (and inventions) in her playwriting. *Meet Vera Stark* is a transmedia endeavor that not only cites film history, but also requires a film screening (and, therefore, the making or staging of a short film) and an onstage recreation of a 1970s television show. In addition, Nottage created companion websites to keep the illusion of Vera Stark's life alive and to provide additional background or story elements from her fictional world. *Meet Vera Stark* is a mixed and multi-media text. Its formal experimentation deserves extended consideration. This chapter has focused on the women in Nottage's play not because it is the only way of engaging the play but rather because it is a compelling topic worthy of investigation. Nottage has spoken extensively about the importance of valuing the labor and embodied experiences of black women. It is her recuperative labor, work centering the fabrication and enactment of social identities, that has been the focus of this study.

Notes

1 Concerning the latter, Marlene Dietrich ghosts *Meet Vera Stark* through *The Belle of New Orleans*, which clearly borrows its title from one of her films (which also featured actress Theresa Harris), *The Flame of New Orleans* (1941).
3 I use "play" here rather than "pass as" to signal that these characters continue to be seen as "black" by other characters who witness their performances.
4 With the exception of Lottie, the "passing" women drink alcohol. Gloria is introduced "nursing a healthy glass of gin" and Anna Mae "pours herself a healthy drink" and "belts back her cocktail" (Nottage 7, 51–52). Carmen Levy Green notes that Vera "battled alcoholism" (Nottage 74).

Works cited

Bogle, Donald. *Bright Boulevards, Bold Dreams*. New York: One World/Ballantine, 2006. Print.

Brantley, Ben. "A Black Actress Trying to Rise Above a Maid." *The New York Times*. May 9, 2011. Print.

Dargis, Manohla. "Just a Maid in Movies, but Not Forgotten." *The New York Times*. April 21, 2011. Print.

DelGaudio, Sybil. "The Many in Hollywood Film; I'd Walk a Million Miles – For One of Her Smiles." *Jump Cut* 28 (April 1983): 23–25. Print.

DuBois, W. E. B. *The Souls of Black Folk*. Chicago: A. C. McClurg and Co, 1903. Print.

Imitation of Life. Dir. John M. Stahl. Prod. Carl Laemmle Jr. and Henry Henigson. By William Hurlbut. Perf. Claudette Corbert, Warren William, Louis Beavers, Fredi Washington. Universal-International, 1934. DVD.

Imitation of Life. Dir. Douglas Sirk. Prod. Ross Hunter and Jean Louis. By Eleanore Griffin, Allan Scott, and Mahalia Jackson. Perf. Lana Turner, John Gavin, Sandra Dee, Dan O'Herlihy, Susan Kohner, Robert Alda, Juanita Moore, Troy Donahue, Sandra Gould, and Jack Weston. Universal-International, 1959. DVD.

Jones, Chris. "'By the Way, Meet Vera Stark' at the Goodman Theatre." *The Chicago Tribune*. May 6, 2013. Print.

Koppes, Clayton R. and Gregory D. Black. "Blacks, Loyalty, and Motion-Picture Propaganda in World War II." *The Journal of American History* 73.2 (1986): 383–406. Print.

Krasner, David. *Resistance, Parody and Double Consciousness in African American Theatre, 1895–1910*. St. Martin's Press: New York, 1997. Print.

Leff, Leonard J. "Gone with the Wind: The Negro Problem." *The Georgia Review* 38.1 (1984): 146–164. Print.

Levitt, Aimee. "*By the Way, Meet Vera Stark* Pulls the Mask Off Old Hollywood." *Chicago Reader*. May 2, 2013. Print.

McBride, Joseph and Stepin Fetchit. "Stepin Fetchit Talks Back." *Film Quarterly* 24.4 (1971): 20–26. Print.

Nottage, Lynn. *By the Way, Meet Vera Stark*. New York: Theatre Communications Group, 2013. Print.

Saltz, Rachel. "The Triumph and Pain of a Hollywood Trailblazer." *The New York Times*. August 21, 2008. Print.

Smith, Valerie. "Reading the Intersection of Race and Gender in Narratives of Passing." *Diacritics* 24.2–3 (1994): 43–57. Print.

Steele, Claude. *Whistling Vivaldi: How Stereotypes Affect Us and What We Can Do*. New York: W.W. Norton & Company, 2011. Print.

Young, Harvey. *Embodying Black Experience*. Ann Arbor: University of Michigan Press, 2010. Print.

Zeisler, Andi. *Feminism and Pop Culture*. Berkeley: Seal Press, 2008. Print.

Special section: *Ruined*

Chapter 7

Melodrama, sensation, and activism in *Ruined*

Jennifer-Scott Mobley

The idea for *Ruined* (2009) was born in 2004 during a conversation between frequent collaborators, playwright Lynn Nottage and director Kate Whoriskey, about Brecht's *Mother Courage*. Both women were drawn to Brecht's heightened style and theory of epic dramaturgy to convey a political message. Nottage and Whoriskey were compelled by the notion of exploring women's complicated relationship to war (Whoriskey ix). Nottage, who previously worked for Amnesty International, was disturbed by the ongoing conflict over natural resources in the Democratic Republic of the Congo. This conflict, which has been raging for many years, has resulted in one of the highest death tolls of any war, as well as widespread grotesque human rights violations against women in particular. These acts of violence have been perpetrated with very little media coverage. Nottage imagined that staging a "Mother Courage of the Congo" could potentially call attention to the crisis. She and Whoriskey traveled to Uganda to an Amnesty International office in Kampala and set out to interview Congolese refugee women as a starting point for an adaptation of *Mother Courage*. However, as research progressed, Nottage began to feel confined by Brechtian dramaturgy rooted in politics and *verfremdungseffect*. She wanted to portray the lives of Central Africans as accurately as possible and Brecht's *Mother Courage* began to feel like a "false frame" (Whoriskey xi). While Nottage deploys some Brechtian devices in *Ruined*, much of her dramaturgy is intentionally antithetical to Brechtian theory. I argue for an alternate reading of *Ruined* as a text that revisits key strategies popular in nineteenth-century melodramatic formations, a contested genre held to be apolitical by many scholars, but which has recently received renewed attention and increased currency as a popular form of activist drama in U.S. theatre.[1] This essay identifies *Ruined* as a melodrama and its impact as a politically active and feminist "dramaturgy of reform."

In *Spectacles of Reform: Theater and Activism in Nineteenth-Century America*, Amy Hughes argues that spectacle – or sensation – scenes, which were a fundamental convention in melodrama, played a role in American activism in the nineteenth century and suggests that spectacle remains central to what she calls the "dramaturgy of reform" (12). In other words, the very structure of melodramatic storytelling, including theatrical conventions such as music, suspense, and the sensation scene, all of which appeal to the senses, engenders socio-political transformation in spectators. She asserts that spectacle is instrumental in activism and social reform because of "its potential to destabilize, complicate, or sustain ideological beliefs" (Hughes 4). Specifically, the "spectacular instant" onstage presents "a heightened, fleeting, and palpable moment in performance that captivates the spectator through multiple planes of engagement, emotionally, intellectually, bodily, affectively" (Hughes 8). Thus, *Ruined* resists adhering to the model of Brechtian dramaturgy that initially inspired Nottage, and instead instigates socio-political change through the methodology of melodrama. Rather than deploying alienation techniques, Nottage leverages the impact of spectacle and spectators' embodied, visceral responses and encourages the audience to identify with her characters in order to inspire political action. The play's widespread international production record suggests its potential to generate political awareness and spark feminist activism.

I begin by exploring the dramaturgical intersections and divergences among Brecht's *Mother Courage*, *Ruined*, and nineteenth-century melodrama. In doing so I will highlight correlations among the tropes used by Nottage and those used by American melodramatists such as George L. Aiken, David Belasco, and Augustin Daly. Clearly *Ruined* shares with *Mother Courage* anti-war themes and a story told through a female protagonist caught in the middle of a war zone. But what does *Ruined* have in common with its nineteenth-century ancestors? It is a classically structured well-made play that adheres to the basic mechanics of early melodrama. For example, *Ruined* features a tightly knit, climatic plot and employs many elements of realism to trace the tribulations of a heroine, Mama Nadi, struggling against forces of evil, in a world of corrupt patriarchal authority in which violence threatens the equilibrium of the community – in this case, her bar-brothel. In the context of the play, the brothel is the domestic sphere, the home, created and inhabited entirely by women; it is a domain of non-violence and relative calm. The dangerous enemy threatening the harmony of domestic "tranquility" is the war outside and the soldiers who perpetuate it. In addition to featuring a spectacular climax scene, *Ruined* concludes with a traditional dénouement in which there is a restoration of heteronormative social order and the community is "safe" from evil, if only for a while. As in a classic domestic melodrama, it is only through heroic cleverness and fortitude that Mama Nadi is able to keep the place running, protect herself and the girls from violence, find romance, and reestablish harmony at least within her domestic sphere.

Nineteenth-century (and, to some degree, contemporary) melodrama is also known for its stock characters, including the hero/heroine and the villain, as well as for maintaining a highly moral tone and a clear delineation between the forces of good and evil in the world of the play. As the heroine, Mama Nadi may be morally ambiguous relative to some of the stock heroes of early melodrama – she does profit from the war by pimping out the girls who work for her – yet it is very clear from the context of the play that they are indeed safer with her than on their own; the women under her roof have all been raped by soldiers and shunned by their families and villages. Their choices are difficult and few: to live alone in the bush as undefended targets for sexual assault, slavery, and likely murder, or to live under Mama's roof with her protection, where they receive food and shelter and have community at the price of prostituting themselves to soldiers as commodities.

Mama Nadi is an anti-hero in the truest sense, thrust into the role of savior against her will. Her income from her brothel doesn't constitute war profiteering as much as survival wages. The ethics of running a brothel must be contextualized in the world of the play; this is a world in which soldiers patronizing prostitutes in an "honest transaction" is a civilized step up from acts of rape and violence that they perpetrate daily on innocent women in the course of fighting the war. As constructed by Nottage, Mama Nadi is a psychologically complex character whose motivation is pragmatically humanistic. Audience members can emotionally identify with her predicament and empathize with her choices, recognizing her as a force for better if not for best. Arguably, Nottage's characterization of Mama Nadi is more nuanced than the stock "hero" of early melodrama. In creating the world depicted in *Ruined* her "strategy was, get you interested in the characters so you care about them" (Berton). In one interview Nottage claimed, "I believe in engaging people emotionally, because I think they react more out of emotion than when they are preached to, told how to feel" (McGee). This emotional identification with the protagonist is somewhat antithetical to Brechtian theory, which discourages both actors and audiences from identifying with a character. Brecht reminds us that "even if empathy or self-identification with the character can be usefully indulged in rehearsals, it is something to be avoided in performance" (194). But, as constructed by Nottage, Mama Nadi and all the female characters are nuanced enough for actors and audiences to identify emotionally with them.

While the characters are crafted with empathetic care, *Ruined* still keeps within the melodramatic tradition of featuring characters that can be readily categorized on the good/bad binary. For example, Mama Nadi, Sophie, Josephine, Salima, and Christian are clearly morally good in the world of the play. The women all look out for one another and share resources. They offer comfort to each other in moments of grief or pain. They seek to avoid violence as much as possible. Christian, the lead male figure is starkly contrasted from the other male characters in the play as a pacifist and a romantic. He takes on Sophie and Salima and delivers them to Mama Nadi at the risk of his own safety. Throughout the play he speaks out against violence and tries to diffuse conflict. In the following exchange he moves to protect Sophie and placate an angry soldier:

(Sophie carries two beers over to the Soldier. . . . The drunken soldier grabs her onto his lap. Christian protectively rises. Sophie skillfully extracts herself from the soldier's lap.)
CHRISTIAN: Are you okay?
SOPHIE: Yes.
(Sophie, shaken, exits. Christian smiles to himself, and lights a cigarette. The drunken Solider, annoyed, plops down next to Christian.)
GOVERNMENT SOLDIER #1: You give me a cigarette, my friend?
CHRISTIAN: (*Nervously*) Sorry, this is my last one.
GOVERNMENT SOLDIER #1: Yeah? You buy me a cigarette?
CHRISTIAN: What?
GOVERNMENT SOLDIER #1: (*Showing off*): Buy me a cigarette!
CHRISTIAN: Sure.
(Christian reluctantly digs in his pocket and places money on the counter. Mama drops a cigarette on the counter. The soldier scoops it up triumphantly and walks away.)

(Nottage 46–47)

This is just one of several instances where Christian chooses the path of non-violence. He is also a recovering alcoholic who abstains from alcohol, recognizing its ill effects on him. However, later in this scene he is compelled by Commander Osembenga (and Mama Nadi) to drink whiskey as a show of solidarity. Rather than risk retribution or start a fight for refusing Osembenga's "hospitality," Christian drinks and as a result relapses into alcoholism for a time.

The character of Christian aside, most of the other male characters in the play – the soldiers – are anonymous forces of senseless violence and destruction. Many of the male roles are identified only as "soldier" or "miner" and are played by the same actors doubling in different parts (Nottage 2). This lends an everyman quality to these male characters and paints them all broadly as agents of evil. Besides Christian and the rebel leaders, the only other named male characters are Mr. Harari, who is also distinct in his passivism and kindness to the girls, and Fortune, Salima's husband. We learn in Salima's monologue that she was captured and made a sex slave for five months by soldiers, who also killed her child. She was eventually released and she returned to her husband who shamed her and drove her away from their village with a switch. But during the course of the play, Fortune regrets his actions and attempts to find Salima. He waits several days, even standing sentinel in the rain outside the brothel to see Salima, but she hides from him and knowingly allows Mama to tell him she is not inside. Fortune eventually instigates violence against all of the women by outing Mama to Osembenga as harboring his rival Kisembe. This vengeful act results in the shocking violence of the play's climax, which I discuss later. Overall, the male characters are somewhat interchangeable and constructed as corrupt and immoral in contrast to the female characters who are unique individuals, each with their own emotional life and backstory, all of whom are on the side of good.

Despite this distinction between good/evil in *Ruined*'s dramaturgy, it is important to note that Whoriskey and Nottage view the men and boys embroiled in this conflict as equally victimized as the women; many of them have also been victims of violence, traumatized physically and psychologically, and forced to fight as soldiers against their will (Whoriskey xi). However, the lack of character development for most of the male soldiers/miners paints them somewhat generically as forces of destruction, further highlighting the humanity of the female characters. The stock soldiers have little dialogue and their lines are characterized as belligerent, threatening, bragging, or trying to gain sexual attention. The following is a typical exchange in Mama's bar. Sophie is singing, the soldiers and the other girls are drinking and fraternizing.

REBEL SOLDIER #1: Another! Hey!
MAMA: I hear you! . . .
(He clumsily slams the bottle on the counter. He gestures to Sophie)

REBEL SOLDIER #1: Psst! Psst! Psst!

(Another Rebel Soldier gives Sophie a catcall. Sophie ignores him. Rebel Soldier #1 turns his attention back to Mama.)

Her! Why won't she come talk to me?

MAMA: You want to talk to her? Behave, and let me see your money. . . .

REBEL SOLDIER #1: The damn beer drained my pocket. It cost too much! You're a fucking thief!

MAMA: Then go somewhere else. And mind your tongue. *(Turns away)*

REBEL SOLDIER #1: Hey. Wait. Wait. I want her to talk to me. Mama, lookie! I have this.

(Proudly displays a cloth filled with little chunks of ore)

MAMA: What is it? Huh? Coltan? Where'd you get it?

REBEL SOLDIER #1: *(Boasting)*: From a miner on the reserve.

MAMA: He just gave it to you?

REBEL SOLDIER #1: *(Snickering)*: Yeah, he gave it to me. Dirty poacher been diggin' up our forest, we run 'em off. Run them good, gangsta style: "Muthafucka run!" Left 'em for the fucking scavengers.

(Nottage 21)

The Soldier/Miners are nearly allegorical in their construction. They are men involved in this senseless conflict and could be on either "side" of it; it does not matter. Their motivations and aggressive behavior are all the same. In production, the distinction between conflicting factions is further blurred by double-casting. Because both sides of the conflict lack official uniforms, the soldiers' costumes are a similar hodgepodge of military and civilian street-wear that make it difficult for spectators to visually identify which military force is in Mama's bar in any given scene. This not only emphasizes the mutability of the combat situation, but also reinforces the universal destructiveness perpetrated by all men involved regardless of affiliation.

However, audiences can recognize the female characters as "good" and identify with their emotions and circumstances. One aspect that contributes to this identification with Mama specifically is her refusal to abandon her bar-brothel. She is motivated by the universal desire to have a "home" where she can keep herself and her "children" – her girls – safe. These protective, maternal instincts transcend cultural boundaries and help audiences identify with Mama and her motivations. Although Mama Nadi is at times a stern madame, she is often compassionate toward the girls. She diffuses situations when the soldiers get inappropriately aggressive, she takes in Sophie despite her "ruined" status, and she does not throw her out when she catches her stealing.[2] In fact, returning to the melodramatic tropes that Nottage employs, Sophie functions as a kind of damsel in distress to be rescued by Mama Nadi; not only does Nadi take Sophie in at Christian's behest knowing that the girl cannot safely engage in sex with customers and therefore is not a valuable commodity, but later in the play Nadi attempts to orchestrate another kind of unforeseen rescue akin to many last-minute saves we see in earlier melodramas such as Daly's *Under the Gaslight* (1867). In this case it is the mother figure doing the rescuing.

Scholar Daniel Gerould notes that early American melodrama was "matriarchal in its pieties," which at the time was distinct from European models that were more patriarchal and driven by paternalistic themes (26). American plots frequently were bound up with mother-daughter love, and female heroines were often depicted as asexual; sexual activity was generally only ascribed to the lecherous villain. Memories of a deceased mother or the maternal instinct of a female protagonist to protect her child, such as when Eliza risks her life crossing the Ohio River to save her infant in George L. Aiken's *Uncle Tom's Cabin* (1852), were frequent tropes. However, Gerould points out that as melodrama developed in the United States, a "new melodramatic heroine" emerged. Heroines such as The Girl in David Belasco's *The Girl of the Golden West* (1905), are "sympathetic portraits of self-reliant heroines who manage to combine wildness and femininity" (Gerould 26). These heroines look after themselves without a man's protection and are not afraid of men and sexuality, reflecting the "New American Woman" figure emerging in the nineteenth century. Mama Nadi is certainly a postmodern echo of this melodramatic heroine. She is capable, self-sufficient, frank about sexuality and sex as a commodity, and (largely) unmoved by romantic overtures. For the most part she dominates all of the men who enter her domain and is fiercely protective of her home as well as the women she harbors. Thus, Nottage expands on the tradition of the melodramatic heroine, developing Mama Nadi and the other female characters more fully to establish embodied subjectivity, which increases audience identification with them. Because the narrative of *Ruined* focuses almost exclusively on women's experiences and the plight of the female characters, thereby expanding melodramatic conventions to include rich female subjectivity, it encourages a feminist reading of the play.

Still another similarity *Ruined* bears to melodramatic form is its use of music. Music was an essential component of the first eighteenth-century melodramas in the boulevard theatres of Paris, where music underscored dialogue to heighten dramatic impact. Perhaps more importantly, music also distinguished these plays from operas or straight plays and thus circumvented the regulations that established theatre monopolies. The term itself, melodrama, means a play with music. Unlike Brecht, who employed songs to jar the audience out of complacency and call attention to the theatricality of his play, Nottage uses music more in the spirit of melodrama to heighten the action and create tension and suspense. Nottage, who wrote the lyrics for the haunting tunes, expands on the effect of music, using soulful poetry to draw us more deeply into the emotional world of the characters and intensify our physiological response to the action. The tunes composed by Dominic Kanza who is Zairen, have a Congolese sound that also contributes to the authenticity of the environment (Nottage, Appendix). Moreover, productions such as the 2009 New York premiere at Manhattan Theatre Club that use live musicians to play the music, further contribute to the immediacy and liveness of the performance by appealing to spectators' senses on a non-verbal level.

In addition to the sensual effect of the music, which heightens audience anticipation and emotion, the songs that Sophie sings also give us a window into her character. For example she sings:

> A Rare bird on a limb
> Sings a song heard by a few,
> . . .
> A sound that haunts the forest,
> A cry that tells a story, harmonious,
> . . .
> To be seen, is to be doomed
> It must evade, evade capture,
> And yet the bird
> Still cries out to be heard.

(Nottage 38)

At this moment Sophie's musical interlude, a metaphor for the plight of women in the Congo, teaches us about her character while at the same time contributing to a sense of calm that marks the beginning of Act One, scene four. In this scene there is a kind of order as the girls genially socialize with the patrons, who drink and play pool. The melancholy song underscores the relative "peacefulness" of the moment. At other times, however, such as at the top of Act Two scene one, Sophie sings a more frenetic tune in which the rhythm and lyrics generate a chaotic, violent atmosphere:

Hey, monsieur, come play, monsieur,
The Congo sky rages electric
As bullets fly like hell's rain
Wild flowers wilt and forest decays,
But here we're pouring champagne.

(Nottage 63)

Indeed, Josephine, who is fraternizing with customers, responds to this song with a frenzied dance of anger that eventually overtakes her emotionally, and the ambiance in the bar is electrified with her pain. The rhythm of the music impacts the audience viscerally and they feel the imminent danger of the circumstances of living in an active war-zone where the rules of combat and the hierarchy of forces change daily. Thus, the lyrics offer a window into the characters' emotions, while the music appeals to audiences' senses and heightens their bodily engagement with the performance.

In addition to the aforementioned features of melodramatic dramaturgy that Nottage employs, *Ruined* also features a spectacular climax that includes a kind of "sensation scene" in which the vulnerability of a character/actor's body – their susceptibility to bodily harm – is vividly dramatized as the scene unfolds. One might envision the typical sensation scene in melodrama to include extravagant stage effects such as the last-minute rescue of a character from train tracks as a "life-size" locomotive chugs across the stage, or a narrow escape from a blazing fire. However, scholars of melodrama note that there are other components to the sensation scene that rely not only on acts of bravery in the face of spectacularly engineered catastrophe but also "intense emotional affectivity." As Hughes notes, there is a "tendency in sensation scenes to generate affect by endangering the body at its center" (10). She argues that one of the central components of the sensation scene in early American melodrama was the enactment of a human body in danger, which thrilled audiences. At the time, affectivity was amplified by the very real possibility that the performers were in danger; given the crude stage machinery and the reliance on gas lighting in nineteenth-century theatres, it was not uncommon for actors to be injured by a mechanical failure, dancers to catch fire by the footlights, or an entire theatre to catch fire during the course of the play and subsequently burn down as audiences fled. The real and present threat that a performer might be injured before their eyes heightened audiences' anxiety and excitement and called attention to the vulnerability of the human body in the scenario.

Many theorists have examined how the actor's liveness – their physical and emotional vulnerability in a given stage moment – is central to the theatre experience. Bert O. States describes this element as a "creatural bond with the actor." He goes on to say that "[o]ur sympathetic involvement with the characters is attended by a secondary and largely subliminal, line of empathy born of the possibility that the illusion may at any moment be shattered by a mistake or accident" (119). Hughes asserts that "for the body in the spectacle, the possibility of death is omnipresent. Actors on stage, especially those performing in melodramas, constantly flirt with disaster. Sensation scenes, in particular, aggressively highlight the body's vulnerability. This suggests that the body in extremity is another defining feature of spectacle" (14). Hughes's argument that "to be unequivocally sensational, a scene requires a virtual/ actual body experiencing fictional/factual peril" precisely describes the sensational effect of the climactic scene in *Ruined* (32).

The harrowing climax of *Ruined* stages the very real dangers that women in the DRC face daily and thus positions the characters/actors in the context of this danger. As the action reaches its peak, Mama Nadi secretly and selflessly gives up her financial nest-egg to procure an operation for Sophie that will repair the damage to her genitals that she suffered when she was assaulted. This scene is only the beginning of the tense climax. The sequence bears all the traditional hallmarks of a melodramatic rescue: bullets are audibly raining outside, the fighting is dangerously close to the brothel, and Mr. Harari, the conduit to the more civilized city of Bunia, must depart immediately with an aid worker in order to escape from the fighting. Mama Nadi surprises Harari with her last minute request of him. She gives him a raw diamond – her only "insurance policy" – with explicit instructions to use the money to get Sophie to safety and get her medical treatment. Tension mounts as Mama hurries to the back room to fetch Sophie (who is unaware of Mama's plan to send her away for care). Meanwhile, the bullets sound ever closer. The aid worker runs in and tells Harari that they must leave now because vehicles carrying soldiers who will kill them are approaching. Harari calls to Mama to hurry. The bullets get louder. Will Sophie escape in time? In fact, Harari panics and leaves without her. Sophie rushes out the door to try to catch the truck and returns a few beats later, totally defeated. Ultimately, this unit of action serves as a preliminary, mini-climax, raising audience tension in anticipation of the forthcoming sensation scene. Nottage expertly manipulates the melodramatic trope of the last-minute rescue, thwarting audience expectations only to raise the stakes higher.

The audience barely has time to process what has happened before the brothel generator blows, shrouding the stage in darkness. Osembenga, the ferocious commander, storms into the bar with his men, accusing Mama Nadi of serving and knowing the whereabouts of his rival, Jerome Kisembe. The scene reaches a peak of tension when Osembenga threatens Mama Nadi and the three girls bodily. The stage directions read "*a Soldier drags Josephine from the back. They throw Mama, Sophie, and Josephine onto the floor*" (Nottage 93). When Mama is unable to tell Osembenga where his rival is, he points to Josephine and says: "Take that one." The stage directions read "*a Soldier grabs Josephine. He is ready to sexually violate her. Josephine desperately struggles to get away. The Soldier tears away at her clothing. The women scream, fight*" (93). This struggle is harrowing not only because of the violence enacted before the audience's eyes, but for the implied violence that is imminent in this moment. Given previous exchanges in the play and what the audience has already learned about how soldiers treat women after raping them, the war tactic lingers menacingly over the scene. The implied threat is not only rape, but that the soldier will violate Josephine with his bayonet. No audience member can contemplate that action without being viscerally affected. It is horrifying. Indeed, Nottage has herself written about her "strong visceral response" to hearing the stories of Congolese rape victims (Nottage, *On Ruined*). Yet, in this moment of extreme tension, the stakes are raised even further when Salima emerges, "*A pool of blood forms in the middle of her dress, blood drips down her legs*" (94). Her appearance stops the soldiers from attacking Josephine and impacts the audience with the gore and bodily recognition that she has mutilated her own body to destroy the baby (conceived of rape) within her womb.

She screams, "STOP it! Stop it. For the love of God, stop this! Haven't you done enough to us. Enough! Enough!" (Nottage 94). The soldiers do stop and her estranged soldier-husband rushes to hold her in his arms where she utters her dying words, "You will not fight your battles on my body anymore" (94). This moment is dramatic on the page and it is a "show-stopper" in performance. In the aforementioned 2009 MTC production when Quincy Tyler Bernstine, who played Salima, appeared, she was literally covered in blood from the mid-section down. She staggered downstage amidst the chaos of the threatening soldiers and the presence of her crumpling, bloody body, as well as her relative calm and stillness surrounded by turmoil, not only halted the onstage action but elicited gasps from the audience. This moment, in which the threat of violence to the other women is juxtaposed with Salima's gore-smeared body, foregrounding the women's bodies in danger, results in a post-modern, feminist sensation scene. Director Kate Whoriskey's staging generated powerful audience affect; we were brought to the highest level of fear and tension as we contemplated unspeakable violence toward Josephine and the other women. Salima's surprising entrance created a tableau of a bloody, sexually mutilated female body. Although we did not witness soldiers violating a character onstage in this moment, the audience read Salima's self-inflicted bodily harm as synonymous to sexual mutilation that stems from this kind of sexual assault; Bernstine as Salima embodied that damage in performance before our eyes.

The appearance of Salima's ravaged body and her spectacular act of despair is the culmination of *Ruined*'s narrative in which we finally see the brutality that we have previously only heard about enacted onstage. Nottage deploys the most powerful of melodramatic tropes to engage audiences on multiple planes: intellectual, emotional, and visceral. If, as Hughes asserts, spectacle can "function as a methodology in reform," then the graphic depiction of sexual violence perpetrated on characters with whom the audience has come to identify, can only incite powerful affect (14). In demanding that audiences bear witness to this unspeakable cruelty, Nottage's dramaturgy escalates political awareness and mobilizes feminist activism for intervention.

Here, I return briefly to Hughes's argument that audience concern for the health and safety of human bodies was central to the sensation scene in classic melodramas, and that many melodramas concerned with social reform relied on sensation scenes to produce audience affect. For example, the *delirium tremens* scene was the wildly popular sensation scene in W.H. Smith's *The Drunkard* (1844) during which the performer enacted the symptoms of detoxification from alcohol and the temporary insanity it was thought to induce. Temperance lectures often featured performances of this scene – the horrifying spectacle of a man in the throes of the DTs. Another example was the stage adaptation of *Uncle Tom's Cabin* (1858) by George Aiken, which aimed to humanize blacks in support of the anti-slavery movement. The spectacular sensation scene in this play featured Eliza, the quadroon slave mother, pursued by bounty hunters, crossing the Ohio River by jumping on a series of (mechanically) moving ice floes while clutching her infant to her breast. The universality of a mother risking her life for her child and the sympathetic depictions of blacks contributed momentum to the abolitionist cause. Spectacles in which the character and the actor are endangered exemplify how nineteenth-century sensation scenes generated audience effect to stimulate social reform. Likewise, the aforementioned sensation scene in *Ruined* deploys the body as spectacle as a methodology of reform, raising audiences' awareness of atrocities committed against women in the Congo conflict by viscerally impacting them with the vulnerability of Salima/Bernstine's performing body.

When I attended the Manhattan Theatre Club production in 2009, there were more audible vocal responses and tears from the audience than during any other performance I can recall attending. At the time, I wondered if the primarily white audience was going to experience their catharsis in the theatre, satisfied that they had somehow participated in a solution just by seeing the show. However, as time passes it seems that *Ruined* has indeed successfully employed spectacle as a methodology of social reform. Reporting on *Ruined*'s 2008 debut at Chicago's Goodman Theatre, *The Seattle Times* noted that the play not only pleased critics but sparked feminist activism. "A group of women in Chicago did a fund-raising drive for Tanzi Hospital in the Congo [which performs surgeries to reverse sexual mutilation]" (Berson). Furthermore, Whoriskey writes in the introduction to the play that the New York production of *Ruined* attracted "the attention of the United Nations and the United States Senate. Several delegates from the United Nations, including General Ban-Ki Moon have attended the performance" (Whoriskey xiii). Nottage and actress Quincy Tyler Bernstine were invited to attend the Senate Foreign Relations Committee hearing of the subcommittee on International Operations and Organizations, Democracy, Human Rights and Global Women's Issues, and the subcommittee on African Affairs, which was designed to examine the use of violence against women, particularly rape, as a tool of war in conflict zones and to "explore what steps are being taken to stop the horrific practice once and for all" (Berton). That the actress who originated the role of Salima as well as Nottage were invited, suggests the affective blurring of the performer's body with the character's body in which Bernstine became the voice of the actual victims.

In another example of *Ruined* gaining national attention, the Enough Project at the Center for American Progress, a peace advocacy organization that runs a campaign to end sexual violence and exploitation in Eastern Congo, also sponsored a reading and a discussion of *Ruined* at the Kennedy Center in Washington in November 2009 (Olepade). Beginning her term as Secretary of State in 2009, Hillary Clinton also worked to raise awareness.[3] She toured Africa twice during her tenure, visiting organizations that care for women who have been raped. Subsequently Clinton brought further attention to the crisis when she publicly refused to visit Rwanda, a country that has played a significant role in perpetu-ating the violence (Wilson). She also declared rape a weapon of mass destruction in contemporary warfare. *Ruined* continues to demonstrate through its longevity and success that there is indeed potential in melo-dramatic dramaturgy for raising awareness and engendering activism.

Moreover, because *Ruined* won the Pulitzer Prize for Drama, it has been "canonized." The production record of the play and the dissemina-tion of the text in anthologies enables instructors to readily incorporate *Ruined* into curricula, which creates opportunities to raise awareness on a local scale in the university classroom. I frequently assign *Ruined* to my undergraduates in the context of my dramaturgy and dramatic literature classes as well as in studies of feminist theatre. The play never fails to electrify the women and men in my classroom. Students routinely (even when it is not part of the assignment) engage in additional research to better understand the circumstances of the conflict in the Congo. Nottage has stated that she hopes the play encourages students to think more glob-ally, noting that many American college students would be hard-pressed to identify African countries on a map (Depalma 2). In fact, this is exactly the kind of conversation her play has evoked in my classrooms. Students become eager to look at maps and discuss the modern uses of coltan (one of the key commodities in the war) in cell phones and laptops and pos-sibly for the first time, consider their ethical position as consumers of global commodities and resources. Aside from the fact that *Ruined* deals with an ongoing conflict that is immediate to students, I believe that one of the reasons this play resonates so powerfully is because the melodra-matic structure is familiar as a staple of American theatre and film. Stu-dents can focus more deeply on the issues the play presents because they are not grappling with alienating aspects of form and structure.

Furthermore, *Ruined* is an appealing play to produce at the uni-versity level because it provides substantial and meaningful roles for actresses of color. This, of course, is a major tenet of feminist playwrit-ing. Because the play is rooted in part in realism, which remains the one of the pillars of undergraduate actor training, students can apply their Stanislavski-based training to develop the rich characters that Nottage has created. The socio-political scope of the play also offers student dra-maturgs a wealth of research and outreach opportunities within local and global communities. Just one of many anecdotal examples of *Ruined*'s impact at the college level occurred when Marymount Manhattan Col-lege staged the play in 2013.[4] The students involved in the production were so inspired by the material that the cast and crew raised $2,700 for the Fistula Foundation, a non-profit organization that partners with the

Panzi hospital in the DRC to help victims of assault and birth-related fistula injuries.[5]

Ruined proves the potential for melodrama and spectacle to function as a contemporary methodology of reform and, given its accessible dramaturgy, will continue to do so in classrooms and on university, regional, and international stages. Lynn Nottage has crafted a play that not only champions humanitarian values, but also carries on the legacy of spectacles of reform within the tradition of melodrama. Thus, *Ruined* offers a contemporary feminist model for melodrama as a mode of theatre for social change.

Notes

1 See *Melodrama and the Myth of America*, in which Jeffrey D. Mason asserts that popular melodrama was part of a national discourse surrounding ideology, and served as an affirmation of culturally constructed myths of America, but is highly skeptical of the potential for melodrama to inspire reform (Mason). Similarly, in *Melodramatic Formations,* Bruce McConachie offers a Marxist critique arguing that melodrama reflected dominant social and political attitudes of the period rather than the seeds of sociopolitical reform.

2 The term "ruined" can refer generally to women who have been raped and therefore marked with shame. More specifically, as in Sophie's case, it refers to rape victims who have been violated with a bayonet, bottles, sticks or other objects resulting in a fistula, or damaged tissue in the vagina. Essentially, the trauma results in a breach or hole between the victim's vagina and nearby anatomy including the anus, colon, or bladder and culminates in various health complications in addition to emotional suffering.

3 I spoke with representatives at Clinton's campaign office in Brooklyn, and also reached out to Clinton via her public/campaign email to certify that she has seen *Ruined*. Unfortunately, I have not been able to verify that she has seen the production and that her efforts in Africa in 2009 were inspired by the play. Given the timing of her trip and the proximity of the Kennedy Center production, it seems likely that Clinton was at least aware of the piece if she had not actually seen or read it. Many articles discussing productions of *Ruined* link Clinton's efforts in 2009 to the impact of the play.

4 Directed by David Mold.

5 For more information, see: www.fistulafoundation.org/students-at-marymount-manhattan-college-raise-funds-for-women-in-dr-congo/.

Works cited

Bentley, Eric. *The Life of Drama.* New York: Applause Books. 1964. Print.

Berton, Misha. "The Road to 'Ruined': Drama at Intiman Is a Powerful Tale of Human Resilience in Wartime." *The Seattle Times.* July 8, 2010. Web. Accessed July 31, 2014.

Blau, Herbert. *The Dubious Spectacle: Extremities of Theater, 1967–2000*. Minneapolis: University of Minnesota Press, 2002. Print.

Brecht, Bertolt. *Brecht on Theatre: The Development of an Aesthetic*. Trans. John Willet. New York: Hill and Wang, 1964. Print.

Depalma, Julia. "Arena's Page." *ArenaStage.org*. June 6, 2011. Web. Accessed August 13, 2014.

Gerould, Daniel, ed. "Introduction." *American Melodrama*. New York: Performing Arts Journal Publication, 1983. 7–29. Print.

Hughes, Amy. *Spectacles of Reform: Theater and Activism in Nineteenth-Century America* Ann Arbor: University of Michigan Press, 2012. Print.

Hurwitt, Robert. "Lynn Nottage's 'Ruined,' 'Fabulation' Open." *SFGate*. February 27, 2011. Web. Accessed August 7, 2014.

Mason, Jeffrey, B. *Melodrama and the Myth of America*. Bloomington: Indiana University Press, 1993. Print.

McConachie, Bruce. *Melodramatic Formations: American Theater and Society 1820–1870*. Iowa City: University of Iowa Press, 1992. Print.

McGee, Celia. "Approaching Brecht by Way of Africa." *The New York Times*. January 25, 2009. Web. Accessed November 11, 2014.

Nottage, Lynn. "On Ruined." *Know Before You Go*. La Jolla Playhouse, November 2010. Web. Accessed July 17, 2014.

———. *Ruined*. New York: Theatre Communications Group, 2009. Print.

Olopade, Dayo. "The Root Interview: Lynn Nottage on 'Ruined' Beauty." *The Root*. March 1, 2010 Web. Accessed August 1, 2014.

Pixérécourt, Rene Charles de. *Four Melodramas*. Trans. Marvin Carlson and Daniel Gerould. New York: Martin E. Segal Theatre Center Publishing, 2002. Print.

Schneider, Rebecca. "Performance Remains." *Performance Research: A Journal of Performing Arts* 6.2 (2001): 100–108. Print.

States, Bert. O. *Great Reckonings in Little Rooms: On the Phenonomenology of Theater.* Berkeley: University of California Press, 1985. Print.

Whoriskey, Kate. "Introduction." *Ruined*. New York: Theatre Communications Group, 2009. ix–xii. Print.

Wilson, Emily. "The Power of 'Ruined." *Women's Media Center*. April 14, 2007. Web. Accessed August 6, 2014.

Chapter 8

Renegotiating realism

Hybridity of form and political potentiality in *Ruined*

Jeff Paden

In her work for theatre, Lynn Nottage articulates connections between bodies, histories, and ethnicities by examining the impulses and institutions that have erased them. Her plays constitute projects of reclamation that sift through the sediment of society to unearth cultural artifacts that have gone missing or unnoticed. Nottage continues this ethic by (re)locating the under-examined experiences of Congolese women in *Ruined* (2009). The play's unflinching depiction of the epidemic of rape plaguing the Democratic Republic of the Congo (DRC)[1] during its brutal civil war materialized from a series of interviews Nottage conducted in Uganda with women who survived brutal sexual attacks by Congolese militia. This focus on survivor testimony disrupts the dominant narrative of the civil war in the DRC as a conflict over natural resources and territory by grafting the violations of these women into a public discourse that has widely dismissed or underreported them. Nottage explained in a 2010 interview that *Ruined* constitutes an effort to retain the complexity of the situation in the DRC, and that there is more to these stories than strict binaries of rapist/survivor, militia/rebel: "I wanted to paint a three-dimensional portrait of the women caught in the middle of armed conflicts; I wanted to understand who they were beyond their status as victims" (Gener 118). This politic of bringing the experiences of women of color to bear in the theatre has informed Nottage's story of a masterful seamstress at the dawn of the twentieth century (*Intimate Apparel*), a young woman coming into womanhood and political awareness in 1950s Brooklyn (*Crumbs from the Table of Joy*), and a wife who with one word reduces her abusive husband to a smoldering heap of ashes (*POOF!*). Yet what distinguishes *Ruined* in Nottage's oeuvre is her desire for the play to galvanize political action from spectators: "I wanted to have a conversation with an audience who may not necessarily know what was going on, or who does know what is going on but didn't feel compelled to act" (Nottage). While an argument can be made that many playwrights considering human rights violations hope their work will bring about some semblance of change in policy or some abatement of pain for the survivors, Nottage, as amply documented in interviews and the introduction to the published text of the play, sought to engineer such outcomes through an ethnographic, activist dramaturgy. For instance, Nottage famously abandoned her initial Brechtian concept for the play's form out of concern that its didactic, agitprop demands would diffuse the potential for political action, reasoning that, "[people] react more out of emotion than when they are preached to, told how to feel" (McGee 4).[2] Nottage's intention for *Ruined* to bring about sociopolitical agency out of the alchemy of dramatic form and political content has garnered a large degree of cultural capital. In 2009, representatives from various human rights organizations as well as United Nations officials attended the play's premiere production at Manhattan Theatre Club in New York City. A few months later, the United States Senate invited Nottage to testify before the Foreign Relations joint subcommittee entitled "Rape and Violence Against Women in the Democratic Republic of the Congo."[3] At a reception following the hearing, Quincy Tyler Bernstine, the actress who originated the role of Salima in both the Goodman Theatre and Manhattan Theatre Club productions, performed the play's most explicit monologue regarding the sexual and emotional violence in the DRC.[4] *Ruined* went on to dominate the 2009–10 theatre awards season by earning the Drama Desk Award, the Obie Award, and the Pulitzer Prize for Drama, among others.[5] These instances of the play's widespread visibility and positive reception by both artistic and political institutions suggest the efficacy of Nottage's strategy to instigate political activism through the play's realistic elements.

Despite this recognition from influential governing bodies and activist entities, critics of the play remain skeptical about the disparity between the play's horrific subject matter and its innocuous conclusion. At the end of the play Mama Nadi, Nottage's departure from Brecht's ethically conflicted Mother Courage, finally accepts merchant/smuggler Christian's persistent professions of love, and the two dance, timidly but tenderly, as the strands of colored lights that snake across the ceiling of Mama's brothel dim to black. Robert Feldberg of *The Herald News* cites the conclusion as evidence that "Nottage succumbs to a desire to project hope and happiness both of which she's established as extremely unlikely by having Christian playfully woo the reluctant Mama Nadi in a scene set out of an old-fashioned

romantic comedy. It's too trivial, a cuddly ending to an otherwise resonant, deeply felt evening of theatre" (D09). Robert Cushman of the
National Post made the case more bluntly: "In *Ruined*, form and content are at war, and content wins" (T07). Feldberg and Cushman question whether the play's conclusion acclimates audiences to atrocity at
the very moment it must ignite their moral outrage, and whether the
cessation of the play's story of trauma signals (perhaps unconsciously)
the cessation of actual trauma in the DRC. However, the implication
that the play falls victim or surrenders to realism's demands for a satisfying, dance-back-into-society dénouement dismisses not only how
Nottage harnesses the form for her particular political aims, but also
the potentiality for realism to productively and ethically stage human
rights violations.

Ben Brantley's review of *Ruined* for *The New York Times* provides a
more nuanced yet no less conflicted consideration of this approach to the
play. While he characterizes it as "a comfortable, old-fashioned drama
about an uncomfortable of-the-moment subject" (C1), he also hypoth-
esizes that Nottage cleverly deployed the play's form as a strategy for
garnering her audience's sentiment: "Nottage . . . hooks her audience
with promises of a conventionally structured, purposefully plotted play,
stocked with sympathetic characters and informative topical detail"
(C1). Brantley acknowledges the impact of this strategy: "precisely for
its artistic caution, *Ruined* is likely to reach audiences averse to more
adventurous, confrontational theatre" (C1). A strange duality exists
within Brantley's to and fro argument: on the one hand, he champions
the play's elements of realism as a conduit for bringing the horrors of the
DRC to bear for audiences unaccustomed to encountering such violence
in the theatre; on the other, his concern for the political efficacy of
the play's conclusion implies that Nottage's "artistic caution" might
not go far enough and, consequently, may sanitize rather than accentuate the terrors of the war waging in the DRC. Brantley's observations
suggest that *Ruined* inhabits an ethically complicated space – between
the playwright engineering an audience's confrontation with atrocities
that play on national stages, and the choice to package those violations in a culturally recognizable theatrical form. As such, the critical
response to the play questions whether realism – which maintains a
strict boundary between performer and spectator via the fourth wall –
compromises the political potentiality of the play and therefore dismantles rather than manufactures the audience's political action. That
being said, while Brantley sees caution, and where Feldberg and Cushman see capitulation in regards to the play's dramaturgical form, I see

Lynn Nottage maneuvering realism's limitations, renegotiating the form to accomplish a particular activist agenda. She achieves this by drawing attention to the act of witnessing itself.

I propose that in an effort to instigate political action, the play's deployments of songs and representations of violence (in the staging of bodies in pain, and the staging of an actual act of violence) work in tandem to disrupt the boundary between performer and spectator that realism seeks to abide. Through this cracked barrier, what Nicholas Ridout calls "the rupture in the machinery of illusion" (88), *Ruined* employs a hybridity of form that clears space for Nottage's ethnographic activist dramaturgy to take root. Marla Carlson and Kaja Silverman each provide a theoretical apparatus for examining how this process of ethical witnessing works.

In *Performing Bodies in Pain*, Carlson proposes a theoretical counterpoint to Elaine Scarry's argument that pain remains distinctive among human sensations because of its inexpressibility and therefore its unshareability.[6] She situates theatrical performances of pain as a potent strategy for marshalling an audience's political response to scenes of atrocity:

> Because pain so powerfully solicits the spectator's engagement, aestheticized physical suffering plays a vital role in communities of sentiment and consolidating social memory, which in turn shapes the cultural and political realities that cause spectators to respond in different ways at different times.
>
> (Carlson 2)

Carlson's theory helps elucidate what pained bodies do onstage and how Nottage's staging of multiple bodies in pain – women who have been raped and remain perpetually wounded – elicits audience empathy and therefore "serves a vital function in producing concerted public action" (9). Alongside Carlson, Kaja Silverman's *World Spectators* details how audiences may interpret pained bodies onstage and how recognition of suffering in the world mobilizes into actual political action. She links the ontology of pained bodies to spectatorship: "it is only insofar as creatures and things appear that they can be" (Silverman 7). Here Silverman reinterprets Martin Heidegger's "being-there" or "dasein" as an action rather than simply an ontological position. In *Being and Time*, for instance, daesin entails not only "to be in the world," but also "alongside the world" (Heidegger 155–6). Being in the world and alongside the world occurs concomantly rather than exclusively or sequentially, indicating that recognizing the presence of another person in the world demands that one takes action on behalf of that person. Silverman calls this witnessing an ethic of care – "we make room for other creatures and things. . . . to come into the light: to move from invisibility to visibility" (32). Applied to the theatre, this ethic of care as an act of world spectatorship reminds both artist and audience that they are not exonerated from coming to terms with and intervening in the catastrophes of the world. To be more precise, world spectatorship demonstrates that a gaze that takes full account of the pain of others functions as a conduit through which theatre audiences may consider strategies for alleviating or stemming violence against society's most vulnerable citizens.

Considering Carlson and Silverman in tandem foregrounds my proposal that Nottage circumvents realism's limitations by renegotiating what realism expects from audiences. With this in mind, I want to resituate the play's conclusion as a messy, complicated, unfinished dénouement that dramatically calls for audience intervention rather than placates the viewer. The critical reaction to the play fixates on the conclusion as a barometer for the play's political success, but by reading the conclusion through the critically unattended violent acts that precede it, a more nuanced understanding of the play's efficacy in delivering on Nottage's political and ethical hope emerges.

Illuminating the play's use of songs functions as an important precursor to analyzing moments where *Ruined* recalibrates realism's form by deploying scenes of pained bodies and staged violence. The action of the play occurs in Mama Nadi's bar-brothel in "a small mining town [in] the Ituri rain forest [of the] Democratic Republic of the Congo" (Nottage 5). As the first scene commences, Mama Nadi reluctantly strikes a deal with merchant/smuggler Christian to take on two new employees in exchange for continued access to the lipstick and other scarce commodities he provides: Salima, whose husband Fortune exiled her when Congolese militia captured and then repeatedly raped her over the course of five months; and Sophie, Christian's niece and the survivor of a rape with a bayonet that has obliterated her womb and therefore her capacity to bear children. Christian turns to Mama Nadi because "here at least I know she'll be safe. Fed" (15). Mama Nadi puts Salima to work as a prostitute; Sophie must sing while the bar's patrons drink and carouse. In Act One, scene two, a month has elapsed since the women's arrival, and Salima and Sophie are still adjusting to life in the brothel. "*Salima, wearing a shiny gold midriff, a colorful traditional wrap and mismatched yellow heels, shoots pool, doing her best to ignore the occasional lustful leers of the Soldiers. . . . Sophie plows through an*

upbeat dance song, accompanied by guitar and drums" (Nottage 19–20).
She sings,

> You come here to forget,
> You say drive away all regret
> And dance like it's the ending
> The ending of the war.

(Nottage 20)

The song's buoyant, festive tempo seems antithetical to this environment, serving as a strange backdrop to the taut tension within the bar as
rebel soldiers greedily drink beer and aggressively dance with Salima
and another prostitute, Josephine. The song concludes abruptly when
a belligerent rebel soldier roughly grabs Mama Nadi's hand after she
refuses to accept a small piece of coltan as payment for sex with Sophie.[7]
In an effort to restore relative calm and protect Sophie, Mama Nadi
convinces the soldier to dance with Salima instead: "Salima is better
dancer. I promise" (Nottage 23). In Act One, scene four, Sophie sings
another song, a slow, soulful ballad about "A rare bird on a limb [who]
sings a song heard by a few, a few patient and distant listeners" (Nottage 38). Her lyrics about yearning to be recognized and rescued fall on
distracted ears, as the miners and soldiers inhabiting the bar think only
of pleasure, not politics. Mama Nadi's place seems anything but the safe
space Christian envisioned for Sophie and Salima. In fact, this moment
makes his hope seem foolishly misguided. The bar remains perpetually
permeable, a tinderbox of potential brutality toward these women. How
can one possibly think about the ending of the war in this place where the
conflict seems so acute and near?

On the surface these songs may function, as Ben Brantley observes,
as "a means for excavating character, of uncovering scars" (C1).
However, I read the songs as a remnant of Nottage's original Brechtian
vision and a marker of the play's hybridity of form since they comment on the gendered violence at the core of the play's dramatic action
while simultaneously commenting on the audience's ability to witness
these staged acts of violence without acting. The theatre of modernity –
in which realism has thrived – facilitates a specific mode of spectatorship where brilliantly lit stages and darkened auditoriums afford a
large degree of privilege (and therefore power) for the spectator and
a small degree of privacy (and therefore power) to the performer. In
this dialectical relationship, the hypervisibility of the performer onstage
facilitates a concealing of the spectator in the unlit house; the performer

works, the spectator watches. Consequently, plays that utilize elements of realism to configure moments of atrocity run the risk of perpetuating a system of looking where audiences may consume images of pained bodies without a thought for what action that kind of looking demands. Nottage deploys the songs in *Ruined* as a counterbalance to this tendency. Thus, Sophie's song about forgetting and dancing like it's the end of war indicts spectators that considered an evening at the theatre an escape from the travails of the world. The song "A Rare Bird" speaks even more directly, inquiring as to whether the audience will really see these survivors and really hear these accounts of violations in the DRC *without* acting on their behalf. By exposing the audience's gaze in this reworking of realism, the play takes the first steps in initiating an ethic of care. Furthermore, in relation to the critical reception of the play, these songs signal that *Ruined* intends to expose and instigate rather than accommodate and placate.

The play's songs trouble the privileged gaze of the spectator, enabling Nottage to lay a foundation for ethically staging pained bodies as a means of assembling a political, activist response from the audience. *Ruined* sets this in motion by exploring the range of the corporeal ramifications of the civil war and rendering the wounded body hyper-visible. The stage directions make multiple references to Josephine's "enormous disfiguring black scar circumventing her stomach" (Nottage 34), and that this scar remains apparent to the audience when she dresses in the backroom and when she seductively dances for Mama Nadi's customers. As a "ruined" woman, Sophie's scars mark both internal and external wounds. Mama Nadi, for instance, comments that Sophie must clean "down below" because "it smells like the rot of meat" (Nottage 17).[8] These repeated manifestations of the range of pain that Josephine and Sophie endure underscores the personal and political realities of the play – how these women are forced to continue on with their lives in the midst of war, despite the sufferings they carry in and on their bodies; how they struggle to dance, sing, make love with profound physical, emotional, and psychic pain. These references to pained bodies might seem less horrific than the more brutal, explicit attempted rape that follows, but these embodied narratives of pain are no less staged, no less immediate, and no less connected to the empathetic reaction Nottage hopes to garner from the spectator. Marla Carlson argues that the formation of communities of sentiment and therefore the mobilization of political action requires repeated confrontations with the pained body: "the community of sentiment doesn't begin to coalesce until someone reperforms the pain by speaking it, writing it, displaying its image, or acting it out – all forms of public speech that constitute a politics of pity and contribute to a plan of action in response to the pain" (155). By staging the repeated ramifications of the civil war directly on the bodies of these women, *Ruined* signifies and materializes the wide array of costs such violence engenders. As a result, the survivors of this violence emerge so that spectators may see them fully and, according to Carlson and Silverman, be moved to act. Most importantly, Nottage's deployment of the pained body foreshadows the play's staging of an act of violence that asks the audience to witness and either accept and be complicit with it, or contest it with action and advocacy.

As the play's deployment of violence shifts from representations of pained bodies to the staging of a violent act, Nottage makes greater demands on both her dramaturgical form and her spectators. As part of her business strategy and in order to keep the civil war at bay, Mama Nadi takes great pains to regulate some semblance of security within the bar. She meticulously monitors any discussion of politics while maintaining a pragmatic egalitarianism that accommodates the pleasures of both the militia (led by the charming yet ferocious Commander Osembenga) and the rebels (led by Jerome Kisembe). Her business and her safety hinge on her ability to successfully negotiate these two leaders, particularly Osembenga, who delivers a strict command to "keep your doors closed to rebel dogs" (Nottage 45). She is astonishingly adept at this intricate dance. She creates a space where the war temporarily suspends – this respite of relative peace and escape is, after all, the product she sells to both sides of the conflict. However the immediate threat of violence, signaled in the sporadic AK-47 gunfire that reverberates beyond the confines of the canteen, seems to creep closer and closer with each scene. As the play progresses, Mama Nadi struggles to keep the constituents of her business – the women she simultaneously protects and exploits and her warring clientele – from colliding.

At the beginning of Act Two, scene six, Mr. Harari, an affable but opportunistic Lebanese jewel merchant, desperately attempts to persuade Mama Nadi to abandon the business and flee the escalating violence. He attempts to reason with her, "there is no shame in leaving, Mama. Part of being in business is knowing when to cut your losses and get out" (Nottage 89). Unsurprisingly, Mr. Harari's forewarning comes to fruition. Osembenga enters the bar, furiously accusing Mama Nadi of entertaining Kisembe and his rebels against his orders. With Osembenga's arrival, the relatively calm environment of the canteen rapidly disintegrates. *"The sound of chaos, shouting, gunfire, grows with intensity. Government soldiers pour in. A siege. A white hot flash. The generator blows!*

Streams of natural light pour into the bar" (Nottage 92). The secluded enclave Mama carved out of this brutal civil war has been penetrated. Up until this moment, the play has obliquely presented the ubiquitous brutality and sexual violations of the DRC, explained in dreadful detail by Sophie, Salima, and Josephine, but always left unseen. However, that structure alters dramatically here. The violence becomes explicit: one of Osembenga's soldiers grabs Josephine's arm, forces her to the floor, tears the clothes from her body, and attempts to rape her. The chaos only stalls when Salima emerges from the backroom "A pool of blood forms in the middle of her dress, blood drips down her legs" (Nottage 94). She has self-aborted the child conceived following the repeated rapes she suffered at the hands of the soldiers. With a triumphant smile on her face, she proclaims what could be the play's refrain, "You will not fight your battles on my body anymore" (Nottage 94).

Prior to this moment, scenes inside Mama Nadi's bar have been replete with those elements Brantley identifies as enticing for audiences: Sophie's sad but soulful singing; Josephine's erotic dancing for the brothel customers; the flirtatious repartee between Mama Nadi and Christian. While the play alludes to the ramifications of rape through Josephine's scars and Sophie's fistula, actual violent acts of the civil war remained distant because they remained unseen. During this scene, however, the bar transforms into a contested space. Osembenga's violence and Salima's abortion and suicide both expose the false pretense of Mama Nadi's political neutrality and indict the political/military institutions of the DRC that repetitively terrorize and brutalize Congolese women. Marla Carlson positions this kind of plot structure which demarcates victims and perpetrators as an imperative for plays (like *Ruined*) that set out to transform audiences into empathetic allies with the survivors of unspeakable violations. Such plays:

> typically embed scenes of torture and execution within a narrative framework designed to position spectators on the side of the character who suffers, drawing us into a community of sentiment with respect to an issue of social justice. We are most often wooed to pity the character's suffering and to oppose the agent who inflicts it.
>
> (Carlson 158)

In this way, Salima's proclamation, "you will not fight your battles on my body anymore," marshals the spectator's political will and thereby fortifies Nottage's political hopes for the play.

That being said, I recognize an even more complex and complicating layer of the play's dramaturgical and political tactics in this moment: Salima's pronouncement could also configure the audience not as political allies but as co-conspirators in the socioeconomic underpinnings of the civil war in the DRC. In an interview with *American Theatre*, Nottage reveals that *Ruined* calls attention to how U.S. audience members are subjects of a nation state that participates in the conflict through a desire for easy access to affordable electronic products:

> I want Americans to understand that they have a very deep investment in what happens in Africa and in the Congo. We're beneficiaries of the abundance of resources that exist there. About 90 percent of coltan . . . comes from the Congo. We're invested in the instability there. As long as they can extract coltan cheaply, we continue to buy our cell phones and laptops for very little. I want Americans to acknowledge that we have a stake in the war that's being fought there.
>
> (Gener 122)

Berkeley Repertory Theatre's 2011 production of *Ruined* made this connection more overt with the program insert "Coltan: From the Congo to You," which traced linkages between the rape of Congolese women and the wrangling for coltan and other natural resources that power the smartphones resting in audience member's pockets and bags. Here the play script and a production of it successfully suture what happens onstage to what happens in the world, thereby opening up possibilities for spectators to regard the pain of others and, as Silverman argues, forge an ethic of care that makes political action more likely.

Yet, it is possible to raise the stakes of this moment even further. While Salima's declaration and subsequent death, according to Nottage, function as implicit indictments of the United States' involvement with the civil war in the DRC, the play also leaves open the possibility for a more provocative engagement with the audience. While the stage directions stipulate that Salima speaks her final lines to the male characters who have harmed her (Osembenga, his soldiers, and Fortune), there is also the possibility that Salima delivers these dying words to the audience. As a result, both the play and performer, for the first time, unsettle realism's protocol by acknowledging the gaze of the spectator. Nicholas Ridout argues that when the fourth wall is breached in this way – perhaps the most fiercely fortified element of realism – the political economy of the theatre crumbles ever so slightly as the spectator's desire and expectation to remain unseen dissipate:

The theatre invites and seduces this desire and then, in the reverse gaze which is perhaps the key signifier of its ontological distinction from film and television, betrays it, dumping you back where you are, in your seat, to nurse the shame of having your desire thus exposed. Dumped back in your seat, thrown back upon yourself. (88)

When the boundary between performer and audience gives way, the spectator experiences a startling moment of self-reflexivity, coming to terms with the loss of a theatrical illusion that differentiates events that occur onstage and those that occur in the world. In regards to *Ruined*, this moment has the potential to further crystallize Nottage's political intentions for the audience by weakening their ability to regard the pain of others and turn away or remain politically inert. As a result, Salima's death functions as the play's climax not simply because it stages violence so starkly, but because here Nottage renegotiates realism's limitations so dramatically. The play's hybridity of form through the deployment of songs, the staging of pained bodies, and the spectators' visceral confrontation with their involvement in the violence ravaging the DRC, makes a reconsideration of the critical response to the play's conclusion necessary.

As noted earlier, the core concern of the critical reception to the play's conclusion centers on whether the romanticized, classical dance-back-into-society ending marks a hollow humanity that skews Nottage's political intents. Feminist critic Jill Dolan laments that the conclusion seemingly dismantles the gender politics so earnestly forged throughout the play, resulting in a diminished sense of political immediacy:

> Suddenly, the play becomes a heterosexual romance, in which Mama and her girls are redeemed by the love of a good man. . . . Would that Nottage had maintained her singular, Brechtian vision of the consequences of war for women to a more bitter end, instead of capitulating to realism's mandate that narratives resolve with heterosexual marriage that solves everything. The gender politics of the Congo that *Ruined* describes with such force are compromised by this conservative happy ending.
>
> (Dolan)

Dolan's critique of this apparent reinscription of heteronormativity misses how the play draws attention to skepticism about this type of outcome. Early on, Mama Nadi ridicules a romance novel given to Sophie by her uncle, Christian: "No, the problem is I already know how it's going to end. There'll be kissing, fucking, a betrayal, and then the woman will foolishly surrender her heart to an underserving man" (Nottage 51). In the last scene of the play, when Christian proposes to Mama Nadi that they work and love together, she remains cynical and defensive: "What would we do, professor? How would it work? The two of us? Imagine. You'd wander. I'd get impatient. I see how men do. We'd argue, fight, and I'd grow resentful. You'd grow jealous. We know this story. It's tiresome" (99). This resistance, the audience learns moments later, is because Mama herself is ruined. Her dismissal of Christian is rooted in shame and fear of the past violence that has marked her body. Here the play complicates the tidy resolution that Dolan excoriates. Since the play traverses the boundary between performer and spectator that realism fiercely maintains, first in its deployment of songs, then by staging bodies in pain, and finally by more starkly staging acts of violence when Osembenga attacks Josephine and Salima perishes, this conclusion rings strange, hollow. Likewise, the conclusion appears incompatible with the fierce independence Mama maintains throughout the play in order to survive. Does she actually love Christian and take a leap of faith to trust him? Or, does she choose the best survival option available to her within this landscape of perpetual violence and violations? Since the play has deliberately and meticulously marked the violence plaguing the DRC, Mama's decision to accept Christian is not altogether unencumbered.

Additionally, by focusing so intently on Mama Nadi and Christian's union, the critical reception of the play overlooks Sophie, who remains on the scene's periphery. In many readings and in the Manhattan Theatre Club production, Sophie looks on hopefully and happily, pulling Josephine into the room to watch too, as childlike symbols of realism's traditional heteronormative familial resolution. However, could another reading of this moment also fulfill Nottage's political intention for the play? Sophie's presence here also serves as a reminder of victims in the DRC who may never see a happy cessation to the conflict. Viewed in this way, Sophie appears silent, guarded, a reminder that this new pairing might deteriorate into a catastrophic disunion similar to that between Salima and Fortune. While Mama Nadi tentatively entertains the possibility of resolution, Sophie looks on, hopeful but still ruined. Here the play renders hope and love as very ambivalent things, interweaving and overlapping with uncertainty. Since uncertainty and irresolution remain, spectators are compelled to consider ways to act on behalf of women like Sophie, Mama Nadi, and Salima. Within this final framework, Nottage sparks an ethic of care that empowers a community of sentiment to not only recognize the necessity for concerted political action on behalf of victims of war and sexual violence, but also to enact it in material ways.

The critical response to *Ruined* reflects a long-standing tension between the ethics and aesthetics of representing violence. Theodor Adorno's frequently cited argument that "to write poetry after Auschwitz is barbaric" (34), and Giorgio Agamben's dictate that representation and language always buckle under the sheer scale of atrocity, with "facts so real that, by comparison, nothing is truer" (12), have rendered the theatre a laboratory where artistic forms are tested and retested, reconstituted and recycled until an equivalent image or gesture or utterance for that atrocity emerges. Postmodernism has been the beneficiary of this creative labor: Brecht's *verfremdungseffekt*, Ernst Toller's expressionistic dramaturgy, and Erwin Piscator's collapsing of film and live performance functioned as efforts to conceptualize the devastations of the two world wars; Jane Taylor's employment of puppets in *Ubu and the Truth Commission* (1997) sought both to protect the identities of commission witnesses, and to focus audience attention on the testimonies themselves rather than the actor's skill in delivering and embodying them. These "fractures and fragmentations" of theatrical forms, according to Leshu Torchin, "supply the favored aesthetics for their ability to hint at the violence of the event upon self and expression" (6). Robert Skloot, in *The Theatre of Genocide*, goes beyond Torchin's prescription by calling for a disposal of reliance on realism by "replacing it with other forms that arouse conscience and deeper understanding" (23). However, this kind of embargo on realism or any other style as an appropriate frame for staging atrocity seems counterintuitive to the theatre's capacity for extending the limitations of language and dramaturgical form. Playwright Erik Ehn confirms this point by acknowledging that theatre's attempts at representing atrocity will always be messy and unresolvable because atrocity proves equally unordered and irresolute. Unlike Adorno and Skloot, he positions the limitations of language and representation as a fertile place. "Because [language] is inadequate, it is right. There is plenty of room. There is only room" (Ehn 10). While the theatre continues to discover ways to unmoor itself from the constraints of language and form, it will also continue to reconstitute its capacity for staging and speaking those things to which the world often shows an unwillingness to listen. In fact, it must do this.

Lynn Nottage joins these and other artists testing representational strategies for staging violence in order to bring awareness to violations that play out on international stages, and to ally with the survivors of these devastations. With *Ruined*, she renegotiates realism's and language's limitations and, like her artistic predecessors and contemporaries, puts these dramaturgical implements to work in compelling ways. By expanding realism's capacity to ethically represent atrocity, *Ruined* not only makes a clearing from which other forms, plays, and tactics will sprout, it also insures that the atrocities and survivors in the DRC remain visible rather than forgotten. In the fight for human rights, this kind of visibility remains an indispensable tool, for it renders crimes against humanity as actual and witnesses to these violations as accountable. The Human Rights Watch underscores this point in their mission statement: "We scrupulously *investigate* abuses, *expose* the facts widely, and *pressure* those with power to respect rights and secure justice" (Human Rights Watch, emphases mine). The theatre likewise has the potential to facilitate such relentless and multiperspectival witnessing through its public exchanges between performers and spectators. Yet Leshu Torchin cautions that "witnessing publics are not enduring, eternal, or general formation, but temporary and contingent collectives hailed through address and encouraged into an active engagement and responsibility with what they see" (14). As a result, the world requires a steady stream of plays, performances, and encounters to reform and reactivate these communities of witnesses. *Ruined* must be accompanied by other artistic works that publically address images of the ruptured body in an effort to make sense of the world, its catastrophes, and potential responses. Lynn Nottage's hybridity of form provides an ethically and artistically productive schematic for future playwrights that hope to advocate for the survivors of atrocities, both at home and abroad.

Notes

1 For a clear and concise explication of the civil war in the DRC, see Kiernan, Ben. *Blood and Soil: A World History of Genocide and Extermination from Sparta to Darfur* (New Haven: Yale University Press, 2007): 542–56. Print.

2 In the preface to the published play, Kate Whoriskey, who directed both the world premiere at the Goodman Theatre in Chicago and the New York premiere at Manhattan Theatre Club, traces the trajectory of this shift in form from Brecht to realism. She remarks that after Nottage interviewed the first group of women it became impossible to imagine how to distance audiences from these harrowing accounts of violence and survival.

3 The full transcript of the hearing, "Confronting Rape and Other Forms of Violence against Women in Conflict Zones; Spotlight: The Democratic Republic of Congo and Sudan" is available at www.foreign.senate.gov/hearings/2009/hrg090512p.html.

4 A video recording of the performance is available at: www.youtube.com/watch?v=SsqyhiaacO8.

5 These include the Outer Critics Circle Award for Outstanding Play, the New York Drama Critics Circle Award, and the Lucille Lortel Award for Outstanding Play.

6 See Scarry, Elaine. *The Body in Pain: The Making and Unmaking of the World* (New York: Oxford University Press, 1985).

7 Coltan (or columbite-tantalite), a dull black metallic ore is a precious commodity in the DRC because as a high-charge conductor it proves essential in the manufacture of mobile phones, video gaming systems, microprocessors, and vast arrays of electronic equipment. Some estimates place 80% of the world's coltan resources in the Congo. As a result, the demand for coltan has bred struggle and brutality as warlords and the military commit staggering atrocities in an effort to control coltan mines and their enormous profits.

8 This also seems to be a reference to fistula, the medical condition affecting many rape survivors in the DRC. Fistula occurs from a perforation in the tissues separating the vaginal wall from the urinary tract and/or rectum. Typically, the result is uncontrollable leakage through the vagina of urine, feces, or both. An incessant rotting smell accompanies this condition. In the *American Theatre* interview cited in this essay, Nottage recounts that many Congolese women did not want to speak with her out of embarrassment because of this condition.

Works cited

Adorno, Theodor, Samuel Weber, and Shierry W. Nicholsen. *Prisms*. Cambridge: MIT Press, 1981. Print.

Agamben, Giorgio. *Remnants of Auschwitz: The Witness and the Archive*. New York: Zone Books, 2000. Print.

Brantley, Ben. "War's Terrors, Through a Brothel Window." *The New York Times*. February 11, 2009. C1. Print.

Carlson, Marla. *Performing Bodies in Pain: Medieval and Post-Modern Martyrs, Mystics, and Artists*. New York: Palgrave Macmillan, 2010. Print.

Cushman, Robert. "The Great Escape: Reality of *Ruined* Is Both Powerful and Overpowering." *National Post*. January 29, 2011. T07. Print.

Dolan, Jill. "*Ruined*, by Lynn Nottage." Web blog post. *The Feminist Spectator*, March 13, 2009. Web. Accessed April 6, 2014.

Ehn, Erik. *Soulagraphie*. Chicago: 53rd Street Press, 2012. Print.

Feldberg, Robert. "Drama Brings Home Violence Against Women in War-Torn Congo." *The Herald News*. February 11, 2009. D09. Print.

Gener, Randy. "In Defense of *Ruined*." *American Theatre* 27.8 (October 2010): 118–22. Print.

Heidegger, Martin. *Being and Time*. New York: Harper, 1962. Print.

Human Rights Watch. "About Us." www.hrw.org/about. Web. Accessed June 17, 2014.

McGee, Celia. "Approaching Brecht, by Way of Africa." *The New York Times*. January 25, 2009. 4. Print.

Nottage, Lynn. "Lynn Nottage on Her Play *Ruined.*" Interview by Dayo Olo-
    pade. *TheRoot.com.* March 1, 2010. Web. Accessed May 2, 2014.
————. *Ruined.* New York: Theatre Communications Group, 2009. Print.
Ridout, Nicholas P. *Stage Fright, Animals, and Other Theatrical Problems.*
    Cambridge: Cambridge University Press, 2006. Print.
Silverman, Kaja. *World Spectators.* Stanford: Stanford University Press, 2000.
    Print.
Skloot, Robert. *The Theatre of Genocide: Four Plays About Mass Murder in
    Rwanda, Bosnia, Cambodia, and Armenia.* Madison: University of Wisconsin
    Press, 2008. Print.
Torchin, Leshu. *Creating the Witness: Documenting Genocide on Film, Video,
    and the Internet.* Minneapolis: University of Minnesota Press, 2012. Print.

Chapter 9

Land rights and womb rights

Forging difficult diasporic kinships in *Ruined*[1]

Esther J. Terry

In *Ruined* (2009), Lynn Nottage invites audiences to reorder African diasporic kinships by attending the journeys of Mama Nadi, Salima, and Sophie in the Central African forest zone. She deploys a dramaturgy imbricated in "diaspora's very form itself, the transgressive and often unexpected loops of circulation that cannot easily be traced to fixed points of origin" (Pinto 3–4). Nottage charts difficult diasporic choices for the African women who must heal to survive, and who cannot return to territorial or lineal authenticities for safety in belonging. By establishing a house of ruined kinships and ruined bodies amidst ruined lands, Nottage disorders originary claims of belonging to Africa and African diasporas. Who belongs to where? Where belongs to whom? Roots do not hold answers for the women in this play. While national and local militias battle to rule female-bodied reproductive capacities, dispossessing those who do not belong in their imagined futures, corporate and foreign miners strip natural resources.

Nottage uses the play's chaotic terror to interrogate the bases of knowledge that define belonging in order to evict, or dispossess women from landed and familial bonds. She reveals how epistemological restrictions justify the violence in particular kinds of rule, whether imperial or local, regional or national, military or corporate. Mama Nadi, Salima, and Sophie navigate the terrors of war by deflecting militant Swahili and metaphorical equivalencies of lands and female bodies. Throughout, the women ally with and against one another to enact a performative African diaspora, or kinship as always already in the process of becoming. In the final dance, Mama Nadi enacts love, through which Nottage resolves and disarms the violent action of the play. As they shift alliances, the women must grapple with their arrivals at Mama Nadi's as roots/routes of no return, in order to have a chance at navigating the dispossessive chaos that threatens their embodied and territorial existences.

> *Our bodies are our first homes. If we are not safe in our bodies, we are always homeless.*
>
> (Patel, quoted. "Indecent Act")

In *Ruined*, Mama Nadi operates a bar and brothel for the miners, militias, and businessmen who travel around the Ituri Region of the Democratic Republic of the Congo.[2] The residents of Mama Nadi's house, Josephine, Salima, and Sophie, have been sexually assaulted by soldiers and subsequently evicted by their families. They sell food, alcohol, and sex, except Sophie who manages the books. Soldiers sexually assaulted Sophie with a bayonet, leaving her ruined.[3] Businessmen like Christian and Mr. Harari travel through, along with assorted miners. Jerome Kisembe leads a Mayi-mayi militia, defined as rebel by the government, but not necessarily treated as rebel by the locals. General Osembenga leads government forces in the region. Nottage uses historical events, like "Mobutu's brand of chaos," to contextualize the world of the play, but the characters are not restricted or bound by historical events (Nottage 89).[4] Regardless of whether or not a house like Mama Nadi's actually existed in the forest zone does not prevent Nottage from placing the women there.

Violence pervades the resource-rich Central African forest zone, which lies in the eastern regions of the Democratic Republic of the Congo. In the midst of converging, unceasing conflicts, Mama Nadi enforces her house rules: no weapons, no political talk, and Mama always eats first. As the play continues, it becomes challenging for her to enforce neutrality and leisure. In her house, where all forces of violence rest at some point, the women must maneuver while holding the knowledge of imminent disposability in their memories and scars. In previous times and places, perhaps last week in their home or last year at market, miners and soldiers went through women's bodies to acquire lands, and went through lands to acquire resources. Throughout the history of the Central forest zones, European colonizers, national governments, and local militias have all claimed terra nullius, or unmastered lands, as justification for evicting occupants as illegal tenants (Mudimbe 152). The women, victims of recent waves of dispossessive violence, cannot inherit roots, or their families' imagined pasts and ancestral lands. They cannot reproduce children into imagined futures, or grant them routes toward legitimate, landed belonging. Overlapping, conflicting spatiotemporal

restrictions on kinship bind the women as female bodies in multiple illegitimate times and spaces.

In illegitimate spatiotemporalities, African kinship does not exist
and, by extension, the African diaspora also ceases to exist. A locality
may order who belongs where according to multiple variables, such as
paternity, and empire may order who belongs where according to others,
such as available raw materials. A woman then, can both belong as a
reproductive female body and disappear as a ruined lineage, whether or
not she retains her reproductive capacity. She inhabits an epistemological murk, oscillating between (non)existence and (dis)belonging (Hunt,
"Placing African Women's History" 360). This arbitrary murk simmers
as a quagmire through which soldiers distinguish and enforce difference
through mud and blood. Lineages and territories can be designated as
both disposable and critical resources, depending on the day. In the context of the play, Kisembe belongs locally as a legitimate leader, but does
not belong (is not legitimated) nationally. Mama Nadi does not belong
locally to lineages or lands, but rather profitably in her own house. Moreover, Mama Nadi's house stands because the clashes between episte-
mologies of belonging also expose disorders of power, or opportunities
to evade further dispossession.[5]

By invoking a reordering of roots/routes, an allusion to Paul Gilroy's
The Black Atlantic (1993), I mean to draw out epistemological and spatiotemporal assumptions within African and African diasporic belonging. As Samantha Pinto notes:

> Diaspora demands the specificity of times, places, names, and dates,
> all the while claiming its multitudes as its . . . global significance.
> The African Diaspora . . . as a historical phenomenon was formed
> through radical experimentations . . . that built on the political and
> ethical worlds that preceded them and yet demanded their suspen-
> sion in configuring new and frequently terrible categories of knowl-
> edge around difference. (7)

African diaspora, historiographically, evokes inherited continuity and
fosters imagined continental difference across time periods and geographic locations. African diaspora often correlates to Early Modern
roots/routes of transatlantic slave trade, with inherited cultural difference
traced in known sub-Saharan bloodlines.[6] To map a difficult diaspora,
in this chapter, entails imagining networks of cultural production and
alliances of kinship that co-exist in multiple times and spaces.[7] I use the
phrase "difficult diaspora" to emphasize the performativity of African

diasporic kinships in *Ruined*, or the characters' abilities to re-stake kinships despite their disordered, illegitimated existences.

The world of *Ruined* entails a lack of permanence. None of those who reside in Mama Nadi's house can benefit from or bestow geographic or temporal stability. They must seek kinship and healing outside of "fixed points of origin," beyond their ancestral lands and lineages, and outside of their bodies being valued and assaulted as female reproductive networks of kinship. Accordingly, I take up moments where the characters encounter epistemological and spatiotemporal conflicts of belonging: where Swahili appears in the multilingual dialogue, the reproductive equivalencies between bodies of land and females, and the final dance between Mama Nadi and Christian. When characters reorder belonging in these moments, they negotiate and stake new terms for existence. In all of these moments, characters' choices amplify the difficulty of forging African diasporic kinships, and Nottage roots/routes healing through the women's choices to refuse ruinous requirements of arbitrary difference.

> *Millions who are home*
> *are crying*
> *for home*

> (Mugo 80)

Swahili inhabits a difficult murk of linguistic-cultural exchange often surrounded by or enabling violence, from Afroasiatic exchange to European conquests and African resistance networks. Swahili evidences roots/routes of longstanding Afroasiatic networks, based in centuries of trade among Arabic, Shirazi, and Bantu people groups.[8] Swahili also remains implicated in Afroasiatic and European conquests.[9] Swahili slave traders pushed the coastal language up-country. European missionaries and corporations forcibly implemented Swahili as intelligible difference, using it to facilitate their Scramble so they understood what African laborers said.[10] In the early twentieth century, African people groups used the spread of Swahili to mobilize against German and English imperial encroachments.[11] In the mid-twentieth century, leaders like Idi Amin and Julius Nyerere enforced an independent and African difference. They silenced dissidents, implemented Swahili, and dispossessed residents.[12]

In a transatlantic African diaspora, Swahili circulates in the theatre and philosophy of intellectuals like Lorraine Hansberry, Maulana Karenga, and Aimé Césaire.[13] They rooted/routed locatable and inheritable African continuities through Swahilized dialogue and concepts. Their work provides dramaturgical and philosophic precedent for Nottage's deployment of Swahili in her play, even as the historical valences of Swahili make visible the imbrication of ruinous violence and dispossession in the play. Swahili rarely occupies a neutral space in historically imagined worlds. Based on prior adoptions of Swahili by varying political interests, the Swahili in *Ruined* motivates solidarity and oppression, alliance and conflict.

The dialogue occurs mainly in English, with additional words and phrases from French, Swahili, and Lingala. The published script contains a glossary defining Swahili phrases used in the play. The glossary includes sante, a French salutation for cheers, and banga liwa, a Lingala invocation for fear death.[14] The glossary does not include Mayi-mayi, Swahili for Water-water.[15] Yet Mayi-mayi invokes crucial given circumstances for Salima and the play's chaos. Swahili's capability to incorporate French and Lingala, as well as jettison a phrase marked with Swahilized histories, amplifies the arbitrary convergence of claims on who belongs where, by troubling fixed origins of language. Banga liwa, in particular, evidences strategic Swahili roots/routes of dispossession at work in the play.

On his first appearance in Mama Nadi's house, General Osembenga drops banga liwa to instantiate the rightness of the government's presence in the region.

OSEMBENGA: Make a joke, but Kisembe has one goal and that is to make himself rich on your back, Mama. He will burn your crops, steal your women, and make slaves of all your men in the name of peace and reconciliation. Don't believe him. He, and men like him, these careless militias wage a diabolical campaign. They leave stains everywhere they go. And remember the land he claims as his own, it is a national reserve, it is the people's land, our land. And yet he will tell you the government has taken everything, though we're actually paving the way for democracy.

MAMA: I know that, but the government needs to let him know that. But you, I'm only seeing you for the first time. Kisembe, I hear his name every day.

OSEMBENGA: Then hear my name, Commander Osembenga, *banga liwa*. You will hear my name quite a bit from now on.

MAMA: Commander Osembenga, forgive me for not knowing your name. *Karibu.*

(Nottage 44, emphasis in original)

In this moment, Mama Nadi and Osembenga parry verbal blows, negotiating the names that matter in the region. Mama Nadi sidesteps Osembenga's interrogations through tactical feints. Osembenga tries to recruit

Mama by disparaging Kisembe. He accuses the militias of carnage that stains and disrupts kinship through coerced trafficking of sex and labor. The slippage between damaged people and damaged lands points to the central image of the play, where conflicts are "waged not just over women's bodies, but over the ruined body of the Congo herself" (Gener 122). This connection configures governmental forces as protecting and defending the national forest reserve, with Kisembe and Mayi-mayi militias transgressing the feminized forests.

Mama Nadi counters with a thinly veiled critique of Osembenga's absence. Her tactical thrust underscores how epistemological enactments of ownership, usage, and access ensure unceasing conflict. Mama Nadi situates Osembenga within a violence of conquest; the governmental order, as a newcomer, has yet to be legitimated in the region.[16] She situates the already audible Kisembe as an established and authenticated violence. By playing on occupancy in her critique, she reminds him that both imperial and national legal precedents in the area demanded occupancy to prove residency and the right to own forest lands. But Osembenga is still an unestablished newcomer.

Her critique stems from imperial and national legal precedents that defined occupancy according to their own aims, as a strategy to create forest reserves. These precedents passed over people groups who accessed the forests for common usage (such as the Twa and Mbuti), and did not count them as legal occupants (Long 3–11). In effect, Mama Nadi undermines Osembenga's assertion of morally defending the national reserve, by interrogating the spatiotemporal limits of occupancy from which the reserve boundaries were drawn. The reserves are the people's land, according to the comparatively recent government, but not the lands of the Twa or Mbuti, the people groups who remained in the forests during the Bantu migrations thousands of years ago.

In so doing, Mama Nadi insinuates that the government is not the only authority on ownership and occupancy. Her engagement in the debate further signals that residents will not submit without protest; they will challenge illegitimate dispossession. She, and all the characters in the play, *know* Osembenga's kind of violence through the ways his forces root/route disposability in and through lands and bodies. She reminds Osembenga that making the land vacant still requires violence; Kisembe is not his only opposition. Local names and knowledge matter too, and residents can choose to support Kisembe, Osembenga, or neither.

Since Mama does not concede based on derogations of Kisembe, and levels the arbitrary designation of vacant national reserves against the government, Osembenga wields his name and banga liwa to raise the stakes. He changes from recruiting Mama Nadi to pacifying her. He maps nation-state bases of ruling within an already legitimated and authenticated violence from Mobutu Sese Seko, who forcibly implemented Lingala in eastern Zaïre. He re-ordered the audible networks of Zaïrian life to disorder the nation's eastern alliances with French and Swahili (Goyvaerts 309–312). And Mobutu's full name, which he took as an authentic displacement of his baptized Joseph-Désiré, was Mobutu Sese Seko Kuku Ngbendu Wa Za Banga:

> Each name has an ancestral reference. Mobutu Sese means the inveterate defender of the forefathers' land. Mobutu Seko, the audacious warrior who ignores the defeat because his endurance wins. Mobutu Kuku Ngbendu, or Mobutu Wa Za Banga means the powerful warrior going from conquest to conquest without being stopped.
> (Inongo, transl. by Yanga 240)[17]

For Osembenga, Mobutu's nation-state stands as the conquering violent precedent to the ruling government in the play. Osembenga replicates governmental claims to national reserves as authentic conquests, which he and his soldiers will defend as "audacious warriors," "without being stopped." He rejects Mama Nadi's reclamation of the forest reserves, and reminds her to fear death, a command based on knowledge of how Mobutu historically dealt with trespassers.[18] This final thrust motivates Mama Nadi to change her tactics; she requests forgiveness, ceding his legitimated order of the reserves. She welcomes him in with karibu, the Swahili-language greeting for welcome or come near.

By categorizing banga liwa as Swahili, Nottage enables the command to more broadly occupy a cross-continental Bantu kinship. She troubles clear-cut containments of languages that underpin linguistic disciplines and imperial orders of continental African societies (Gardner-Chloros 1–6).[19] A Lingala command to a Swahili welcome engenders implications of Zaïrian nation-state reordering, from west to east. Those who grew up with Lingala and Swahili as one of their mother tongues would recognize the historic conflict embedded in juxtaposing Lingala and Swahili in the Central African forest zone. While this relationship remains, Nottage primarily situates this scene as a Swahili command to a Swahili welcome, inviting a lack of certainty in linguistic difference and shifting the stakes of the confrontation between Osembenga and Mama Nadi.

Each character deploys Swahili toward his or her own claims. Osembenga leverages the play's Swahili to replicate past claims of ownership from Mobutu's reign. Mama Nadi engages Swahili to de-escalate the

tension, and welcome Osembenga's authority over the region. It is a calculated move, and one made in a space where Osembenga has already
agreed to follow Mama's rules by leaving his bullets and weapons at the
door (Nottage 42). Mama Nadi's claim on her business and home remains
firm and substantiated in her Swahili welcome, even as she allows Osembenga's claims to order the world outside her door with a Swahilized
precedent from Mobutu, at least for the moment. In this scene, Swahili
provides roots/routes of ruling authority for government forces and for
Mama Nadi's place. Nottage employs Swahili to further complicate a
murk of overlapping times and spaces, from African diasporic imaginaries in theatrical worlds to violently imposed imaginaries in historical
worlds. Nottage makes visible the performative potential of Swahili as a
tactic for becoming violence and for becoming stability. Swahili becomes
a weapon in the fight over categories of difference, and a tool for position-
ing Central African worlds in transatlantic African diasporic theatre.

The whole land
is crying:
"the waters are bitter
what shall we drink?"

(Mugo 80)

Land-female metaphorical equivalents foster an imperial-local quagmire of heteropatriarchies. Equating reproductivities and fertilities invites
European imperial valences of a passive land, and Bantu or Nilo-Saharan
conventions that require land and women as the spatiotemporal anchors of
legitimated existence.[20] Salima and Sophie must navigate these requirements, with ruined and poisoned bodies, or reproductive fertilities designated as illegitimate networks of belonging. Nottage emphasizes that
the women's families, Osembenga, and Kisembe, will not offer security
and peace from disposability. In Bantu constructions of existence, *to be*
is always defined in relation to *where* or *as what* (Kagame 95).[21] In Bantu
thought, land locates a person and a people group in relation to ancestors and material resources and traditions (Kagamae 91). Women locate
persons and people groups in relation to ancestral alliances and their
growth over time (p'Bitek, Zarowsky). Without these anchors of being,
the residents of Mama Nadi's belong nowhere and to no one; dispossession lives on and in their bodies.

In the play, the scars and wounds of the women echo the damage
exacted on the surrounding forest lands, and amplify the outcomes of
converging ruinous campaigns. As Méndez García notes, "words used
to refer to the mining of coltan can also be used when talking about

sexuality and the female body: the miners plough, penetrate the earth, and, in the process, ruin it for agriculture" (133).[22] Both Mama Nadi and Sophie are ruined, even though Mama Nadi does not reveal her full circumstances until the final scene. Josephine has a disfiguring abdominal scar, and Salima's body grows with "the child of a monster," conceived during her forced concubinage (Nottage 70). Likewise, the land near Yaka-yaka, formerly teeming with life, now "looks like God spooned out heaping mouthfuls of earth, and every stupid bastard is trying to get a taste" (Nottage 40). Just as multiple militant penetrations into female bodies leave permanent scars, multiple mining penetrations into the land engender poison and barrenness.

In Act One, Salima and Sophie enter Mama Nadi's house as trafficked by Christian, a traveling businessman and Sophie's uncle. He introduces Salima: "from a tiny village. No place really. She was, captured by rebel soldiers, *Mayi-mayi*, the poor thing spent nearly five months in the bush as their concubine" (Nottage 12, emphasis in original). Christian affirms the dislocation that qualifies Salima for work and refuge at Mama Nadi's. Salima has "no place," no home and no kin, no roots in the past or routes toward the future. Even though Salima can still reproduce, she cannot give her children an ancestral past or plot of land. Later, she refers to "the child of a monster" in her womb, insisting "there's no telling what it will be" (Nottage 70). Just as the child itself was conceived in volatility and will be birthed into illegitimate belonging, so too does Salima's future appear to hold even greater instability and illegitimacy.

At the top of Act Two, Sophie urges Salima to go out and reunite with her husband, Fortune, who holds vigil outside the brothel's entrance. Salima remains in the back rooms and retraces her route to Mama Nadi's. "I lay there as [the Mayi-mayi soldiers] tore me to pieces . . . Chained like a goat. These men . . . fighting for our liberation" (Nottage 69). Salima uses seemingly paradoxical imagery here, a woman chained and subject to the sexual assaults of local liberation fighters, to rebut Sophie's prediction of a happy, marital reunion. Salima's presence in the play, as a woman who retains her reproductive capacity but still belongs nowhere and to no one, challenges the claims of those who take up the names and practices of freedom fighters. Her physical trauma comes from soldiers in a local militia, like the one headed by Kisembe, Mayi-mayi who assert their local residence and ritual immunity to claim their actions as defensive tactics.

Mayi-mayi invokes historical moments when water was called upon for protection in battle, or for a ritual immunity that would turn bullets into water. In the early twentieth century, Maji Maji named the anti-German uprisings of inland Bantu people groups, such as the

Matumbi, Ngoni, and Hehe (Giblin and Monson 19–23). In Central African Maï-Maï groups, ritualized immunity emerged as a banner against Belgian and United States forces in 1964, Mobutu's forces in the late 1980s, and foreign exploitation of minerals in the early 1990s (Wild 452–454). By linking Salima's trauma to histories of African freedom fighters, Nottage interrogates the consequences of local soldiers fighting over land and women. She exposes Kisembe as an additional cause of ruination in the play. And so, in the middle of Salima's account, Sophie changes tactics. She listens, witnessing and affirming the senselessness of dispossessive violence. "Those men were on a path and we were there. It happened" (Nottage 69).

In Salima's account and Sophie's witnessing, Nottage emphasizes the lack of available alliances, or networks of belonging, for the women in the play. Even though soldiers brought violence on and within the women's bodies, Sophie and Salima would not need to seek refuge in Mama Nadi's house if their families had taken them in. Salima grieves the lack of familial reconciliation:

> I walked into the family compound expecting open arms. An embrace. Five months, suffering. I suffered every single second of it. And my family gave me the back of their heads. And he, the man I loved since I was fourteen, chased me away with a green switch. He beat my ankles raw. And I dishonored him? I dishonored him? . . . He was too proud to bear my shame . . . but not proud enough to protect me from it. Let him sit in the rain.
>
> (Nottage 70)

Even though Salima returned home, damaged but able to heal, her husband Fortune only saw her as a poisoned, shamed body. "He called me a filthy dog, and said I tempted them. . . . I was made poison by their fingers, that is what he said" (Nottage 67). Salima's grief aligns with Christian's choice to bring her and Sophie to Mama Nadi's: the women there can never exist within, return to, the structures of belonging enforced by the nation-state, local leaders, or their own husbands.

In the play, to know ruined earth and to know ruined female bodies is to chart (in)fertile or monstrous futures. No character embodies this more than Sophie. Throughout much of the play, Sophie's ruined body provides the metaphorical equivalent to the land. She endures Josephine belittling her, "so many men have had you that you're worthless." Even Mama Nadi describes Sophie as "damaged goods" (Nottage 37, 16). Mama Nadi extends this metaphor later in the play, by linking virginal value in unconquered women and lands: "My mother taught me that you can follow behind everyone and walk in the dust, or you can walk ahead through the unbroken thorny brush. You may get blood on your ankles, but you arrive first and not in the residue of others" (Nottage 53). And so Sophie, like the overused land, becomes dust. Neither Sophie nor the damaged forests can be located as a beginning or root; they cannot pass on futures.

The play's juxtaposition of land-becomes-dust and female-becomes-dust evokes the concept of "nature-as-conquerable-feminine" from European heteropatriarchies, and the control of female-bodied sexuality under Congolese heteropatriarchies (Fox 9–11; Dolan; Hunt, *Colonial Lexicon*).[23] Yet, the choices Sophie makes with her body defy the apparent finality with which she, as dust, may be conquered. In the middle of Act Two, Sophie threatens Osembenga, "I am dead! Fuck a corpse! What would that make you?" (Nottage 83). Sophie wagers her dispossessed existence as a toxic offensive; she has no locative or reproductive being left that would matter to the times and spaces of governmental heteropatriarchy. Osembenga holds no threat to her. And Sophie's threat, wielding her toxic and evicted body and refusing fear, foreshadows Salima's terminal wager.

At the end of the play, Salima goes so far as to reject her female-bodied reproductive capacity as any kind of battleground. She fatally injures herself and the uncertain future she carries within her body (Nottage 94). In doing so, Salima refuses the ruinous difference that binds her body and child into illegitimate being, apart from recognizable kinships. She removes her body from arbitrarily legitimated inheritances and futures, leaving one less woman and child for the soldiers and miners to dispossess.[24] Sophie's and Salima's ability to reject the fertile orders of belonging, forced on them and the lands around them, exposes the underside of the militant and mining offensives. By assaulting women and the earth based on fertile and reproductive capacities, the soldiers fail to defend against the potential poison that their violence generates.[25] Salima and Sophie deploy a performativity of the female body through their very knowledge of land-female metaphorical equivalents. The female body, like the land, becomes a site of origin and a site of death, a reproductive order of belonging and a toxic network of disbelonging with the ability to poison those who stripped it.

And build
new homes
On whatever
patch of ground
your feet tread

(Mugo 81)

Mama Nadi threatens and refuses heteropatriarchal reproductivities by establishing a place of her own. "I didn't come here as Mama Nadi . . . I stumbled off of that road without two twigs to start a fire. I turned a basket of sweets and soggy biscuits into a business. . . . This is my place, Mama Nadi's" (Nottage 86). Rejecting landed and heteropatriarchal orders of belonging, she forged her own sovereignty of belonging in her house, re-staking her existence. In the play, she welcomes all customers, to keep the fighting outside her doors. She also holds her house as a protected and recognized bastion of legitimated belonging for the women within. For if she herself did not *belong* in Mama Nadi's place, if she was not recognized as occupying it, then Mama Nadi would not exist in the same way the Twa and Mbuti did not *exist in* (occupy) forest lands under imperial and national definitions. By extension, then, the women in the house would also not exist.

Moreover, Mama Nadi stakes a legitimate location for being by drawing on the knowledge that hostilities and chaos will persist. Someone somewhere will always want the resources in the forest zones. Others elsewhere will always be undergoing eviction from their homes. Understanding the lack of cessation in hostilities and the constant displacements wrought through terror enables Mama Nadi to strike a profit by maintaining a fixed establishment in the unsettled region. Her house emphasizes the performativity of located belonging, or the time and place of existence as always already in the mode of becoming un/stable. Furthermore, her home becomes a secure position from which she fights the very dispossession that drove her and her employees there.

> We will not wait until everything has been destroyed.
> We are tired of being disbelieved and disappeared.
> We will have our homes back.
> We will have our bodies back.
> We will have them back.
>
> (Muriithi)

Nottage alters the rules of engagement in the final scene. The bar and boardinghouse stand bereft of customers and clients. Christian enters, tired and sober, and proposes to Mama Nadi, "settle down with me" (Nottage 98). Mama Nadi resists, protesting, "love is too fragile a sentiment for out here. It isn't worth it" (Nottage 99). In the exchange that follows, Mama Nadi finally reveals that she too is ruined. Instead of rejecting her as dust, Christian expresses his love for her, thereby dismantling the conflation of damaged female bodies and land that is woven throughout the play. She agrees only to dance with him (Nottage 102). Because of Mama Nadi's insistence on her independence and the legitimization of her profitable existence, the ending dance surprised critics, scholars, and audiences. Some critics praised the ending's hopeful but unguaranteed happiness, while Nottage herself claimed the resolution as "radical and confrontational" (Brantley; Feingold; Nottage qtd. Timpane). Scholars expressed frustration over this melodramatic romance, this happy, heter-normative, and individualized resolution (Fox 1, 11, 12; Dolan).

Given this contested ending, I am asking, as did Lorraine Hansberry of *A Raisin in the Sun:* what does happy mean in a *Ruined* world?[26] In *Raisin*, the Younger family defies segregated oppression in a moment of suc-cessful home purchase. They will be in danger in the play-to-come, from their new neighbors in their new neighborhood, where they do not belong. And yet they celebrate. In *Ruined*, Mama Nadi and Christian defy local heteronormativities in their un-landed, un-reproductive partnership. They dance, "a celebration of freedom from fixity, a momentary triumph over gravitational pull" (Thiong'o, "Towards a Performance Theory" 7). But they will also be in danger in the world of the play-to-come, where their love does not belong. To fulfill Bantu or Nilo-Saharan heteronormativities, Mama Nadi and Christian would still require children, ancestral pasts, and landed futures (Macharia, "African Queer Studies"; p'Bitek). They have none of these, and will be adjudged as failures by their communities (Macharia, "African Queer Studies").

Yet by ending on a note of hope, Nottage invites her audiences to consider "Love is more than tolerance, more than equality, more than freedom. It is an embedding, a valuing, a risking, a demand" (Macharia, "Love" 10). Neither Nottage nor Mama Nadi want love granted as a concession for women's equality, or merely tolerated. With love, they demand that we value their orders of belonging, that we risk imagin-ing a future where lands and women are not rended and discarded in the name of profit or a nation. Moreover, we must imagine a future where language, women, and homes wield love as "incoherent attach-ment and revolutionary persistence," so that love no longer serves as a weapon to enforce arbitrary divisions (Macharia, "Love" 7). Instead, like the women in the play, we would be able to map improbable routes to wend through the murk of disordered chaos. By reordering belonging, we would find an incoherent strength to disarm the poison of arbitrary difference and sustain us in the battles that are sure to come. And then we would discover that "this is the most precious gift true love offers—the experience of knowing we always belong" (hooks 164).

Notes

1 Acknowledgments: I am especially grateful to Jocelyn L. Buckner for curating and editing this collection. Kasongo Kapanga, Isaac Ngere Konguka, Evan Mwangi, and Keguro Macharia provided valuable contexts for Kiswahili dialects, love, and gender in African worlds. Jessica Finney, Shailja Patel, Aaron Bady, Matthew Durkin, Shana Russell, and Rohini Chaki responded generously to many conversations over email and social media. Kantara Souffrant, Kristin Moriah, David Bisaha, and Emma Freeman commented on several early drafts, helping clarify the work. I am profoundly grateful to Mwalimu Leonora Kivuva and all who have facilitated my Kiswahili education over the years, in Kenya, Tanzania, and the U.S.

2 On Ituri: Wilkie, "Life Amidst Chaos"; Kisangani, *Civil Wars in the Democratic Republic of the Congo*. On Congolese popular music: Mbembe, "Variations." On foreign direct investment/mining: Alden et al., *China Returns to Africa*; Fantu and Cyril, *The Rise of China and India in Africa*.

3 Fox, "Battles on the Body," 4, 7.

4 Nottage has been clear that she did not use verbatim testimony.

5 Mbembe, *On the Postcolony*, 2.

6 Smallwod, *Saltwater Slavery*; Zeleza, "Rewriting the Diaspora."

7 Pinto intervenes in a masculine-centric Black Atlantic, by analyzing Black female poets, writers, and playwrights whose aesthetic strategies transgress "fixed points of origin."

8 Whiteley, Swahili; Blommaert, *Grassroots Literacy*, 35, 69, 37 n4, for forest zone dialects. I use "people groups" throughout, as opposed to "tribe." See Ngugi, "The Myth of Tribe in African Politics."

9 Mazrui, *Swahili State and Society*, 35–49; Fabian, *Language and Colonial Power*, 6, 17, 42, 65, 70, 88.

10 Mazrui, *Swahili State and Society*, 35–49; Mudimbe, "African Gnosis Philosophy"; Fabian, *Language and Colonial Power*, 6, 17, 42, 65, 70, 88. By Scramble for Africa, I mean the Berlin Conference division of Africa into European areas of control.

11 Fabian, *Language and Colonial Power*; Giblin and Monson, *Maji*; Pugliese, "Complementary or Contending Nationhoods?" in *Mau & Nationhood*, 97.

12 Tordoff and Mazrui, "The Left and the Super-Left in Tanzania"; Patel, *Migritude*, 10–12, 64, 78; Macharia, "Nothing Has Changed in the Post-Moi World."

13 Hansberry, *Les Blancs*; Césaire, *A Tempest* and *A Season in the Congo*; Karenga, *The African-American Holiday of Kwanzaa*.

14 Goyvaerts, "Emergence of Lingala in Bukavu," 303–305. See also Ngugi wa Thiong'o, *Decolonising the Mind*; Evan Maina Mwangi, "Gender and the Tactics of Eroticism in Ngugi wa Thiongo's Drama"; Achebe, "English and the African Writer."

15 Over the course of several email conversations, Kasongo Kapanga clarified Central African usages and contexts for the Swahili, French, and Lingala in the play.

16 Mbembe, *On the Postcolony*, 24–27.

17 Yanga cites and translates, Sakombi, Inongo. *Authenticité à Paris* (Kinshasa: Départment de l'Orientation Nationale) Print. 1973. See http://elanguage.net/journals/sal/article/viewFile/1043/1101, 240.

18 Hooi, "Congo's Civil War Imperils Livelihood," for more on Mobutu.

19 Gardner-Chloros, *Code-switching*, 9, "'Languages' are often treated as if they were discrete, identifiable, and internally consistent wholes, and we forget how historically recent and culturally selective such a view is." See also 13–18, 21–30, 54–56.

20 Historical contexts of Central African forest zones include Bantu peoples and Nilo-Saharan peoples, among others. The play's dramaturgy closely follows Bantu-centric conflicts over land and reproductivity, e.g., *The Wound in the Heart*, Ngugi wa Thiong'o, and *Aminata*, Francis Imbuga. Links between lands, ancestry, and futures are not exclusive to Bantu peoples. See p'Bitek, "Song of Lawino"; Zarowsky, "Isn't This My Soil?" and "Writing Trauma." In contrast, West African plays like *Anowa* and *The Broken Handcuff* link impotency as a consequence for African men working as slave traders.

21 Macharia, "Fugitivity" and "How Does a Girl Grow into a Woman?" 8; and Wiredu, "The Need for Conceptual Decolonization in African Philosophy."

22 Cf Nottage 25, I.ii.

23 For more on imperial efforts to control and/or boost reproductivity, Hunt "An Acoustic Register," and "Noise Over Camouflaged Polygamy"; Schumaker, *Africanizing Anthropology*, 35; Thomas, *Politics of the Womb*.

24 This moment echoes, for example, Sethe's female ancestors in *Beloved*, who speak of throwing away the children conceived from sexual assaults by slavers and masters. See Morrison, *Beloved*, 74.

25 Mbembe, *On the Postcolony*, 4.

26 "Lorraine Hansberry talks with Studs Terkel: 1959/05/12." See also the letter from "white native Georgian" who "can't imagine what the future holds for [the Younger] family . . . whether the white neighborhood supposedly accepts them, or whether life continues to be the futile struggle it has always been." *To Be Young, Gifted, and Black*, 127. See also Keppel, *The Work of Democracy*, 200, 205; and Mbembe, Variations: "In such a torrid space, what then is jubilation?"

Works cited

Achebe, Chinua. "English and the African Writer." *Transition* 18 (1965): 27–30. Print.

Aidoo, Ama. *Anowa*. Alexandria: Alexander Street Press, 2015. Print.

Alden, Chris, Daniel Large, and Ricardo Soares, eds. *China Returns to Africa: A Rising Power and a Continent Embrace*. New York: Columbia University Press, 2008. Print.

Blommaert, Jan. *Grassroots Literacy: Writing, Identity and Voice in Central Africa*. Abingdon: Routledge, 2008. Print.

Brantley, Ben. "War's Terrors, Through a Brothel Window." *New York Times*. Feb. 10, 2009. Web.

Césaire, Aimé. *A Season in the Congo*. Trans. Gayatri Chakravorty Spivak. New York: Seagull Books, 2010. Print.

————. *A Tempest*. Alexandria: Alexander Street Press, Sept. 2014.

Cheru, Fantu and C. I. Obi, eds. *The Rise of China and India in Africa: Challenges, Opportunities, and Critical Interventions*. Uppsala: Zed, 2010. Print.

DeSouza George, Raymond E. *The Broken Handcuff (Give Me Free)*. n.d. TS.

Dolan, Jill. "*Ruined*, by Lynn Nottage." Web blog post. *The Feminist Spectator*, March 16, 2009. Web. Accessed September 2014.

Edmondson, Laura. "Uganda Is Too Sexy: Reflections on *Kony 2012*." *TDR: The Drama Review* 56.3 (2012): 10–17. Print.

Fabian, Johannes. *Language and Colonial Power: The Appropriation of Swahili in the Former Belgian Congo, 1880–1938*. Berkeley: University of California Press, 1991. Print.

Feingold, Michael. "*Ruined*'s Women Face a Congo Civil War." *Village Voice*. Feb. 18, 2009. Web. Accessed September 2014.

Fox, Ann M. "Battles on the Body: Disability, Interpreting Dramatic Literature, and the Case of Lynn Nottage's *RUINED*." *Journal of Literary & Cultural Disability Studies* 5.1 (2011): 1–16. Print.

Gardner-Chloros, Penelope. *Code-switching*. Cambridge: Cambridge University Press, 2009. Print.

Giblin, James and Jamie Monson, eds. *Maji Maji: Lifting the Fog of War*. Leiden, Netherlands: Koninklijke Brill NV, 2010. Print.

Gilroy, Paul. *The Black Atlantic: Modernity and Double Consciousness*. Cambridge: Harvard University Press, 1993. Print.

Goyvaerts, Didier L. "The Emergence of *Lingala* in Bukavu, Zaïre." *The Journal of Modern African Studies* 33.2 (1995): 299–314. Print.

Hansberry, Lorraine. *Les Blancs: The Collected Last Plays: The Drinking Gourd/What Use Are Flowers?* Ed. Robert Nemiroff. New York: Vintage, 1994. Print.

————. *To Be Young, Gifted, and Black: An Informal Autobiography of Lorraine Hansberry*. Adapted, Robert Nemiroff. New York: Signet, 1969. Print.

Hooi, Alexis J. "Congo's Civil War Imperils Livelihood." *Cultural Survival Quarterly* 1.4 (2001): 1. Print.

hooks, bell. *All About Love: New Visions*. New York: Harper Collins, 2000. Print.

Hunt, Nancy R. "An Acoustic Register, Tenacious Images, and Congolese Scenes of Rape and Repetition." *Cultural Anthropology* 23.2 (2008): 220–253. Print.

————. *A Colonial Lexicon: Of Birth Ritual, Medicalization, and Mobility in the Congo*. Durham: Duke University Press, 1999. Print.

————. "Noise over Camouflaged Polygamy, Colonial Morality Taxation, and a Woman-Naming Crisis in Belgian Africa." *The Journal of African History* 32.3 (1991): 471–494. Print.

————. "Placing African Women's History and Locating Gender." *Social History* 14.3 (1989): 359–379. Print.

Imbuga, Francis. *Aminata*. Alexandria: Alexander Street Press, Sept. 2014. Web. Accessed September 2014.

Journalists for Justice. "Indecent Act Allegedly Committed by Tony Mochama Upon the Person of Shailja Patel." Sept. 2014. Web. Accessed September 2014.

Kagame, Alexis. "The Empirical Apperception of Time and the Conception of History in Bantu Thought." *Cultures and Time: At the Crossroads of Cultures*. Paris: UNESCO Press, 1976. 89–116. Print.

Karenga, Maulana. *The African American Holiday of Kwanzaa: A Celebration of Family, Community & Culture*. Los Angeles: University of Sankore Press, 1988. Print.

Keppel, Ben. *The Work of Democracy: Ralph Bunche, Kenneth B. Clark, Lorraine Hansberry, and the Cultural Politics of Race*. Cambridge: Harvard University Press, 1995. Print.

Kisangani, Emizet. *Civil Wars in the Democratic Republic of the Congo, 1960–2010*. Boulder: Lynne Rienner, 2012. Print.

Long, Cath. "Land rights in the Democratic Republic of the Congo – A New Model of Rights for Forest-dependent Communities?" *Global Protection Cluster*. Web. Accessed June 2014.

"Lorraine Hansberry Talks with Studs Terkel." Web. Accessed September 2014.

Macharia, Keguro. "African Queer Studies." *Gukira*. Web. Accessed September 2014.

———. "Fugitivity." *Gukira*. Web. Accessed September 2014.

———. "How Does a Girl Grow into a Woman?" Girlhood in Ngugi wa Thiong'o's *The River Between. Research in African Literatures* 43.2 (2012): 1–17. Print.

———. "Love." n.d. TS.

———. "Nothing Has Changed in the Post-Moi World." *The Star Kenya*. Jan. 2015. Web. Accessed February 2015.

Mazrui, Alamin M. *Swahili Beyond the Boundaries: Literature, Language, and Identity*. No. 85. Athens: Ohio University Press, 2007. Print.

———. *Swahili State and Society: The Political Economy of an African Language*. London: James Currey Ltd, 1995. Print.

Mbembe, Achille. *On the Postcolony*. Berkeley: University of California Press, 2001. Print.

———. "Variations on the Beautiful in the Congolese World of Sounds." *Politique Africaine* 4.100 (2005): 69–91. Web. Accessed September 2014.

Méndez García, Carmen. ""This is my place, Mama Nadi's": Feminine Spaces and Identity in Lynn Nottage's *Ruined*." *Investigaciones Feministas* 3 (2012): 129–139. Print.

Morrison, Toni. *Beloved*. New York: Vintage Books, 2004. Print.

Mugo, Micere. *My Mother's Poems and other Songs*. Nairobi: East African Educational Publishers, 1994. Print.

Muriithi, Wairimu. "#mybodymyhome (iv)." *The New Inquiry*. Web. Accessed February 2015.

Mwangi, Evan. "Gender and the Erotics of Nationalism in Ngugi wa Thiong'o's Drama." *TDR: The Drama Review* 53.2 (2009): 90–112. Print.

Nottage, Lynn. *Ruined*. New York: Theatre Communications Group, 2009. Print.

Nurse, Derek. "The 'Indigenous Versus Foreign' Controversy about the Sources of *Swahili* Vocabulary." *Studies in African Linguistics* 9 (1985): 245. Print.

Patel, Shailja. *Migritude*. New York: Kaya Press, 2010. Print.

p'Bitek, Okot. *Song of Lawino & Song of Ocol*. Nairobi: Heinemann, 1966. Print.

Pinto, Samantha. *Difficult Diasporas: The Transnational Feminist Aesthetic of the Black Atlantic*. New York: New York University Press, 2013. Print.

Pugliese, Cristiana. "Complementary or Contending Nationhoods? Kikuyu Pamphlets & Songs 1945–52." *Mau Mau & Nationhood*. Eds. E.S. Atieno Odhiambo and John Lonsdale. Oxford: James Curry Ltd, 2003. 97–120. Print.

Schumaker, Lyn. *Africanizing Anthropology: Fieldworks, Networks, and the Making of Cultural Knowledge in Central Africa*. Durham: Duke University Press, 2001. Print.

Smallwood, Stephanie. *Saltwater Slavery: A Middle Passage from Africa to American Diaspora*. Cambridge: Harvard University Press, 2007. Print.

Sommers, Marc. *Fear in Bongoland: Burundi Refugees in Urban Tanzania*. Oxford: Berghahn Books, 2001. Print.

Thiong'o, Ngugi wa. *Decolonising the Mind*. London: James Currey, 1986. Print.

———. "The Myth of Tribe in African Politics." *Transition: An International Review* "Looking Ahead" 101 (2009): 16–23. Print.

———. "Towards a Performance Theory of Orature." *Performance Research* 12.3 (2007): 4–7. Print.

———. *The Wound in the Heart*. Alexandria: Alexander Street Press, 2014. Web.

Thomas, Lynn. *Politics of the Womb: Women, Reproduction and the State in Kenya*. Berkeley: University of California Press, 2003. Print.

Timpane, John. "Wide, Wide War." *Philadelphia Inquirer*. May 29, 2011. Web. Accessed September 2014.

Tordoff, William and Ali A. Mazrui. "The Left and the Super-Left in Tanzania." *The Journal of Modern African Studies* 10.3 (1972): 427–445. Print.

Whiteley, Wilfred. *Swahili: The Rise of a National Language*. London: Metheun & Co Ltd, 1969. Print.

Wild, Emma. "'Is it Witchcraft? Is it Satan? It is a Miracle.' Mai-Mai Soldiers and Christian Concepts of Evil in North-East Congo." *Journal of Religion in Africa* 28.4 (1998): 450–467. Print.

Wilkie, David S. "Life Amidst Chaos." *Cultural Survival Quarterly* 29.1 (2005): 37–38. Print.

Wiredu, Kwasi. "The Need for Conceptual Decolonization in African Philosophy." *Foundation for Intercultural Philosophy and Art*. Web. Accessed September 2014.

Yanga, Tshimpaka. "Language Planning and Onomastics in Zaire." *Studies in African Linguistics* 9.2 (1978): 233–44. *ELanguage*. Linguistic Society of America. Web. Accessed September 2014.

Zarowsky, Christina. "'Isn't This My Soil?' Land, State, and 'Development' in Somali Ethiopia." *Cultural Survival Quarterly* 22.4 (1999): 47–51. Print.

———. "Writing Trauma: Emotion, Ethnography, and the Politics of Suffering among Somali Returnees in Ethiopia." *Cultural Medicine and Psychiatry* 28 (2004): 189–209. Print.

Zeleza, Paul T. "Rewriting the African Diaspora: Beyond the Black Atlantic." *African Affairs* 104.14 (2005): 35–68. Print.

Chapter 10

On creativity and collaboration

A conversation with Lynn Nottage, Seret Scott, and Kate Whoriskey[1]

Jocelyn L. Buckner

JOCELYN L. BUCKNER: Let's begin by talking about history. Your plays take place in a range of historical periods. *Intimate Apparel* takes place in New York at the beginning of the last century, *Las Meninas* in France in the eighteenth century, *Crumbs from the Table of Joy* in New York in the mid-twentieth century, *Ruined* and *Mud, River, Stone* are set in contemporary African countries but deal with the legacy of colonial exploitation, and *By the Way, Meet Vera Stark* is situated in Hollywood in the 1930s and the new millennium. Where does your interest in periodization come from? What draws you to write about historically based characters like Esther, Nabo, or Vera Stark?

LYNN NOTTAGE: I think the majority of my plays, which one could call history plays, begin with a question. Usually they begin with a question that's very difficult to answer. Often my plays revolve around my search for answers to vexing questions, as was the case with *Las Meninas*, which is about Queen Marie-Therese, the wife of Louis XIV, and a scandalous affair that she had with an African dwarf, whose name we believe was Nabo. A female child was produced from their union, and immediately sequestered at a convent. I first read about their affair in a book called *African Presence in Early Europe* written by Ivan Van Sertima. It was only mentioned in a tiny paragraph, but I became obsessed with knowing the truth. I thought, "Mm? Can this possibly be true?" That was the simple initial question that led to my crazy play. If it *was* true, what ended up happening to both Queen Marie Therese and their child? So, I went in search of the answer to these questions. I began my research in the Sterling Library at Yale University and continued for about a year there, until I graduated from Yale School of Drama. But I still didn't have the answer to the question. I think it ended up being a five year journey from when I first asked the question to when I finally found information that satisfied my appetite. Incidentally, it was in the New York Public Library at 42nd Street. I found this book, which I was the first person to check out since 1810. The book was written in 1792, and it was a primary text that was directly translated from a French memoir of one of the King's mistresses. In it she outlines a relationship that the Queen had with an African dwarf. I thought, "Oh, there it is!" The play was my investigation of a question.

The same was very much true with *Intimate Apparel*, which is set at the turn of the last century in New York City. My mother and my grandmother, at about the same time, could no longer answer questions about our past. My mother developed, relatively young, ALS, which is Amyotrophic Lateral Sclerosis. This disease slowly renders one immobile and eventually robs you of your speech. Just when I was prepared to ask questions about our family history, she was no longer able to answer them.

At the same time my mother was struggling with Lou Gehrig's disease, with ALS, my grandmother was in the depths of alcoholism, which eventually led to her dementia, so she was incapable of answering these questions. Slowly, I found that my family history had completely slipped out of my reach, primarily because my relatives, the last links to that part of my life, were physically incapable of sharing the stories. While I was cleaning out my grandmother's house, I found a picture that I had never seen before. It was a picture of my grandmother, and her mother, and my grandmother's sister. My great-aunt. I realized I knew nothing about this woman, other than she was a seamstress who came to New York at the turn of the century. She was an incredibly resourceful woman who managed to build a life.

And, so, *Intimate Apparel* was really me trying to come to terms with not a forgotten family history, but an absent family history, because my family had never really bothered to talk about the details of their lives. My grandmother was one of the most amazing raconteurs. This was a woman who could weave a story out of nothing. I mean, thin air! She was a very big personality, and she spoke a lot about herself as a little girl, but not in the context of family.

I ended up spending a great deal of time in the New York Public Library, trying to piece together the lives of African Americans who came to New York in the first big wave of immigration. Because I think there's a lot that's been written about the second wave, the

Great Migration, which peaked in the 1940s and 50s, but there's far less information about the wave that came just after Reconstruction through the early Industrial Revolution. This is the period when my family came to New York. They came in the late 1800s and early 1900s, so we're very much rooted in New York City. As I was digging through texts at the Library, I found that our stories were not present. There was very little literature documenting the lives of everyday African Americans at the turn of the twentieth century. I'm talking about a period just before the Harlem Renaissance – when we finally had the opportunity to sing our songs on the page and the stage.

I think in the case of *By the Way, Meet Vera Stark*, and to a lesser extent *Crumbs from the Table of Joy*, once again it began with a question: "Who are these women in early Hollywood? These beautiful, talented, African American women who were very much ingénues, but were unfortunately pushed to the margins. What were their lives like? What were their aspirations?"

JLB: I'm glad you mentioned the Migration because it is so present in a number of your works: the Crump family in *Crumbs* moves from Pensacola to Brooklyn; in *Intimate Apparel* Esther leaves North Carolina for Manhattan; and Vera Stark moves from Harlem to Hollywood. What about this specific American geographical movement is attractive to you as a storyteller?

LN: I think the history of the African American in America in the story of movement. We were brought here on ships against our will, and I think that since we came here, we've always been in search of a place to settle and to be. As a result, once we were freed, I think we went on a hunt for a place, and constantly found that we were not welcomed, and thus picked up our bags and continued to move. In many ways, what I write about parallels that; my characters are always in search of identity. I think place and identity are intertwined, because we feel so displaced in this country that we're constantly looking for a place to settle, which ultimately translates into a place to be ourselves.

JLB: Your plays land in a variety of places in the African diaspora, from the continent, to the Caribbean, to New York, even in Europe. Do you seek to tell stories in specific locales, or do locations emerge from your readings, research, current events, or your own travels?

LN: I think the locale often comes last. In the case of *Mud, River, Stone*, it is a play that takes place in Mozambique, which involves an African American couple on a romantic holiday who find themselves in a very remote, dangerous location – in a war zone. They are people who are extremely bourgeois, and have a very idealized and romanticized notion of Africa and that region in particular. When they arrive, they discover that it's very different from what they imagined. When I wrote the play, I had never been to Africa, so I was really filtering my own fears and desires through these characters. In many ways when I wrote the play I still had a very romantic and slightly cantilevered view of Africa, because it was the Africa in my imagination, not a place that I had been. It was still "Africa" and not individual countries. When I wrote the play it was this continent that was big and looming, and represented motherland, and fears and dreams and desires and all of those things. The way that play came about was that I read an article in the back of the *New York Times* about this town in Mozambique where everyone who passed through for a period of time was kidnapped and held hostage. All the locals wanted was some food and a blanket that had been promised to them. When the United Nations finally came to negotiate, they too, were taken hostage. I found it fascinating that in this place, in this little town, the demands were so small and achievable. They wanted food and a blanket, which should be a basic right of every human being. I began writing that play and I did not do as much research as I usually do because I wanted it to be pure fantasy. I wanted to see where my imagination was going to lead me. I wanted to go to extremes that research would only hinder. Though the play was based on a real incident, it was entirely conjured from my imagination.

I think it's true of all the settings of my plays. They begin with an idea or a notion, and some form of inquiry. Then I go about finding a place to set them. Unless, of course, it's the Court of Louis XIV, then it can only take place in the Court of Louis XIV. Mostly, my locations come out of necessity, they help serve the narrative.

JLB: The scope of diaspora in your plays brings to mind additional themes like displacement, as you've already mentioned, longing and belonging, as well as home and homeland. How does knowing our past and origins help fingerprint our contemporary identities, and what do you think the dramatization of these questions in your plays helps audiences to discover about themselves?

LN: I feel strongly that in order for us to feel fully centered in the present, we have to take ownership of our history. For so long, as an African American woman, I was not allowed to own history because my narrative was consciously excluded from the public record. So,

I think that my plays are trying to firmly place women of color, in particular woman of diaspora, in key historic moments so that we can reclaim history, and therefore, reclaim ourselves in the present tense.

I don't know whether you felt this way, and I imagine all women do to a certain extent, but when I was growing up and reading the history books, I had a real sense of not having been thought of as a participant. It's as though women appeared suddenly and spontaneously in the 1960s. But we were present, and there's no sense of us having any kind of agency prior to the 1960s, with the notable exceptions of women like Sojourner Truth and Susan B. Anthony, etc.

JLB: But you don't see the everyday experience.

LN: You don't see everyday women. I really think, in order for us to feel fully empowered, that we have to understand the roles that we've played in the shaping of America. We played an enormous role. My plays are about ordinary, extraordinary women. I'm fully aware of that. Many people like to imagine that their ancestor was a prince or a king. But what I recognize is that I come from a long line of really hard-working women who did not write books, and who tended to other people's children. Who washed laundry and sewed clothing, and picked cotton, and cut sugar cane, but who were extraordinary in their own right, and were the building blocks for who I am, and the building blocks for this country itself because they were raising white children, who became the leaders of this country. These women, in their own remote way, helped shaped the sensibilities of this country.

Early on, one of the criticisms of my work was, "Why aren't you singing songs of our heroes?" I thought, "These *are* my heroes." These women, my ancestors, they're my heroes. There are so many versions of what a hero should be, or what constitutes a remarkable story. These are the remarkable stories, the stories of self-reliance and ingenuity that show how women took advantage of small opportunities, and transformed situations that were incredibly imperfect, and triumphed in the midst of adversity.

I feel the character of Esther is the definition of one of these women. At the very beginning of *Intimate Apparel*, she sits down at her sewing machine and feels absolutely trapped and a victim of circumstance. She cannot recognize the beauty of self and doesn't even understand, fully, her own power. But, the journey of the play is her discovery of love, she's the most loved person in the play.

And, she's perhaps the most powerful person, because she has the power to determine her own future.

JLB: Yes! Which is extraordinary for a woman in 1905.

LN: Which is extraordinary. I think of my great-grandmother when she came to the U.S. as a very, very young woman, and how incredibly terrifying it must have been to come here from Barbados, to get off the boat at Ellis Island. She stepped onto the island of Manhattan not knowing anyone, and probably only having three or four dollars in her pocket. Imagine being a black woman having to find a place to live and forge a life, knowing the many obstacles that you'd face because of your gender and your color, and succeeding so well. I think it's extraordinary. Sometimes, I think about what an incredibly privileged life I have because of the courageous choices that that woman made. And, I also think that's true of my mother, who was a feminist, and in many ways, it's her brave choices that gave birth to me as a writer. Sometimes if we don't know our history, we can't fully appreciate and take advantage of our own circumstances. One of my favorite phrases is "sustaining the complexity of what it means to be a woman." I'm interested in all of the facets of womanhood, and how that empowers me as a storyteller.

JLB: That sentiment seems to resonate in much of your work.

LN: I gravitate toward that phrase because early on in my writing, I felt a bit criticized as being an African American writer who was not necessarily always portraying, in particular women, or African American men in a heroic light. I thought, well, that's not real life, and if we're going to be truthful we have to sustain the complexity of our reality and show ourselves in all of our textures. No matter how difficult it is to digest.

JLB: Your characters resist stereotypes. When there is a stereotype addressed in your plays, there's always a complication of it, or a twisting of it, so that it becomes apparent that the stereotype is a distortion. Do you intentionally set out to address or complicate stereotypes, or is that a natural by-product of creating rich, three-dimensional characters?

LN: In two of my plays, *Fabulation, the Reeducation of Undine*, and *By the Way, Meet Vera Stark*, I wanted to get inside of those stereotypes, and explore them more thoroughly. Once inside, I can then explode them. I think it was very specifically part of my agenda when I sat down to write those two plays. I wanted to confront stereotypes and toy with audience expectations.

JLB: Perhaps one of the most interesting and familiar traits of many of your characters is their struggle with class and economic issues. Class is one of our main identity traits that can change. At least that's what we're told in the U.S., right?

LN: I think that's very much what my new play *Sweat* is about. There are certain assumptions about American identity and our collective narrative, such as the fact that we live in a culture in which we have upward mobility. We all are deeply invested in the Horatio Alger myth, we embrace the notion that if we work hard we can transform ourselves and ascend the economic ladder. *Sweat* is about a group of people who have fully invested in the American myth and discover that it no longer exists. They no longer have a narrative that they can interpret and understand.

Sweat came out of wanting to understand what was happening in America and how poverty was and is reshaping our narrative. It began in 2012, with a friend who wrote a letter to me. She's a single mother of two, who was basically confessing to the fact that she hadn't worked in a long time and was completely broke. She said in this letter, "I'm not asking for anything, I don't want a hand out. I just need people to be aware of my situation and to be sensitive." It broke my heart. It made me want to go in search of stories like hers and try to understand why this is happening in our country. I received a commission from the Oregon Shakespeare Festival for the American Revolution Cycle, and I decided I wanted to focus on the de-industrial revolution.

JLB: I like that phrase, because we don't have a word for it yet, but that's exactly what it is happening all over the country.

LN: That is the word. It's the de-industrial revolution. In many ways we think of modern America as the America at the turn of the twentieth century. That was an America in which you had this big influx of immigration. In which you had black folks migrating from the South. European immigrants coming from Europe. Asian immigrants coming from Asia. In this way, really, the modern definition of America is the twentieth century America. It's about the Industrial Revolution in America.

Now, the new, postmodern definition of America centers on the de-industrial revolution, in which new technologies have triumphed and the country now rewards people who have an advanced education, and devalues people who work with their hands. And all of those people who are invested in using their hands as a means of living no longer have a place in the economic food chain. Unfortunately, that's the majority of America. And it's changing the shape of our culture in ways that we can't quite even comprehend yet. But, it's happening right now, and I think we're in the midst of a big cultural revolution. I wanted to write about this major cultural shift, and I use Reading, PA as my focal point.

JLB: What made you choose Reading in particular, when there are, unfortunately, so many empty and struggling factory towns?

LN: It was a city that once had a very strong narrative and was at the center of the Industrial Revolution in Southeastern Pennsylvania. It had textiles, it had steel, it had agriculture, and was a magnet for new immigrants. Then it so absolutely collapsed. Within a matter of decades it went from being an affluent city to a city that now can't economically support itself. Many factories closed, moved out of state or out of the country. Reading can't even resurrect itself, because it has absolutely no tax base left.

What's interesting is that Pittsburgh and Detroit are big, iconic cities, so there's an investment in them succeeding. It's like we need Detroit to succeed because it's so representative of our aspirations as Americans. The difference between a Detroit and a Pittsburgh, versus cities like Camden and Reading and Newburgh, is that they are very small cities. At some point they were thriving, but they began to decline, and there wasn't the same investment in rescuing them. They become these ghost towns in which you have inhabitants who are stuck. They're not able to live in the present; they're haunting their own lives.

We began visiting Reading in 2012, which coincided with the inauguration of the city's first African American mayor. We interviewed as many people as possible to find out what was happening in the city, from the police chief, to the homeless, to small business owners, to social workers. We targeted a real wide cross-section of folk who represented the range of people living in Reading. At first we were hoping to find these incredible stories of resilience, because that's what I'm drawn to as an artist. We found a few poignant stories of resilience, but not stories in which people triumphed. After two years of spending time there, I thought, "Wow, this is a really fractured, broken place." We need to examine this more deeply, why can't this city resurrect itself, because if it continues down this tragic path, like our country, it's going to completely crumble.

JLB: Obviously this is a compelling story, and a national tragedy, because Reading isn't the only city that's experiencing this. How do you think addressing these kinds of issues of class in a relatively luxurious art form like theatre helps bring attention to the social issue of economic disparity?

LN: I'm a storyteller and this is what I do, so this is the tool that I have. If I was a social activist I'd go and organize in the factories, but unfortunately, I don't have that skill. I think that what I can do is bring these stories to an audience, and perhaps put them in space where they feel empowered to effect change.

Yeah, when people are sitting in the comfort of their seats it's easy for them to say, "Oh, it's them, not me." But I do think that there are a handful of people who come to the theatre, who'll see my characters, and become invested in their stories. I think that's what we have the power to do. I really do think that theatre should be at the vanguard of change, because it's one of the few mediums where we can gather collectively, and actually experience a collective catharsis, and we can't underestimate the impact and power of that. I think that there is something magical that happens when we're able to laugh together, we're able to cry together, and that's what excites me about the medium.

My hope is that in a show like *Sweat* we'll see these strong, working-class folk, whose stories don't get told that often on the stage, and we can feel empathy, and we can feel invested in their journey, and somehow when we read a news story or when we sit across from someone on the bus, that we will look in their eyes, and understand something about who they are.

JLB: We've been discussing aspects of history, diaspora, and identity in your works, and now I'd like to draw directors Seret Scott and Kate Whoriskey into the conversation, to hear their perspectives on collaborating with you and staging your plays. How did your collaborations begin?

LN: With Seret Scott the beginning was *POOF!*, which was my very, very first professional production. I had no idea what to do, so I just allowed this very wonderful, very gentle, collaborator to be my guide. In many ways she became my introduction to theatre. She was wonderful, she was enormously generous to me as a very young, naïve artist trying to negotiate new territory, and taught me the rules of the room, and the rules of making theatre. We did *POOF!* and then we did *Mud, River, Stone* together. She also directed *Crumbs from the Table of Joy*, and a number of my other plays. Early on, she was my go-to director. She's someone who works incredibly well with actors. She knows how to speak their language and as a result solicit incredible and nuanced performances from them.

SERET SCOTT: I met Lynn very early in my directing career; she was working with Amnesty International as the on-site producer of a ten-minute play festival highlighting the organization. Lynn helped me sort through information about the political climate that my play explored. We stayed in touch socially, and she never once mentioned she was a writer. *POOF!* was the first play of hers I directed, and years later I learned it was her first professional production! Her writing was dramatically savvy from the start. Early on we did a fair amount of feeling each other out, especially since we were both so new to our crafts, but there was a real sense of trust from the beginning. We talked, shared personal stories, laughed a lot. I think it was her trust in me that allowed me to first, embrace her words, and then, explore the fantasy of her worlds, to go further.

JLB: What about you, Kate?

KATE WHORISKEY: We began on a blind date arranged by the then literary manager of South Coast Rep, Jerry Patch. The theatre had commissioned Lynn to write a play. She handed in the first act of what would become *Intimate Apparel*. Jerry read it and was thrilled by it. He enthusiastically gave me a call saying he had found some terrific material. I gave it a read and was completely taken with how Lynn carved out language that carefully crafted two people falling in love in a pre-Freudian time. After an hour-long conversation at New Dramatists, we decided to work together on the premiere of *Intimate Apparel,* co-produced by South Coast Repertory Theatre and Baltimore's Center Stage.

LN: I was looking for a new collaborator, because at that point, Seret had gotten very busy. Kate has a very strong visual sensibility, and at that moment for *Intimate Apparel*, I felt like it needed a strong visual eye, because the story's so simple. I wanted someone who would understand the visual vocabulary of the piece. I met her, and I just felt safe with her. I felt like it was going to be a good collaboration.

One of the things that I really love about working with Kate is that we see the same thing. If something's not working, I don't have to say, "It's not working." I know she sees it. She really can plug into my language and knows how to read it on the page and then translate it to the stage. I don't know that every director can do that.

JLB: As directors, how do you access Lynn's characters and stories in order to communicate to an audience? Do you focus on universal themes in the text, or do you think that, because the specificity of her plays is well-crafted, the stories are inherently accessible to anyone who sees them?

KW: I think why so many people respond to Lynn's writing is because of her skill in crafting character. She has a real gift for revealing a person's actions over time. What the audience thinks they understand about a character at the beginning of the play is often radically shifted by the end. I see one of my central jobs as carefully taking the audience through a progression of character. In this way, many of the themes Lynn writes about are articulated.

SS: I'd say initially I focus on the characters because their choices make the story. Her stories are so ethnically rich and diverse that audiences, no matter their background, recognize, relate, and travel through Lynn's worlds as if on both familiar and foreign ground.

JLB: How do you work to illuminate the human components of hope and resiliency in Lynn's plays, which so often focus on serious subject matter? Even *Ruined*, for example, contains moments where there is pleasure in that world, despite its devastation. In *Intimate Apparel* there are also moments of richness, humor, and beauty despite the kind of violation and betrayal that happens to Esther. How do you find and celebrate those humorous and pleasurable moments in the work?

SS: It's textual. I build on what's on the page, the silences, emotional energy, humanity, candor, humor, and pathos. I find that actors in her plays internally identify with their roles; nothing feels manufactured. Many times I've had the good fortune to observe an actor/audience connection that wasn't easy for the viewer to turn away from, wasn't easy to dismiss.

KW: I would say, similarly, in *Intimate Apparel* and *Fabulation*, it's really within the text. It is also in the text of *Ruined* but I would say *Ruined* has more room for interpretation. One of the phrases that Lynn and I would repeat to each other was "sustain the complexity." We didn't want the piece to become an overtly political play. We wanted to tell a story about people in a circumstance. We wanted to show the range of human behavior and not concentrate only on the subject of war.

When we went to interview Congolese women in Uganda, we were struck by how the women approached telling us their stories. Their stories, which often included horrific detail, were told in a quiet, controlled way. When we gave [the play] to American actors, they tended to look for catharsis. That's what we learn in drama school. How do we basically make something sing? Where is the aria? That is not what we experienced when we did the interviews. We wanted to stay true to the way in which the women confided in us. In a way, *Ruined* was so much about finding the humor, the life, and the joy, so that these moments of quiet could hold dramatic tension.

JLB: Lynn's approach to tackling difficult subject matter has evolved and changed since she began writing professionally in the 1990s. Can you describe your approach to working together in staging texts that deal with significant topics like domestic abuse, stereotypes, and war? What is your process in making these stories palatable for an audience while maintaining the integrity and the complexity of the script?

KW: I would say that Lynn gives quite a few clues. With *Ruined,* she knew that subject matter would not be easy for an American audience so she, very cleverly, crafted a well-made play with a love story at the end. That was intentional. She knew that the audience needed some kind of grounding, some sort of way into the world so that she could actually express the lives of these women. I think the thing with her writing is that she is very intentional about the form. If you support that form the work will live in a robust way. I think you have to play the notes on the page in a way. She's given you a great score, so play those notes. To me, with certain writing, directing requires a muscularity. Directors try to help writing by supporting certain things that are not actually on the page. I think with Lynn the opposite is true, you actually have to really listen to what is on the page in order to direct it well.

SS: There's poetry in Lynn's use of language and that language seems to organically hit her ear in the context of the moment. I've seen Lynn uneasy about a phrase or line that wasn't working for her. At a table rehearsal years ago, Lynn spoke to me about a passage, it "Wasn't what she wanted to say, she'd take a look at it." The actor in the role, thinking he was being helpful said, "Well I could just say this instead," and offered his own words. Lynn said quietly, "No, you can't." There was no ego, it was simply about the right words and the next day, three words were added that made the difference.

JLB: Can we talk about new play development? How involved do you become in the first staging of a work, Lynn? Are you hoping for a particular kind of specificity in capturing that story in the initial embodiment on stage, or are you interested in seeing how others approach the story?

LN: The wonderful thing about theatre is that it's such a thoroughly collaborative process. To a certain extent, once you tell the story, you have to be willing to let go of aspects of it. Otherwise you will constantly be frustrated. But, yes, for the very first production I'm very much involved. I'm there at casting, and I like to be there, occasionally, at the design meetings, so I'm part of shaping the play's first interaction with the audience. As a playwright, you like to be there for the very first production to shape its sensibility, not just what the audience hears, but what the audience sees. You want it to be a complete and absolute rendering of your vision for the first time. After that, I surrender to the universe, and allow directors and actors to do what they will because I think that's the fun of being a playwright, is that you can let it go and rediscover the play years and years down the road. But, for the first production, I think it's important for my voice to be present in all aspects of it, and to have the production come as close to the vision, initial impulse as possible. That's not to say that I'm not open to discovery, but I do think it's important. As a result, I think when I'm trying to decide on whom to work with, I tend to gravitate to directors who are really interested in being absolute collaborators and who are interested in helping me, as a playwright, bring my vision to the stage.

JLB: What kind of characteristics does that encompass for you, for directors?

LN: Someone who is interested in dialogue. A lot of times you'll meet people who are monologists, and when I meet a director who's a monologist, I know instantly that they're not someone who I want to work with. Or, if they're absolutists, they're overly conceptual directors who are interested in imprinting on the piece and not necessarily interested in the storytelling. I have a mantra that is "everything has to be in service of a narrative." If it's not in the service of a narrative, then it doesn't belong on the stage, at least in the first few productions. When I'm looking for a director, I'm looking for someone who understands the story that I'm telling and understands the sensibilities and aesthetics of that story.

JLB: Kate and Seret, can you share your perspective on the collaborative process for new productions, particularly a work that is still in development?

KW: That's a hard question because it seems to change from project to project and moment to moment. I think the central thing is to really listen to the intent of the writer and to try to craft his/her impulses as specifically as possible.

SS: In *Crumbs*, a phrase in Aunt Lily's dialogue didn't sound period-1950s to me, and I mentioned it to Lynn. She listened to the dialogue several times and disagreed. The next day she showed me a passage in a book on jazz (specifically bebop) that supported the phrase. I mention this because it was early in our working relationship, and we were still developing creative communication. I was able to adjust the actor's delivery of the line to keep it from sounding too contemporary; a solution both Lynn and I were very satisfied with. There was never a defensive position from Lynn I think about anything I questioned. After reading a new scene, sometimes I'd ask to switch a line and read it again, or do an improvisation of the scene and read it again. There was never an objection and on several occasions Lynn said, "I like that!" It was a great feeling.

KW: To me something that is so telling about Lynn is how she went about the five year process of creating *Ruined*. We had done so many readings, we had done the show at the Goodman, we had done the show at Manhattan Theatre Club. She was awarded the Pulitzer Prize, the Drama Desk, the Lortel, and multiple other awards for it. Then we were doing a production in Seattle. And after all of this, after she received so many accolades and it was clearly seen as a successful piece of writing, Lynn came in to the first day of rehearsal and said, "I just have two or three line changes." That is exactly who Lynn is. It does not matter what anyone else has to say about how good it is . . . for her, it's not complete until she thinks it's complete. There's something about the level of thought she devotes and how tireless she is which, to me, is her gift.

JLB: Lynn, do you find yourself collaborating with female directors more than male directors?

LN: I have worked with male directors, for example, I've worked with Roger Rees and with Daniel Sullivan, who are amazing collaborators. I would definitely work with them again, but there's something . . . It's like you talk about your comfort zone? I feel very safe when I'm working with female directors. I feel like there's a shorthand and that we have similar goals. I think that it's the fact that they're female that is the glue that ties us all together.

JLB: What about your working relationship has made you want to, or made it possible, to work together on multiple productions?

KW: I think Lynn is one of the most compelling writers today, so it's very exciting to be in the room with her. She's one of the absolute most adventurous people I know, and one of the most compassionate. She loves complexity. It's in every character she creates. So having the chance to be part of the research process and the developmental process is extraordinary. Lynn is constantly evaluating the work, honing in on the story. She creates worlds that she wants people to see that are as yet unseen. I think she has a drive to be very specific in the creation of the worlds. For me, that's why I love working with her and will always say yes, because I feel like she's pushing the boundaries of what theatre is and also who the audience is for theatre.

SS: Lynn has a wonderfully wicked sense of humor; you'll find it in the turn of a phrase, the double meaning of a word. Things aren't what they seem on the surface and that goes for the darkness as well. In the final scene of *Crumbs*, Ernestine says that Aunt Lily was found dead, her "cold body poked full of holes." Now, based on Aunt Lily's lifestyle there were many reasons, drugs, gunshots, a disease that ate away at her, that she'd be poked full of holes, so I asked Lynn what she was suggesting, what happened to Aunt Lily? Lynn said with a wry smile, "Her body was poked full of holes." That was a diamond for me, not knowing the exact details of Lily's end allowed me to explore Lily's earlier behavior without limits. Rich.

JLB: Did you anticipate *Ruined* sparking the conversations that it has, and earning the critical attention that it has received?

LN: No. I was hopeful that it would. I didn't anticipate the extent to which it would succeed. But I was hopeful that it would somehow start a conversation and that was important.

KW: It was a project that we were very interested in doing, but we did not know whether we would even find a producer. When we talked to people about it before it got the roots it did, people would be very polite, but you could tell that they were thinking, "Oh my god, I never would want to see a play about that." Then I remember – Lynn and I were walking after the first preview at the Goodman Theatre, and I said to her, "Lynn, I think this might be your best play," and she said, "I don't know." But I insisted, I said, "I think it might be, I think you've written a great play," and she was so dismissive. "Whatever," she said. (*laughs*)

JLB: Lynn and Kate, you are working together on *Sweat*, and you worked together on the creation of *Ruined*, from the research and development process through production. Can you describe the dynamic of these collaborative processes? How is your relationship different in the field, when you're in the research and development phase of a project, so to speak, versus when you are working together in a rehearsal room?

LN: I think *Ruined* was a really unique process for both of us, because it was the first time that either of us had worked as intently to develop a piece from its inception on up. We decided that we were going to take this trip to East Africa to interview the women together, because we both had a certain level of ownership of it. One of the things that we both did is keep lists of what we experienced on our travels in Uganda. At the end, we compared lists, which were very different. Her list was very visual and mine was very experiential. It's like the two sides of the brain.

At that point, we realized that to tell the story, we needed both. The production ultimately reflected the fact that both of us had been there. Little details, like the generator, the way the lights hung, I don't think that Kate could have arrived at that if she hadn't been there, and vice-versa. I think that the fact that we traveled together also emboldened us to ask certain questions and to press each other when we were producing the play. We shared a frame of reference and could go back very quickly and say, "Remember when we there and we heard that little piece of music?" Or, "We saw that thing. How can we work it in?"

I think that, somehow, it was very, very important for the production to reflect our shared references. I think it's also true in *Sweat*; it's about the textures. We have a view of the same landscape from which we draw our inspiration. Very often when you work with a director, their sole landscape is what is painted on the page. When Kate and I collaborate in this way, we share the outer landscape.

KW: What's been nice about working in Reading is we could have more than one conversation with people. We could go down and talk to people a little more, which is great.

JLB: Speaking of the landscape of the texts, let's talk about form and genre. Lynn, critics sometimes categorize your dramaturgy as traditional in structure, meaning that it speaks to a tradition of American realism. And yet, when viewing your plays in production, there always seems to be an element of surprise and a transcendence of that.

LN: One of the things I pride myself on is that I don't think the work is easily classifiable, so when critics try to do it, they can't. I feel, to a certain extent, that the work succeeds with audiences because it is surprising, and it's not easily classifiable. I can't think of one play that I have written that would fall into the realm of naturalism in its pure sense. I think that my work is much more akin to someone like Tennessee Williams, where it's a kind of heightened, lyrical reality, but it's not naturalism. It's often misread, I think, based on preconceived notions about what black theatre is and should be. I think that the work does not necessarily fall into convenient categories. As a result, it vexes critics who, when they're writing and they have a limited amount of time to describe it, might have to spend a tiny bit more effort and they don't want to do that.

JLB: Or they want people to have a point a reference.

LN: A point of reference, yes. Early on critics always compared my writing to August Wilson, but it's as far away from August Wilson as possible. It's just not what I do. I think of my style as being more direct, and being less self-conscious about language. The poetry comes in the relationships of the characters and not in the way in which they say it. It's in the language itself. I do think of the work as very poetic, but it's in the spareness of what the characters say, as opposed to the abundance of the language, and in the way in which they say it.

JLB: Seret and Kate, how do you approach building those transcendent moments onstage that must move beyond a particular time or place?

SS: The last category I'd put Lynn's work in is realism. The story may be realistically based, such as spousal abuse in *POOF!*, but as written, when the abusive husband goes up in a puff of smoke, the play is *anything* but realistic. And yes, *POOF!* is visually funny! There's a magical element to Lynn's writing that makes the unusual seem possible. Her plays give me an opportunity to explore enchanted circumstances and landscapes.

KW: I was just thinking about design. Part of directing is intuitive. In thinking about the designs that we did for *Fabulation* and *Intimate Apparel* and *Ruined,* there's always an element that cues the audience that we are not in a fully realistic setting. For example, with *Ruined*, Mama Nadi's place was surrounded by black plexiglass. The trees came from black plexiglass so that there was always some element that was visually cuing the audience about what they're going to see, that there is something that is slightly different about the world. In *Intimate Apparel* it was the idea of dress forms floating above Esther – the thought being – what does she create every day? In *Fabulation* there was half of a cab that was mounted to the back wall. None of those elements, to me, feel like they're realistic. It feels like each visual metaphor is trying to describe to the audience what the vocabulary is for the piece and it is not solely one fully realized location.

SS: In *POOF!* and *Mud, River, Stone* the heightened story elements challenged me. As an actress and (new) director, I hadn't often worked in theatrical forms that weren't postured in realism. I initially approached both plays with a *real-ness*, even though the scripts had a fair amount of suggested fantasy. Eventually I lightened up and began to confidently explore scenes that lent themselves to enhanced imagery, although I checked in with Lynn often to gage her reaction. She was quite onboard with exploration, and indeed was eager to enhance what we were finding. War, loneliness, abuse, fame, all manner of the human condition, are backdrops to her characters, many of whom are the least educated, most humble, most forgotten human beings among us. Lynn's stories are intimate, with universal themes in scope and character.

JLB: Let's talk about some of your recent dramaturgical innovations. With *Vera Stark*, and now with *Sweat*, Lynn, you've engaged with a practice you call transmedia storytelling. *Vera Stark* engages with film and television, a website that accompanies the play, and there is the device of an academic conference in the show. All of these elements mediate the story about Vera and the messages in the play. With *Sweat*, you're creating a social sculpture in Reading, PA, and an interactive transmedia installation that is a kind of living, breathing documentary of Reading. What was the impetus to work with multiple media dramaturgically? How does engaging with transmedia technologies change the way you write?

LN: As a writer I'm interested in meeting the audience where they live, and the audience is living across multiple platforms now. Art comes from many different dynamic forms, and I'm interested in telling stories across these platforms. How do you meet audiences that have very short attention spans, that are on their cell phones, looking at the screen? I find it fascinating to capture the attention of those folks and pull them back into the theatre. Something that I am exploring is this impulse to be connected in a certain way, which I think ties into the way in which we're connected in the room. We still long for human connection. The device that we're holding in our hand can bring us back into the room and into the present, into a dialogue.

I think new media is absolutely changing the way all of us write. You see certain playwrights, like Annie Baker, who choose to explore silence and attenuated moments in response to how quickly the world is moving outside and how impatient we are when we come to the theatre now. Is it that we want theatre to move at the same rate that television and film move? What she's done to confront that is to say, "I'm going to pause, and so, when you're here, you're really forced to be in the present moment."

JLB: How do you envision the transmedia elements of your plays influencing their staging? For example, in *Vera Stark* there's a film – does anyone producing that play have to also create film footage?

LN: They have to create it, yes. Or they don't. I don't say they have to in the script. It just says you see a film. One can choose to stage it. I think it's exciting that it opens up other possibilities for staging when we're playing with transmedia. Nowadays, I think that there are more people who are interested in spectacle. There's more devised theatre, there's more theatre that's physical. I think that the theatre will constantly be evolving, and that it will move with trends, and there may come a time when we absolutely reject technology and theatre gets back to basics. But I think that right now, people are exploring new technology because it's so much a part of how we live our lives today. We're completely plugged in and connected. I think it would be a mistake not to acknowledge it.

JLB: Lynn, I'd like to end by asking how you see yourself positioned in the landscape of American theatre. You've spoken throughout our conversation about being an African American woman deliberately writing previously untold or unheard stories. How do you situate and maintain your voice and perspective in the conversation of the American canon?

LN: I see myself as part of the American storytelling tradition. I am writing stories that haven't been told, but they're very much American stories. My writing, my stories fit into a larger conversation about our culture; I am telling stories about people who have been marginalized. I feel I'm telling American stories that are filtered through an African American female's lens. Still, for whatever reason, the culture needs to subdivide and compartmentalize our narratives. Which I don't think is entirely healthy and speaks to the problems of the fragmentation of our culture, that we, African American women, still aren't entirely welcome in the full American narrative.

I don't understand this reluctance to include us. But fortunately times are slowly changing; there are many black writers who are insurgent.

JLB: Do you see yourself in conversation with those writers?

LN: I do. I continue to mentor a number of playwrights of color, who are becoming important writers in their own right. I think in some ways, they probably may not exist if there weren't writers like us who cracked open the regional theaters with plays that became incredibly successful and allowed artistic directors to say, "Hey, we have an audience for this work." I feel proud to be part of the frontline of change in the theatrical landscape.

Note

1 This interview is transcribed and condensed from conversations conducted at Manhattan Theatre Club in New York, NY and in Lynn Nottage's home in Brooklyn, NY in 2014, and via email in 2015.

Afterword

Lynn Nottage's futurity

Soyica Diggs Colbert

In "On Creativity and Collaboration," Lynn Nottage states, "the majority of my plays . . . one could call history plays" (180). Ranging in time period, from the eighteenth to the twenty-first century, and location, from Mozambique to Hollywood, her drama focuses on the complex and untold stories of women. Although many of the chapters in *A Critical Companion to Lynn Nottage* accurately describe her feminist practice of recuperating stories that have been lost in and to the annals of history, the activist impulse essential to her work also directs the temporal focus of the drama toward the future. Nottage's drama details underexplored and undocumented pasts in an effort to expand Black women's possibilities. As a part of her process, she goes to great lengths to recover women's voices, either digging through the archives of the New York Public Library or traveling with her collaborator Kate Whoriskey to Uganda to collect the stories of women ravaged by the genocidal war in the Congo. Her research practice of recuperation results in drama that contains temporal and spatial disjunction in order to remap connections between the past and present, and to imagine political possibilities in the future.

By the Way, Meet Vera Stark is set in 1933 and 2003, with footage of the title character taped in 1973, creating a toggling effect back and forth through time. The second act explicitly engages with the Third Wave feminist practice of recuperating the history of Black women artists that begins in the 1970s, asking: what happened to Vera Stark? The answers that the play provides, however, are in the service of cultural production in the present. It challenges the audience's ability to see the characters in the play outside of the stereotyped racial roles that attend all cultural production. The play suggests that knowing what happened to Vera requires shifting how we see the evidence, not uncovering new evidence to see. Disjuncture also informs the settings of Nottage's works. In "On

Creativity and Collaboration," Whoriskey explains how the set design in *Ruined* (2009) disallowed easily folding the play into the genre of realism. She explains, "with *Ruined*, Mama Nadi's place was surrounded by black plexiglass. The end of the trees came from the black plexiglass so that there was always some element that was visually cuing the audience about what they're going to see, that there is something that is slightly different about the world" (196). Nottage's practice entails not only crucial archival research but also acts of innovation. Through the deployment of her imagination and her choice to create worlds that draw upon, but are purposefully distinct from those found in the archive, Nottage demonstrates how artists function as activist visionaries.

Nottage's ethnographic and archival research grounds the voices of her women characters and enables expression of "the complexity of what it means to be a woman" (185). This complexity emerges from Black women's experience of emerging at intersections. As contributing author Harvey Young argues, "Although it can be difficult to single out a particular embodied sense of being from all others, within certain situations distinct aspects of our social identities may trigger a particularly strong affective experience of difference or otherness" (114). Young concludes that the individual's affective relationship to difference, as experienced in the social sphere, produces shorthand for identity lined to "those identity markers that most render us potential targets of harassment, abuse, or discrimination" (114). I would add to Young's artful description of the "habitus as a woman," *Vera Stark's* depiction of all the phenotypically Black women characters appearing as servants. As Young argues, "In *Meet Vera Stark*, Nottage presents characters who consciously invoke performance to challenge the negative contingencies of identity" (114). The play pokes fun at Vera's inept rendering of the slave in order to challenge her automatic association with the role, but the casting, nevertheless, demonstrates the way Vera's perceived race *and* gender inform her habitus as a woman.

Faedra Chatard Carpenter makes a similar point about the complexity and multiplicity of characters in Nottage's *Fabulation, or the Re-education of Undine*. She explains, "In *Fabulation*, surface assumptions regarding characters' inherent value within both personal and professional ecosystems are taken to task, thereby disrupting all-too-familiar stereotypes and trite notions based on race, class, and gender" (99). While not explicitly stated, *Fabulation* calls into question Undine's purported superiority based on her class position, and suggests, conversely, that her upward mobility does not belie her personal or cultural histories. The play depicts these pasts as sources of wealth *and* baggage, rather than one or the other. It also disrupts the cohesion of neat ecosystems, demonstrating the inherent contradictions at the heart of each character's identity. The characterization works alongside the layering of time periods and location in Nottage's plays, together presenting a multifaceted experience that accounts for contradiction, disjunction, progression, regression, and feelings of home and homelessness.

In Nottage's dramaturgy, depicting the intersectional perspectives of Black women such as those highlighted above requires a new structure, a new form. Her innovate manipulation of dramatic forms, whether melodrama in *Ruined,* or the Greek chorus in *Mud, River, Stone,* or heightened realism in *Fabulation,* models structural critique and engages with the long held feminist debate over the utility of the master's tools. In Audre Lorde's essential essay, "The Master's Tools Will Never Dismantle the Master's House," she makes the case for inventing new structures that will support the freedom dreams of Third Wave women of color feminists, responding to the heteronormativity, whiteness, and middle class bias of Second Wave feminists of the mid-twentieth century. Lorde laments the exclusion of "poor women, Black and Third World women, and lesbians" from the proceedings of the New York University Institute for the Humanities conference she was invited to address (110). She argues that feminists emphasize their identity as women and overlook the distinct experiences of women to create solidarity. She asserts:

> Those of us who stand outside the circle of this society's definition of acceptable women; those of us who have been forged in the crucibles of difference – those of us who are poor, who are lesbians, who are Black, who are older – know that survival is not an academic skill. It is learning how to take our differences and make them strengths. For the master's tools will never dismantle the master's house. They may allow us temporarily to beat him at his own game, but they will never enable us to bring about genuine change. And this fact is only threatening to those women who still define the master's house as their only source of support. (112)

Lorde's argument is radical and totalizing. It calls for a complete rethinking of social organization in order to achieve the possibility of dismantling racism, patriarchy, homophobia, and class hierarchies.

Nottage's commitment to representing the intersectional perspectives of women requires that she at least remodel the tools of theatrical storytelling, and at most invent new ones. Her most recent productions, *By The Way, Meet Vera Stark* (2011) and *Sweat* (2015) include "interactive transmedia installation[s]" (197). Websites and video exist alongside and are incorporated into the plays' live performances, thereby augmenting the theatrical event. The websites designed to accompany the shows offer backstories of the characters, histories, and speculation surrounding the play. Through these transmedia projects, Nottage expands the world of the play and the space and temporality of the event. Rupturing the tight seams and sequences of her drama, Nottage invites the viewer into her world of meaning-making to continue the practice of imagining the world anew, once the curtain falls. Nottage explains:

> I really do think that theatre is a vanguard of change because it's one of the few mediums where we can meet collectively, and actually have a collective catharsis and we can't underestimate the impact of that. I think that there is something magical that happens when we're able to laugh together, we're able to cry together, and that's what excites me about the medium.
>
> (188)

Her experimentation with form is not separate from her dual investment in telling women's stories and creating spaces within the theatre to advocate for women's rights, but rather is integral to those commitments. Nottage's formal innovation not only clears space for women's voices but also helps to build a theatre house that mitigates the displacement associated with diasporic subjects. The drama calls attention to how diaspora functions as a temporal and spatial disjunction. Jocelyn L. Buckner and Adrienne Macki Braconi consider how Nottage's theatre reimagines space to address the feeling of homeless resulting from forced and voluntary migrations. My addition to these insights is a philosophical one. The drama creates temporal disjunctions in order to mitigate the spatial ones of diaspora while also cultivating the physical spaces of the theatre and transmedia performance. Nottage's formal interventions align with the metaphor of homemaking to address the displacement of diaspora. Lorde's essay suggests that Third Wave feminists need new tools to dismantle the master's house. I suggest that Nottage is creating new tools to build a new house. The theatre, in Nottage's rendering, becomes a response to the alienation of homelessness.

Nottage clears space in which to view a world emerging from the intersection of womanhood. She comments, "I'm a storyteller and this is what I do, so this is the tool that I have. If I was a social activist I'd go and organize in the factories, but unfortunately, I don't have that skill. I think that what I can do is bring these stories to an audience, and perhaps put them in space where they feel empowered to effect change." (188). Nottage likens her skill as a playwright to a union organizer in a factory, distinguishing and specifying the commonality of her aesthetic work with other skills. The skills Nottage does possess include not only telling women's stories, but also offering new ways for them to unfold. Turning, redirecting, and realigning bodies in space and time, Nottage's drama encourages artists, scholars, and audience members to see Black women with fresh eyes.

Works cited

Lorde, Audre. *Sister Outsider: Essays and Speeches*. New York: Ten Speed Press, 2007. Print.

Index